DATE			

FINAL JUSTICE

ALSO BY W. E. B. GRIFFIN

Honor Bound

Honor Bound
Blood and Honor
Secret Honor

Brotherhood of War

Book I: The Lieutenants
Book II: The Captains
Book III: The Majors
Book IV: The Colonels
Book V: The Berets
Book VI: The Generals
Book VII: The New Breed
Book VIII: The Aviators
Book IX: Special Ops

The Corps

Book I: Semper Fi
Book II: Call to Arms
Book III: Counterattack
Book IV: Battleground
Book V: Line of Fire
Book VI: Close Combat
Book VII: Behind the Lines
Book VIII: In Danger's Path
Book IX: Under Fire

Badge of Honor

Book I: Men in Blue
Book II: Special Operations
Book III: The Victim
Book IV: The Witness
Book V: The Assassins
Book VI: The Murderers
Book VII: The Investigators

Men at War

Book I: The Last Heroes
Book II: The Secret Warriors
Book III: The Soldier Spies
Book IV: The Fighting Agents

G. P. PUTNAM'S SONS

NEW YORK

FINAL
JUSTICE

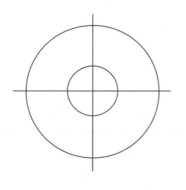

W.E.B.
GRIFFIN

G. P. Putnam's Sons
Publishers Since 1838
a member of
Penguin Putnam Inc.
375 Hudson Street
New York, NY 10014

Library of Congress Cataloging-in-Publication Data

Griffin, W. E. B.
Final justice / W.E.B. Griffin.
p.   cm.
ISBN 0-399-14926-0
1. Payne, Matt (Fictitious character)—Fiction.   2. Police—Pennsylvania—
Philadelphia—Fiction.   3. Philadelphia (Pa.)—Fiction.   I. Title.
PS3557.R489137 F56   2003   2002068266
813'.54—dc21

Printed in the United States of America
1   3   5   7   9   10   8   6   4   2

This book is printed on acid-free paper. ∞

Book design by Jennifer Ann Daddio

IN FOND MEMORY OF

Sergeant Zebulon V. Casey

Internal Affairs Division

Police Department, the City of Philadelphia, Retired

"There came a time when there were assignments that had to

be done right, and they would seek Zeb out. These assignments

included police shootings, civil-rights violations, and he tracked

down fugitives all over the country. He was not your

average cop. He was very, very professional."

—HOWARD LEBOFSKY

DEPUTY SOLICITOR OF PHILADELPHIA

FINAL JUSTICE

CHAPTER
1

[ONE]

It was Sunday night, and at quarter after eleven the Roy Rogers restaurant at South Broad and Snyder Streets in South Philadelphia was just about full.

Amal al Zaid, who was five feet seven inches tall and weighed 145 pounds, and who had spent sixteen of his twenty-one years as Dwayne Alexander Finston before converting to Islam, was mopping a spill from the floor just outside the kitchen door when he glanced at the clock mounted high on the wall near the front entrance to the restaurant.

The first thing he thought was that he had forty-five minutes to go on his shift, and then he would be free to ride his bicycle home to the apartment he shared with his mother, two brothers, and a sister in the Tasker Homes Project a few blocks away, grab a quick shower, and then go by the mosque to see what was happening.

The second thing he thought was, *Those two is bad news.*

Amal al Zaid had seen two young men enter the restaurant. Both were in their early twenties. One was of average height and build, and the other short and overweight. Both of them stopped, one at a time, just inside the door, and looked around the restaurant, and then at each other, and then nodded.

The average-looking one slid into a banquette near the door. The sort-of-fat one, who had something wrapped in a newspaper sticking out of his jacket pocket, walked all the way through the restaurant toward where Amal al Zaid was mopping the floor by the kitchen door. Amal al Zaid then pushed the right door to the kitchen open, and held it open while he pushed his mop bucket on wheels through it.

After a moment, Amal al Zaid peered carefully through the small window in the kitchen door. He saw that the short fat guy had taken a seat in the last banquette on the left, with his back to the kitchen wall. And he saw the short fat guy pull whatever he had wrapped in newspaper from his pocket, and lay it on the banquette seat. And then Amal al Zaid saw what it was: a short-barreled revolver.

"Holy shit," Zaid said, barely audibly, and turned and looked around the kitchen.

The kitchen supervisor, Maria Manuela Fernandez, a thirty-five-year-old in immaculate kitchen whites, who carried 144 pounds on her five-foot-three frame, was a few steps away, examining the latest serving trays to come out of the dishwasher.

Zaid went to her, touched her arm, and when she turned to him, said, "Manuela, I think we're getting stuck up."

Mrs. Fernandez's eyebrows rose.

"There's a fat guy with a gun in the last booth," Zaid said, pointing at the wall, "and there's another guy—they came in together—in the first booth on the right by the front door."

Mrs. Fernandez walked quickly and looked through the window in the door, then went to a wall-mounted telephone near the door and dialed 911.

Mrs. Fernandez's call was answered on the second ring by Miss Eloise T. Regis in the radio room of the Philadelphia police department, on the second floor of the Police Administration Building at Eighth and Race Streets in downtown Philadelphia.

The Police Administration Building is universally known in Philadelphia as "The Roundhouse," because the building has virtually no straight walls—exterior or interior—or corridors. Even the interiors of the elevators are curved.

Within the radio room are rows of civilian employees who, under the supervision of a few sworn police officers, sit at telephone and radio consoles receiving calls from the public and from police vehicles on the job, and relaying official orders to police vehicles.

There are twenty-two police districts in Philadelphia, and six divisions of detectives. There is also the Special Operations Division, which includes the Highway Patrol—despite its name, far more of an elite force than one concerned with highway traffic—and the Special Investigations Unit.

The Traffic and Accident Divisions actually have the primary responsibility for the public's safety on the highways and streets of Philadelphia. Their tools include a fleet of radio-equipped tow trucks and other special vehicles. The Juvenile Division is charged with dealing with crimes committed against—or by—juveniles.

Additionally, there are special-purpose units, such as the K-9 Unit, the Marine Unit, the Airport Unit, and the Vice, Narcotics, Organized Crime, and Dignitary Protection Units—and others.

Each district, division, and special unit has its own complement of radio-equipped police vehicles of all sorts.

And on top of this, of course, is the communications network necessary to maintain round-the-clock instantaneous contact with the vehicles of the senior command hierarchy of the police department, the commissioner and his staff, the deputy commissioners and their staffs, the chief inspectors and their staffs, and a plethora of other senior police officers.

With hundreds of police and support vehicles on the job at any one time, it was necessary to develop, both by careful planning and by trial and error, a system permitting instant contact with the right vehicle at the right time.

The police commissioner—or the commanding officer of the Marine Unit—is not really interested in learning instantly about every automobile accident in Philadelphia, nor is a request from the Airport Police for a paddy wagon to haul off three drunks from their bailiwick of much interest to a detective investigating a burglary in Chestnut Hill.

Philadelphia is broken down, for police department purposes, into eight geographical divisions and the Park Division. Each division is headed by an inspector, and contains from two to four districts, each commanded by a captain. Generally, each division has its own radio frequency, but in some divisions, really busy districts—the Twenty-fifth District in the East Division, for example—have their own separate frequencies. Detectives' cars and those assigned to other investigative units (Narcotics, Intelligence, Organized Crime, et cetera) have radios operating on the "H-Band." All police car radios can be switched to an all-purpose emergency and utility frequency called the "J-Band." Special Operations Division has its own, the "S-Band."

For example, a police officer in the Sixteenth District would routinely have his radio switch set to F-1, which would permit him to communicate with his (The West) division. Switching to F-2 would put him on the universal J-Band. A car assigned to South Philadelphia with his switch set to F-1 would be in contact with the South Division. A detective operating anywhere with his switch set to F-1 would be on the Detective's H-Band, but he too, by switching to F-2, would be on the J-Band.

Senior police officers have more sophisticated radios, and are able to communicate with other senior police brass, the detective frequency, or on the frequency of some other service in which they have a personal interest. Ordinary police cars are required to communicate through the dispatcher, and forbidden to talk car-to-car. Car-to-car communication is authorized on the J-, H-, and S-Bands.

"Communications discipline" is strictly enforced. Otherwise, there would be communications chaos.

There is provision, however, for a radio room dispatcher—simply by throwing the appropriate switch—to send a radio message simultaneously to every radio-equipped police vehicle, from a police boat making its way against the current of the Delaware River through the hundreds of police cars on patrol to the commissioner's and mayor's cars.

This most often happens when an operator takes a call in which the calling party says, "Officer needs assistance. Shots fired."

Not every call to 911 requesting police assistance is legitimate. Philadelphia has its fair share of lunatics—some say more than its fair share—who like to involve the cops in any number of things having nothing whatever to do with maintaining the peace and tranquillity within the City of Brotherly Love. And Philadelphia's youth, having watched cop movies on television to learn the cant, dial 911 ten or twelve times every day to report a murder, a body, a robbery, a car accident, anything that will cause a flock of police cars, lights flashing and sirens screaming, to descend on a particular street corner and liven up an otherwise dull period of the day.

The people who answer the telephones didn't come to work yesterday, however—Miss Eloise T. Regis, for example, had been on the job for more than twenty years—and usually they *know,* from the timbre of the caller's voice, or the assurance with which the caller raises the alarm, that *this* particular call is legitimate.

When Miss Regis answered the call from an excited Latino-sounding lady reporting a robbery in progress at the Roy Rogers at Broad and Snyder, she had *known* the call was genuine.

At 11:21, a call went out from Police Radio.

"Possible armed robbery in progress, Roy Rogers restaurant, Broad and Snyder. Unknown civilian by phone."

Officer Kenneth J. Charlton, of the First District, then patrolling the area, responded, "One seven. In on the Roy Rogers."

As Mrs. Fernandez was speaking excitedly with Miss Regis, there was the sound of a shot, and some unintelligible shouts.

The door to the kitchen burst open, and the fat guy with the gun came through it. He saw Mrs. Fernandez on the telephone, and when she saw him, she dropped the handset and moved away from the telephone, placing her back against the wall near the telephone.

. The fat guy went to the handset dangling from the wall phone, put it to his ear, listened a moment—just long enough to be able to determine with whom Mrs. Fernandez was speaking—then grabbed the coiled expansion cord and ripped it free from the telephone.

Then he looked at Mrs. Fernandez and said, "You fucking bitch!" and raised his revolver to arm's length and fired at her. The bullet struck her just below her left ear and exited her skull just above her right ear.

Her convulsing body slid down the wall until her knees were fully bent, and then it fell forward onto the floor.

The fat guy then brandished his revolver at the other kitchen workers. There were six: three men and three women. The fat guy had not seen Amal al Zaid when he had shoved the kitchen door open. He had done so with such force that it went past the spring stop, causing it to remain in the open position at a right angle to the doorway. Amal al Zaid was behind it, his back pressed against the wall, literally paralyzed by fear.

"In the fucking cooler, motherfuckers!" the fat guy said, waving his revolver and gesturing toward the walk-in refrigerator.

When the kitchen staff—stumbling in their haste, one of the women moaning in terror as she held both hands to her mouth—had gone inside the walk-in refrigerator, the fat guy walked quickly toward it, closed the door, and looked around the kitchen.

Holy Christ! Amal al Zaid thought. *That crazy nigger's going to see me!*

The fat guy found what he wanted—a wooden-handled sharpening steel— on a worktable right behind him, picked it up, and jammed it in the loops intended for a padlock in the refrigerator door. Then he turned and started for the kitchen door.

In the logical presumption that he would be seen by the guy who'd just shot Manuela, Amal al Zaid lost control of his bladder, and momentarily forgot that he was no longer a Christian.

Our Father, Who art in heaven, hallowed be Thy name . . .

The fat guy looked to the left as he made his way across the kitchen, paused briefly to look down at the body of the goddamn bitch who had called the motherfucking cops, and then went through the open kitchen door into the dining area.

Amal al Zaid finally found the courage to look through the narrow crack between the door and the doorjamb, and saw that the fat guy was working his way though the dining room, collecting wallets and coin purses and watches and rings from the customers.

The other sonofabitch was at the cashier's station by the front door, taking the paper money from the cash register.

The fat guy finished robbing the four people at the banquette he was working, then walked toward the front of the restaurant.

"Let's get the fuck out of here," the fat guy said.

"Fuck, fuck, *fucking* fuck, it's a fucking cop!" the guy at the register said, gesturing through the window.

He squatted down behind the cash register. The fat guy slid into the banquette nearest to him on the right.

At 11:26, Officer Charlton entered the restaurant, holding his service pistol at his side. He glanced at the cashier's station, saw the man crouching behind it, and took a half-dozen steps around the cashier's station.

The guy at the cash register suddenly stood up, lunged at Officer Charlton, and wrapped his arms around him, preventing Officer Charlton from raising his pistol to fire it.

The fat guy jumped from the banquette, ran to them, shoved the muzzle of his pistol under Charlton's "bulletproof" vest, and fired.

Officer Charlton stiffened, then went limp and fell to the floor. The guy who had been behind the cash register then stepped over Charlton's body. Then he turned and fired twice at the body. Then he ran out of the restaurant onto South Broad Street after the fat guy.

After a moment, Amal al Zaid pushed himself off the wall and ran to the employees' locker room.

Shit! Oh, fuck, I pissed in my pants!

In the employees' locker room, he opened his locker and took his cellular telephone from his jacket, punched in 911, and when the voice said, "Police Radio?" blurted: "This is the Roy Rogers restaurant at Broad and Snyder. Two black guys just shot the kitchen lady and a cop who walked in while they was robbing us."

This call too, coincidentally, was answered by Miss Regis. And again, her experience told her the call was legitimate.

"Sergeant!" she called, raising her voice just to get his attention, not to ask his permission. Then she threw the appropriate switch.

Three fast, short beeps, signifying an emergency message, were broadcast to every police radio in Philadelphia.

Miss Regis pressed the switch activating her microphone.

"Assist the officer, Broad and Snyder, inside the Roy Rogers, report of an officer shot. Assist the officer, Broad and Snyder, inside the Roy Rogers, report of an officer shot. This is a civilian by phone, we have officers responding to a previous call of a possible armed robbery at that location."

[TWO]

The second vehicle to reach the Roy Rogers restaurant at South Broad and Snyder Streets in response to the first "possible armed robbery in progress" call over the F-Band was a new Buick Rendezvous CXL Sport Utility Vehicle, on the roof of which were three antennas capable of listening to police radio frequencies. A fourth antenna was mounted on the rear window, and just before getting close to Synder Street, the driver of the car switched off a flashing blue light with a magnetic base that he had put on the roof after hearing the call.

The driver, however, was not a sworn police officer of the Philadelphia police department, and—as had often been pointed out to him—using the flashing blue light on the roof to speed one's way through traffic was in violation of at least four laws of the Commonwealth of Pennsylvania, ranging from violation of Paragraph 4912 of the Criminal Code of Pennsylvania—impersonation of a public official, such as a police officer—to violation of Paragraph 6504 of the Criminal Code—setting up a nuisance in public.

The Rendezvous itself, and all the expensive radios and scanners, were the property of the *Philadelphia Bulletin,* with whom the driver, Michael J. "Mickey" O'Hara, a wiry, curly-haired man in his late thirties, was professionally associated. The magnetic base flashing blue light was the property of the Philadelphia police department, having been removed by Mr. O'Hara from a wrecked and burned unmarked car, rendering him liable to charges of having violated one or more of Paragraphs 3921, 3924, and 3925 of the Criminal Code, which deal with the unlawful taking of property.

Mr. O'Hara's association with the *Bulletin* went back twenty-one years, to his sixteenth year, when he was hired as a copyboy, shortly after having been expelled from West Catholic High School. Monsignor Dooley had caught Mickey with a pocketful of Francesco "Frankie the Gut" Guttermo's numbers slips, and when Mickey had refused to name his accomplice in that illegal and immoral enterprise, the monsignor had given him the boot.

Mickey had immediately found a home in journalism, and had become a reporter—the *Bulletin* said "staff writer"—before he was old enough to vote. As he had risen in the *Bulletin* city room hierarchy, his remuneration had naturally increased. He had been perfectly happy with his relationship with the *Bulletin* and the compensation he was given until his childhood friend, Casimir Bolinski, had brought the subject up.

"Face it, Mickey, those bastards are screwing you," Casimir had said when passing through Philadelphia to visit his parents.

It was more than an idle observation; it was a professional one. Because Mickey had refused to name him as his fellow numbers runner, Casimir, already known as "The Bull," had graduated from West Catholic High, gone on to Notre Dame on a football scholarship, and from Notre Dame to the Green Bay Packers.

There, while his Packers teammates had spent their off seasons in various nonproductive if pleasant pursuits, Casimir had studied the law. He hadn't wanted to, if the truth be known, but Mrs. Antoinette Bolinski, who weighed approximately one third as much as her husband, was a woman of great determination, and The Bull knew better than to argue with her.

To his surprise, Casimir liked the study of law, and immediately showed a flair for the business aspects of the profession. The day after the Packers—in an emotional ceremony—retired The Bull's jersey, Casimir J. Bolinski, *D. Juris,* announced the opening of his law offices, in which he intended to deal with the relationships between professional athletes and their employers. He started, rather naturally, by representing professional football players, but as word spread throughout the world of sports about how successful The Bull had been in securing pay far beyond the expectations of the players, professionals from baseball, basketball, and even a number of jockeys—the crème de la crème, so to speak, of the world of sports—began to beat a path to his door.

"The way it is, Mickey," Casimir had explained, "is when I first quit the game, the guys would come to see me and say 'How they hanging, Bull? What's this bullshit about you being a lawyer?' and now they come in, shaved and all dressed up in suits, and say, 'Thank you very much for seeing me, Dr. Bolinski.'"

Antoinette Bolinski had been thrilled to find out that *D. Juris* stood for "Doctor of Law," and that she was thus entitled to refer to Casimir as "my husband, Dr. Bolinski." She immediately began to do so. The phrase had a really classy ring to it, and if the other lawyers didn't want to use the title, screw them.

As once the fabled defense of the Detroit Lions had crumpled before The Charging Bull in that never-to-be-forgotten 32–zilch game, the assembled legal counsel of the *Bulletin* gave way before Dr. Bolinski's persuasive arguments that the few extra dollars they were going to have to spend on Mickey were nothing compared to the dollars they would lose in lost circulation if Mickey moved over to the *Inquirer* or the *Daily News*.

"Jesus, you're dumb, Mickey," Casimir had said later. "You've got the fucking Pulitzer, for Christ's sake. You should have known that's worth a whole lot of dead presidents' pictures."

As a result of the negotiations by Dr. Bolinski on behalf of Mr. O'Hara with the *Bulletin*, Mr. O'Hara's compensation was quadrupled, and it was agreed that the *Bulletin* would provide Mr. O'Hara with a private office and an automobile of Mr. O'Hara's choice, equipped as Mr. O'Hara wished; and that he would be reimbursed for all expenses incurred in his professional work, it being clearly understood this would involve a substantial amount of business entertainment.

With one exception, however—Mickey was the sole supporter of his widowed mother, and had been having a really hard time paying her tab at the Cobbs Creek Nursing Center & Retirement Home—his new affluence didn't change his life much.

After toying with the suggestion of Dr. Bolinski that he have the *Bulletin* buy him either a Mercedes or a Cadillac, Mickey had chosen the Buick Rendezvous. A Caddie, or a Kraut-mobile, he reasoned, would piss off most of the people with whom he worked. By that he meant the police officers. It was said—with more than a little justification—that Mickey knew more cops by their first names than anyone else, and that more cops knew Mickey by sight than they did the police commissioner.

Mickey knew that most—certainly not all—of Philly's cops liked him, and he attributed this to both reciprocation—he liked most cops—and to the fact that he spelled their names right, got the facts right, and never betrayed a confidence.

As he did most nights, Mickey O'Hara had been cruising the city in the Rendezvous when one of the scanners had caught the "possible armed robbery" call. He was then five blocks south of the Roy Rogers on South Broad Street.

"Possible, my ass," he had said, aloud, then put the gumball machine on the roof, glanced in the rearview mirror, and made an illegal U-turn on Broad Street.

When he reached the Roy Rogers, he saw there was a blue-and-white, door open, parked on Snyder, which told him the cops had just arrived, and the possible robbery in progress was probably still in progress, because the cop wouldn't have left his car door open if he hadn't been in a hell of a hurry.

He double-parked on Snyder, beside the police car, grabbed his digital camera from the passenger seat, and quickly got out of the Rendezvous. Two black guys were coming out of the restaurant in a hurry. In a reflex action, Mickey put the digital camera to his eye and snapped a picture.

The short fat black guy saw him, raised his arm, and took a shot at Mickey with a short-barreled revolver. He missed, but Mickey, as a prudent measure, dropped to the ground beside the Rendezvous. When he looked up, both of the doers were hauling ass down Snyder Street.

Mickey got to his feet, ran quickly to the Roy Rogers, and went inside.

Just inside the door there was a cop on the floor, facedown, in a spreading pool of blood.

Mickey snapped that picture, and then as he was waiting for the camera to recycle, to take a second shot, realized he knew the dead cop. He was Kenny Charlton of the First District.

Son of a bitch! Kenny was a good guy, seventeen, eighteen years on the job. His wife works for the UGI. They have a couple of kids.

The green light in the camera came on, and he took another picture.

He was about to step around the body when he sensed motion behind him and looked over his shoulder.

A very large black man, in the peculiar uniform of the Highway Patrol, had entered the restaurant, pistol drawn. Another highway patrolman was on his heels.

"I think the doers just ran down Snyder," Mickey said, pointing. "Two black guys, one short and fat . . . two black guys."

Sergeant Wilson Carter turned to the highway patrolman behind him. "Get out a flash," he ordered.

The second highway patrolman—Mickey knew the face but couldn't come up with a name—left the restaurant quickly.

Sergeant Carter looked down at the body of Officer Charlton, dropped to his knees, felt his carotid artery, and shook his head.

"Jesus, Mickey, what happened?" he asked.

"I got here just before you did," O'Hara said, shrugging in a helpless gesture.

There were now the sounds of approaching sirens, at least two, probably three, maybe more.

"They shot somebody in the kitchen, too," one of the restaurant patrons called out.

Sergeant Carter looked around to see who had called out, and when he did, one of the patrons, a very tall, very thin, hawk-featured black man, stood up and pointed to the kitchen.

Sergeant Carter headed for the rear of the restaurant. Mickey followed him, holding the digital camera in his hand, concealing it as well as he could.

Carter pushed open the door and went in the kitchen. Mickey caught it before it closed and followed him in.

There was a body of a chubby woman, some kind of Latina, on the floor, her head distorted and lying in a pool of blood.

"Jesus Christ!" Sergeant Carter said.

"One of them came in the kitchen," a young black guy in kitchen whites said. "Manuela was calling the cops. He shot her."

"They all gone?" Carter asked.

"There was just the two of them," the young black guy said. "They're gone."

"You get a good look at him? Them?"

The young black guy nodded.

Carter went back into the dining room.

Mickey didn't follow him. He took a picture of the young black guy, then held up his finger, signaling him not to go anywhere, and then took two pictures, different angles, of the body on the floor.

Then he slipped the digital camera into his pocket.

"What's your name?" he asked.

"Amal al Zaid."

"You want to spell that for me?" Mickey asked, and wrote it down, and then asked where he lived.

Then he asked Amal al Zaid what had happened, and had just about finished writing that down when three other police officers entered the kitchen—a lieutenant, a detective, and a uniform.

Lieutenant Stanley J. Wrigley was acquainted with Mr. O'Hara.

"Jesus Christ, Mickey, how did you get in here?" he asked.

"I got here before Highway," Mickey replied. "The doers were two black guys. Carter put out a flash."

"You have to get out of here, Mickey, you know that," Lieutenant Wrigley said.

"Yeah."

"Do me a favor," Wrigley said. "Go out the back door. Otherwise the rest of the media will bitch you're getting special treatment again."

"Yeah, sure, Stan."

"You get a pretty good look at the doers?" the detective asked.

"Not good. Two young black guys, one of them short and fat."

"You told that to Carter?" Wrigley asked.

Mickey nodded.

"Thanks, Mick," Wrigley said, and O'Hara went to the rear door of the kitchen and went through it.

[THREE]

Twelve minutes later, Mickey O'Hara walked into his glass-walled office just off the city room of the Philadelphia *Bulletin,* adjusted the venetian blinds over the glass of the windows and doors so that he could not be seen from the city room, locked the door, and then sat down at his personal computer, switched it on, and waited for it to boot up.

He had two computers. One was tied into the *Bulletin's* network, and the other was his personally. While he was waiting for his personal computer to boot up, he spun around in his chair and faced the *Bulletin* computer terminal keyboard and rapidly typed:

CE
Hold me space for the double murder at the Roy Rogers.
I was there and may have pics.
O'Hara

He read what he had typed, then pushed the Send key.

Then he spun around in his chair again and faced his own computer. This state-of-the-art device, which fell under the provisions of his contract for personal services with the *Bulletin,* requiring the *Bulletin* to provide him with "whatever electronic devices and other tools he considered necessary to the efficient performance of his duties," was brand new. It had a twenty-one-inch liquid crystal diode color monitor, and provided more than a hundred different typefaces, each clearer and more legible than the single typeface available on the *Bulletin's* computer terminals.

Mickey took his digital camera—another $1,200 electronic device he considered necessary for the performance of his duties—from his trouser pocket, carefully removed the memory chip, replaced it with another $79.95 64-megabyte memory chip, and shoved the chip he had removed into the mouth—it reminded him of a feeding goldfish—of a device connected to the keyboard of his computer.

He tapped some keys, which caused the JPG images on the memory chip to be transferred into his computer. The quick tapping of more keys brought the images up on the LCD monitor.

He then removed the memory chip from the goldfish's mouth, unlocked a drawer in his desk and unlocked a metal box in the drawer, dropped the memory chip into it, relocked it, closed the desk drawer, and relocked that.

Mickey was thinking of writing a book—Casimir Bolinski said he was sure he could sell it for him—*for big bucks, Mick, if you ever get off your lazy Irish ass and write a proposal*—and if he did, he would need the pictures.

He tapped keys again and a photo-editing program came up on the LCD monitor's screen. The first picture, of the two black guys coming out of the Roy Rogers, appeared.

It was really a lousy picture, understandable in the circumstances.

For one thing, he had thrown the viewfinder to his eye with such haste that the picture was cockeyed; the two doers appeared in the lower right quarter of the picture, and only from the waist up.

Far worse, the camera's internal light meter had detected the bright light coming from the door, decided that was the ambient light, and set the camera accordingly. The entrance to the restaurant appeared in near perfect clarity, but the two doers were not in the light from the door, and consequently they could hardly be seen. You could see it was two guys, but you couldn't see any facial details.

Mickey quite skillfully tried to fix it, using all of the capabilities of the photo-editing program. He "lightened" the two guys. That didn't work. Neither did darkening the perfectly captured restaurant entrance. He tried everything else he could think of, but nothing worked.

Finally he gave up. He cropped out the unnecessary background, typed keys that renamed "00001.JPG" to "DoersXRR.JPG," then pressed the Enter key. Then he pushed other keys, which ordered yet another electronic device necessary to the performance of his duties, to print three copies, eight by ten inches, 1,200 dots per square inch. A $5,300 electronic device hummed and clicked as it began to execute the order.

00002.JPG and 00003.JPG—the pictures of the body of Officer Kenneth J. Charlton, the poor bastard, lying dead at the entrance of the Roy Rogers—also required editing.

He first made a copy of each as they had come from the camera, renaming them Chardwn1.JPG and Chardwn2.JPG respectively, and ordered three eight-by-ten copies of each at 1,200 dots per square inch.

Then he went back to each picture in turn, cropped out unnecessary background, very carefully edited the picture so that Officer Charlton's eyes appeared to be closed, not twisted in agony, and then made the pool of blood in which Charlton's head was lying disappear. He then renamed these pictures Charbul1.JPG and Charbul2.JPG, ordered the printing of one eight-by-ten of each, and also sent the pictures by the Internet to O'Hara@PhillyBulletin.com.

He did much the same thing with the other pictures—those of that poor dame in the kitchen and the young black kid—that he had made with the digital camera.

Although a somewhat complicated process, doing everything took him less than ten minutes. He had a good deal of experience doing the same sort of thing, and of course he had, literally, the best equipment the *Bulletin*'s money could buy to do it with.

Mickey knew that some people—just about any cop—would think what he should have done was simply turn the memory chip over to the cops, to assist them in their search for the murderers.

Mickey had several problems with that. For one thing, if the cops had the memory chip, there was no way he could get copies of the pictures before the *Bulletin* went to bed at 3 A.M. For another, while Mickey thought it was important that the public get to see the bodies of Kenny Charlton and the Puerto Rican, Latina, whatever, lady lying where they had fallen, there were families involved, and there was no reason the families had to see how fucking gruesome it actually was. Seeing Daddy and Momma in the *Bulletin* lying dead was going to be bad enough.

When he had finished, he picked up his telephone with one hand, and with the other slid out a shelf on his desk to which a list of telephone numbers was affixed under celluloid. He found what he wanted and punched it in.

"First District, Corporal Foley."

"Mickey O'Hara, Jerry. Did they pick up the Roy Rogers doers yet?"

"Not yet, Mick. They're still looking."

"You're sure, Jerry?"

"Jesus, yeah, I'm sure. I thought they would have something by now. Every cop in Philadelphia's down here looking for them."

"Thank you, Jerry."

He dropped the telephone into its cradle, looked at the gray monitor before him, a cursor blinking on it, and then tapped the balls of his fingers together as he searched for the lead sentence of what he was about to write. He wanted to get it right.

After a moment, it came to him.

CE
Slug Massive Manhunt Begins for Roy Rogers Murderers

By Michael J. O'Hara
Bulletin Staff Writer
Photos by Michael J. O'Hara

Philadelphia April 27—Philadelphia police began a massive manhunt just before midnight, confident they would quickly apprehend the two young black men eyewitnesses say first shot to death Mrs. Maria Manuela Fernandez, kitchen supervisor of the Roy Rogers restaurant at South Broad and Snyder Streets, during a robbery and then shot Police Officer Kenneth J. Charlton, of the First District, who responded to the call, killing him instantly. Amal al Zaid, a maintenance worker at the restaurant, told this reporter Mrs. Fernandez, a single mother of three, was shot without warning by one of the robbers as she was on the telephone reporting the robbery to police authorities, and then ambushed Officer Charlton as he entered the restaurant a few minutes later.

Five minutes and 250 words later, Mickey gave the computer screen a quick read, cursed the goddamn sci-fi movie typeface, then inserted a missing comma and pushed the Send key.

Then he turned to the printer, picked the photographs from the tray, put the ones intended for the cops into a large manila envelope, and, carrying the ones from which he had deleted the blood, walked out of his office and across the City Room to the city editor.

"These the pics?" the city editor asked.

"I thought you should see them in color," Mickey said. "I appended them to my piece, but they'll look black-and-white on the El Cheapo network."

The city editor examined the photographs.

"No blood," he said. It was both a question and a statement.

"You noticed, did you, you perceptible sonofabitch?"

"Nice work, Mickey," the city editor said.

Mickey O'Hara held up his hands in a *what are you going to do?* gesture, then walked out of the City Room.

He got in his car, which was parked in a slot marked with a RESERVED FOR MR. O'HARA sign, and drove to the Roundhouse, where he parked in a slot marked with a RESERVED FOR INSPECTORS sign, and then entered the building.

The uniforms behind the plate-glass window pushed the solenoid that opened the door to the lobby.

One of the uniforms, a corporal, called: "I thought you'd be out at the Roy Rogers, Mickey."

Mickey waved the manila envelope in his hand.

"Been there, done that," he said, and walked across the lobby to the elevator. He rode it to the first floor, and then walked down the corridor until he came to a door marked HOMICIDE.

He pushed it open, then made his way past a locked barrier by putting his hand behind it and pushing the hidden solenoid switch.

There was only one detective in the room, a younger man who looked like he needed both a new razor and a month's good meals.

"Got you minding the store, have they, Fenson?"

"What can I do for you, O'Hara?" the detective asked.

"Washington's the lieutenant?"

"This week at least," Fenson said.

Lieutenant Jason Washington had taken the examination for promotion to captain. It was universally expected that he would pass.

"I hear the results of the sergeant's exam will be out tomorrow," he said. "The lieutenant's and captain's should be right after that."

"Can you imagine him in a uniform, addressing some uniform roll call in a district?" Fenson asked.

"No, I can't," O'Hara admitted. "Is Washington here?"

"He's out at the Roy Rogers scene. What can I do for you?"

"It's a question of what I can do for you," O'Hara said. "Can you get Washington on the horn and tell him I've got a picture of the doers? A lousy picture, I admit, but a picture."

He laid it on the detective's desk.

"You're sure this is them? And you're right, it's a lousy picture."

"I'm sure," O'Hara said. "I took it."

"Washington called a couple of minutes ago and said he was coming in," the detective said.

Mickey O'Hara used the gentlemen's rest facility, then sipped on a paper cup of tepid coffee.

Eight minutes after that, an enormous—six feet three, 225 pounds— superbly tailored, very black man came into Homicide. Known behind his back as "The Black Buddha," Lieutenant Jason Washington regarded himself—and was generally regarded by others—as the best homicide detective in Philadelphia, and possibly the best homicide detective between Bangor, Maine, and Key West, Florida.

"Michael, my friend, how are you?" he greeted O'Hara with obvious sincerity, plus a warm smile and a friendly pat on the shoulder.

"Hey, Jason," O'Hara said. "I have a lousy picture of the doers."

He pointed to the photograph lying on the detective's desk.

Washington picked it up, examined it carefully, then looked at O'Hara.

"I concur in your judgment of the quality," he said. "And the source, Mickey?"

"I went in on the robbery-in-progress call," O'Hara said. "When I got there, these two were leaving. I took that picture."

"And you believe these were the doers?"

"Yeah, that's them," O'Hara said. "They match the description I got from one of the employees."

"The camera zeroed in on the light in the doorway," Washington said. "Pity."

"It's twelve hundred dots to the inch. Maybe the lab'll be able to salvage more than I could," Mickey said.

"Detective Fenson," Washington said. "Didn't you think, considering Mr. O'Hara's reputation as one of the more skilled photographers of the dark side of our fair city, that it behooved you to get this photograph to the lab as quickly as possible?"

"That's a pretty bad picture, Lieutenant."

"But a picture nevertheless, Detective Fenson," the Black Buddha said softly. "I constantly try to make the point that no stone should ever be left unturned."

Fenson picked up the picture and walked out of the room.

"I am grateful for the photograph, Mickey," Washington said. "Even if others may not be. I have a feeling that this case isn't going to be as easy to close as everyone else seems to feel it will be."

"Why's that?"

"Intuition," Washington said. "Nothing concrete."

"Your intuition is . . . what? Legendary?"

"That has been said," Washington said, smiling, then added, "I just have the feeling, Mick. I really hope I'm wrong."

"I got a couple of shots of the bodies, too," O'Hara said, and handed him the manila envelope.

Washington looked at them, then raised his eyes to O'Hara.

"I presume that these will shortly appear in the *Bulletin*?"

"I cleaned them up some," O'Hara said. "But yeah, they will."

Washington took O'Hara's meaning.

"Thank you, Mickey."

O'Hara gave a deprecating shrug.

"Buy you a cup of decent coffee, Jason?"

"Café Royal? In the Four Seasons?"

"Why not? The *Bulletin*'s paying."

"Then I accept your kind offer," Washington said.

CHAPTER
2

[ONE]

When Deputy Commissioner (Patrol) Dennis V. Coughlin, a tall, heavyset, ruddy-faced man who still had all of his curly silver hair and teeth at age fifty-nine, walked into his office on the third floor of the Police Administration Building, he saw that there were three documents on his desk demanding his immediate attention.

They were in the center of his leather-bound desk blotter, held in place by a heavy china coffee mug bearing the logotype of the Emerald Society, a fraternal organization of police officers of Irish heritage.

Denny Coughlin had joined "The Emerald" thirty-seven years before, right after graduation from the Police Academy and coming on the job, and had twice served as its president.

Coughlin peeled off the double-breasted jacket of his well-tailored dark blue suit as he walked toward his closet, exposing a Smith & Wesson snub-nosed .38 Special revolver worn, butt forward, on his right side.

Except for those rare times over the years when he wore a uniform, Denny Coughlin had slipped that same pistol's holster onto his belt every morning for thirty-three years, since the day he had reported on the job as a rookie detective.

He hung his jacket carefully on a hanger in his closet, closed the door, and turned to his desk.

Captain Francis Xavier Hollaran, an equally large Irishman who at forty-nine still had all of his teeth but not very much left from what had once been a luxurious mop of red hair, entered the room carrying a stainless-steel thermos of coffee.

"I went by Homicide," he greeted the commissioner. "Nothing that's not in there."

Hollaran indicated with a nod of his head the documents on the green blotter on Coughlin's desk.

"It's only nine hours," Coughlin replied. "They'll get something soon." He paused, then added, "Jesus Christ, won't they ever learn?"

"Wolf, wolf, boss," Frank Hollaran said. "You answer so many calls like that that are false alarms, you get careless."

"And dead," Coughlin said, more than a little bitterly.

Two of the documents on the green blotter under the Emerald Society mug detailed the events surrounding the death on duty of Officer Kenneth J. Charlton of the First District. (In Philadelphia, "districts" are what are called "precincts" in many other major police departments.)

One was an "Activities Sheet," which listed every move detectives of the Homicide Bureau had made in the case, including a listing of every interview conducted. The Activities Sheet was a "discoverable document," which meant it would have to be made available to the defense counsel of anyone brought to trial in the case. Attached to it was a teletype message known as a "white paper," which was a less formal, less precise report. As an unofficial, internal memorandum, the white paper was not "discoverable." The two documents together presented the details of the case as it had so far developed.

According to them, Officer Charlton had, at 11:26 the previous evening, responded to a radio report of a robbery in progress at the Roy Rogers restaurant at South Broad and Snyder Streets in South Philadelphia. That was a fact and was listed on the Activities Sheet. It was also a fact that Officer Charlton had not waited for backup to arrive before going into the restaurant.

The white paper theorized that Officer Charlton had been close to the scene when the call came, and had probably decided that he would have backup within a minute or two, but that waiting for it before entering the restaurant would give the robbers a chance to escape. It was further theorized that the doers had probably *seen* his patrol car coming. Charlton had been on the job seventeen years, and if he had used his siren and flashing lights at all, he was experienced enough to have turned them off before getting close to the scene. One of the doers had then ducked behind the cashier's counter, waited until Officer Charlton started to come behind the register, then grabbed him and held him while the other doer had shoved a pistol under Charlton's body armor and fired and shot him in the spine.

After the doer who had grabbed Charlton had paused long enough to fire two shots at Charlton's body, both doers had then fled from the restaurant. An autopsy might be able to determine if the first shot had killed Charlton, or whether he had still been alive when the second doer had shot him twice again.

It was splitting legal hairs.

Under Paragraph 2501(a) of the Criminal Code of Pennsylvania, Criminal Homicide is defined as the act of intentionally, knowingly, recklessly, or negligently causing the death of another human being.

Paragraph 2502(b) of the Criminal Code of Pennsylvania further defines Criminal Homicide to be Murder of the Second Degree when the offense is committed by someone engaged as the principal, or an accomplice, in the perpetration of a felony. Armed robbery is a felony.

So if it was determined that Officer Charlton died immediately as a result of being shot by Doer Number One at the cash register, Doer Number Two was guilty of the crime of Murder in the Second Degree because the act occurred while he was an accomplice in the commission of a felony.

If Officer Charlton was still alive when Doer Number Two shot him twice again, killing him, then Doer Number Two was guilty of Murder in the Second Degree because he was the principal, and Doer Number One was guilty as the accomplice.

The Activities Sheet reported that by the time other police arrived at the scene, both Doer Number One and Doer Number Two had disappeared into the night and that a very poor-quality photograph had been taken of them as they left the scene by a citizen, and turned over to the Homicide Bureau.

Both Commissioner Coughlin and Captain Hollaran were familiar with all the details in the report on Coughlin's desk. They had been at the Roy Rogers before Officer Charlton's body had been taken away by the coroner.

There was a standing operating procedure that Commissioner Coughlin— who exercised responsibility for all the patrol functions of the department— would be immediately notified in a number of circumstances, whatever the hour. Those circumstances included the death of a police officer on duty.

There was an unofficial standing operating procedure understood and invariably applied by the police dispatchers. Whenever a call came in asking to be connected with Deputy Commissioner Coughlin so that he could be notified of the death of a police officer on duty—or something of almost as serious a nature—Captain F. X. Hollaran was notified first.

After he was notified of such an incident, Hollaran would wait a minute or two—often using the time to put on his clothing and slip his Smith & Wesson snub-nose into its holster—and then call Coughlin's private and unlisted number to learn from Coughlin whether he wanted to be picked up, or whether he would go to the scene himself, or whether there was something else Coughlin wanted him to do.

The procedure went back many years, to when Captain Denny Coughlin had been given command of the Homicide Bureau and Homicide detective Frank Hollaran had become—without either of them planning it—Coughlin's right-hand man.

As Coughlin had risen through the hierarchy, Hollaran had risen with him, with time out for service as a uniform sergeant in the Fifth District, as a lieutenant with Northeast Detectives, and as district commander of the Ninth District.

Last night, when Hollaran had called Coughlin, Coughlin had said, "You better pick me up, Frank. It's going to be a long night."

It had turned out to be a long night. The commissioner himself, Ralph J. Mariani, had shown up at the Roy Rogers minutes after Coughlin and Hollaran. He had immediately put Hollaran to work organizing the notification party. The mayor, who was out of town, was not available, so Mariani would be the bearer of the bad news.

When finally the party was assembled, it consisted of Mariani, Coughlin, the police department chaplain, the pastor of the Methodist Episcopal Church attended by the Charlton family, the First District captain, and Officer Charlton's lieutenant and sergeant.

Captain Leif Schmidt, the First District commander, telephoned Mrs. Charlton and told her that he had had a report her husband had been injured and taken to Methodist Hospital, and that he had dispatched a car to pick her up and take her there.

Sergeant Stanley Davis, Officer Charlton's sergeant, accompanied by police officer Marianna Calley, went to the Charlton home and suggested to Mrs. Charlton that it might be a good idea if Officer Calley, who knew the kids, stayed with them while she went to the hospital.

The notification protocol had evolved through painful experience over the years. It was better to tell the wife at the hospital that she was now a widow, rather than at her home. There were several reasons, high among them being that it kept the goddamn ghouls from the TV stations from shoving a camera in the widow's face to demand to know how she felt about her husband getting killed.

It also allowed the notification party to form at the hospital before the widow got there. The mayor would normally be there, and the police commissioner, and other senior white shirts, and it was better for them to hurry to a known location than descend one at a time at the officer's home, which sometimes might not have space for them all, and would almost certainly be surrounded by the goddamn ghouls of the fourth estate, all of whom had police scanner radios, and would know where to go.

Telling the widow at the hospital hadn't made the notification any easier, but it was the best way anyone could think of to do it.

The third document on Deputy Commissioner Coughlin's desk, which had been delivered to his office shortly before five the previous afternoon—just after Coughlin had left for the day—was in a sealed eight-by-ten manila envelope, bearing the return address "Deputy Commissioner (Personnel)" and addressed *"Personal Attention Comm. Coughlin ONLY."*

Coughlin tried and failed to get his fingernail under the flap, and finally took a small penknife from his desk drawer and slit it open.

It contained a quarter-inch-thick sheaf of stapled-together paper. Coughlin glanced at the first page quickly and then handed it to Hollaran.

"I think this is what they call a dichotomy," Coughlin said. "The good news is also the bad news."

Hollaran took the sheaf of Xerox paper and looked at the first three pages. It was unofficially but universally known as "The List."

It listed the results of the most recent examination for promotion to sergeant. Two thousand seven hundred and eighty-two police officers—corporals, detectives, and patrolmen with at least two years' service—had taken the examination. Passing the examination and actually getting promoted meant a fourteen percent boost in basic pay for patrolmen, and a four percent boost for corporals and detectives.

A substantial percentage of detectives earned so much in overtime pay that taking the examination, passing it, and then actually getting promoted to sergeant—who put in far less overtime—would severely reduce their take-home pay. Many detectives took the sergeant's examination only relatively late in their careers, as a necessary step to promotion to lieutenant and captain, because retirement pay is based on rank.

The examination had two parts, written and oral. Originally, there had been only a written examination, but there had been protests that the written examination was "culturally biased" and an equally important oral examination had been added to the selection process.

Passing the written portion of the examination was a prerequisite to taking the oral portion of the examination, and a little more than five hundred examinees had failed to pass the written and been eliminated from consideration.

Oral examinations had begun a month after the results of the written were published, and had stretched out over four months.

Six hundred eighty-four patrolmen, corporals, and detectives had passed the oral portion of the sergeant's examination and were certified to be eligible for promotion.

That was not at all the same thing as saying that all those who were eligible for promotion would be promoted. Only fifty-seven of the men on The List—less than ten percent—would be "immediately"—within a week or a month—promoted. A number of factors, but primarily the city budget, determined how many eligibles would be promoted and when. The eligibles who weren't promoted "immediately" would have to wait until vacancies occurred—for example, when a sergeant was retired or promoted.

What that translated to mean was that if an individual ranked in the top 100, or maybe 125, on The List, he or she stood a good chance of getting promoted. Anyone ranking below 125 would almost certainly have to forget being promoted until The List "expired"—usually after two years—and a new sergeant's examination was announced and held.

The first name on The List in Hollaran's hand—the examinee who had scored highest—was Payne, Matthew M., Payroll No. 231047, Special Operations.

"Why am I not surprised?" Hollaran asked, smiling, and then added, unctuously, "Detective Payne is a splendid young officer, of whom the department generally, and his godfather specifically, can be justifiably proud."

"Go to hell, Frank," Detective Payne's godfather said, and then added, "What he needs is a couple of years—more than a couple: three, four years—in uniform, in a district."

"You really didn't think Matt would ask for a district assignment? In *uniform*?" Hollaran asked, chuckling.

When Police Commissioner Mariani had announced the latest examination for promotion to sergeant, he had added a new twist, which, on the advice of other senior police officials and personnel experts, he believed would be good for morale. The five top-ranking examinees would be permitted to submit their first three choices of post-promotion assignment, one of which would be guaranteed.

Deputy Commissioner Coughlin had at first thought it wasn't a bad idea. And then he had realized it was almost certainly going to apply to Matthew M.

Payne, and that changed things. Matty's scoring first—which meant that there would be no excuse not to give him the assignment he had chosen—made it even worse.

"I had lunch with him last Thursday," Coughlin said. "I told him, all things considered, that he stood a pretty good chance of placing high enough on The List. . . ."

"How prescient of you, Commissioner," Hollaran said, smiling.

"How do you think you're going to like the last-out shift in Night Command, Captain?"

The last-out—midnight to eight A.M.—shift in Night Command was universally regarded as the department's version of purgatory for captains. Those who occupied the position usually had seriously annoyed the senior brass in one way or another. There was no relief from the midnight-to-morning hours; the occupant was required to be in uniform at all times while on duty, and he was the only captain in the department to whom the department did not issue an unmarked car.

Some Night Command captains took their lumps and performed their duties without complaint, while waiting until they were replaced by some other captain who had annoyed the hierarchy, but many heard the message and retired or resigned.

"Come on," Hollaran said, not awed by the threat. "Matt took the exam, grabbed the brass ring, and he's a good cop and you know it."

". . . and would be given his choice of assignment," Coughlin went on, ignoring him. "And that he should seriously consider a couple of years in uniform."

"And?"

"He said his three choices were going to be Special Operations, Highway, and Homicide."

"Somehow, I can't see Matt on a motorcycle," Hollaran said.

"And Highway's under Special Operations, and he's been in Special Operations too long as it is," Coughlin said.

"Which leaves Homicide," Hollaran said.

"Which, since he knows he can't stay in Special Operations forever, is really what he wants. He's got the system figured out."

"And that surprises you? With you and Peter Wohl as his rabbis?"

Coughlin flashed him an annoyed look.

Hollaran suddenly smiled.

"You're having obscene thoughts again, Frank?" Coughlin asked. "Or something else amuses you?"

"The Black Buddha," Hollaran said. "Wait till he finds out the empty sergeant's slot in Homicide will be filled by brand-new Sergeant Payne."

Coughlin smiled, despite himself.

"They're pretty close," Coughlin said. "Which makes their situation even more uncomfortable for both of them."

"They'll be able to handle it," Hollaran said.

(TWO)

At 9:05, Detective Matthew M. Payne—a six foot tall, lithely muscled, 165-pound twenty-six-year-old with neatly cut, dark, thick hair and dark, intelligent eyes—arrived in the parking lot behind the Roundhouse, at the wheel of an unmarked, new Ford Crown Victoria.

He was neatly dressed in a tweed jacket, gray flannel slacks, a white button-down-collar shirt, and striped necktie, and when he finally found a place to park the car and got out of the car, carrying a leather briefcase, he looked more like a stockbroker, or a young lawyer, than what comes to mind when the phrase "police detective" is heard.

There seemed to be proof of this when he entered the building and had to produce his badge and identification card before the police officer guarding access to the lobby would pass him into it.

But as he was walking toward the elevator, he was recognized by a slight, wiry, starting-to-bald thirty-eight-year-old in a well-worn blue blazer. He was not a very imposing-looking man, but Matt—and others—knew him to be one of the best homicide detectives, in the same league as Jason Washington.

"As I live and breathe, the fashion plate of Special Operations," Detective Anthony C. Harris greeted him. "What brings you here from the Arsenal down to where the working cops work?"

"Hey, Tony!" Payne said, smiling as they shook hands. He looked quickly at his watch. "Got time for a cup of coffee?"

Harris shook his head.

"Guess who wants me to take a look at the Roy Rogers scene," Harris said.

"South Broad? That one? I saw Mickey's piece in the *Bulletin*."

Harris nodded.

"I thought they'd have them by now," Payne said. "Mickey said 'massive manhunt.'"

"It would help if we knew who we're looking for," Harris said. "No one's picked anybody out of the mug books, and there's no talk on the streets."

"I thought there were a bunch of witnesses?"

"There were. I have just been looking at police artist sketches. To go by them, twenty-five different people shot Kenny Charlton."

Payne picked up on the use of Charlton's first name.

"You knew him?"

"One of the good guys, Matt," Harris said, just a little bitterly. "With a little bit of luck, right after I get a positive ID on these two bastards, they'll resist arrest."

I'm a cop, a detective—hell, I think I'm going to be a sergeant—and I don't know if he means that or not.

Harris, too, was quick to pick up on things on other people's faces. The subject was changed.

"So what's new with you, Matt?" he asked.

"A famous movie star is coming to Philadelphia," Matt said.

"I thought all movie stars were famous," Harris said. "Which one?"

"They haven't told me yet," Matt said. "I'm on my way to the auditorium for the preliminary meeting with Gerry McGuire of Dignitary Protection. And just for the record, there are also infamous movie stars."

"Score one for the fashion plate," Harris said. "Don't let this go to your head, but the Black Buddha and I miss you, Matt, now that we're back with the police department . . ."

Both Jason Washington and Tony Harris, over their bitter objections, had been transferred to the Special Operations Division when it was formed, and only recently—after they had trained other Special Operations detectives to Inspector Peter Wohl's high standards—had been allowed to return.

"Fuck you, Tony!"

". . . and we don't see much of you. Why don't you—not today, wait 'til we get the Charlton doers—come by when you have the time and buy us lunch?"

"Yeah. I will."

"Give my regards to the movie star," Harris said, touched Payne's arm, and walked across the lobby to the exit.

Matt walked across the lobby toward the auditorium.

The Dignitary Protection Unit, as the name suggests, is charged with protecting dignitaries visiting Philadelphia. Philadelphia's own dignitaries—the mayor, for example, and the district attorney—are protected by police officers, but those officers are not under the Dignitary Protection Unit.

Staffing the unit poses a problem. Sometimes there are several—even a dozen—dignitaries requiring protection, and sometimes only one or two, or none at all.

What has evolved is that only a few men—a lieutenant, two sergeants, and half a dozen detectives—are assigned full time to Dignitary Protection.

When needed, additional detectives—who don't wear uniforms on duty, and thus already have the necessary civilian clothing—are temporarily reassigned from their divisions, then returned to their regular duties after the visiting dignitary has left town.

Over time, most of the detectives placed on temporary duty with Dignitary Protection had come from the Special Operations Division, as had uniformed officers of the Highway Patrol, which was part of Special Operations. Special Operations had citywide authority, for one thing, which meant that its officers knew more about the back alleys and such of the entire city than did their peers who spent their careers in one district. That was useful to Dignitary Protection.

And the department had yet to hear a complaint from any visiting dignitary that en route from Pennsylvania Station or the airport to his hotel his car had been preceded and trailed by nattily uniformed police officers mounted on shiny motorcycles with sirens screaming and blue lights flashing.

But the Roman Emperor spectacle was really a pleasant by-product of the fact that Highway Patrol officers were the elite of the department. It was hard to get into Highway, hard to stay there if you didn't measure up, and while there you could count on being where the action—heaviest criminal activity—was.

The dignitary in his limousine, in other words, was protected by four—or eight, or even twelve—of the best-trained, best-equipped streetwise uniforms in the department.

Consequently, Dignitary Protection had gotten in the habit of requesting temporary personnel from Special Operations first, because the commanding officer of Special Operations almost always gave Dignitary Protection whatever it asked for, without question.

There had been a lot of talk that the smart thing to do would be to simply transfer the unit—if dignitary protection wasn't a special operation, what was?—to Special Operations.

That hadn't happened, for a number of reasons never really spelled out, but certainly including the fact that Inspector Peter Wohl, the commanding officer of Special Operations, probably could not have won an election for the most popular white shirt in the department.

For one thing, at thirty-seven, he was the youngest inspector in the department. For another, he already had, in the opinion of many inspectors and chief inspectors, too much authority. And in the course of his career—especially when he had been a staff inspector in Internal Affairs, again the youngest man to hold that rank—he had put a number of dirty cops, some of them high ranking, in the slam.

Almost all police officers of all ranks, although they don't like to admit it, have ambivalent feelings toward dirty cops, and the cops who catch them and send them to the slam. Dirty cops deserve the slam, and the guys who put them there deserve the gratitude and admiration of every honest police officer.

On the other hand, *Jesus Christ, Ol' Harry was a good cop for seventeen years before this happened, and how's his family going to make out while he's doing time? And when he gets out, no pension, no nothing. I'm glad he's not on my conscience.*

When Wohl—after having placed second of eleven examinees on the written examination for promotion to inspector—appeared before the senior officers conducting the oral part of the exam, his ability to handle the conflicting emotions that dealing with dirty cops evoked was one of the reasons he got promoted.

So while just about everyone agreed that Dignitary Protection belonged in Special Operations, it didn't go there. It stayed a separate unit.

There was so much going on between Dignitary Protection and Special Operations, however, that Inspector Wohl had decided there should be one man charged with liaison between the two. He had assigned this duty—in addition to his other duties—to Detective Matthew M. Payne.

It was no secret anywhere in the department that Inspector Wohl was Detective Payne's rabbi, and there were many who thought that this was the reason Payne was given the assignment. And to a degree, the suspicions had a basis in fact.

The function of a rabbi is to groom a young police officer for greater responsibility—and higher rank—down the line. As he had risen upward in the police department, Inspector Wohl's rabbi had been Inspector, then Chief Inspector, then Deputy Commissioner Dennis V. Coughlin.

As Commissioner Coughlin had risen upward through the ranks, his rabbi had been Captain, and ultimately the Hon. Jerome H. "Jerry" Carlucci, Mayor of the City of Philadelphia, who had liked to boast that he had held every rank in the police department except policewoman, before answering the people's call to elective public office.

And His Honor, too, had had a rabbi. His had been—ultimately, before he retired—Chief Inspector Augustus Wohl, whose only son Peter had entered the

Police Academy at twenty, two weeks after he had graduated from Temple University.

Wohl did think that learning about Dignitary Protection would do Detective Payne some good—the more a cop knew about the department, the better—but another major reason was efficiency.

Whoever sat in at the meetings at Dignitary Protection would be expected to report to Wohl precisely what had happened, and what would be asked of Special Operations.

Matt Payne not only had the ability to write a report quickly and accurately, but he had almost permanently attached to his right wrist a state-of-the-art laptop computer, on which and through which the final reports of what happened at the Dignitary Protection meeting would be written, and transmitted to Inspector Wohl's desktop computer long before Detective Payne himself could return to Special Operations headquarters in what once had been the U.S. Army's Frankford Arsenal.

As Payne was about to push open the door to the auditorium, Sergeant Al Nevins, a stocky, barrel-chested forty-five-year-old, trotted across the lobby and caught his arm.

Nevins was one of the two sergeants permanently assigned to Dignitary Protection.

"God loves me," he said. "You're early. I was afraid you'd show up on time, and I put out the arm for you, and radio reported they couldn't find you." He offered no explanation, instead turned and, raising his voice, called across the lobby, "Lieutenant Payne's here."

Lieutenant Gerry McGuire, the commanding officer of Dignitary Protection—a somewhat plump, pleasant-looking forty-five-year-old—walked across the lobby to them. He was—surprising Matt—in uniform.

"I tried to have Al reach out for you, Matt," McGuire said. "I'm glad you're here. We're going to do this, now, in the Ritz-Carlton."

"Who's coming to town, sir?" Matt asked.

"Stan Colt," Lieutenant McGuire said.

"My life is now complete," Matt said.

Stan Colt was an almost unbelievably handsome and muscular actor who had begun his theatrical career in a rock band, used the fame that had brought him to get a minor part in a police series on television, and then used that to get his first role in a theatrical motion picture, playing a detective. That motion picture had been spectacularly successful, largely, Matt thought, because of the special effects. There had been a half-dozen follow-ons, none of which Matt had seen—the first one had reminded him of the comic books he'd read as a kid; in one scene Stan Colt had fired twenty-two shots without reloading from a seven-shot .45 Colt, held sideward—but he understood they had all done exceedingly well at the box office.

"Matt," McGuire said, "be aware that the mayor and the commissioner look upon him as a Philadelphia icon, right up there with Benjamin Franklin." He looked at his watch and added, "I mean now, we're due there at nine-thirty."

He waved Matt ahead of him across the lobby. Sergeant Nevins followed them.

"What's going on at the Ritz-Carlton?" Matt asked.

"Mr. Colt's advance party is there," Lieutenant McGuire replied. "And possibly the archbishop, though more likely Monsignor Schneider. And the commissioner said he might drop by. Colt's people are calling it a 'previsit breakfast conference.'"

"What's going on?"

"West Catholic High School is going to give Mr. Colt his high school diploma," McGuire said. "Which he apparently didn't get before he went off to show business and fame. In connection with this, there will be two expensive lunches, two even more expensive dinners, and a star-studded performance featuring Mr. Colt and a number of friends. The proceeds will all go to the West Catholic Building Fund. The archbishop, I understand, is thrilled. And the mayor and the commissioner are thrilled whenever the archbishop is thrilled."

"I get the picture," Matt said.

The elevator door opened and Lieutenant McGuire led the way out of the building to the parking lot.

"Where's your car, Al?" McGuire asked. "Mine's in the garage again."

"Mine's right over there," Matt said, pointing, and immediately regretted it.

The assignment of unmarked cars in the Philadelphia police department—except in Special Operations—worked on the hand-me-down principle. New cars went to the chief inspectors, who on receipt of their new vehicles handed down their slightly used vehicles to inspectors, who in turn handed down their well-used, if not worn-out, vehicles to captains entitled to unmarked cars, who passed their nearly worn-out vehicles farther down the hierarchy.

Special Operations had a federal grant for "Experimental Policing Techniques," which, among other things, provided money for automobiles. Special

Operations vehicles were not provided out of the department budget, in other words, and the grant was worded so that "unneeded and unexpended funds" were supposed to be returned to the federal government.

The result of that was that not one dollar of "unneeded and unexpended funds" had ever been returned to Washington, and everyone in Special Operations who drove an unmarked car—down to lowly detectives and patrol officers in plainclothes assignments—drove a new vehicle.

When the annual grant money was received, new cars were purchased by Special Operations, and the used Special Operations cars were turned over to the department motor pool for assignment.

From Matt's perspective, it was a good deal for the department all around. Once a year, the department got thirty-odd cars—most of them in excellent shape—for nothing. And the department did not have to provide—and pay for—thirty-odd unmarked cars to Special Operations.

However, from the perspective of Lieutenant McGuire—and of most other lieutenants and captains, and even more than a few more senior officers— lowly detectives and officers in plainclothes should not be driving new cars when captains and lieutenants were driving cars on the steep slope leading to the crusher.

All Lieutenant McGuire said, however, when he got in the front seat of the car beside Matt, was "I love the smell of a new car."

They drove up Market Street to City Hall, and then around it, to the Ritz-Carlton, whose main entrance was on the west side of South Broad Street just across from City Hall.

McGuire looked at his watch again and said, "Park in front. I don't want to be late."

Matt pulled into space normally reserved for taxis, put a plastic covered POLICE OFFICIAL BUSINESS sign on the dashboard, and then hurried after McGuire and Nevins.

The Stan Colt advance party was in a large suite, the windows of which looked down on the statue of William Penn atop City Hall.

A buffet had been laid out—an impressive one, complete to a man in chef's whites manning an omelet stove—and there were seven or eight people in the room, including two men in clerical collars. Matt knew the archbishop by sight, and he wasn't one of the two, so the gray-haired one in the well-tailored suit had to be Monsignor Schneider.

In an adjacent room was a long conference table, on which water and coffee carafes, cups and saucers, and even lined pads and ballpoint pens had been laid out. There were two telephones on the table, and television sets mounted on the walls.

This suite was designed not for luxury—although it's no dump—but as somewhere the boss can gather the underlings together and inspire them.

Matt walked into the conference room, took a telephone cord from his briefcase, and looked along the walls for a telephone jack. Finding none, he dropped to his knees and got under the table. There were two double telephone jacks, and he plugged the telephone cord into one of them.

As he backed out, he became aware of nylon-sheathed legs.

"Can I help you?" a female voice asked as he got to his feet.

"No, thanks," he said. "I managed to get it in . . ." *Jesus Christ! Will you look at this!* ". . . the hole with only a little trouble."

"Laptop?" the blonde asked.

"Yes, ma'am."

"To take notes?"

"Yes, ma'am."

She's probably Stan Colt's squeeze. Far too beautiful for a common man. Jesus Christ, she's stunning!

She put out her hand.

"I'm Terry Davis," she said. "With GAM."

"Is that one 'r' and an 'i,' or two 'r's and a 'y'?"

"Not that it matters, but two 'r's and a 'y.'"

"And what's GAM?"

"Global Artists Management," she answered, making her surprise that he didn't know evident in the tone of her voice.

"Of course," Matt said, "I should have known."

"If you need anything else, just let me know."

"Thank you very much."

"Have you had your breakfast?"

Not quite an hour before, Detective Payne had had two fried eggs, two slices of Taylor ham, two bagels, a glass each of orange juice and milk, and two cups of coffee.

"I could eat a little something, now that you mention it."

"Well, when you have your laptop up and working, won't you please have some breakfast?"

"You're very kind," Matt said.

She smiled at him and walked back to the room with the buffet, in the process convincing Payne that both sides of her were stunning.

He turned the laptop on, pushed the appropriate buttons, thought a moment about whether he wanted to make this official or not, decided he didn't, and then typed, very quickly, for he was an accomplished typist, the private screen name for Inspector Wohl, and then his own; he wanted a copy of what he was about to type.

> 0935 dignitary is stan colt, coming to town to raise money for west catholic high school. So far two $$dinners, two $$lunches, and a $$benefit performance. will know dates locations etc after breakfasting upper floor suite ritz carlton with mcguire, monsignor schneider, terry davis of gam, others. I think I'm in love. 701.

In a moment, the computer told him his mail had been sent. Probably less than a minute later, the computer on the table behind Inspector Peter Wohl's desk at Special Operations headquarters would give off a ping, and a message would appear on his monitor telling him he had an e-mail message from 701, which was Detective Payne's badge number. A similar action would take place on Detective Payne's desktop, and when he got back to the office, he would copy the message into his desktop.

Leaving the computer on, Payne went into the room with the buffet. Lieutenant McGuire, seated at a table with Monsignor Schneider and the other priest, waved him over.

"Yes, sir?"

"Payne, do you know the monsignor?"

"No, sir."

"Monsignor, this is Detective Payne, of Special Operations, which will be providing most of the manpower for Mr. Colt's security while he's here."

"I'm very pleased to meet you," the monsignor said, smiling and standing up to offer his hand. "Your boss and I are old friends."

Was that incidental information, to put me at ease, or are you telling me that if I displease you in any way, you'll go right to Wohl?

"Detective Payne, this is Father Venno, of my office," the monsignor went on, "who'll be my liaison, representing the archdiocese."

"How do you do, Father?" Matt said politely, putting out his hand and looking over Venno's shoulder, finding Terry Davis at a table with two empty chairs, and wondering if he could get away with joining her.

"Why don't you get a plate—the omelets are wonderful—and join us?" Monsignor Schneider said.

Shit!

"Thank you very much, sir," Payne said.

Although he didn't have nearly as much appetite as he'd had when contemplating taking breakfast with Miss Davis, the omelets offered did have a certain appeal, and Detective Payne returned to the table with a western omelet with everything, an English muffin, and a large glass of orange juice.

"That was an unfortunate business on South Broad Street last night, wasn't it?" Monsignor Schneider said. "At the Gene Autry?"

"The Roy Rogers, Monsignor," Father Venno corrected him.

"Wasn't it?" the monsignor repeated, directing the question to Matt Payne, his face making it clear he didn't like to be corrected.

"Yes, sir, it was," Matt said.

"Have there been any developments in the case?"

"They're working on it, sir," Matt said. "I think they'll wrap it up pretty quickly."

"Greater love . . . ," the monsignor said, somewhat piously.

"Officer Charlton was a good man," Lieutenant McGuire said. "A very sad situation."

Over Father Venno's shoulder, Matt saw that the two empty chairs at Terry Davis's table were now occupied by Sergeant Al Nevins and another man—presumably from GAM—and that everyone was smiling at one another.

"I've just placed you," Father Venno said, a tone of satisfaction in his voice.

"Excuse me?" Matt said.

"You were involved in that . . . unfortunate incident . . . in Doylestown a couple of months ago, weren't you?"

"Unfortunate incident?" And it was six months ago, not "a couple," and I was just starting to think I'd be able to start really forgetting it. Thanks a lot, Father!

"What unfortunate incident was that?" Monsignor Schneider asked.

"At the Crossroads Diner, Monsignor," Father Venno said. "The FBI and Detective Payne were attempting an arrest—"

"Of a terrorist," the monsignor interrupted, remembering. "A terrorist armed with a machine gun. Several people lost their lives." He looked at Payne. "You were involved in that, were you?"

"Yes, sir, I was," Matt said.

"As I recall," the monsignor said, "three people died, and another young woman was shot."

"I believe there were just two deaths, Monsignor," Lieutenant McGuire said. "The terrorist, a man named Chenowith, and a civilian, a young woman who was cooperating with the FBI. What was her name, Matt?"

"Susan Reynolds," Matt answered.

And I loved her, and she loved me, but we didn't make it to that vine-covered cottage by the side of the road because that lunatic Chenowith let fly with his automatic carbine.

He had a sudden painfully clear mental image of Susan on her back in the parking lot behind the Crossroads Diner, her mouth and her sightless eyes open, her blond hair in a spreading pool of blood. The carbine bullet had made a small, neat hole just below her left eye, and a much nastier hole at the back of her head as it exited.

He laid his fork down, put his napkin on the table, and stood up.

"Will you excuse me, please?" he said, and looked around the room in search of a bathroom.

As he walked across the room, he heard Monsignor Schneider ask, "Detective Payne has experience working with the FBI, does he?" and heard Lieutenant McGuire's answer.

"Yes, he does, Monsignor."

Then he was in the bathroom, hurriedly fastening the lock, and hoping that he could splash cold water on his face quickly enough to force back the bile and nausea he felt rising.

Ninety seconds later, he was leaning with his back against the bathroom wall, wiping his face with a towel, exhaling audibly. He had managed to keep from throwing up, but there had been a cold sweat, and he could feel the clammy touch of his undershirt on his skin.

You're going to have to stop this shit, Matthew. That was a long time ago, Susan is not going to come back, and you're going to have to really put all of that out of your mind, or they'll put you in a rubber room.

Finally, he hung the towel back on its rack, and then, after purposefully taking several slow, deep breaths, unlatched the door and went out of the bathroom. Everyone was filing into the conference room—*how the hell long was I in the john?*—and he joined the line at the end, taking his seat at the table where he had left the laptop.

He saw a dark blue plastic folder lying beside his laptop. There was a neatly printed label on its cover: **Stan Colt's Visit to Philadelphia.** Matt looked around the table and saw that everyone had been provided with a folder, and that there was another laptop on the table, in front of a man about his age wearing a gray business suit.

Matt's seat turned out to be beside Monsignor Schneider.

"Are you all right, son? You look a little pale."

"A little indigestion, sir. I'm afraid I gulped the omelet."

"If I may have your attention," a natty, intense-looking man in a dark suit said, waited until everyone was looking at him, and then went on. "I think it might be a good idea if we all knew each other. I'll start with me. My name is Rogers Kennedy, and I'm a senior vice president of Global Artists Management, heading up GAM's New York office. Let me say that I'm delighted to be here, and it's my intention to see that Mr. Colt's activities here raise just as much money as possible for West Catholic High School, which is really dear to Mr. Colt's heart, and to see that that's done in such a manner that Mr. Colt will look back on the experience fondly. To make sure that any bumps in the road, so to speak, are smoothed out beforehand, or that the best possible detour is set up.

"This lovely young lady, who is living proof that there is such a thing as the opposite of the dumb blonde of fame and legend, is Miss Terry Davis, of GAM's West Coast Division. *Vice President* Davis has been charged with the hands-on management of Mr. Colt's visit . . ."

**1005 head gam man is rogers kennedy senior vp from nyc
terry davis gam vp from la is hands-on boss**

". . . and this is Larry Robards," Rogers Kennedy went on, indicating the young man with the other laptop, "my administrative executive, who takes things down so we don't forget anything."

Mr. Robards smiled around the table.

"Administrative executive"? What the hell is that?

larry robards is kennedy's 'administrative executive' read male secretary

"Monsignor?" Kennedy asked.

"I'm Monsignor Schneider," Schneider said, smiling but not standing up. "The archbishop has asked me to handle Stanley's visit and the fund-raising events . . ."

Stanley? Is that Stan Colt's real name—Stanley?

". . . and this is Father Venno, who is under my orders to make himself available to Stanley from the moment he gets off the plane until he gets back on," Monsignor Schneider said.

Venno smiled around the table.

mons. schneider representing archbishop
father venno his surrogate . . . available to colt around the clock while he's here.

"I'm Lieutenant McGuire," McGuire said, getting to his feet. "I command the Dignitary Protection Unit. This is Sergeant Al Nevins, who will handle the paperwork. Both of us—all of the Philadelphia police department—are determined to make Stan Colt's time in Philadelphia, to use your phrase, Mr. Kennedy, as bump-free as possible. Let me assure you that you will have our complete cooperation."

He sat down.

lieut gerry mcguire for dignitary protection

"Thank you, Captain, that's good to hear," Kennedy said, and added: "Mr. Colt will have his own security, of course. Wachenhut, I believe, Terry?"

"Wachenhut Security Services, right," Terry Davis confirmed

"I'll have them liaise with you, Lieutenant McGuire, as soon as possible."

"Yes, sir," McGuire said.

wachenhut rent-a-cops

Kennedy looked around the table, and smiled at Matt.

"And this gentleman?"

"My name is Payne, Mr. Kennedy. I'm with Special Operations."

"I don't think I quite understand."

"We're going to provide the detectives, and highway patrol officers—and just about whatever else Lieutenant McGuire asks for. I'm here to get a preliminary idea of what that might be."

"You're with the police department?" Kennedy sounded surprised.

"Yes, sir."

"*Detective* Payne, Mr. Kennedy," Monsignor Schneider said, "if I may put it this way, is one of the finest of Philadelphia's finest . . ."

Jesus, where did that come from?

"*Detective* Payne?" Terry Davis asked in surprise.

". . . whose real-life exploits could really serve as the basis for one of Stanley's films," the monsignor went on. "I'm delighted the police department has assigned him to this project."

Hey, I'm not assigned to this "project."

"No offense intended, certainly, Detective," Kennedy said. "We're delighted to have you."

I think I have just been had. And I really don't want to baby-sit a movie actor.

Matt looked at Lieutenant Gerry McGuire, who, smiling at Matt's discomfort, sarcastically gave him a hidden-behind-his-hand thumbs-up gesture. Matt returned it with a hidden-behind-his-hand gesture of his own, the third finger of his balled fist held upright. Lieutenant McGuire smiled even more broadly.

"If you'll open the folder before you," Rogers Kennedy went on, "you'll find the tentative schedule we have worked out for Mr. Colt's visit, and I think it would be a good idea to go over it now, to see if there are any potential bumps in Stan's road we may have missed."

Matt opened the folder.

Wohl's going to want at least three copies of this. I can take it to the office and xerox it. Better yet, scan it into the computer, so when the inevitable changes are made to it, they won't have to be written on it, and the whole thing re-xeroxed. Or I can type it into the laptop now, and skip the scanning.

He immediately began to type, and was finished long before Rogers Kennedy, Monsignor Schneider, and Lieutenant McGuire had worked their way through it, item by item. When he looked up, he saw that Terry Davis was looking at him. When he smiled at her, she looked away.

Think about this, Matthew: If your life was really over when that sonofabitch Chenowith killed Susan, would you now be wondering what Vice President Davis looks like in her birthday suit? Or considering the possibilities of getting her into that condition?

Peter Wohl said, Dad said, Amy said, just about everybody—including the second-rate shrink with the bad breath they made me go see—told me that it would take time, but I would get over Susan.

If that is the case—and Jesus, that would be great—then why, when Father Venno "placed" me in "that unfortunate incident," was I instantly back in that

*goddamned Crossroads Diner parking lot, with Susan's blood sticky on my hands?
Followed, as usual, with the cold-sweat-and-nausea business?*

He looked across the table at Terry Davis again.

As if sensing his eyes on her, she looked at him.

*Are you going to be the salvation of M. M. Payne, you stunning, long-legged
blonde goddess? Or have I already slipped over the border into LaLa Land?*

He winked at her.

She looked away, shaking her head, but he could see she was smiling.

He walked up to her when the meeting was over.

"Well, I guess we'll be seeing more of one another," she said. "Is there any-thing I can do for you?"

"You mean in connection with this?" he asked.

"Yes, of course."

"I don't think that's going to happen," he said. "The only reason I was here was because my boss had other things to do."

"And didn't want to come in the first place?"

"You said that, not me," Matt said. "But there is something you can do for me."

"Name it."

"Have dinner with me."

"No."

"That's getting right to the point, isn't it?" he said. "You didn't leave your-self any wriggle room."

"I'm on a red-eye back to the Coast at twelve-thirty," she said. "And between now and then I'm going to go make the appropriate noises over a girl-friend from college's toddler I've never seen."

"Dare I hope that changes your response from 'hell, no' to 'maybe some other time'?"

"We'll be working together. I'm sure we'll take some meals together."

"Matt," Lieutenant Gerry McGuire called, "I've got to get back to work."

He looked at her and shrugged, then walked out of the suite.

CHAPTER
3

Matt Payne dropped Lieutenant McGuire and Sergeant Nevins at the Round-house, and then—after thinking it over for a moment at the parking lot exit—headed back toward Center City rather than toward the Delaware River and Interstate 95, which would have taken him to Special Operations headquarters.

Inspector Wohl would expect him to come to the Arsenal—still called that, although the U.S. Army was long gone—directly from the meeting with Dignitary Protection, but that couldn't be helped. He needed a quick shower and a change of linen. The cold sweat he had experienced had been a bad one, and had produced an offensive smell. Sometimes, the cold sweats just left him clammily uncomfortable, but sometimes they were accompanied by an unpleasant odor, which he thought was caused by something he had eaten. He hoped that was the reason; he didn't want to think of other unpleasant possibilities.

He went over to Spruce Street, and west on it past Broad Street to Nineteenth, where he turned right and then right and right again onto Manning. Manning was more of an alley than a street, but it gave access to the parking garage beneath the brownstone mansion on Rittenhouse Square that housed the Delaware Valley Cancer Society.

The 150-year-old building had been converted several years before to office space, which, as the owner of the building had frequently commented, had proven twice as expensive as tearing the building down and starting from scratch would have been.

Inside, the building—with the exception of a tiny apartment in the garret—was now modern office space, with all the amenities, including an elevator and parking space for Cancer Society executives in the basement. Outside, the building preserved the dignity of Rittenhouse Square, thought by many to be the most attractive of Philadelphia's squares.

When the owner—the building had been in his family since it was built—had authorized the expense of converting the garret, not suitable for use as offices, he thought the tiny rooms could probably be rented to an elderly couple, perhaps, or a widow or widower, someone of limited means who worked downtown, perhaps in the Franklin Institute or the Free Public Library, and who would be willing to put up with the inconvenience of access and the slanting walls and limited space because it was convenient, cheap, and was protected around-the-clock by the Wachenhut Security Service.

It was instead occupied by a single bachelor, the owner's son, Matthew M. Payne, because the City of Philadelphia requires that its employees live within the city limits, and the Payne residence in Wallingford, a suburb, did not qualify.

The owner of the building had decreed that two parking spaces in the underground garage be reserved for him. Both his wife and his daughter, he thought, would appreciate having their own parking spaces in downtown Philadelphia, and it was, after all, his building.

Matt Payne pulled the unmarked Crown Victoria into one of the two reserved parking spots. The second reserved parking spot held a silver Porsche 911 Carrera, which had been his graduation present when he had finished his undergraduate work at the University of Pennsylvania.

He carefully locked the car, then trotted to the elevator, which was standing with its door open. He pressed 3, the door closed, and the elevator started to move. Once he was past the ground floor, he pulled his necktie loose and began to open his shirt. The buttons were open nearly to his belt when the door opened, and he started to step out onto what he expected to be the third floor.

It was instead the second. Two female employees of the Delaware County Cancer Society had summoned the elevator to take them to the third floor, which was occupied by the various machines necessary to keep track of contributors, and the technicians—all of whom were male—and was seldom visited by anyone not connected with the machines.

The ladies recoiled at the unexpected sight of a partially dressed male—obviously in the act of undressing even further, and from whose shoulder was slung a rather large pistol—coming out of the elevator at them.

"Sorry," Matt Payne said, gathering his shirt together with both hands, and indicating with a nod of his head that they were welcome to join him in the elevator.

The ladies smiled somewhat weakly and indicated they would just as soon wait for the next elevator, thank you just the same.

He pushed 3 again, and the elevator rose one more floor.

When the door opened, there was no one in sight. Matt crossed the small foyer quickly, pushed the keys on a combination lock on a door, shoved it open, and went up the stairs to his apartment two at a time.

Not quite ninety seconds later, he was in his shower—a small stall shower; there wasn't room for a bathtub—when his cell phone went off.

He stuck his head and one arm out from behind the shower curtain. "Payne."

There was no direct response to that. Instead, Matt heard a familiar voice say, somewhat triumphantly, "Got him, Inspector!"

A mental picture of police officer Paul T. O'Mara came to Payne's mind. Officer O'Mara, a very neat, very wholesome-looking young officer in an immaculate, well-fitting uniform, was sitting at his desk in the outer office of the commanding officer of Special Operations. Officer O'Mara was Inspector Wohl's administrative assistant.

He had assumed that duty when the incumbent—Officer M. M. Payne—had been promoted to detective.

Officer O'Mara, like Inspector Wohl, was from a police family. His father was a captain, who commanded the Twenty-fifth District. His brother was a sergeant in Civil Affairs. His grandfather, like Peter Wohl's father and grandfather, had retired from the Philadelphia police department.

More important, his father was a friend of both Deputy Commissioner Dennis V. Coughlin and Chief Inspector (Retired) Augustus Wohl. When Officer O'Mara, who had five years on the job in the Traffic Division, had failed, for the second time, to pass the examination for corporal, both Commissioner Coughlin and Chief Wohl had had a private word with Inspector Wohl.

They had pointed out to him that just because someone has a little trouble with promotion examinations doesn't mean he's not a good cop, with potential. It just means that he has trouble passing examinations.

Not like you, Peter, or, for that matter, Matt, the inference had been. *You're not really all that smart; you're just good at taking examinations.*

One or the other or both of them had suggested that what Officer O'Mara needed was a little broader experience than he was getting in the Traffic Division, such as he might get if it could be arranged to have Personnel, with your approval, of course, assign him to Special Operations as your administrative assistant, now that Matty got himself promoted, and the job's open.

Officer O'Mara's performance as Wohl's administrative assistant had been satisfactory. He was immensely loyal, hardworking, and reliable. The trouble with Officer O'Mara, as Detective Jesus Martinez had often pointed out, was that he had been at the end of the line when brains were passed out, and an original thought and a cold drink of water would probably kill him.

Inspector Wohl came on the line a moment later.

"When's the meeting going to be over?" he asked without any preliminaries.

"It's over, sir."

"You're en route here?"

"Actually, sir, I'm in the shower."

"You had planned to come to work today?"

"Yes, sir. I will be there directly."

The line went dead.

Shit! Another three minutes, and when he asked, "You're en route here?" I could have said, "Yes, sir."

I wonder what's going on?

Why did he put the arm out for me?

[TWO]

Twenty minutes later—after having twice en route responded to radio requests for his location—Detective Payne entered the walled collection of aging red-brick buildings once known as the U.S. Army Frankford Arsenal and now somewhat hopefully dubbed the "Arsenal Business Center" by the City of Philadelphia.

When business had not rushed to the Arsenal, the city had given its permission for two units of the police department to occupy some of the buildings. One was the Sex Crimes Unit, and the other the far larger Special Operations Division, which previously had been operating out of a building at Castor and Frankford Avenues. Built in 1892, the Frankford Grammar School had rendered the city more than a century of service before being adjudged uninhabitable by the Bureau of Licenses & Inspections.

It had then served as Special Operations Division Headquarters—with Inspector Peter Wohl installed in what had been the principal's office—until space had "become available" in the Arsenal Business Center. Just as soon as funds became available, the city intended to demolish the old school. Unless, of course, it *really* died of old age and fell down by itself, thereby saving the city that expenditure.

Matt drove through the collection of old and mostly unused Arsenal buildings until he came to one of the "newer" buildings—the cornerstone was marked 1934—and drove around it, looking for a place to park. There were none. Even the spot reserved for COMMISSIONER was occupied.

He finally parked a block away and then trotted to the Special Operations headquarters building. Inspector Wohl was now housed in the ground-floor office of what had once been the office of the Arsenal's commanding officer.

He pushed open the door from the corridor to Wohl's outer office.

Officer O'Mara pushed a lever on his intercom.

"Sir, Detective Payne is here."

"Send him in."

Matt knocked politely at the door and waited for permission to enter.

"Come in, please," Inspector Wohl called.

Matt pushed the door open.

There were five people in the room. Inspector Peter Wohl, sitting behind his desk; Captain Michael J. Sabara, fortyish, a short, barrel-chested Lebanese, who was Wohl's deputy; Captain David Pekach, the weasel-faced, fair-skinned, small, wiry thirty-seven-year-old commanding officer of the Highway Patrol; and, sitting side by side on Wohl's couch, two white shirts Matt was really surprised to see in Wohl's office: Deputy Commissioner (Patrol) Dennis V. Coughlin and his Executive Officer, Captain Francis X. Hollaran.

What the hell is going on?

"I'm delighted, Detective Payne," Inspector Wohl said, sarcastically, "that you have managed to squeeze time for us into your busy schedule."

"There's one bastard I would really like to see shuffling around in shackles," Captain Hollaran said, handing something to Captain Pekach.

"You'd like to see him in shackles?" Captain Sabara replied. "I'd like to see him fry. I'd strap him in the chair myself."

Despite his somewhat menacing appearance, Captain Michael Sabara was really a rather gentle man. Matt was surprised at his vehemence.

"Fry"? "I'd strap him in the chair myself"?

Who are they talking about?

"You were saying, Detective Payne?" Inspector Wohl went on.

"Sorry, sir. I had to change my clothes," Payne said.

"When was the last time you got a postcard, Dave?" Commissioner Coughlin asked.

"I get one every couple of months," Pekach replied. "The one before this was from Rome. This one's from someplace in France."

"Probably from where he lives," Coughlin said, shaking his head. "The sonofabitch knows the French won't let us extradite him."

"Unless it had something to do with Monsignor Schneider, I don't think I want to hear why you had to change your clothes," Inspector Wohl said.

"Nothing to do with the monsignor, sir."

"Good," Inspector Wohl said. "I presume everything went well at the meeting?"

"Everything went well at the meeting," Matt said. "I e-mailed you, sir."

"So you did," Wohl said. "And I was delighted to hear that you think you're in love, but wondered why you thought you should notify me officially."

"You're in love, are you, Payne?" Captain Pekach asked.

"No, sir, I'm not."

"Then why did you tell Inspector Wohl you were, and as part of your official duties?" Commissioner Coughlin asked.

"It was a little joke, sir," Matt said.

Jesus, why the hell did I do that?

And damn it, I sent it to his personal e-mail address, so it wasn't official.

"You have to watch that sort of thing, Matty," Commissioner Coughlin said, his tone suggesting great disappointment in Matt's lack of professionalism.

"Who are you in love with, Payne?" Captain Sabara asked.

"There was a girl at the meeting," Matt said. "I . . ."

"The sort of girl you could bring home to dinner with your mother?" Sabara pursued.

"Or to dinner with my Martha?" Captain Pekach asked.

Martha was Mrs. Pekach.

"Sir?"

"More important," Sabara asked, "what makes you think this female is in love with you?"

I am having my chain pulled. Just for the hell of it? Or is there more to this?

"Actually, sir, I knew she was in love with me from the moment she saw me. I seem to have that effect on women."

There were smiles, but not so much as a chuckle.

"Let me put it to you this way, Matty," Commissioner Coughlin said, very seriously. "The *one* thing a detective—or a newly promoted sergeant—*doesn't* need is a reputation as a ladies' man . . ."

What did he say—"or a new sergeant"?

". . . it tends to piss off the wives of the men they're working with," Coughlin finished.

Now there was laughter.

"Congratulations, Matty," Coughlin said. "You're number one on the list."

He stood up, went to Matt, shook his hand, and put his arm around his shoulders.

"I'll be damned," Matt said.

"Damned? Probably, almost certainly," Wohl said. "But for the moment, we're all proud of you."

"Yeah, we are, Matt," Pekach said. "I don't think even our beloved boss was ever number one on a list."

"Yeah, he was," Coughlin corrected him. "Peter was number one on the lieutenant's list."

Officer O'Mara appeared at the door with a digital camera, lined them all up, with Matt in the middle, and took four pictures of them.

"There's a dark side to this," Pekach said. "Matt, you know Martha's going to have a party for you."

"She doesn't have to do that," Matt said.

"She will want to," Pekach said.

"I've got to go back to work," Coughlin said. He looked at Hollaran. "Frank and I would have been out of here long ago if Detective Payne hadn't found it necessary to take a bath in the middle of the morning."

"It was a matter of absolute necessity," Matt said.

"So we'll leave just as soon as Matty calls his father and mother and lets them have the good news."

"Sir?" Wohl asked, confused.

"You don't mind if I borrow him for a couple of hours, do you, Peter?"

"No, sir."

"I'll wait for you outside, Matty," Coughlin said.

"Yes, sir."

There was a round of handshakes, and in a moment Matt and Wohl were alone in the office.

"Sit down, have a cup of coffee, and call," Wohl said. "You seem a little shaken."

Matt said aloud what he was thinking.

"I thought I was going to pass," he said. "Not number one, but pass. But now that it's happened . . . *Sergeant* Payne?"

"You'll get used to it, Matt," Wohl said, poured him a cup of coffee, and pointed to the couch, an order for him to sit down.

"Coughlin will wait," he said. "Prepare yourself for another 'what you need is a couple of years in uniform' speech."

"Another? You know about the first?"

Wohl nodded. "And for the record, Matt, I think he's right."

"I don't want to be a uniform sergeant," Matt said.

"You need that experience," Wohl said. "End of my speech."

"Thank you," Matt said, sat down, took out his cellular, and started pushing autodial buttons.

It didn't take long.

Mrs. Elizabeth Newman, the Payne housekeeper, said:

"I thought you knew, Matt, your mother went to Wilmington overnight."

Goddamn it, I did know!

"Thanks, Elizabeth. I did know. I forgot."

On the second call, Mrs. Irene Craig, Executive Secretary to Brewster Cortland Payne, Esq., founding partner of Mawson, Payne, Stockton, McAdoo & Lester, arguably Philadelphia's most prestigious law firm, said, a certain tone of loving exasperation in her voice, "I left two messages on your machine, Matt. Your dad went to Washington on the eight-thirteen this morning, and is going to spend the night with your mother in Wilmington."

And I got both of them, too, goddamn it!

"I'm sorry to bother you, Mrs. Craig. Forgive me."

"No, I won't. But I love you anyway."

On the third call, a nasal-voiced female somewhat tartly informed him that Dr. Payne would be teaching all day, and could not be reached unless it was an emergency.

"Thank you very much. Tell Dr. Payne, please, that unless we have her check within seventy-two hours, we're going to have to repossess the television."

"Amy always teaches all day on Monday," Inspector Wohl said.

Inspector Wohl knew more about Dr. Payne's schedule than her brother did. They were close friends, and on-and-off lovers.

Matt looked at him but said nothing.

"Low-ranking police officers should not keep Deputy Commissioners waiting," Wohl said. "You might want to write that down."

"Yes, sir. Thank you very much, sir."

Deputy Commissioner Coughlin was standing on the stairs to the building waiting for him.

"You drive, Matty," he ordered. "Frank had things to do. You can either drop me at the Roundhouse later, or I'll catch a ride somehow."

"Yes, sir. Where are we going?"

"The Roy Rogers at Broad and Snyder," Coughlin said. "You heard about that?"

"Yes, sir. I ran into Tony Harris at the Roundhouse this morning. Did they get the doers?"

"Not yet," Coughlin said. "We will, of course. We should have already. I'd like to know why we haven't."

And en route, I will get the speech.

I really hate to refuse anything he asks of me.

And he's right—and Peter made it clear he agrees with him—I probably would learn a hell of a lot I don't know and should if I went to one of the districts as a uniform sergeant.

But I don't want to be a uniform sergeant, spending my time driving around a district waiting for something to happen, getting involved in domestic disturbances, petty theft, and all that.

I like being a detective. I like working in civilian clothing.

And I didn't come up with that ruling that the high-five guys get their choice of assignment. They offered that prize, and I won it, fair and square, and I want it.

That's what I'll tell him.

When all else fails, tell the truth.

"What did your mother have to say?" Commissioner Coughlin asked.

"My father went to Washington," Matt replied. "He's going to meet Mother in Wilmington, and they'll spend the night. So I'll have to wait until they get back to tell them. And I couldn't get Amy on the phone; she teaches all day on Monday."

"Is he still pushing you to go to law school?"

Here it comes: "Maybe you should think about it, Matt."

"With great subtlety and even greater determination."

"He means well, Matty," Coughlin said.

"I know."

"What's Peter got you working on?" Coughlin asked.

I'm not supposed to tell you. But on the other hand, you're Deputy Commissioner Coughlin. You have every right in the world to ask.

"A cop-on-the-take question. Captain Cassidy, of the Eighteenth, is driving to his new condominium at Atlantic City in his new GMC Yukon XL. He gave his old one—last year's—to his daughter, who is married to a sergeant in the Eleventh. They also have a condo at the shore."

"Peter got it from Internal Affairs?" Coughlin asked.

"Until just now, I thought he got it from you," Matt said. "Either you or Chief Lowenstein. He said he wanted answers before Internal Affairs got involved."

Chief Inspector Matthew L. Lowenstein was chief of detectives.

"And have you? Come up with any answers?"

"Not so far."

"What have you got so far?"

"His major expense is the condo," Matt said. "The payment on the mortgage—$325,000—is about $2,400 a month. They furnished it from scratch, and the furniture payment is $323 a month. The Yukon—"

"What's a *Yukon*?" Coughlin interrupted.

"I'm not really sure. What Cassidy has—and the old one, too, that he gave to his daughter—is the big GMC. Until I started this, I thought they called them 'Suburbans.'"

"Okay," Coughlin said.

"Anyway, he bought the new Yukon—no trade-in—with no money down, on a four-year note. That's $683 a month. That's about—"

"Thirty-four hundred a month," Coughlin interrupted. "Which is a large chunk out of a captain's pay."

"His house is paid for," Matt said. "He lives in Northeast Philly, not far from Chief Wohl."

"I know."

"He has two kids in school, one in Archbishop Ryan High School and the other in Temple. I don't know yet what that costs."

"It's not cheap."

"On the income side, in the last nine months, his mother, who lived with him, died. And so did a brother. An unmarried brother, in Easton. There was some insurance—I'm working on how much—and some property. I'm working on that."

"Gut feeling?"

"I don't think he's on the take," Matt said. "Not the type."

"You think you can tell by looking, do you, Matty?"

"The Black Buddha told me that just because you can't take your gut feeling to court, doesn't mean you should ignore it," Matt said.

"You better get out of the habit of calling him that, if you're going to Homicide."

"It doesn't make him mad," Matt argued. "He told me that Buddha was a very wise man, and 'God knows, I'm black.'"

Coughlin chuckled.

"Have you thought what *Lieutenant* Washington is going to think if you go to Homicide?"

That's two "if you're going to Homicide"s. Come on, Uncle Denny. Get the speech over with.

"Sure," Matt said.

"Aside from the fact that Captain Patrick Cassidy is an affable Irishman who is good to his wife and daughter, and probably has a dog named Spot, why aren't you made suspicious by his sudden new affluence?"

"There could be a number of explanations for it."

"I'm all ears."

"He cared for his mother for years. She could have left him money. Or the brother. Even if they didn't, I can hear his wife saying, 'Okay, that's over. Your mother's gone. I want a place at the shore.'"

"Even if they can't afford it?"

"I hope to find out they can," Matt said. "I was going to go to Easton today to check the brother's will."

"Was?"

"Here I am, at your orders," Matt said.

"We won't be at the Roy Rogers long," Coughlin said. "I just wanted a look around after the crime scene people did their business. I thought you might want to have a look, since you may go to Homicide."

That's two "if"s and a "may." Where's the speech?

"I would. Thank you."

They rode in silence for a minute or two, and there was no speech, which both surprised and worried Matt.

There has to be a hook in the two "if"s and a "may."

What's he done? Had a word with the commissioner, who will call me in and say that while I'm certainly entitled to go to Homicide, "the Department has a real problem. They really need a sergeant with your experience in the Special Victims Unit and you'll certainly understand that the needs of the department are paramount, and I give you my word that you'll get to Homicide one day."

If that's what he's done, he certainly won't tell me.

Shit!

"Who were they talking about when I walked in?" Matt asked.

"Who's who?"

"The 'bastard' Frank Hollaran said he'd really like to see in shackles, that Mike Sabara wants to personally strap in the electric chair."

"Isaac 'Fort' Festung. The sonofabitch keeps sending Pekach postcards."

"Who is he?"

"You really don't know?" Coughlin asked, his surprise evident in his voice.

"No, I don't," Matt confessed. "The name sounds familiar . . . but no, I really don't know. What did he do?"

"How old are you, Matty?"

"Twenty-seven."

"I guess that's why you never heard of him. When you were seven years old—no, six; she was in the trunk for a year—Fort Festung beat his girlfriend to death, stuffed her body in a trunk, and put the trunk in a closet. When they finally found her, her body was mummified."

"Jesus! And he sends Dave Pekach postcards from prison?" Matt asked, and then, remembering, added, "I thought Dave said from France."

"He did," Coughlin said. "Festung never went to prison. After Dave got a search warrant, found the body, and arrested him, his lawyer, now our beloved Senator Feldman, got him released at his arraignment on forty thousand dollars bail, and he jumped it."

"He was charged with murder and got out on bail?" Matt asked, incredulously.

"Yeah, that's just what he did," Coughlin said, "and he's been on the run ever since. A couple of months ago, they found him in France. "

"And now he'll be extradited and tried?"

"He's already been tried. The only *in absentia* trial I ever heard about. The jury found him guilty, and Eileen Solomon sentenced him to life without possibility of parole."

"The D.A.?" Matt asked, surprised.

The Hon. Eileen McNamara Solomon had just been reelected as district attorney of Philadelphia, taking sixty-seven percent of the votes cast.

"Before she was D.A., she was a judge," Coughlin said. "And no, Matty, it doesn't look as if he'll be extradited. He's got the French government in his pocket. And knows it. And likes to rub it in our faces, especially Dave Pekach's. That's what the postcard was all about. He's still thumbing his nose at the system."

"I'll be damned," Matt said.

"Get the case out and read it. It's interesting," Coughlin said, and then, nodding out the windshield, "I wonder if they're just slow, or they got something."

Matt followed his glance. The crime scene van was parked on Snyder Street, fifty yards past the Roy Rogers restaurant.

"I think there's a place to park right in front of the van," Coughlin said. "You can drop me here."

"You want me to come in?" Matt asked, as he pulled to the curb.

"That's the idea," Coughlin said, as he got out of the car. "If you're going to Homicide, you might find this educational."

That's three *"if"'s and a "may."*

[THREE]

Matt had to show his badge to the uniform standing outside to get past him into the Roy Rogers, and then was surprised to find Coughlin waiting for him just inside the door.

The restaurant was empty except for a man Matt guessed was the manager, sitting with a cup of coffee at one of the banquettes near the door, and a forensic technician trying to find—or maybe lift—prints from a banquette at the rear of the restaurant, by the kitchen door.

And then the kitchen door opened, and Detective Tony Harris came through it, and saw Coughlin. He walked up to him.

"Commissioner," he said.

"Tony," Coughlin said, as they shook hands. Then Coughlin asked, "They found something?"

"Jason didn't think they found enough," Harris said. "That's why he sent them back."

"The famous Jason Washington's 'never leave a stone unturned' philosophy?"

"Never leave the stones *under* the stone unturned," Harris said.

"Can you walk it through for me, Tony? Bright Eyes here just might learn something."

"Sure," Harris said. "Two doers. They came through that door. Two young black guys, one of them fat. They—I got this primarily from a guy who works here—took a look around, then the fat one walked to the last booth on the left and sat down, and the other one sat in the first booth—where you are, Matt. My eyewitness, who was mopping the floor by the door, ducked into the kitchen. He looked out, saw the fat guy take a revolver—wrapped in newspaper—from his jacket, and told the kitchen supervisor. She called 911.

"The next thing my eyewitness knew, there was a shot." Harris pointed to the ceiling above where Matt was standing. "We recovered the bullet. Full jacket .38.

If we can find the gun, we can most likely get a good match. Then the fat doer went into the kitchen. . . ."

"Let's have a look," Coughlin said.

"Yes, sir," Harris said, and led them through the restaurant to the kitchen doors.

"We have a bunch of prints from both sides of the doors," Harris said. "All the employees had been fingerprinted, so we're running the ones we lifted against those."

He pushed the door open.

"My eyewitness was behind the door, with his back against the wall," Harris said. "He saw the fat doer grab the telephone, listen a moment—presumably long enough to hear she was talking to police radio—rip the phone from the wall, call her an obscene name, hold his revolver at arm's length, and shoot her. She slid down the wall, and then fell forward."

He pointed to the chalked outline of a body on the floor, and to blood smeared on the wall.

"Then the fat doer herded everybody but my eyewitness, who he didn't see, into the cooler, and jammed a sharpening steel into the padlock loops."

He pointed to the cooler door, then went on. "Then he went back into the restaurant, not seeing my eyewitness, and started to take wallets, et cetera, from the citizens. Doer Number One, meanwhile, is taking money from the cash register.

"Right about then, Kenny Charlton came through the door. Doer Number One is crouched behind the cashier's counter. Kenny saw him, the doer jumps up, wraps his arm around Kenny, wrestles with him. The fat doer then runs up, sticks his gun under Kenny's bulletproof vest, and fires. Kenny goes down. Doer Number One steps over Kenny's body, takes two shots at it, and then follows Doer Number Two out the door and down Snyder. Mickey O'Hara got their picture, but it's a lousy picture. No fault of Mickey's."

"Why did the fat doer stick his gun under Charlton's vest?" Matt asked. "Why not just shoot him in the head? Or the lower back, below the vest?"

Coughlin gave him a look Matt could not interpret, and finally decided it was exasperation at his having asked a question that obviously could not be answered.

Tony Harris held up both hands in a helpless gesture.

The restaurant manager walked up to them with three mugs of coffee on a tray.

"I thought you and the other detectives might like . . ."

"That's very nice of you," Coughlin said.

"Mr. Benetti, this is Commissioner Coughlin," Harris said.

"Oh, Jesus, I'm sorry. . . ."

"I like to think I'm still a detective," Coughlin said. "No offense taken."

"I . . . uh . . . don't know how to say this," Benetti said. "But I'm glad to see you here, Commissioner. I would hate to have what those animals did to Mrs. Fernandez and Officer Charlton . . . wind up as an unsolved crime."

"We're going to try very hard, Mr. Benetti, to make sure that doesn't happen," Coughlin said.

Benetti looked at Coughlin, then put out his hand.

"Thank you," he said, and walked away.

Coughlin looked over his shoulder, then pointed to one of the banquettes. He slid in one side, and Tony Harris and Matt into the other.

"Still no idea who these animals are?" Coughlin asked.

Harris shook his head, "no."

"The police artist's stuff is just about useless," Harris said. "Everybody saw somebody else. We're going to have to have a tip, or make them with a fingerprint."

Coughlin shook his head.

"One question, Tony. I want the answer off the top of your head. How would you feel about having Sergeant Payne in Homicide?"

Harris chuckled, then smiled.

"I heard the list was out," he said. "Good for you, Matt!"

"That doesn't answer my question, Tony," Coughlin said.

"Welcome, welcome!" Tony said.

"I should have known better than to try that," Coughlin said. "In law school, they teach you never to ask a question to somebody on the stand unless you know what the answer's going to be."

"Commissioner, you asked," Harris said. "What's wrong with Matt coming to Homicide?"

"He's too young, for one thing. He hasn't been on the job long enough, for another. I can go on."

"He's also smart," Harris said. "And he's a stone-*under*-the-stone turner. *I* didn't wonder why this bastard didn't shoot Kenny in the head, or lower back. Matt already thinks like the Black Buddha. The other stuff, we can teach him."

Coughlin snorted.

"And he's going to make a good witness on the stand," Harris said. "Think about that."

"I'll be damned," Coughlin said. "For a moment, I thought—I guess, to be honest, hoped—you were pulling my leg. But you're serious, aren't you?"

Tony Harris nodded his head.

"I thought you'd be all for him coming to Homicide," he said.

Coughlin looked between the two of them but didn't respond directly.

After a moment, he asked, "Are you about finished here, Tony?"

"Just about."

"I need a ride to the Roundhouse."

"My pleasure."

"Matt's going to Easton on a job I gave Peter Wohl and Peter gave to Matt," Coughlin said. "And he'd better get going."

"What job's that?" Harris asked.

"One of those I'd rather not talk about," Coughlin said, looking at Matt. "But the sooner you *know* something, Matt, the better."

"Yes, sir. I understand."

"You sore at me, Matt?" Coughlin said.

"I could never be sore at you," Matt said.

Coughlin met his eyes and then nodded.

Then he pushed himself out of the banquette.

[FOUR]

Matt started to head for the Schuylkill Expressway as the fastest way out of town. When he turned onto South Street, he punched the autodial button on his cellular, which caused Inspector Wohl to answer his cellular on the second ring.

"Matt, boss. Commissioner Coughlin's on his way back to the Roundhouse, and I'm on my way to Easton. Okay?"

"From the cheerful sound of your voice, I guess you again refused to listen to his sage advice?"

"He didn't offer any," Matt said. "He tried to sandbag me with Tony Harris."

"And?"

"Tony said I already think like the Black Buddha, they can teach me what I have to know, and 'welcome'—no, 'welcome, welcome'—to Homicide."

There was a moment's silence.

"He also told me he gave you the Cassidy job," Matt said.

Again there was a perceptible pause.

"If you come up with something unpleasant, give me a call," Wohl said. "Otherwise fill me in in the morning."

"Yes, sir," Matt said.

Wohl broke the connection without saying anything else.

At the next intersection—South and Twentieth Streets—Matt changed his mind about the Schuylkill Expressway and instead drove back to Rittenhouse Square, where he drove into the underground garage, parked the unmarked Ford, and got in the Porsche.

It had occurred to him that he hadn't driven the Porsche much lately, and it needed a run. What he liked best about the Porsche—something he somewhat snobbishly thought most people didn't understand—was not how easily you could get it up to well over 100, 120 miles per hour—a great many cars would do that—but how beautifully it handled on narrow, winding roads, making 60 or 70 where lesser cars would lose control at 50 or less. Such as the twenty miles or so of Route 611 between Kintnersville and Easton, where the road ran alongside the old Delaware Canal.

With the winding road, and a lot else on his mind—

God, that was an unexpected compliment from Tony Harris, me thinking like Jason . . .

And it couldn't have been timed better. Uncle Denny had egg all over his face . . .

I wonder when the promotion will actually happen?

What am I going to do if Captain Cassidy's brother's will hasn't been filed in the courthouse? Some people don't even have wills. What do they call that, intestate, something like that?

With a little luck, the courthouse'll have a computer and I can do a search for all real estate in the name of John Paul Cassidy. . . .

I've got to find out more about Whatshisname who stuffed his girlfriend in a trunk and sends Dave Pekach taunting postcards from Europe. . . .

Uncle Denny said the body was (a) mummified and (b) in the trunk for a year? Didn't it smell?

I'll have to find out when Stan Colt is going to grace Philadelphia with his presence. I really would like to see more—a hell of a lot more—of Vice President Terry Davis. . . .

Nice legs. Nice everything. . . .

—he didn't think about Route 611 passing through Doylestown, right past the Crossroads Diner, until the diner itself came into view.

Shit, Shit, Shit!

The mental image of Susan with the neat hole under her sightless eyes jumped into his mind.

No, goddamn it. No! Not twice in one day!

Think of something else.

Terry Davis in the shower.

A mummified body in a trunk. If you want to feel nauseous, think of a stinking, mummified body.

But (a) mummies don't stink. They look like leather statues, but they don't smell, (b) mummies are bodies that have gone through some sort of preservation process. They gut them, I think I remember from sixth grade, and then fill the cavity with some kind of preservatives—or was it rocks? sand?—and then wrap them in linen.

The body in this weirdo's trunk might have been dried out after a year, but, technically speaking, it wasn't mummified. After a year, why wasn't it a skeleton? Wouldn't the flesh have completely decomposed—giving off one hell of a stink—in a year?

There is a lot you don't know about bodies. And ergo sum, a sergeant of the Homicide Bureau should know a lot about dead bodies.

Maybe I can take a course at the university.

Not a bullshit undergraduate course, a course at the medical school. Amy's a professor. She should (a) know and (b) have the clout to have her little brother admitted.

Christ, I'm going seventy-five in a fifty-five zone!

Sorry to be speeding, Officer. What it was, when I passed the Crossroads Diner, was that I naturally recalled my girlfriend with the back of her head blown out in the parking lot. . . .

Terry Davis has long legs. Nice long legs.
Why do long legs turn me on?
Why do some bosoms, but not others, turn me on?
Why did Terry Davis turn me on like that?
She really does have nice legs.
And she smelled good, too.

He recognized where he was. What he thought of as "the end of Straight 611 out of Doylestown." The concrete highway turned into macadam, made a sharp right turn, then a sharp left turn, and then got curvy.

Right around the next curve is where we pick up the old canal.
I'll be damned! I'm not going to throw up.
And I'm not sweat-soaked.
Thank you, God!
He made the left turn and shoved his foot hard against the accelerator.

CHAPTER
4

Johnny Cassidy's Shamrock Bar was on The Hill in Easton, near—and drawing much of its business from—Lafayette College. Even at four in the afternoon, there were a lot of customers, mixed students and faculty and other staff of the college.

Matt took a stool at the bar and ordered a beer, a pickled egg, and a Cassidy Burger—"Famous All Over the Hill"—and struck up a conversation with the bartender, who had a plastic nameplate with a shamrock and "Mickey O'Neal Manager" printed on it pinned to his crisp, white, open-collar, cuffs-rolled-up shirt. Matt thought he was probably thirty-five or forty, and was not surprised that he was talkative.

When Matt asked how Johnny Cassidy was, O'Neal shook his head sadly and said the Big C had gotten him, five, no six, months before. Johnny kept feeling tired, and he finally went to the doctor, and six weeks later he was dead. Died the same week as his mother, in fact.

"So what's going to happen to the bar?"

"It's going to stay open," Mickey O'Neal said, firmly, and then went on to explain that he'd worked in the place for fifteen years before Johnny died, starting out as an afternoon bartender and working his way up to assistant manager, and got to know him real well. Johnny had been godfather to two of his kids. "They called him Uncle Johnny."

When Johnny knew his time was up, he made a deal with Mickey and his brother—Johnny's younger brother, nice guy, who's a cop in Philadelphia, and who had cared for their mother until she died; Johnny had never married—which gave twenty-five percent of the place to O'Neal and the rest to his brother.

"We're talking about me buying him out, over time, you know, but right now, I'm just running the place for the both of us. Once a month, I write him a check for his share of what we make. It's a pretty good deal all around. The bar stays open, which means I have a job, and his brother gets a check—a nice check, I don't mind saying—once a month. Which is nice, too. Johnny figured he owed his brother—did I say he's a cop in Philly?—for taking care of their mother all those years."

There were now answers to the questions raised by what Detective Payne had learned at the Northampton County Court House: Seven months before, for one dollar and other good and valuable consideration, all assets, real estate, inventory and goodwill of the property privately held by John Paul Cassidy at 2301 Tatamy Road, Easton, had been sold to the Shamrock Corporation. The building at 2301 Tatamy Road housed both Johnny Cassidy's Shamrock Bar and, above it, four apartments on two floors.

It would appear on the surface—he would nose around a little more, of course—that there was a perfectly good reason for Captain Cassidy's sudden affluence. If the brother had insurance, which seemed likely—and the mother did, which also seemed likely—that would explain where he had gotten the cash to buy the condominium at the shore. And it seemed reasonable that getting a check every month for his share of the profits would explain why Captain Cassidy felt he could afford to give his old Suburban to his daughter and buy a new Yukon XL, no money down, to be paid for with the monthly check.

Detective Payne had a third beer "on the house" and another pickled egg, and then got back in his Porsche to return to Philadelphia.

[TWO]

The temptation to take the very interesting winding road beside the old Delaware Canal was irresistible. But he didn't want to go back through Doylestown—past the Crossroads Diner—so he turned off Route 611 onto Route 32 a few miles south of Riegelsville, and followed it along the Delaware.

A few miles past New Hope, his cellular phone tinkled. He looked at his watch and saw that it was quarter to five.

That's probably Peter. Despite what he said about filling him in in the morning, he wants to know what I found out.

"Yes, sir, Inspector, sir. Detective Payne at your service, sir."

"Hey, Matt," a familiar voice said. It was that of Chad Nesbitt. They had been best friends since kindergarten.

"The Crown Prince of tomato soup himself? To what do I owe the honor?"

"Where are you?" Chad asked, a tone of exasperation in his voice.

"About five miles south of picturesque New Hope on Route 32. I presume there is some reason for your curiosity?"

"What are you doing way up there?"

"Fighting crime, of course. Protecting defenseless citizens such as yourself from evildoers."

"Daffy wants you to come to supper. Can you?"

Daffy was Mrs. Nesbitt.

"Why does that make me suspicious?"

"Matt, for Christ's sake, make peace with her. It gets to be a real pain in the ass for me with you two always at each other's throat."

"What's the occasion?"

"There's a girl she wants you to meet."

"Not only no, but hell no."

"This one's nice. I think you'll like her."

"She's a nymphomaniac who owns a liquor store?"

"Sometimes, Matt, you can be a real pain in the ass," Chad said.

There was a perceptible silence.

"Come on, Matt. Please."

"If you give me your solemn word that when I get there, we can go directly from 'How do you do?' to carnal pleasures on your carpet without—"

"Fuck you. Come or don't."

"When?"

"As soon as you can get here."

"Okay," Matt said. "Take me half an hour, depending on the traffic on Interstate 95."

The Wachenhut Security guards who stood in the Colonial-style guard shack at the entrance to Stockton Place in Society Hill were chosen by Wachenhut with more care than their guards at the more than one hundred other locations Wachenhut protected in the Philadelphia area.

Not only was Wachenhut's regional vice president for the Philadelphia area resident in one of the luxury apartments behind the striped-pole barrier, but so were executives of other corporations, which employed large numbers of Wachenhut Security personnel.

Number 9 Stockton Place, for example, a triplex constructed behind the facades of four of the twelve pre-Revolutionary brownstone buildings on the east side of Stockton Place, was owned by NB Properties, Inc., the principal stockholder of which was Chadwick Thomas Nesbitt III and was occupied by Mr. and Mrs. Chadwick T. Nesbitt IV.

Mr. Nesbitt IV was working his way upward in the corporate ranks—he had recently been named a vice president—of Nesfoods International, of which his father was chairman of the executive committee. Four of Nesfoods International's Philadelphia-area manufacturing facilities employed the Wachenhut Corporation to provide the necessary security, as did many other Nesfoods establishments around the world.

It therefore behooved Wachenhut to put its best security foot forward, so to speak, on Stockton Place.

It wasn't only a question of providing faultless around-the-clock security— Wachenhut had learned how to do that splendidly over the years—but to do so in such a manner as not to antagonize those being protected, and their guests.

The senior security officer on duty in the shack when the Porsche Carrera rolled up was a retired soldier who had spent twenty years in the Corps in the military police. His retirement pay wasn't going as far as he'd thought it would, and since he had enlisted at seventeen and retired at thirty-eight, he'd still been a young man who wanted to work.

Wachenhut had been glad to have him, assigned him—with a raise in pay—to Stockton Place after only six months on the job, and made him a supervisor eighteen months after he had joined the firm. His superiors thought he would be capable of handling the sometimes delicate Stockton Place assignment, and he had proven them right.

When the silver Porsche Carrera slowed as it approached the barrier, the senior security officer on duty nodded at it, then spoke softly to the trainee.

"Now this guy doesn't look like he's either about to break into an apartment, or try to sell something. Very few burglars drive cars like that. So you smile at him, ask him who he wishes to see, and then for his name. Then you say 'Thank you very much, sir,' raise the barrier, and call whoever he said he's going to see and tell them he's coming."

"Got it," the trainee said, and stepped out of the guard shack.

"Good evening, sir," he said to the driver. "How may I help you?"

"Matthew Payne to see Mr. Nesbitt," Matt said.

"Thank you, sir," the trainee said, and stepped inside the guard shack, and pushed the button that raised the barrier. Before the Porsche was past the barrier, the Wachenhut supervisor was on the interior telephone.

"Like this," he said, and then when the phone was answered, said, "This is the gate. We have just passed a Mr. Payne to see Mr. Nesbitt."

Matt pulled the Porsche to the curb in front of Number 9, got out, walked to the red-painted door, and pushed the doorbell.

The door was opened almost immediately by Mr. Nesbitt IV, who looked very much like Matt Payne but a little shorter and a little heavier.

"Hello, you ugly bastard," he said. Then he raised his voice. "Dump the dope! The cops are here!"

Then he embraced Matt.

"Thanks for coming. And for Christ's sake, behave yourself."

The ground floor foyer of Number 9 was open to a skylight in the roof, invisible from the street. To the right was the door to the elevator, and to the left the door to the stairs. There were balconies on the first and second floors of the atrium.

Mrs. Chadwick T. Nesbitt IV, the former Daphne Elizabeth Browne, known for most of her life as "Daffy," a tall, attractive blonde, appeared on the upper balcony, looked down, smiled, and called, "Matt, how nice! Come up."

Matt and Chad got on the elevator, and when the door closed, and he was reasonably sure he couldn't be heard, Matt asked, "How nice? Is she into the sauce?"

Chad laughed.

"Looketh not ye gift horse in ye mouth," he said.

The elevator stopped, and the door opened, revealing the living room of the apartment. Floor-to-ceiling tinted glass walls provided a view of the Delaware River, the Benjamin Franklin Bridge, and on the New Jersey shore, mounted on now-disused buildings, a huge illuminated sign showing a steaming bowl of soup and the legend "Nesfoods Delivers Taste and Nutrition!"

Daffy Nesbitt kissed Matt on the cheek, then turned and cried, "Terry, this is Chad's and my oldest friend in the world."

Sitting on the thickly carpeted floor with Miss Penelope Alice Nesbitt, aged twenty-two months, was Terry Davis.

She smiled at Matt's pleased surprise.

Matt looked at Mrs. Nesbitt.

"Get it over with, Daffy," he said.

"Get what over with?"

"Whatever you're going to say next in the mistaken belief that it will either be clever or terribly amusing."

"Hey, Matt, she's being nice," Chad said.

"That's what worries me," Matt said.

"Hello, again," Terry said.

"Again?" Daffy asked.

"We met this morning," Terry said.

"I'd tell Daffy we had breakfast together, but she would read something into that," Matt said, smiling at Terry.

"Now who's being clever and terribly amusing, you prick?" Daffy snapped.

"Daffy, please, try to control your vulgarity in front of my goddaughter," Matt said, unctuously.

Terry Davis laughed.

"Is she really?" she asked. "Your goddaughter?"

"Yeah," Matt said.

"She's adorable."

"Yeah."

"What do you mean you had breakfast?" Daffy asked.

"At the Ritz-Carlton, no less," Matt said.

"Anybody for a drink?" Chad asked.

"You got any champagne?" Matt asked.

"You hate champagne," Daffy said.

"Not on those days on which I get promoted, I don't," Matt said. "But I'll settle for scotch."

"Promoted to what?" Daffy asked.

"To sergeant, thank you for asking."

"No shit! Hey, good for you, Matt!" Chad said. He went behind a wet bar and came up with a bottle of champagne. "I knew there was one in here."

"Terry," Daffy said, "Matt is a police officer."

"I know. 'One of Philadelphia's finest,'" Terry said.

"Who said that?" Daffy asked in disbelief.

"The monsignor. What was his name?"

"Schneider," Matt said. "I think he's a closet cop groupie."

He dropped to the carpet and picked up the toddler, and tickled her.

She shrieked in delight.

"Matt, you know you're not supposed to do that with her," Daffy said.

"She obviously hates it," Matt said. "What have you got against tickling?"

He nonetheless handed the child to Terry and got up.

"It hyperexcites her," Daffy said.

"Oh," Matt said.

The champagne cork popped, and Matt walked to the wet bar and took a glass, then handed it to Terry.

"Thank you," she said. "Congratulations."

"Thank you," he said, and turned to Daffy.

"Yes, thank you very much, I'd love to."

"You'd love to what?"

"Stay for supper," Matt said.

"Would you believe, wiseass, that Chad tried to call you to ask you to supper? He said they said you were out of town, and they didn't know when you'd be back," Daffy said.

"I talked to him, but I didn't know if he could make it," Chad said. "So I didn't tell you."

"Daffy has this terrible habit of offering me up to the ugliest women," Matt said. "I think they pay her."

"That's what I thought she was doing to me when she said someone was coming she really wanted me to meet," Terry said. "You're not nearly as ugly as I thought you would be."

"Then you can't ask for your money back, can you?"

Terry laughed.

"You really are a bastard, aren't you?" she asked.

He took a second glass of champagne from Chad, then, making a show of thinking it over carefully, shrugged and handed it to Daffy.

"In these circumstances, I will give you a walk," he said.

"Which means what?"

"That tonight I will not wring your neck for playing cupid," Matt said. "Half the police department already knows I'm in love with Terry."

"Damn you, you're embarrassing Terry!"

"Are you embarrassed, Terry?" Matt asked.

"I'm still having trouble getting used to the idea that you're a policeman," she said. "And that you showed up here. Did you know I was here?"

"Of course. I had you under surveillance from the time you left the Savoy-Plaza. That man in the overcoat who exposed himself to you on Broad Street? One of my better men."

Terry laughed.

"Baloney!" she said.

"I'll prove it to you. He has a camera . . . delicacy forbids my telling where. I'll send you a print."

He mimed opening an overcoat, focused his hips, and then mimed pushing a shutter cord.

"Say 'Cheese.' Click. Gotcha!"

Chad laughed.

"Oh, God!" Terry said.

"I can't believe you did that!" Daffy said.

"But you're smiling, Daffy darling!"

"We thought we'd eat in," Daffy said, quickly changing the subject. "Terry has to be at the airport at eleven-thirty. I bought some shrimp at the Twelfth Street Market, but Monday the cook is off."

"That's Daffy's way, Terry," Matt said, "of asking whether I will be good enough to prepare my world famous Wild Turkey shrimp."

"*Wild Turkey* shrimp?"

"Over wild rice," Matt said. "Yes, Daffy, I will. But *you'll* have to peel the slimy crustaceans. That's beneath the dignity of a master chef such as myself."

"I've got to give Penny her bath," Daffy complained.

"I'll peel the shrimp," Terry said. "I have to see this. Wild Turkey—you're talking about the whiskey? . . ." Matt nodded. ". . . shrimp?"

"Bring your glass, I'll bring the bottle. The kitchen for some unknown reason is on the ground floor."

Matt led Terry into the kitchen, turned on the fluorescent lights, and then took his jacket off and laid it on a counter. Then he took his pistol from its shoulder holster, held it toward the floor, away from Terry, removed the clip, and then ejected the round in the chamber.

"I'm impressed," Terry said. "If that was your intention."

He gave her a dirty look but didn't reply. He reloaded the ejected round in the magazine, put the magazine in the pistol, the pistol in the shoulder holster, then shrugged out of that and hung it on an empty hook of the pot rack above the stainless-steel stove.

Then he looked at her.

"I wasn't trying to impress you. I don't like leaving guns around with a round in the chamber."

"Sorry," she said, and then asked, "What kind of a gun is that?"

He looked at her for a moment before deciding the question was a peace offering.

"It's an Officer's Model Colt," Matt said. "A .45. A cut-down version of the old Army .45."

"That's what all the cops carry?"

"No. Most Philadelphia cops carry Glocks. They're semiautomatic, like this one, but nine-millimeter, not .45."

"Then?"

"I think this a better weapon."

"And they let you do that?"

"With great reluctance. I had to go through a lot of bureaucratic bullsh— difficulty before I got permission to carry this."

"What is it with Colt?" Terry asked.

"Excuse me?"

"There's some sort of significance, obviously. Stan actually changed his name legally to Colt. And he always carries a Colt automatic in his films."

"What was his name before?"

"Coleman."

"Stan Colt, née Stanley Coleman?"

"Yeah."

"Whatever works, I guess," Matt said, chuckling. "To answer your question, I suppose there is a certain romance to 'Colt.' They call the old Colt .44 revolver 'The Gun That Won the West,' and then the Colt Model 1911—the big brother of my pistol—was the service weapon right through Vietnam. Now the services use a nine-millimeter Beretta."

"You ever shoot anybody with that pistol?"

"Not with that one."

"But you have shot someone?"

"Why don't we just drop this subject right here?" Matt flared.

"Sorry," she said, offended and sarcastic.

He found a plastic bag of shrimp in the refrigerator, took it to the sink, tore the bag open, and started to peel them.

After a long moment, Terry went and stood beside him and took a handful of shrimp.

He glanced at her but said nothing.

They peeled shrimp in silence for perhaps three minutes, and then Matt said, "That's not the first time you've peeled shrimp."

"How can you tell?"

"Most people don't know how to squeeze the tail that way."

"My dad has a boat. We have a place on Catalina Island. I practically grew up peeling shrimp."

"Your father's a movie star? Producer? Executive?"

"Lawyer," she said. "With connections in the industry. Enough to get me my first job with GAM."

"So's mine," Matt said. "A lawyer with connections."

"Daffy told me—when she was selling me on the blind date."

"Actually, he's my adoptive father," Matt said, as he took a large skillet from an overhead rack.

"Your parents were divorced? Mine too."

"My father was killed before I was born," Matt said. "He was a cop, a sergeant named John X. Moffitt, and he answered a silent alarm and got himself shot. My mother married my dad—that sounds funny, doesn't it?—about six months later. He'd lost his wife in a car crash. A really good guy. He adopted me legally."

"Is that why you're a policeman? Because of your father?"

"That's one of the reasons, certainly," Matt said, as he unwrapped a stick of butter. "I like being a cop."

"Daffy doesn't approve," Terry said.

"I know. Daffy would be delighted—because of Chad—if I married a nice young woman, such as yourself, went to law school, and took my proper role in society."

"Yeah," Terry replied thoughtfully. "I picked up a little of that. Tell me about your promotion."

"The sergeant's examination list came out today," Matt said. "With underwhelming modesty, I was number one, and get to pick my assignment."

"Which is?"

"Homicide."

"What is that, some sort of a death wish?"

"Huh?"

"Homicide sounds dangerous," she said. "Killers, right?"

"I never thought about it," Matt said. "But now that I do . . . Homicide's not dangerous. Being on the street is dangerous. My father was a uniform sergeant in a district. That's dangerous. Cops get hurt answering domestic-disturbance calls. Stopping speeders. Homicide's nothing like that. You've been watching too many Stan Colt movies."

"I don't really understand."

"Street cops face the bad guys every day. Last night, a uniform cop answered a robbery-in-progress call at the Roy Rogers restaurant on Broad Street. One of the two bad guys shoved a revolver under his bulletproof vest and killed him. The first homicide guy didn't get to the scene for maybe fifteen minutes. By then, the bad guys were long gone."

She looked at him but said nothing.

"The trick to this is to sauté them slowly in butter with a little Cajun seasoning," he said. "You add the booze just before serving, and flame it. And since the rice isn't done, we can put this on hold and have another glass of wine while we wait for the rice and the bathers to finish with the bathee."

"What about when they arrest . . . the bad guys? Isn't that dangerous?"

"First you have to find out who the bad guys are. Then make sure you can—to the district attorney's satisfaction—make the case against them. Then, if they're not already in the Roundhouse surrounded by cops, if you have to go out to arrest them, you take enough uniforms with you to make sure nobody gets hurt."

"That's not much like one of Stan's movies, is it?" she asked.

"Not much," he agreed, as he filled her glass.

"Then why does Homicide have the prestige? You were as proud as a peacock to tell me you were going to Homicide."

"Homicide detectives are the best detectives in the department," he said. "When you're trying somebody for a capital offense, all the 't's have to be crossed and the 'i's dotted. There's no room for mistakes. People who kill people should pay for it."

"And homicide sergeants?"

"Modesty precludes my answering that question."

"Modest you ain't, Sergeant."

"Sergeant I ain't, either. I'm just number one on the list. God only knows when I'll actually get promoted and sent to Homicide."

"And in the meantime, you'll have to do something beneath your dignity, like protecting Stan from his adoring fans? Or vice versa."

"Meaning?"

"Now that we're going to be professionally associated, I think I should tell you that Stan likes young women. Very young women."

"That ought to go over big with the monsignor and the cardinal. And I'm not—I am now really sorry to say—going to be involved in that. That's Dignitary Protection, and sometimes, since the subject came up, that can be really dangerous. Dignitaries, celebrities, attract lunatics like a magnet."

"You're not going to be involved?"

"No. I was just there this morning to see—for my boss—what the triumphal visit will involve. I'm with Special Operations, and we usually provide the bodies needed."

"I'm sorry, too," she said.

"We will solve that problem when you come back," he said. "I really want to see more of you."

"So what do you do in Special Operations?" she said, obviously changing the subject.

"Today, for example, I think I proved that a cop who's been spending more money than a cop makes came by it entirely honestly."

"Internal affairs?"

"No. This was unofficial, before Internal Affairs got involved. Now there won't be an Internal Affairs investigation. A good thing, because just being involved with Internal Affairs makes people look bad."

Mr. and Mrs. Chadwick T. Nesbitt IV and a freshly bathed Penelope in her nightgown appeared in the kitchen at this point, and Detective Payne resumed his preparation of Wild Turkey shrimp over wild rice.

At 10:45 Matt said that he would be happy to deliver Terry to the airport to catch the red-eye to the coast.

At 11:17, as he closed the trunk of the Porsche after having taken Terry's luggage from it, and she was standing close enough to him to be kissed, a uniform walked up and said, "You're going to have to move it, sir. Sorry."

Matt took out his badge and said, "Three sixty-nine," which was police cant for "I am a police officer."

The uniform walked away. Matt looked at Terry, saddened by the lost opportunity.

Terry stood on her toes and kissed him chastely on the lips.

"Thanks," she said, then quickly turned and entered the airport. She turned once and looked back at him, and then he lost sight of her.

He got back in the Porsche, and on the way to Rittenhouse Square decided that, all things considered, today had been a pretty good day.

[THREE]

The Hon. Alvin W. Martin, Mayor of the City of Philadelphia, a trim forty-three-year-old in a well-cut Harris plaid suit, smiled at Police Commissioner Ralph J. Mariani and waved him into his City Hall office.

"Thank you for coming so quickly, Ralph," he said. "Have you had your coffee?"

The mayor gestured toward a silver coffee service on a sideboard.

"I could use another cup, thank you," Mariani said. He was a stocky Italian, balding, natty.

"I was distressed, Ralph," the mayor said, "to hear about the trouble at the Roy Rogers."

"Very sad," Mariani said. "I knew Officer Charlton. A fine man."

"And Mrs. Fernandez, who paid with her life for calling 911."

"A genuine tragedy, sir," Mariani said.

"I'm going to the funeral home at three this afternoon," Martin said. "I should say 'homes.' Officer Charlton's first, and then Mrs. Fernandez's. I think it would be a good idea if you went with me."

"Yes, sir. Of course."

"I feel sure the press will be there," the mayor said. "I'd really like to have something to tell them."

"I'm afraid I don't have much news, Mr. Mayor," Mariani said. "We're working on it, of course. And it's just a matter of time until we nail those animals, but so far . . ."

"When you say you're working on it, what exactly does that mean?"

"That we're applying all our resources to the job."

"Who's in charge of the investigation?"

"Lieutenant Washington, of Homicide, sir."

The mayor knew Lieutenant Jason Washington, which was not the same thing as saying he liked him. The mayor thought of Washington as a difficult man who was not able to conceal—or perhaps didn't want to conceal—his contempt for politicians.

Mayor Martin had sought Lieutenant Washington out shortly after taking office. The police department always provides a police officer, sometimes a sergeant, but most often a lieutenant, to drive the mayoral limousine, serving simultaneously, of course, as bodyguard.

He'd toyed with the idea of having a white officer—a very large, happy, smiling Irishman who would look good in the background of news photos came to mind—but before he could make the appointment, he'd seen Washington striding purposefully though the lobby of the Roundhouse, and asked who he was.

That night he had mentioned the enormous lieutenant to his wife, Beatrice, at supper.

"I thought you knew Jason," Beatrice said. "He's Martha's husband."

The mayor knew his wife's friend, Martha Washington. Beatrice, as the mayor thought of it, was "into art and that sort of thing," and Martha Washington was both a very successful art dealer and a painter of some repute.

"No, I don't," the mayor confessed. "How do you think he'd like to be the mayor's driver?"

"I don't think so," Beatrice had said. "I can't imagine Jason as a chauffeur—yours or anyone else's."

"You're going to have to get used to being the mayor's wife, precious."

Mayor Martin had taken the trouble to meet Washington socially, which had proven more difficult to do than he thought it would be.

The mayor had arranged for the Washingtons to be invited to a friend's cocktail party, and when they sent their regrets, to a second friend's cocktail party, which invitation they also declined with regret. On the third try, he finally got to meet them, and Alvin W. Martin's first impression of Jason Washington that night was that he was going to like him, possibly very much, and that he would look just fine in the background of press photos.

Washington was an imposing man, superbly tailored, and erudite without rubbing it in your face. The mayor, studying Washington's suit with the eye of a man who appreciated good tailoring, wondered how he could afford to dress that well on a detective's salary. He decided the artist wife picked up the tab.

He finally managed to get him alone.

"I'd really like to get together with you, Jason. You don't mind if I call you 'Jason,' do you?"

"Not at all."

"I'm in the process of selecting a driver. Would you be interested?"

"With all possible respect, Mr. Mayor, absolutely not."

"Actually, it would entail more than just driving the limo," the mayor had said. "I really need someone around who can explain the subtleties of the police department to me."

"I'm sure you'll have no trouble finding such a person, Mr. Mayor."

"And, specifically, I need input from someone knowledgeable about what I might be able to do for our fellow blacks in the police department."

"I can tell you that, Mr. Mayor, in a very few words: Really support a meaningful pay raise; get it through the City Council. Policemen often have a hard time making ends meet."

"I was speaking specifically of black police officers."

"There are two kinds of police officers, Mr. Mayor. The bad ones—a small minority—and all the others. And all the others are colored blue."

"That's a little jingoistic, isn't it, Lieutenant?"

"Simplistic, perhaps, Mr. Mayor, and perhaps chauvinistic, but I don't think jingoistic, which, as I understand the word, carries a flavor of belligerence I certainly didn't intend."

"Let me be very frank," the mayor said. "When I asked around for the name of an outstanding black officer to whom I could turn with questions regarding the police department generally, and black officers in the department specifically, your name immediately came up. You have a splendid reputation. And I wondered how it is you're a lieutenant."

"'Only' a lieutenant? Is that what you mean?"

"All right, if you want to put it that way. You don't think race had anything to do with you having been a policeman twenty-three years before being promoted to lieutenant?"

"Mr. Mayor, I've spent most of my career in Homicide . . ."

"You've been described to me as one of the best homicide investigators anywhere."

Washington ignored the compliment, and continued:

". . . where, because of the extraordinary amount of overtime required, most detectives make as much as inspectors and some as much as chief inspectors. I was a little late reaching my present rank because I never took the examination until I had assurance, in writing, that should I pass and be promoted, I would not be transferred from Homicide."

Aware that his temper was rising, the mayor said, "I wasn't aware that you could make deals like that."

"They aren't common."

"Frankly, the more you reject the idea, the more it appeals to me. I need someone who will tell me how things are, rather than what they think I want to hear. And I was under the impression that police officers serve where their superiors decide they can be of the most value."

"That's true, of course," Washington had replied. "But it is also true that police officers my age with twenty years or more of service can retire at any time they so desire."

The mayor suddenly saw the headline in the *Bulletin*: ACE HOMICIDE LIEUTENANT RETIRES RATHER THAN BECOME MAYOR'S DRIVER

"Well, I'm disappointed, of course," the mayor had said. "But I will certainly respect your wishes. You will be available, won't you, if I need an expert to explain something to me?"

"I'm at your service, Mr. Mayor," Washington had said.

Mayor Martin now looked across his desk and asked, "And what does Lieutenant Washington have to say about why these people haven't been arrested? It's been two days, Commissioner."

Mariani replied, "I talked to him last night, Mr. Mayor. He says he's doing everything he can think of to do, and that something's bound to turn up. Right now, we don't even know who the doers are."

"There were no witnesses?"

"There were witnesses, sir. Mickey O'Hara of the *Bulletin* even took a picture of them as they left the restaurant. He was one of the first to reach the scene. Unfortunately, it wasn't a very good photograph."

"We have a picture of these people?" the mayor asked, incredulously.

"Not a very good picture, Mr. Mayor."

"I can see the story in the *Bulletin*," the mayor said, unpleasantly. *"Even with a photo provided by the* Bulletin, *police are unable to identify, much less arrest—"*

"O'Hara wouldn't write a story like that," Mariani said. "He understands our problem."

"You have more faith in the press than I do, obviously," the mayor said. "And none of the witnesses can come up with a description of these people?"

"We put police artists on the job immediately, Mr. Mayor. The result of that has been a number of pictures none of which look like any other picture. Everybody saw something else."

"The bottom line, then, is that you don't have a clue as to who these people are."

"We're doing our best, sir."

"That's really not good enough, Commissioner," the mayor said. "I need something for the press, and I need it by three this afternoon."

"What would you like me to say, sir?"

"How about forming a task force?"

"We have one in everything but name now, sir. A cop has been killed. Washington can have anything he asks for. It's just going to take some time, I'm afraid."

"A cop and a single mother of three," the mayor said. "We don't want to forget her, do we?"

"We're not forgetting her, sir. But when a police officer is killed, it sort of mobilizes the entire department."

"Just for the record, Commissioner, the entire police department should be mobilized whenever any of our citizens is brutally murdered."

"Yes, sir. Of course."

"What about Special Operations, Commissioner?"

"Sir?"

"Supposing I announce this afternoon that I have ordered that the Special Operations Division take over the investigation?"

"Sir, it's a homicide," the Commissioner said.

"You don't think it's a good idea, I gather?"

"Mr. Mayor, it won't accomplish anything that's not already been done. If I call Inspector Wohl . . .'

"Who is?"

"The commanding officer of Special Operations, sir."

"Okay."

"If I call him right now and give him the job, he'll say 'Yes, sir,' and then he'll call Lieutenant Washington and ask him how he can help. I don't know this for a fact, but I'll bet Wohl has already done that."

"Let's do it anyway," the mayor said. "Make it official. And tell this Inspector . . . Wohl, you said?"

"Yes, sir."

"To light a fire under Washington."

"Yes, sir. Sir, Inspector Wohl was once a homicide detective. . . ."

"So much the better."

"A *rookie* homicide detective. Jason Washington, as a very experienced, very good, homicide detective, was charged with bringing Detective Wohl up to homicide speed—"

"Commissioner," the mayor interrupted somewhat sharply, "I'm getting the feeling you're dragging your feet, for reasons I can't imagine. So I repeat, call this Inspector Wohl and tell him he is now in charge of this investigation task force, and I expect results."

"Yes, sir, I'll do so immediately."

"There's one more thing," the mayor said. "The cardinal called me at home last night."

"Yes, sir?"

"About the visit of Stan Colt. The cardinal said that Colt being here may raise a half million dollars or more for West Catholic High School."

"It probably will, sir."

"The cardinal wants to make sure Mr. Colt's visit goes smoothly. And in this case, I want what the cardinal wants."

"So do I, Mr. Mayor. After the cardinal called me about Mr. Colt coming here, I gave Mr. Colt 'Visiting Dignitary' status for his trip. He will be under the care of the Dignitary Protection Unit."

"So he told me," the mayor replied. "What he called me about was the assignment to Colt's visit of a particular detective. Apparently this detective made a very good impression on Monsignor Schneider—who's doing the nuts and bolts of Colt's visit for the cardinal—when they met at some sort of preliminary meeting. I'd like this done."

"Certainly, sir. You have the detective's name?"

"Payne," the mayor said. And then he read the commissioner's face. "You know him? Is there going to be some problem with this?"

"We published the sergeant's examination ratings yesterday," the commissioner said. "Detective Payne ranked number one."

"In other words, he's a very bright detective?"

"And a very good one."

"And now he's a sergeant?"

"He will be whenever the promotion ceremony is held."

"And when will that be?"

"Whenever you decide, Mr. Mayor."

"How about . . ." He checked his calendar. "I'm free from nine-fifteen until ten tomorrow morning."

"Sir, we have the funds to promote the top twenty-one men on the list immediately. It would be difficult to get all twenty-one in on such short notice."

The mayor gave him a look that was mingled curiosity and exasperation.

"We could promote the top five," Commissioner Mariani said. "You will recall, sir, we offered the top five examinees their choice of assignment."

"And you can get all five in here tomorrow morning?"

"Yes, sir. I'm sure I can."

"Good. We'll get him in here and promote him, and the others, and then assign Sergeant Payne to Dignitary Protection."

"But there's a small problem there, too, I'm sorry to say. Payne is entitled to his choice of assignment."

"Commissioner, why don't you suggest to Detective Payne that the Dignitary Protection Unit would be a fine choice of assignment?"

"He wants to go to Homicide, sir."

"How do you know that?"

"Deputy Commissioner Coughlin told me, sir. He's Detective Payne's godfather."

"Figuratively speaking, or literally?" the mayor asked, sarcastically.

"Both, sir."

The mayor exhaled in exasperation.

"Then I suggest you suggest to Deputy Commissioner Coughlin that he suggest to Detective Payne that Dignitary Protection would be a fine choice—indeed the only choice—for Detective Payne to make."

"Mr. Mayor, the prize—the choice of assignment—has been widely publicized. If we don't make good on the promise . . ."

"What?"

"I'm afraid the Fraternal Order of Police would—"

"Jesus Christ!" the mayor exploded. "How about this, then, Commissioner? We promote Payne. Sergeant Payne is assigned to Homicide, and then *temporarily* assigned to Dignitary Protection for Stan Colt's visit?"

"That would work fine, sir."

"Then please see that it's done," the mayor said. "I'll look for you here about quarter to three. Thank you, Commissioner."

CHAPTER 5

Inspector Wohl and Detective Payne were alone in Wohl's office at the Arsenal. Payne's laptop was on Wohl's coffee table, and Payne was bent over it, using it as a notebook, as he reported to Wohl on his investigation of the sudden affluence of Captain Cassidy.

Wohl held up his hand to Detective Payne to stop; he was about to answer his cellular phone.

He picked the cellular up from his desk and answered it. "Wohl."

Then he slipped the cellular into a device on his desk, which activated a hands-off system.

"Are you there, Inspector?" Jason Washington's deep, resonant voice came from the speaker.

"Just putting the phone in the whatchamacallit, Jason."

"Lieutenant Washington reporting for duty, sir."

"Do I have to tell you this wasn't my idea, Jason?"

"I understand it was the mayor's inspiration of the day," Washington said.

"Well, just for the record: Lieutenant, you are designated the senior investigating officer for the mayor's task force investigating the murders at the Roy Rogers. You will report directly to me. Now, is there anything you feel you need to facilitate your investigation?"

"No, sir."

"If there is, you will promptly let me know?"

"Yes, sir."

"We now go off the record," Wohl said. "Who told you?"

"The commissioner. Off the record. He also told me about Matt. I thought Matt would have called me."

"Me, too," Wohl said. "Detective Payne, why didn't you telephone Lieutenant Washington and inform him of your spectacular performance?"

"He's there?" Washington asked.

"Bright-eyed and bushy-tailed. Well, Detective Payne?"

"I thought," Matt said, raising his voice so the microphone on Wohl's desk would pick it up, "Tony would tell you."

"As indeed he did. When can we expect your services, Sergeant?"

"Homicide's wastebaskets need emptying, do they, Jason?" Wohl asked, innocently.

"I'm not a sergeant yet."

"You will be, as I understand it, at approximately nine-thirty tomorrow morning. May I assume that you will report for duty immediately thereafter?"

"Your wastebaskets must be overflowing," Wohl said.

"I have nothing so mundane in mind for Sergeant Payne, Inspector. His first duty will be to supervise Detective Harris, and Harris's team."

Matt thought: *That will be a blind man leading the guide dog around.*

"Tony's somehow fallen from grace?" Wohl asked.

"Actually, Peter, it was Tony's idea. He figures Matt can keep other people from looking over his shoulder. And we all know what a splendid typist Sergeant Payne is."

Wohl considered that—*the problem of how rookie sergeant Payne will fit into Homicide has been solved. Jason said it was Tony's idea, but I suspect Jason was involved. Matt will follow Harris around, relieve him of as many administrative details as possible, and since he is both bright and aware of his massive ignorance of homicide procedures, he will keep his mouth shut, do whatever Tony "suggests"— which will include making sure that the rest of Tony's team does what Tony wants them to do, and when—and in the process learn a hell of a lot*—and grunted his agreement.

"Tony hasn't come up with anything on the doers?" Wohl asked.

"They're out there somewhere, Peter," Washington said. "I think it highly unlikely that the mob imported two professionals from New York to stick up a Roy Rogers."

Wohl chuckled.

"One distinct possibility, Peter, is that these two master criminals, once they have gone through the—best estimate—less than fifteen hundred dollars they earned on this job, will do it again."

"Yeah," Wohl agreed, seeing both the likelihood of a second or third or fourth robbery before they were—almost inevitably—caught, and the likelihood that once they were arrested, they could be identified in a lineup as the Roy Rogers doers.

"There is an obvious downside to that," Washington went on. "Their willingness to use their weapons . . ."

"Compounded by the fact they know they are already facing Murder Two," Wohl interjected.

". . . and there will be no greater penalty if they use them again," Washington finished for him.

"Or they may really go underground," Matt said, "knowing they're wanted for Murder Two."

"The cheap seats have been heard from," Wohl said.

"I was about to make reference to wisdom from the mouths of babes," Washington said. "Except, of course, he's right."

"God, don't tell him that. His ego needs no buttressing."

"Actually, Peter, he will bring a fresh approach, which may very well be useful. Yesterday, when Tony walked Coughlin and our new sergeant through the Roy Rogers, Matt wondered aloud why Doer Two put his revolver under Charlton's vest. Tony was somewhat chagrined that question hadn't occurred to him."

"Is that significant?"

"Never leave a stone unturned . . ." Washington began.

". . . or the stone under the stone," Wohl finished.

"You were, as I recall, an apt pupil," Washington said. "It might be. It opens avenues of inquiry. 'Is Doer Two a cop hater?' for example. 'Is he someone who knew, and intensely disliked, Kenny Charlton?' 'Did Stan Colt—which brings us to that—use the under-the-vest technique in one of his cinema fantasies?'"

"Yeah," Wohl agreed. "What about Stan Colt?"

"The commissioner didn't mention that Sergeant Payne's services will be required in Dignitary Protection when Stan Colt comes to our fair city?"

"No," Wohl said, simply. "He didn't."

"He apparently made a very good impression on Monsignor Schneider," Washington said, "as incredible as that might sound. I am to lose his services temporarily whenever the Colt people think they need him."

"Can't you get me out of that?" Matt asked.

On the other hand, that would give me a lot of time with Terry.

"No," Washington said. "Peter—Tony just walked in, shaking his head ruefully—you asked if there is anything I need. I just thought of something."

"It's yours," Wohl said.

"I'm a little short of wheels. Sergeant Payne, obviously, will no longer be needing his sparkling new Crown Victoria."

"Okay," Wohl said. "And to prove what a fully cooperating fellow I am, I will even have Sergeant Payne deliver it to you, tomorrow when he reports for duty."

"It's always a pleasure dealing with you, Inspector," Washington said, and the line went dead.

Peter removed the cellular phone from the hands-off system, laid it on the desk, and turned to Matt.

"Now, where were we?"

The telephone on his desk buzzed, and Wohl answered it.

The conversation was very brief.

Wohl said "Yes, sir" three times, "Yes, sir, at three" once, and "Yes, sir" one final time.

He looked at Matt again. "The commissioner thinks it would be a very good idea if I were to be at the Monti Funeral Home at three," he said, "to coincide with the visit of the mayor, and his announcement that he has formed a task force to quickly get the Roy Rogers doers."

Matt nodded.

"Now, where were we?" Wohl asked again.

[TWO]

When the Hon. Alvin W. Martin got out of the mayoral limousine at the Monti Funeral Home on South Broad Street in Yeadon, just outside the city limits, he paused long enough on the sidewalk to tell the press that he would have an announcement to make as soon as he had offered his condolences to Mrs. Charlton and the Charlton family.

Then he made his way into the funeral home itself, where he found the long, wide, carpeted central corridor of the building about half full of men with police badges on their uniforms, or hanging from breast pockets of suits, from chains around the necks, or on their belts.

Each of the badges had a narrow, black "mourning band"—sliced from the elastic cloth around the bottom of old uniform caps—across it.

The mayor spotted Deputy Commissioner Coughlin at almost the end of the corridor. Commissioner Mariani had told him that Coughlin knew Mrs. Charlton, and would escort him into the "viewing room" where Charlton's body was laid out, wait until the mayor paid his respects at the casket, then introduce him to Mrs. Charlton, and finally lead him out of the viewing room.

Coughlin was in the center of a group of seven men. Mayor Martin recognized first Mr. Michael J. O'Hara of the *Bulletin*—*no camera, and in a suit. What the hell is he doing here? And with these people?*—and then Captain Hollaran, Coughlin's executive assistant—*or whatever the hell his title is*—and Lieutenant Jason Washington. The others he could not remember having met—or, for that matter, even seen—before.

One was in the special uniform of the Highway Patrol, and as Martin drew closer, he saw the insignia of a captain. That made him the Highway Patrol's commanding officer. *That little fellow is the head of Highway Patrol?* There was another captain, a large man with an imposing, even somewhat frightening, mien—*Jesus, I'd hate to get on the wrong side of him!*—in a standard police captain's blue tunic and white shirt uniform.

The other two men—young men, one in his twenties, the other maybe ten years older—in Coughlin's group didn't look like policemen. Both were wearing gray, single-button suits very much like the suit the mayor was himself wearing—*I'll give three to two that they get their clothes in the same place, and that place is Brooks Brothers. They look like lawyers. I'll give even money that's what they are.*

Well, I would have lost that one, he thought, as the older of the lawyers turned toward Commissioner Coughlin—*probably to tell him he spotted me*—and in doing so, his previously concealed breast pocket came into view. There was a black-banded badge hanging from it.

Martin extended his hand and smiled just a little as he reached Coughlin.

"A sad occasion, Commissioner," he said.

"Indeed it is," Coughlin said. "Mr. Mayor, I don't believe you know any of these officers?"

"Aside from Captain Hollaran and Lieutenant Washington, I'm really sorry to say I don't," Martin said. "Good to see you, Jason, Captain."

"Good afternoon, Mr. Mayor," they said, almost in unison.

"This is Inspector Peter Wohl, of Special Operations," Coughlin said, and the older lawyer put out his hand.

"How do you do, sir?"

"Captain Sabara, his deputy," Coughlin went on, "and Captain Pekach of Highway Patrol."

When the mayor had shaken their hands, Coughlin gestured toward the "other lawyer."

"And this is Detective Payne, Mr. Mayor."

"Is it indeed? Congratulations on the exam, Detective Payne."

"Thank you."

What I'm looking at here is the police establishment. A politically correct police establishment. Coughlin and Hollaran, the Irish cops of fame and legend; God only knows what the rough-looking one is, Eastern European, maybe; Wohl sounds German; Payne looks like a WASP. And Jason Washington representing the Afro-Americans—what did Washington say, "all cops are blue"? All we're missing is a Jew.

As if on cue, a large, stocky, ruddy faced, barrel-chested man with a full head of curly silver hair, a badge with a mourning strip on it hanging from his pocket, walked up to the group. He was Chief Inspector of Detectives M. L. Lowenstein.

"Afternoon," he said.

"Thank you for coming, Chief Lowenstein," the mayor said. "I really wanted you here when I make the announcement."

Lowenstein nodded at him, then put out his hand to Detective Payne.

"I saw the list, Matt," he said. "Congratulations."

He knows Payne, too? That young man really gets around.

"Thank you."

"Have you seen Denise?" Coughlin asked Lowenstein.

"Sarah and I went to the house Monday evening," Lowenstein said, and looked at Commissioner Mariani. Neither the commissioner nor the mayor had trouble translating the look: *I've already expressed my condolences, so there's no reason for me to be here again, except for this political bullshit about a task force.*

"Anytime you're ready, Mr. Mayor," Coughlin said. "I'll take you in."

"Right," the mayor said, and nodded, and followed Coughlin into the viewing room.

It was a large room, with an aisle between rows of folding chairs. Up front, the first row of chairs on the right was upholstered. Mayor Martin saw the heads of two children on either side of a gray-haired woman—*the widow and their kids*—and of several other adults—*family members, probably.*

Officer Kenneth J. Charlton was laid out in a gray metal casket in the center of the room. As he walked down the aisle behind Charlton, the mayor could see his face, and then enough of the body to see that Charlton was to be buried in his uniform.

Coughlin stopped in the aisle next to the first row of chairs, and the mayor realized he was expected to approach the casket alone.

There was a prie-dieu in front of the casket, which made the mayor uncomfortable. So far as he was concerned—he had learned this from his father, the Rev. Dr. Claude Charles Martin, now pastor emeritus of the Second African Methodist Episcopal Church—prie-dieux were a Roman Catholic device, or maybe Catholic/Episcopal device, of which he did not approve.

So what the hell do I now? Ignore it, as Pop would have me do, and stand by the casket looking thoughtfully down at the body? Or use the damn thing, and feel—and perhaps look—hypocritical?

He dropped to his knees onto the padded prie-dieu and bent his head. And looked at the face of Officer Charlton.

You poor bastard. God damn the animals that did this to you!

The anger took him by surprise.

Lord, forgive my anger. But what we have here is a good man who put his life on the line to protect other human beings. And lost it.

Lord, take him into Your arms, and give him the peace that passes all understanding.

He's wearing his badge. Will they take it off? Or bury him with it?

Probably take it off.

Give it to his family?

Or is there some sort of memorial with the badges of the other cops who've been killed in the line of duty?

They have their pictures hanging in the lobby of the Roundhouse, but I can't remember if their badges are there, too. *

Lord, protect this man's wife and children, and give them the strength to get through this ordeal.

Make them wise in Your ways, Dear Lord, and grant them Thy peace.

Give the police the wisdom to find the people who did this to this Thy servant, Lord.

And quickly, before they kill someone else.

Lord Jesus, guide my steps with Thy almighty hand.

In the name of the Father, the Son, and the Holy Spirit.

Amen.

The mayor took one more look at the face of Officer Kenneth J. Charlton, and then got somewhat awkwardly off the prie-dieu.

Then he turned and walked toward the widow and the children.

---

*Police officers killed in the line of duty are placed in their caskets in full uniform, including their weapon. The weapon, badge, and frontispiece are all removed just before the casket is closed. Weapons are returned to the police arsenal at the Police Academy and badges and frontispieces (their numbers) are reissued.

Mrs. Charlton stood up, then urged the boy and the girl to their feet.

"Mrs. Charlton, I'm Alvin Martin . . ."

"It was good of you to come, Mayor."

". . . and you have my most sincere condolences, and my . . ."

"This is Kenny Jr., and this is Deborah."

"Kenny, Deborah, your father was a brave man who died a hero. You can be very proud of him."

There was no response.

"If there is ever anything I can do for you, I want you to call me. You understand?"

Kenny Jr. and Deborah nodded their heads but didn't look at him.

The mayor nodded at Mrs. Charlton, then turned and walked to the aisle and then down it.

His press relations officer was waiting for him in the corridor outside the viewing room.

He led the mayor to another viewing room where the press was waiting for him. The press relations officer had arranged Mariani and the other police department brass in a line against the wall, and he handed the mayor two three-by-five cards on which the essence of the announcement had been printed in large letters.

The mayor glanced at them quickly, then turned to face the press.

"This is a very sad day," he began. "Both a citizen—a single mother of three—and a police officer have lost their lives as a result of a brutal attack that affects not only their grieving survivors but every citizen of Philadelphia.

"This sort of outrage cannot be tolerated, and it will not be. I have ordered the formation of a task force to be commanded by Inspector Peter Wohl of the Special Operations Division. . . ."

[THREE]

When Matt Payne, driving the unmarked Crown Victoria, came down Pennsylvania Route 252 and approached the driveway to his parents' home in Wallingford, he looked carefully in the rearview mirror before applying the brake. Two-fifty-two was lined with large, old pine trees on that stretch, and the drives leading off it were not readily visible. He had more times than he liked to remember come uncomfortably close to being rear-ended.

Wallingford is a small Philadelphia suburb, between Media (through which U.S. 1, known locally as the "Baltimore Pike," runs) and Chester, which is on the Delaware River. It is not large enough to be placed on most road maps, although it has its own post office and railroad station. It is a residential community, housing families whom sociologists would categorize as upper-middle-income, upper-income, and wealthy, in separate dwellings, some very old and some designed to look that way.

Brewster Cortland Payne II had raised his family, now grown and gone, in a large house on four acres on Providence Road in Wallingford. It had been in the Payne family for more than two centuries.

What was now the kitchen and the sewing room had been the whole house when it had been built of fieldstone before the Revolution. Additions and modifications over two centuries had turned it into a large rambling structure that fit no specific architectural category, although a real estate saleswoman had once remarked in the hearing of Mrs. Patricia (Mrs. Brewster C.) Payne that "the Payne place just looked like old, old money."

The house was comfortable, even luxurious, but not ostentatious. There was neither swimming pool nor tennis court, but there was, in what a century before had been a stable, a four-car garage. The Payne family swam, as well as rode, at the Rose Tree Hunt Club. They had a summer house in Cape May, New Jersey, which did have a tennis court, as well as a berth for their boat, a fifty-eight-foot Hatteras called *Final Tort V.*

Matt made it safely into the drive, and as he approached the house, saw a two-year-old, somewhat battered, GMC Suburban parked with one of its front wheels on the grass beside the parking area by the garage. It had been Brewster Payne's gift to his daughter, Amelia Payne, M.D., not because she needed such a large vehicle, but in the hope that the truck-sized—and truck-strong—vehicle would keep her alive. Amy Payne's inability to conduct a motor vehicle over the roads of the Commonwealth of Pennsylvania without, on the average of once a week, at least grazing other motor vehicles, street signs, and on memorable occasion, a fire hydrant, was almost legendary.

Amy Payne was in the kitchen with her mother and Mrs. Elizabeth Newman, the Payne housekeeper, when Matt walked in. They were peeling shrimp. Amy was a not-quite-pretty young woman who wore her hair short, not for purposes of beauty but because it was easier to care for that way.

Mrs. Newman was a comfortable-looking gray-haired woman in her fifties. Patricia Payne was older than she looked at first glance. She was trim, for one thing, with a luxuriant head of dark brown, almost reddish hair, and she had the fair skin of the Irish.

"Well, if it isn't the famous soon-to-be Sergeant Matthew Payne," Amy greeted her brother. "How good of you to find time in your busy schedule for us."

"Amy!" Patricia Payne protested.

"Got another fire hydrant, did you, Sigmund?" Matt said, as he walked to the table and kissed his mother.

"You were on television," Patricia Payne said. "I guess you know."

"That wasn't my idea," Matt said. "The mayor's press guy grabbed my arm and said 'You stand there.'"

"You did look uncomfortable," his mother said. "Well, I guess congratulations are in order, aren't they?"

"That's what I came out to tell you," Matt said. "How did you find out?"

"Not from you, obviously," Amy said.

"Hey, I tried to call when I found out," Matt said. "Didn't I, Elizabeth?"

"Yes, he did."

"And she told me you and Dad were going to be overnight in Wilmington," Matt said, and added, "I even tried to call you, Sigmund Freud."

"I thought that had to be you. Sophomoric humor."

"I'm almost afraid to ask," Patricia Payne said.

"He told the receptionist to tell me they were going to repossess my television unless they got paid," Amy said.

"Matt, you didn't," Patricia Payne said, but her face revealed that she found a certain element of humor in the situation.

"I walked into the office, and the receptionist, all embarrassed, whispered in my ear and said that the finance company had called—"

Mrs. Newman laughed out loud.

"I'm going to get you for that, wiseass," Amy said.

"I put a bottle of champagne in the refrigerator after Denny called," Patricia Payne said. "Go get your father and we'll open it. He's in the living room."

"Uncle Denny called?" Matt asked.

"We're invited to the promotion ceremony," Patricia said. "Denny's very proud of you. We all are."

"You, too, Sigmund?" Matt asked.

Dr. Payne gave him the finger.

"And that goes for your boss, too," she said. "We had dinner Monday night and he didn't say a goddamn word."

"All Peter knew was that the list was out. He didn't know when the promotion would come through, except that it wasn't going to be anytime soon. That's probably why he didn't tell you."

She snorted.

Matt walked out of the kitchen, down a narrow corridor, and through a door into a rather small, comfortably furnished room with book-lined walls, and the chairs arranged to face a large television screen.

Brewster C. Payne was sitting with his feet up on the matching ottoman of a red leather armchair, one of two. He was a tall, angular, dignified man in his early fifties.

He had a legal brief in his lap and his right hand was wrapped around a glass of whiskey.

"You were on the boob tube," he said. "You looked distressed."

"I was," Matt said, and then went on: "Amy's pissed that Uncle Denny told you before I did. For the record, I tried to call just as soon as I found out."

"That's not why she's . . . somewhat less than enthusiastic," Brewster Payne said. "I think she was hoping you'd fail the test and leave the police department."

"Mother's got champagne in the fridge," Matt said, changing the subject. "But I'd rather have a quick one of those."

Payne pointed at a bottle of scotch, sitting with a silver water pitcher, a silver ice bowl, and several glasses. Matt helped himself, and while he was doing so, Brewster Payne rose from his chair. When Matt raised his glass, his father held out his glass and touched Matt's.

"It's what you want, Matt, so I'm happy for you. And proud. Number one!"

"Thank you."

"You can stay for supper? We bought some shrimp on the road from Wilmington. . . ."

"Sure. I made shrimp last night for Chad and Daffy, but what the hell. . . ."

"We could thaw a steak."

"Shrimp's fine. Daffy was playing matchmaker again. I'd already met her. She's from Los Angeles. She's handling, I guess is the word, Stan Colt when he comes to town. His real name is Stanley Coleman."

"I saw it in the paper. Are you involved with that somehow?"

"Peter sent me to a meeting to see what Dignitary Protection is going to need to protect Super Cop. Monsignor Schneider—who sitteth at the right hand of the Bishop—was there. I think he's a cop groupie. He knew all about Doylestown. Anyway, he asked for me by name. When Super Cop, aka Colt aka Coleman comes to town, I'll be temporarily assigned to Dignitary Protection. Terry said he's interested in very young women. That ought to make it interesting."

"Is that the young woman's name, 'Terry'?"

"Terry Davis. Two 'r's and a 'y.' She said her father's a lawyer with movie connections, and he got her the job with GAM. Which stands for Global Artists Management."

"I think I know him," Brewster Payne said. "If it's the same fellow, he masterfully defends, whenever challenged, the motion picture industry's amazingly imaginative accounting practices."

"Interesting," Matt said. "If you happen to bump into him . . ."

"I'm getting the impression that you are somewhat taken with this young lady, and therefore not entirely unhappy with the prospect of protecting . . . what did you call him? 'Super Cop'?"

"She's a blonde. Nice legs," Matt said. "And she knows how to peel shrimp. What more can one ask for?"

"What indeed?" Brewster Payne said.

"Matt," Patricia Payne said at the door, "I told you I was going to open a bottle of champagne."

"I needed a little liquid courage to face Sigmund Freud," Matt said.

She turned without replying, and after a moment, her son and husband followed her into the kitchen.

The three women were standing around the chopping block in the middle of the kitchen. They each held a champagne glass, and there were two more on the chopping block. And something else, wrapped in a handkerchief.

Matt and his father picked up the champagne stems.

"To Sergeant Payne," Patricia Payne said, and they all touched glasses.

Matt took a sip and set it down.

"I've got something for you," she said. "I wanted the family to be together when I gave it to you."

She picked up the handkerchief and handed it to him. Even before he unwrapped it, Matt knew what it was. It was a police badge, and he knew whose.

"Your father's," she said.

Matt looked at the sergeant's badge, Number 471, of the Police Department of the City of Philadelphia.

"When Denny called," Patricia Payne went on, "he said that he could arrange for you to be assigned your father's number if I wanted. I told him I thought you would like that. And he asked me if I happened to still have it, and I told him I'd have to look. I found it. It was in the attic. And your father's off-duty gun, the snub-nosed .38."

He looked at his mother but didn't say anything.

"Your father was a good man, Matt," his mother said. "A good police officer."

"I have two fathers," Matt said, his voice breaking. "My other father is a good man, too."

Brewster Payne looked at him.

"Write this down, Matt. Never reply to a heartfelt compliment. You never can come up with something worth saying."

He put his arm around Matt's shoulder, and then embraced him.

"Give that to Denny before the ceremony tomorrow," Patricia Payne said. "He'll know how to handle it."

Matt nodded, and slipped the badge into his pocket.

"Under the circumstances," Brewster Payne said, picking up his whiskey glass, "barring objections, I think I'll have another of these."

"Me, too," Matt said.

"First, we'll finish the champagne," Patricia Payne said. "And then we'll all have a drink."

Matt had just turned onto I-476 in Swarthmore to return to Philadelphia when the S-Band radio in the Crown Victoria went off: "S-Twelve."

He pulled the microphone from under the center armrest.

"Twelve."

"Meet the inspector in the 700 block of North Second."

"Got it. En route. Thank you," he said.

It was entirely possible that a crime had been committed in the 700 block of North Second Street, requiring his professional attention. But it was far more likely that he was going to find Inspector Wohl inside the premises at 705 North Second, which was known as Liberties Bar, and was the preferred watering hole of the Homicide Bureau.

I wonder what that's all about?

I wonder why he didn't call me on the cell phone?

Tomorrow, I will no longer be S-Twelve.

There was a somewhat battered, three-year-old Crown Victoria parked on Second Street in front of Liberties Bar. And a last year's Crown Victoria, three brand-new Crown Victorias, and a Buick Rendezvous.

When Matt walked into Liberties, the drivers of these vehicles were sitting around two tables pushed together along the wall, across from the ornately carved, century-old bar. They were Deputy Commissioner Coughlin, Chief Inspector Lowenstein, Inspector Wohl, Lieutenant Washington, Detective Harris, and Michael J. O'Hara, Esq.

There was a bottle of Old Bushmills Irish whiskey, a bottle of Chivas Regal, a bottle of Jack Daniel's, and two bowls, one with cashews, the other with stick pretzels, on the table.

"What's going on?" Matt asked, slipping into a chair at the table beside Harris.

"I am interrogating a witness to the Roy Rogers job," Harris said, nodding at O'Hara. "And getting nothing out of him."

"Jesus, Tony," Mickey said. "The bastards took a shot at me!"

Matt poured scotch into a glass.

"It would behoove you to go easy on that tonight, Detective Payne," Wohl said. "Which is the reason we put the arm out for you. We didn't want you to go off somewhere and get smashed by yourself."

"Yes, sir," Matt said, and picked up the drink and took a sip. Then he took his father's badge from his apartment and slipped it to Denny Coughlin.

"Mom found that, and said to give it to you," he said.

Coughlin looked at the badge, then laid it on the table.

"What's that?" Lowenstein asked.

"Jack Moffitt's sergeant's badge," Coughlin replied. "I remember the day he got it." He looked at Matt and said, "I don't want to hand this to your mother a second time. You understand me?"

Matt's mouth ran away with him.

"Color me careful."

"Watch your lip, Matty!" Coughlin said.

"That would make a good yarn," Mickey O'Hara said. "'New Sergeant Gets Hero Father's Badge.'"

"Which you won't write, right?" Lowenstein said.

"Okay," Mickey said, shrugging his shoulders and reaching for the bottle of Old Bushmills.

"I loved Jack like a brother," Coughlin said. "And he had a lot of balls. But he wasn't a hero. His big balls got him killed. He answered a silent alarm without backup. . . ."

"I remember," Lowenstein said. "I had North Detectives when it happened."

"Jack knew better," Coughlin said. "He could still be walking around if he'd done what he was trained—ordered—to do."

"Dennis, how would you judge Dutch Moffitt's behavior?" Jason Washington's sonorous voice asked.

Coughlin looked at him, obviously annoyed at the question.

"Was that an excess of male ego—'I'm Dutch Moffitt of Highway Patrol. I can handle this punk by myself'?" Washington pursued. "Or a professional assessment of the situation in which he found himself, with the same result?"

Coughlin looked at him for a long moment before deciding if and what to answer.

"Dutch said, 'Lay the gun on the counter, son. I don't want to have to kill you. I'm a police officer.' Was that the right thing to do? I think so. I would like to think that's what I would have done. I would also like to think I would have looked around for a second doer. Dutch didn't, and the junkie girlfriend shot him."

"I worked with Dutch," Peter Wohl said. "I can't believe he didn't look for a second doer. He had trouble keeping his pecker in his pocket, but he was a very good street cop."

"Your mother never told you, 'Don't speak ill of the dead,' Peter?" Coughlin said. "Especially in front of the deceased's nephew?"

Wohl shrugged, unrepentant. Coughlin had another thought.

"Your grandmother's going to be in the mayor's office tomorrow, Matty. I thought she had a right to be."

"Oh, shit!" Matt blurted.

Coughlin glared angrily at him.

"I was going to tell her later," Matt said, somewhat lamely. "Maybe even go by."

"She's your grandmother, Matt," Coughlin said, on the edge of anger.

"I don't like the way she treats my mother," Matt said.

"Don't tell me she's still pissed that Jack's widow married Payne?" Lowenstein asked.

"It's a religious thing, Matt," Coughlin said. "Patricia raised Matt as an Episcopal after Payne adopted him."

"You Christians do have your problems, don't you?" Lowenstein asked. "How many angels *can* fit on the head of a pin?"

Coughlin gave him the finger.

"I don't agree with her, Matty," Coughlin said. "You know that. But she's still your grandmother."

"Does my mother know she's coming?"

"If your mother knew, she would, being the lady she is, not go."

"Jesus—"

"Before you two continue with what is sure to be an indeterminable discussion of Mother Moffitt," Washington interrupted, "may I finish with my profound observation?"

Matt realized—wondering why it had taken him so long—that while no one at the table was drunk, it was also obvious that no one was on their first—or third—drink, either. He looked at the bottles. The Chivas Regal was half empty; the Jack Daniel's and the Old Bushmills were almost dry.

And Washington had even called Coughlin by his first name.

What the hell is this all about? Why are all these people sitting around here getting smashed?

"How could we stop you?" Mickey O'Hara asked.

Washington continued, "With the given that Sergeant Jack Moffitt was a good street cop, that Captain Dutch Moffitt was a good street cop, and that Officer Charlton had survived almost to retirement as a street cop, what mistake—indeed, what *fatal* mistake—did all three of them make?"

"They weren't as good as they thought they were?" Mickey asked.

"Close, Michael," Washington said.

"Oh, shit, not that 'they didn't turn over the rock under the rock' crap again," Tony Harris said.

"Yes, indeed," Washington said. "That 'turn over the rock under the rock' crap again. If Sergeant Moffitt had looked around the gas station one more time, if Dutch had looked around the Waikiki Diner one more time, if Charlton had taken one more look . . ."

"I don't think that's such a profound observation, Jason," Coughlin said.

"More like self-evident," Lowenstein said.

"I was trying to make the point for Matt's edification," Washington said.

Coughlin looked at him, then at Matt.

"He's right, Matty," he said. "Pay attention."

"Yes, sir," Matt said.

"Would you like to see how your names will appear in tomorrow's *Bulletin?*" Mickey asked. "Or shall we go back to discussing Mother Moffitt?"

He took several sheets of paper from his inside jacket pocket and swung them back and forth.

"Curiosity underwhelms me," Wohl said, and held his hand out for the sheets of paper.

Slug—Mayor Forms Double Murder Task Force

(Jack, don't bury this with the underwear ads. These slimeballs need catching. AND USE THE PICTURES)

By Michael J. O'Hara
Bulletin Staff Writer

Photos by Jack Weinberg
Bulletin Photographer

Philadelphia—Mayor Alvin W. Martin, surrounded by the heavy hitters of the Philadelphia Police Department, and standing not far from where the body of Officer Kenneth Charlton lay in state in the Monti Funeral Home in the 2500 block of South Broad Street, this afternoon announced the formation of a special police task force to bring the two men who murdered Charlton and Mrs. Maria M. Fernandez during the robbery Sunday evening of the Roy Rogers restaurant on South Broad Street.

"Both a citizen—a single mother of three—and a police officer have lost their lives as a result of a brutal attack that affects not only their grieving survivors but every citizen of Philadelphia," the mayor said, adding: "This sort of outrage cannot be tolerated, and it will not be."

(Photo 1 L-R, Lowenstein, Mariani, Martin, Coughlin) Flanked by Police Commissioner Ralph J. Mariani, Deputy Commissioner Dennis V. Coughlin, and Chief Inspector of Detectives Matthew Lowenstein, Martin announced that Inspector Peter F. Wohl, the highly regarded commanding officer of the Special Operations Division, would head the task force.

(Photo 2 L-R, Washington, Wohl, and Harris) Speaking to this reporter later, Inspector Wohl said it was not his intention to take over the investigation from Lieutenant Jason Washington, "who is beyond question the most skilled homicide investigator I know of," but rather to "ensure that Lieutenant Washington and his able team leader, Detective Anthony Harris, get whatever assistance they need from not only Special Operations, but the entire police department, so these criminals can be quickly removed from our streets."

(Photo 3 L-R, Sabara, Wohl, Pekach, Sgt M. M. Payne, and Capt F. X. Hollaran) Wohl's deputy, Captain Michael J. Sabara, and Captain David R.

96 · W. E. B. GRIFFIN

Pekach, commanding officer of the elite Highway Patrol, nodded their agreement with both Wohl's cold determination and with his explanation of the difficulty sometimes encountered—as now—in identifying the perpetrators of a crime.

"The patrons of the Roy Rogers restaurant were terrorized by the cold brutality of these criminals. Shots were fired. Two people were killed, and everyone else's life was in danger. It's regrettable, but I think very understandable, that the horrified witnesses can't really agree on a description of the men we seek.

"This is not to say that we won't apprehend them, and soon, but that it will take a bit longer than we like."

Wohl went on to say that "it's only in the movies that a fingerprint lifted from the scene of a crime can be quickly matched with that of a criminal whose identity is unknown. There are hundreds of thousands of fingerprints in our files, millions in those of the FBI, and the prints we have in our possession will have to be matched to them one at a time until we get a match."

Wohl went on to explain that once the people sought are in custody, their fingerprints can be used to prove they were at the scene of the crime, "but until that happens, fingerprints won't be of immediate use to us.

"And once we have these people in custody, and can place them in a police lineup, there is no question in my mind—experience shows—that the witnesses to their crime will be able to positively identify them. This crime will not go unpunished."

Wohl said that police are already running down "a number of leads," but declined to elaborate.

end

Wohl slid the two sheets of paper across the table to Coughlin. Lowenstein leaned over so that he could read it, too.

"Magnificent story, Mickey," Wohl said. "There's just one little thing wrong with it. All those quotes from me are pure bullshit."

"Is the Black Buddha the most skilled homicide investigator you know of, or not?" O'Hara challenged.

"Of course I am," Washington said. "Let me see that when you're finished, Dennis, please."

"He is, but I didn't tell you that," Wohl said.

"But if I had asked, you would have said so, right? And I'm right about the fingerprints, right?"

"But I didn't even talk to you at the goddamn funeral home!"

"But if you had, you would have said what I said you said, more or less, right?"

"This'll be in the paper tomorrow, Mick?" Lowenstein asked.

"It will, and I wouldn't be at all surprised if it was on page one."

"Pity you couldn't have put in there that we had a late-night conference," Lowenstein said. "Martin would have loved that."

"I didn't know about the 'late-night conference' until I walked in here," O'Hara said. "When I heard on the command band that everybody was headed to the 700 block of North Second, I thought there was a war on here."

"Commissioner Coughlin and myself were conferring privately with Inspector Wohl," Lowenstein said, "when these underlings coincidentally felt the need for a late-night cup of coffee at this fine establishment."

There were chuckles.

"Nice story, Mickey," Coughlin said.

"Presuming the conference is over," Wohl said, as he got to his feet, "I am going home." He looked at Matt. "And so are you."

Coughlin stood up.

"Are we square with the tab here?"

"I'll get the tab," Mickey O'Hara said. "My pleasure."

"Bright-eyed and bushy-tailed and at the mayor's office at quarter to nine, Matty," Coughlin ordered. "And I expect you to be nice to your grandmother."

"I have, as always," Jason Washington said, getting to his feet, "thoroughly enjoyed the company of my colleagues. And I am sure you have all profited greatly from the experience."

Detective Harris shook his head, then chuckled, then giggled, and then laughed. That proved contagious, and each of them was smiling, or chuckling, or laughing as they filed out the door onto North Second Street.

CHAPTER
6

[ONE]

The Hon. Alvin W. Martin looked up from his desk when his executive assistant, Dianna Kerr-Gally, a tall, thin, stylish, thirtyish black woman, slipped into his office.

"It's ten past nine, Mr. Mayor."

"Is everybody in the conference room?"

"Just about, but Commissioner Mariani has someone he wants you to meet."

She nodded toward the outer office.

"Sure, send him in," the mayor replied, with an enthusiasm he really didn't feel. He had things to do, and the less time spent on the promotion ceremony the better.

It wasn't only Commissioner Mariani. He had with him Deputy Commissioner Coughlin and a tall, lean, stern-faced, gray-haired woman in a simple black dress and the young detective who had scored number one.

"Good morning, Mr. Mayor," Mariani said.

"Good morning, Ralph."

The mayor smiled at the woman, who returned it with a barely perceptible curling of her lips.

She looks like that farmer's wife in the Grant Wood painting.

What's that on her dress? Miniature police badges. Three of them.

"Mr. Mayor," Coughlin said. "I thought before the program begins that you'd like to meet Mrs. Gertrude Moffitt. . . ."

"I'm delighted. How do you do, Mrs. Moffitt?"

She nodded, her lips curled slightly again, but she didn't say anything.

"Mrs. Moffitt is the widow of a police officer, and two of her sons died in the line of duty as police officers . . . ," Coughlin said.

Well, that explains the three badges.

". . . Sergeant John X. Moffitt and Captain Richard C. Moffitt . . . ,"
Coughlin went on.

"That's a proud tradition, Mrs. Moffitt," the mayor said. "I'm honored to
meet you."

She nodded again.

". . . and she is Detective Payne's grandmother," Coughlin finished.

"The tradition continues, then," the mayor said. "This must be a proud
moment for you."

"If my grandson still carried his father's name, it would be," she said.

What the hell does that mean?

Detective Payne looked pained.

Whatever the hell it is, I'm not going to get into it here and now.

"Since you know full well, Mrs. Moffitt, that police work never ceases, I'm
sure you'll forgive me if I ask the commissioner if there have been any developments in the Roy Rogers case."

"I'm afraid not, Mr. Mayor . . ."

*Damn! The press will be in the conference room. It would have been a perfect
place and time to announce the cops have finally bagged those animals.*

". . . but Commissioner Coughlin tells me there was a meeting last night of
all the principals of the task force, plus Chief of Detectives Lowenstein."

"Really? Well, I hope something good will come from it."

"I feel sure that it will, Mr. Mayor," Coughlin said. "We all feel there will
be developments in the very near future."

"I hope you're right, Commissioner," the mayor said. "Mrs. Moffitt, when
we go into the conference room"—he looked at his watch—"and we're going to
have to do that right now, I think it would be very appropriate if you were to
pin his new badge on your grandson."

And a picture like that will certainly make the evening news.

"All right," she said.

"Here it is, Mother Moffitt," Coughlin said. "That's Jack's badge."

"That's Jack's badge?" she asked, looking at the badge Coughlin was holding out to her.

"Yes, it is."

"You told me, Dennis Coughlin, that it had been buried with him."

"I was wrong," Coughlin said.

"And where was it all these years? She had it, didn't she?"

"Patricia's Jack's widow, Mother Moffitt."

She snatched the badge out of his hand.

"Well, at least she won't have it now," Mother Moffitt said.

"If you will all go into the conference room now?" Dianna Kerr-Gally asked, gesturing at a door. "We can get the ceremony under way."

When the mayor tried to follow the procession into the conference room, Dianna Kerr-Gally held up her arm, palm extended, to stop him.

He stopped.

Dianna Kerr-Gally, using her fingers and mouthing the numbers, counted downward from ten, then signaled the mayor to go into the conference room.

He walked briskly to the head of the table, where a small lectern had been placed. He looked around the room, smiling, attempting to lock eyes momentarily with everyone.

There were five promotees, all of whom looked older than Detective Payne, and all but Payne were in uniform. Two of the promotees were gray-haired. All the promotees were accompanied by family and/or friends. Dianna Kerr-Gally had put out the word no more than four per promotee, and apparently that had been widely ignored. The large room was crowded, just about full.

There were three video cameras at the rear of the room, and at least half a dozen still photographers. One of them was Michael J. O'Hara of the *Bulletin*.

I'll have to remember to thank him for that front-page story about the task force.

Jesus, is that who I think it is? It damn sure is.

Brewster C. Payne in the flesh.

The last time I saw him was on Monday in Washington, in the Senate Dining Room. He was the "something really important has come up" reason our distinguished senior senator was sorry he couldn't have lunch with me.

What's his connection with Detective Payne?

When Dianna Kerr-Gally came to the lectern to hand him the three-by-five cards from which he would speak, he motioned her close to him and whispered, "The tall WASP in the back of the room?"

She looked at nodded.

"His name is Brewster Payne," she whispered back.

"I know who he is. Ask him if he can spare me a minute when this is over."

She nodded.

"If I may have your attention, ladies and gentlemen?" the mayor began, raising his voice so that it could be heard over the hubbub in the room.

The next time we do something like this, there should be a microphone.

. . .

"I realize you're a busy man, Mr. Payne," the mayor said, as Dianna Kerr-Gally ushered Brewster Payne into his office. "But I did want to say hello. I don't think we've ever actually met, have we?"

"I don't believe we have. But didn't I see you in Washington on Monday?"

"Across the dining room," the mayor said, waving him into a chair. "I need a cup of coffee. Do you have the time?"

"Thank you very much," Payne said. "I'd love one."

"Dianna, please?"

"Right away, Mr. Mayor."

"Would it be impolitic for me to ask what you and the senator seemed to be talking so intently about?"

"My firm represents Nesfoods," Payne said. "The senator chairs the Agricultural Subcommittee. We were talking about tomatoes, United States and Mexican."

Nesfoods gave me one hundred thousand for my campaign. I wonder how much they gave to the senator?

"The tomato growers here are concerned about cheap Mexican tomatoes?"

"That issue has been resolved by the Free Trade Agreement. What I hoped to do—what I think I did—was convince the senator that it's in everybody's best interests for the Department of Agriculture to station inspectors in Nesfoods processing plants in Mexico, so that we can process the tomatoes there, and ship the pulp in tank trucks to the Nesfoods plants here and in California. That will both save Nesfoods a good deal of money and actually increase the quality of the finished product. Apparently, the riper the tomato when processed, the better the pulp."

"And what was the problem?"

"As hard as it is to believe, there are those who are unhappy with the Free Trade Agreement," Payne said, dryly, "and object to stationing Agriculture Department inspectors on foreign soil."

"But after you had your little chat, the senator seemed to see the light?"

"I hope so, Mr. Mayor."

Dianna Kerr-Gally came into the office with a silver coffee service and poured coffee.

When she had left them alone again, the mayor looked over his coffee cup and said, "I wasn't aware until this morning that your son was a policeman."

"I think of it as the firm's loss is the city's gain," Payne said. "Actually, Matt's my adopted son. His father—a police sergeant—was killed before he was born. I adopted Matt before he could walk."

"You'd rather he would have joined Mawson, Payne, Stockton, McAdoo and Lester?" the mayor asked.

"Wouldn't your father prefer to see you in a pulpit?" Payne responded.

"Whenever I see him, he shakes his head sadly," the mayor said. "I don't think he's given up hope that I will see the error of my ways."

"Neither have I given up hope," Payne said. "But in the meantime, I am as proud of Matt as I daresay your father is of you."

"I like to think public service is an honorable, even noble, calling."

"So does Matt," Payne said. "He thinks of the police as a thin blue line, all that separates society from the barbarians."

"Unfortunately, he's probably right," the mayor said.

Payne set his cup down.

"I don't want to keep you, Mr. Payne," the mayor said. "But I did want to say hello. Could we have lunch one day?"

"I'd be delighted," Payne said. "And thank you for the coffee."

He stood up, shook hands with the mayor, and walked out of the room.

Commissioner Mariani told me that if I didn't send that young man to Homicide as promised I could expect trouble from the Fraternal Order of Police. He didn't tell me that the FOP would be represented, pro bono, by Mawson, Payne, Stockton, McAdoo & Lester.

[TWO]

The Hon. Eileen McNamara Solomon, Philadelphia's district attorney, devoutly believed that at least seventy percent of the nurses under fifty in the surgical department of the hospital of the University of Pennsylvania would rush to console Benjamin A. Solomon, M.D., the moment he started to feel sorry for himself because his wife-the-D.A. had become careless about her appearance.

So, although she was always too busy to waste a lot of time in a beauty parlor, she made it to Cathleen's Coiffeurs every Tuesday at 8:00 A.M., watched what she ate, and, weather permitting, jogged on the Parkway for an hour starting at 7:00 A.M. Monday, Wednesday, and Friday.

The result was a rather tall, lithe forty-nine-year-old, who wore her blonde hair cut stylishly but short, and whose husband had no reason to see if the grass was greener in someone else's bedroom.

After graduation—third in her class—from the University of Pennsylvania School of Law, and passing the bar examination, Eileen McNamara had declined offers to join any of the several more or less prestigious law firms because she suspected she was going to become the Token Female.

Instead, she took a job with the Public Defender's Office, which had the responsibility of providing legal counsel to the indigent. She had quickly proven herself to be a highly competent courtroom lawyer.

But she had always been a little uncomfortable after she had convinced a jury that there was reasonable doubt that some miserable sonofabitch had actually pistol-whipped a grandmother while in the process of robbing her corner grocery, or some other miserable sonofabitch had actually been pushing drugs on grammar school kids.

And she had been unhappy in the company of her colleagues, who almost universally believed that having been born into poverty, or to a drug-addict mother, or of Afro-American/Puerto Rican/Latin/Outer Mongolian/Whatever parentage was an excuse to commit robbery, rape, and murder, and to meanwhile support oneself in outrageous luxury by selling what were known as "prohibited substances" to others.

So she had changed sides. Philadelphia's District Attorney was delighted to offer Miss Eileen McNamara a position as an assistant district attorney not only because she was a good-looking blonde, but also because her record of successfully defending people his assistant D.A.s had prosecuted unsuccessfully had made them look even more incompetent than they actually were.

She had been somewhat happier in the D.A.'s office, but not much. The cases she would have liked to prosecute seemed to get assigned to the "more experienced" of her fellow assistant D.A.s, and the cases she was assigned to prosecute were—she quickly figured out—the ones her fellow assistant D.A.s didn't want because the cases were either weak or politically dangerous or both.

But she did her best with the cases she was given, and managed to convince one jury after another that not only was there not any reasonable doubt that some miserable sonofabitch had done what the cops had said he or she had done, but that he or she had done it with full knowledge of what he or she was doing, and in the belief he or she was going to get away with it, and therefore did not deserve much pity from the criminal justice system.

Assistant District Attorney McNamara quickly discovered—as something of a surprise—that as a general rule of thumb, she liked the cops. By and large, they were really what they considered themselves to be, a thin blue line protecting society from the barbarians.

What surprised her in this regard was that they seemed to genuinely share her concern for what she thought of as the other group of innocent victims of a criminal act. The first group was of course those who had been robbed/beaten/murdered by the criminal. The second group was the wives/parents/children of the miserable sonofabitch who had committed the crime.

Eileen McNamara had been an assistant district attorney almost three years when she first ran into Benjamin Solomon, M.D., F.A.C.S. More accurately, when Ben ran into her, rear-ending her Plymouth with his Cadillac as she was looking for a parking place in South Philadelphia.

Ben hadn't been going very fast, just not paying attention, but fast enough to do considerable damage to her trunk and right fender. The accident had taken place within, if not the sight, then the hearing, of Officer Martin Shaugnessy.

Officer Shaugnessy had trotted to the scene. He pretended not to recognize the good-looking blonde assistant D.A. who had once made mincemeat out of the public defender who had decided that the best way to get his client off the hook was to paint arresting Officer Shaugnessy as an ignorant, prejudiced police thug who took an almost sexual pleasure in persecuting young men of Puerto Rican extraction.

"How much have you had to drink, sir?" was his first question now to Dr. Solomon, who had just given Miss McNamara his effusive apologies and insurance card.

"Drink? It's eight-thirty in the morning! I haven't even had my breakfast!"

"People who speed and drive as recklessly as you obviously were, sir, are often driving under the influence. Would you please extend your right arm, close your eyes, and try to touch your nose?"

"Officer, I don't think the doctor has been drinking," Miss McNamara said. "I think this was just a simple fender bender."

"You sure?" Officer Shaugnessy asked, dubiously.

"I'm sure," Miss McNamara said. "And I'm sure the doctor and I can work this out between us."

"Well, if you say so, ma'am."

"Thank you," Miss McNamara said.

"Yes, ma'am," Officer Shaugnessy said. He filled out the Form 75-48, which the insurance companies would need, and then went back to walking his beat.

While they were waiting for the wrecker, Eileen became aware that the doctor kept stealing looks at her. For some reason, it didn't make her uncomfortable; usually when men did that, it did.

As the wrecker hauled her Plymouth away, Dr. Solomon looked directly at her. His eyes on hers did make her uncomfortable.

"What was that with the cop all about?" Dr. Solomon asked. "You know him?"

"I know a lot of cops," Eileen said. "That one looked familiar. But do I know him? No."

"How is it you know a lot of cops?"

"I'm an assistant D.A."

"Really? An assistant D.A.?" Ben had asked, genuinely surprised. "Good-looking blondes don't come to mind when I hear that term."

"On the other hand, you do look like a doctor," Eileen heard herself say, adding quickly, "What kind?"

"Chest-cutter," Ben had said. "Thoracic surgeon. What do you mean, I look like a doctor?"

"Your eyes," Eileen said. "You have intelligent, kind eyes."

When she heard what she had said, she blushed.

"So do you," Ben had said, softly, after a minute. "Can I buy you breakfast?"

"Breakfast?"

"And lunch, and dinner, and whatever else you want to eat for the rest of your life?"

"You're sure you haven't been drinking?"

"I don't drink," he said. "If I sound a little strange, I was at the table all night—until about an hour ago. And then I met you."

Benjamin Solomon, M.D., and Eileen McNamara, L.L.D., were united in matrimony not quite a month later, which caused varying degrees of joy and despair within their respective Eastern European Hebraic and Irish Roman Catholic communities.

They had been married three years when Eileen told Ben the strangest thing had happened the previous afternoon. She had been asked if she would be interested in running for judge in a special election called by the governor to fill two vacancies caused by the incarceration of two incumbent jurists.

"I think you should," Ben had said after a moment. "You've been on both sides of the fence, and I think you'd do a good job straddling the middle. And you already have the name. Judge Solomon the Second."

She won the election handily, primarily, she believed, because nobody had ever heard of her, and there was general contempt for those whose names were known to the voters.

And she liked the bench, at least trying to keep things fair and just.

They hadn't been able to have children—Ben's fault, the gynecologists said, probably because he'd worn Jockey shorts all of his life—and she really regretted that. But she told herself that a child whose parents both had independent careers could not have gotten the attention it deserved, and that made being childless a little easier to bear.

She had been on the bench six years when a delegation of pols came to her and proposed that she run for district attorney. The incumbent had been elected to Congress. Her service as an assistant D.A. and her six years on the bench had taught her that there was considerable room for improvement in the office of the District Attorney.

She talked the offer over with Ben. She was sure that she would make a hell of a good D.A., but she hadn't been at all sure that she could win, and if she lost, she would be out of a job. She couldn't run for reelection to the bench and for D.A. at the same time.

Ben said she should give it a shot; she would always regret it later if she didn't. And, Ben said, it wasn't as if they were going to have to sell the dog to make the car payments if she found herself unemployed. That was a reference to the fact that Ben's scalpel earned more than ten times as much money for them as the government paid her to wield her gavel.

She ran, and won with fifty-two percent of the vote. The first time she ran for reelection, she got fifty-eight percent, and the last time, she'd garnered sixty-seven percent of the vote.

Eileen McNamara Solomon had two cellular telephones, which, when she was there, she placed in rechargers on her desk beside the office phone with all its buttons. One of the cellulars, which buzzed when called, was her official phone. She made herself available with it around-the-clock.

The second Nokia cellular had a green face, and when it was called, it played "When Irish Eyes Are Smiling." This was her private line, its number known to very few people. It had been a gift from Ben, who said that, believe it or not, he had a busy schedule, too, and didn't like to be put on hold.

When the green phone began to play "When Irish Eyes Are Smiling" she thought it was probably Ben, and wondered if he was about to ask her to lunch.

"Hi," she said to the telephone.

"You busy, Eileen?" a female voice inquired. She knew the voice.

"Never too busy for you, Martha. How are you?"

Eileen McNamara and Martha Peebles had met in Art Appreciation 101 at the University of Pennsylvania, and the tall, then sort of skinny eighteen-year-old Irish girl and the seventeen-year-old slight, short WASP with an acne condition had been immediately comfortable with each other.

Eileen had told Martha all about her family, then taken her home to meet "King Kong"—her brother—and her father, both bricklaying subcontractors, and her mother. Martha had been visibly reluctant to talk about her family, except to say that her mother had died and she lived with her father and brother, who was a would-be actor.

Martha had not offered to take Eileen home with her, and Eileen wondered if she was maybe ashamed of her father, or her home, and went out of her way to make sure Martha understood she didn't care if her father "had problems" or what her house looked like, or how much money there was.

It was four months before Martha finally took Eileen home, on a Saturday, and Eileen got to meet the brother, Stephen, who was light on his feet, and her father, Alexander.

Martha had shown her around the house and property, which had taken a little time, as there were twenty-eight rooms in the turn-of-the-century mansion set on fourteen acres behind stone walls on Glengarry Lane in Chestnut Hill, plus a guest house, a hothouse, and stables for Alexander Peebles's polo ponies.

"I never saw anything like this," Eileen had confessed, as they left the stables. "Not even in the movies."

Martha had looked at her.

"I really don't want this to change things between us," Martha said. "You're the best friend I ever had."

Eileen had never forgotten the frightened look in Martha's eyes.

"Don't be silly."

"And don't tell anybody else, please."

"Why should I?"

Eileen had never had a best friend in high school, and neither, Martha said, had she. They became and remained best friends and stayed best friends. Martha was the first person Eileen had told about Ben, right after he rearended her. And Martha had been her only bridesmaid when she married Ben.

And Eileen really worried about Martha, particularly after her father died, cutting the queer brother out of his will, and leaving everything to Martha. Everything included the Tamaqua Mining Corporation, which owned, among other things, somewhere between ten and twelve percent of the known anthracite coal reserves in the United States.

There had been no man; there never had been one in Martha's life seriously. There were several reasons for this, Eileen thought, the primary reason being that Martha, aware that she was no great beauty, suspected that what few suitors she had had were primarily interested in her money, followed closely by Martha's comparison of her young men with her father, and finding that none of them came close to matching up.

Eileen really thought that maybe her best friend was losing it when she began to complain that her house was being burgled on a more or less regular basis, and that the police weren't paying attention.

Eileen called Denny Coughlin and told him she would appreciate it if he would lean on the commanding officer of the Fourteenth District and get him to send enough uniforms around to 606 Glengarry Lane often enough to convince the inhabitant that her property and person were being adequately protected.

Denny Coughlin had called her back within the hour to tell her she could put her mind at rest about Miss Peebles. He'd called the Fourteenth District commander, as she'd asked him to do, and Captain Jessup had told him he was a little late. It seems Miss Peebles's lawyer, Brewster Payne, had talked with his partner, Colonel Mawson, who'd telephoned Police Commissioner Czernich about Miss Peebles's problem.

The commissioner had called Jessup and told him not to worry about Miss Peebles anymore. He had given the problem to Special Operations, and Highway Patrol would now be rolling by 606 Glengarry on a regular—at least hourly—basis. Special Operations had been told the commissioner didn't want to hear of any more problems at 606 Glengarry Lane.

The next morning, just after Judge Solomon had walked into her chambers at nine, Martha Peebles had called.

"Eileen, it happened."

"What happened?"

"My knight in shining armor. He finally came."

"Martha, are you all right?"

"His name is David Pekach, and he's the captain commanding Highway Patrol. And we did it, Eileen!"

Martha reported that Captain Pekach had called to inform her that her property would now be patrolled by Highway Patrol on a regular, frequent basis, and that she could put her mind at rest.

"My God, Eileen. He's so much like Daddy. All man. You just feel safe when you're with him."

"What do you mean you did it, Martha?"

"You know what I mean," Martha said, not even very shyly.

"You're not telling me this cop just walked in the door, and you took him to bed?"

"No, of course not. Not then. What happened was that he said he would swing by at midnight himself, and I said I never went to bed that early, and if he had the time—didn't have to get home to his wife—why didn't he stop in and I'd give him a cup of coffee. And he said he wasn't married, and thank you, he'd like a cup of coffee. And he came back at midnight, and that's when we did it."

"I think you're out of your mind."

"I know. I'm out of my mind with love. His first name is David. And I thought it was going to hurt the first time, and it didn't. God, Eileen, it was wonderful!"

"Denny, tell me about Captain David Pekach of Highway Patrol," was the call that came next.

"What would you like to know, Eileen? And why?"

"The why's my business. Tell me about him."

"What about him? He's a good cop."

"Is he married?"

"No. He's never been married. Before he made captain, and they gave him Highway Patrol, he was a lieutenant in Narcotics. He grew a pigtail, and the dealers thought he was one of them. He's got one hell of an arrest record."

"That's all?"

"When he was a rookie detective in Homicide, just a kid, when the rest of the department didn't think the sainted Fort Festung could possibly do anything like hurt his girlfriend, Dave Pekach finally got a judge to give him a search warrant—"

"I know who he is," Eileen interrupted, remembering him from the trial.

"Like I said, Eileen, he's a very good cop."

"Tell me about him and women. I understand he's quite a swordsman."

"Who told you that?" Coughlin asked. "Eileen, you've seen him. He's a little guy. Looks like a weasel. Women do the opposite of swoon when they see him. I've never even seen him with a woman. What's this all about?"

"Thanks, Denny."

Brewster Courtland Payne, Esq., gave Miss Martha Peebles in marriage to Captain David Pekach three weeks later. The Hon. Eileen McNamara Solomon was the matron of honor.

"Eileen, I realize this is short notice, but I'd really like you and Ben to come for supper tonight," Martha Peebles Pekach said now.

"What's up?"

"Brewster Payne's son—Matt?—just made sergeant, and Precious and I are having a little party for him."

"That kid made sergeant?" Eileen asked, surprised. Very privately, she thought of Detective Matt Payne as the Wyatt Earp—or maybe the Stan Colt—of the Main Line. Most cops never draw their weapons in twenty years of service. Brewster Payne's kid had already shot two critters and been involved in an O.K. Corral shoot-out in Bucks County and he hadn't been on the job much over five years.

And now he's a sergeant?

"He was number one on the list. The mayor promoted him this morning."

"I'll have to check with Ben," Eileen said.

"With or without him, Eileen, please? Sixish."

[THREE]

Lieutenant Jason Washington, who was sitting in his glass-walled office, his feet resting on the open lower drawer of his desk, deep in thought, became aware that Detective Kenneth J. Summers, a portly forty-year-old, who was on the desk, was waving at him.

He raised his eyebrows to suggest that Summers now had his attention. Summers pointed to the telephone. Washington nodded and reached for it.

"Homicide, Lieutenant Washington."

"Dave Pekach, Jason."

"Dare I to hope that you are calling to tell me two critters have flagged down a Highway car and, overwhelmed by remorse, are asking how they can go about confessing to the Roy Rogers job?"

"You don't have them yet?" Pekach asked, surprised.

"You know where we are, David?" Washington said. "In the absence of a better idea, I have four people running down a somewhat esoteric idea proposed by the newest member of our happy little family."

"Matt?"

"Indeed. *Sergeant* Matthew Payne. He wondered—causing Tony Harris some chagrins—and between thee and me, me too—for not having had the same thought first—why Doer Number One took the trouble to put his weapon under Kenny Charlton's bulletproof vest instead of simply shooting him in the head."

"Yeah. I wonder why."

"There may be no reason, but for the moment, we are considering the possibility that he knew Kenny, felt some personal animosity toward him, and wanted to make sure the wound was fatal."

"That's possible. That sounds like a deliberate act, not like something that just happened."

"So we are now compiling a photo album of every young African-American critter Kenny ever arrested. And since Kenny spent many years on the street, there is a large number of such critters."

"It may work, Jason," Pekach said, thoughtfully.

"And I have Tony starting all over again from Step One," Washington said.

"Actually, I was calling about Matt," Pekach said. "My Martha wants to wash down his sergeant's badge. . . ."

"Somehow I don't think Your Martha used that phrase."

"She's having a few people in, is the way she put it. You and Your Martha, of course, and Tony. And My Martha asked me to ask you if it would be a good idea to ask the other guys in Homicide."

"What and where are the festivities?"

"Tonight, here. Six, six-thirty. If it stays nice, outside. Like the last one. Which, come to think of it, Lieutenant, was to wash down your new badge."

"I was about to say, David, that tonight is not the best of times. But then I remembered the profound philosophical observation that all work, et cetera, et cetera. Tony will be there, I'll see to that, and so will My Martha and I. And I will put a card on the bulletin board advising every one that edibles and intoxicants will be available at 606 Glengarry Lane for anyone interested in celebrating Sergeant Payne's promotion."

"You think anyone will come?"

"Edibles and intoxicants may entice one or two. And simple curiosity about Castle Pekach will entice some of the others. I don't want to make it a command performance. Is Henry going to grace the premises?"

Captain Henry C. Quaire was commanding officer of the Homicide unit.

"My Martha called Whatshername."

"Gladys," Washington furnished.

"*Gladys* and Henry will be there," Pekach said.

"Why am I not surprised?" Washington said.

Gladys Quaire regarded an invitation to 606 Glengarry Lane as the Philadelphia equivalent of an invitation to watch the races at Ascot from the Royal Enclosure.

Pekach chuckled, then said goodbye.

[FOUR]

When Dr. and Mrs. Benjamin Solomon drove through the gate at Glengarry Lane, the macadam road to the house was lined with various models of Ford Crown Victoria automobiles. They were in Ben's Cadillac, as Eileen was wearing what she thought of as her Doctor's Wife hat.

But she could not leave her D.A.'s hat very far behind. In the new Ford Crown Victoria that followed the Cadillac into what was still known as the Peebles Estate, Detective Albert Unger of the District Attorney's Squad pushed his microphone button as he rolled past the gate.

"Radio, D-One."

"Go, D-One."

"At 606 Glengarry Lane in Chestnut Hill until further notice."

"Got it."

Philadelphia provides an unmarked detective-driven police car to its district attorney. The detective, of course, also serves as bodyguard to the D.A. Usually, this made sense, and it was nice to be picked up at the house and dropped off by a car. But sometimes—now, for example—it didn't.

There were going to be at least thirty—knowing Martha, probably more—police officers at 606 Glengarry Lane, all of them armed, and many senior enough to be accompanied by their own armed drivers. The person of the district attorney was going to be about as safe as it could be. And if something happened that required the immediate presence of the district attorney, any of the white shirts' unmarked cars would be available to take her there with siren howling.

But, because he went where she went, poor Al Unger would just have to hang around the car waiting for the radio to go off while the D.A. was at the party. He wouldn't be alone. Deputy Commissioner Coughlin's driver and the drivers of the other senior white shirts would also have to hang around waiting for their radios to go off. Martha Peebles Pekach would ensure, of course, that the caterer's waiters would make sure they were fed.

Eileen was not surprised—the weather was wonderful—that the party was being held outside the stables. Alexander Peebles's polo ponies were long gone, and the grass field where they had once played was ideal for an outside party.

Tables had been set up, and waiters moved among them serving drinks and steaks and Italian sausage from charcoal stoves.

Their hostess and her husband greeted them as they walked on the field.

"Sorry to be late, Ben had to work," Eileen said, hugging Martha Peebles.

"You're here, that's all that matters," Martha Peebles said. She kissed Dr. Solomon. "I put you with the Paynes," Martha went on, gesturing toward one of the tables.

"Guess who I got a postcard from?" Captain Pekach said.

"When you get a minute, I've got something to tell you about that," Eileen said.

"In a couple of minutes," Pekach said.

Eileen saw Ben smiling, and she saw why. Amelia A. Payne, M.D., was sitting with her parents. Ben not only would have someone to talk to—he really had little in common with the cops, or for that matter with Brewster C. Payne—and he and Amy Payne both liked each other and shared a disdain for some of their fellow healers at the University of Pennsylvania Medical School and many of UP's bureaucratic procedures, about which they could—and almost certainly would—talk at length.

Deputy Commissioner Coughlin and Brewster C. Payne got to their feet as the Solomons approached the table.

The men wordlessly shook hands. Eileen sat down beside Patricia Payne, and Ben sat down across the table beside Amy.

"Where's the birthday boy?" Eileen asked—and before Patricia could answer, dealt with the waiter. "Irish rocks for me. Diet Coke over there." She pointed at her husband, then added: "Make it a double. I've been a good girl all day."

"One for me, too, please," Patricia Payne said. "Not a double."

"Where is *Sergeant* Payne?" Eileen asked.

Amelia A. Payne snorted.

"I guess you're thrilled, huh?" Eileen asked.

"Not really," Amy said, "truth to tell."

"Matt went into the house for something. He'll be back," Patricia said.

"Is it safe to say you're thrilled?" Eileen asked Patricia.

"Mixed emotions," Patricia replied. "Proud? Sure. Happy for Matt. Sure. But the badge the mayor pinned on him was his father's."

"Ouch," Eileen said. "They kept it all these years?"

"I had it. I thought it was the right—"

"It was," Eileen said, firmly.

"Mother Moffitt showed up at the ceremony," Amy said. "To cast her usual pall on things."

"Amy!" Patricia Payne said.

"Dave got another postcard from our fugitive," Coughlin said, obviously to get off the subject of Mother Moffitt.

"He told me," Eileen said. "There was something today . . . I'll tell you later, when I tell Dave."

"Am I permitted to ask? 'Our fugitive'?" Brewster Payne said.

"Isaac 'Fort' Festung," Eileen said.

"Oh, that chap."

"That despicable sonofabitch," Coughlin said, and added, immediately, "Forgive the French."

A waiter handed the District Attorney a drink. She waited until Patricia Payne had hers, then touched glasses and took a healthy sip.

"To Sergeant Payne," she said.

"Thank you," Patricia Payne said.

"Denny, 'despicable sonofabitch' is an apt description of Fort Festung, so an apology for your language is not necessary," Eileen said. "But if you're asking for a general pardon for our French brothers, *I'm* not about to forgive them."

There were chuckles and smiles.

"She's even stopped buying French perfume," Dr. Solomon said.

"See if you can enlist Patricia in your cause, Eileen," Brewster Payne said.

"What they should have done when he showed up in France—he entered France illegally, by the way, and was using a phony name, also illegal—was deport him on the next plane."

"Didn't that have something to do with the death penalty?" Patricia asked.

"That was their first excuse, but when that didn't wash—we didn't have the death penalty at the time of his trial; there was no way I could have sentenced him to death, as much as I might have liked to—they said they wouldn't let us extradite because he'd been tried *in absentia*."

"I thought the legislature took care of that, and guaranteed him a new trial if he asked for one." Brewster C. Payne said.

"They did. And we so informed the French. Now they're giving us some nonsense about the statute of limitations," Eileen said. "We're appealing that. We expect a decision on that tomorrow, and if it goes our way, we're back to Step One. In other words, we start asking all over again for his extradition."

She stopped, suddenly becoming aware that two men were seeking her attention.

"And there's Dave Pekach waiting for me to tell him what I just told you," she said, nodding at Pekach, who was standing at the edge of the field. "Excuse me."

She got to her feet and turned to a waiter. "Medium rare," she ordered. "One piece of Italian sausage, a sliced tomato. No potatoes. I'll be back in five minutes, or less." She pointed at her husband. "That handsome gentleman will have the same."

She stood up, and walked to Pekach, and followed him into the stable. They walked almost to the end of it.

"Did I interrupt something important?" Pekach asked. "You and Denny Coughlin looked pretty serious."

"We were talking about Saint Isaac," Eileen said. "What did the new post-card say?"

"The usual. 'Having fine time, wish you were here. Best regards, Isaac.'"

"The arrogant sonofabitch!" the district attorney said, and then went on: "I had a call—Tony Casio did—from the State Department today. . . ."

"I have the feeling I'm about to hear something I shouldn't," Matt Payne said, coming into the passageway from inside one of the stalls.

"What the hell were you doing in there?" Pekach asked, curiously.

"I'm gone," Matt said. "Sorry."

"Stay," Eileen said. "There's no reason you shouldn't hear this. Maybe you should."

"What were you doing in there?" Pekach pursued.

Matt looked between them and decided that when you don't know what the hell to say, tell the truth.

"You remember the scene in *The Godfather*, the wedding, where everybody handed the bride an envelope? As a tribute to the Godfather, not because they gave a damn about the bride?"

"Yeah," Pekach said. "So?"

"I felt like the bride," Matt said. "Out of respect to you and Martha and/or my parents and/or Denny Coughlin, everybody was coming to the table and saying, 'Congratulations, Sergeant.' And then Amy would snort. So I came to hide in here."

"You should have waited until Ben and I finally got here," Eileen said. "Our congratulations would have been absolutely sincere."

He looked at her for a moment.

"Thank you," he said, and then added: "Like I said, I wasn't trying to eavesdrop and I'm gone."

"You're not interested in Fort Festung?" Eileen asked.

"I'm becoming fascinated—"

"Okay. Stay. Latest bulletin," Eileen said. "Tony Casio . . ."

"He's Eileen's fugitive guy," Pekach explained.

". . . had a call from the State Department this afternoon. The French are going to rule on the statute of limitations tomorrow, and their 'legal counsel,' read FBI guy, heard that it'll go our way."

"Which leaves us where?"

"We start the extradition business all over again. If the decision comes down tomorrow in our favor, we start the extradition process again tomorrow."

"And this time?" Pekach asked.

"The French can stall only so long, David," Eileen said. "We'll get him."

Pekach looked at her a long moment but didn't say anything.

"Okay, birthday boy," Eileen said. "Back to the table. And smile nice when somebody says 'congratulations.'"

"Yes, ma'am," Matt said.

[FIVE]

At just about the time the last of the unmarked Ford Crown Victorias was leaving the Peebles Estate—somewhere around 1:15 A.M.—Homer C. Daniels, a six-foot-one-inch, 205-pound, thirty-six-year-old Caucasian male, who had once been a paratrooper and still wore his light brown hair clipped close to his skull, was standing in the shadow of a tree in the 600 block of Independence Street in Northeast Philadelphia, in the area known as East Oak Lane.

He was looking up at the second-story windows on the right side of what had been built as a single-family home—not quite large enough to be called a mansion—not quite a century before. It had been empty for a while after World War II, and then had been converted to a "multifamily dwelling" with two apartments on the ground floor, two on the second, and a third in what had been the servants' quarters on the third.

Daniels, who was wearing a black coverall, thought of himself as a businessman rather than a truck driver, although in each of the past several years he had driven a Peterbilt eighteen-wheel tractor-trailer rig 150,000 miles all over the country.

For one thing, he was a partner in Las Vegas Classic Motor Cars, Inc., the company that owned the Peterbilt. And he almost always had the same partner's interest in the truck's cargo, and sometimes he owned all of the cargo.

Las Vegas Classic Motor Cars, Inc., as the name implied, dealt with what they referred to as the "Grand Marques" of automobiles, ranging from the "vintage"—such as Duesenbergs and Pierce-Arrows, no longer manufactured—to the "contemporary"—such as Ferrari, the larger Mercedes-Benz, and Rolls Royce.

As a general rule of thumb, if an automobile was worth less than $75,000, Las Vegas Classic Motor Cars, Inc., was not interested. A boat-tailed Dusey, in Grand Concourse condition and worth, say, $1,250,000, had the opposite effect.

They bought and sold some cars themselves, and accepted some cars on consignment. Often they would buy a "decent" classic, and spend up to $100,000 rebuilding it from the frame up to Grand Concourse condition before offering it for sale. They also provided "frame up" restoration for owners of classic cars, and had earned an international reputation for the quality of their work.

Cars of this sort were genuine works of art, and as one would not entrust a Rodin sculpture or an Andy Warhol painting of a tomato can to the Acme Trucking Company, or even the United Parcel Service, one could not move, for example, a Grand Concourse–condition 1954 Mercedes-Benz 300SL "Gull Wing" coupe worth $275,000 to or from Las Vegas without taking the appropriate precautions.

Dragging such a motorcar along behind a car or truck on one of the clever devices available from U-Haul was obviously out of the question. So was loading such a vehicle on a flatbed trailer, chaining it in place, and covering it with a tarpaulin.

The solution was to ship such a vehicle within a trailer, and for a while Las Vegas Classic Motor Cars, Inc., had done just that. Then it had occurred to the partners that contracting for the transport, "direct, sole cargo" of vehicles, was costing them a lot of money. They crunched the numbers, and concluded the expense of buying and operating their own truck was justified.

They bought the Peterbilt, had a trailer specially modified—essentially the installation padding and means to hold the vehicles immobile while being transported—and hired a professional truck driver.

That had proved to be a disaster. The driver had hit something—he said—on the road, causing him to lose control, go into a ditch, and turn over. The devices installed to keep the 1939 Packard 230 Le Baron bodied convertible in place had not been strong enough to hold the massive car when the trailer had turned over, and massive damage had resulted.

The partners had suspected that what had really happened—truck drivers like to "make miles"—was that the driver had fallen asleep at the wheel. The insurance company had similar suspicions, and although they had—finally— paid up, they had immediately informed the partners that their rates in the future would regrettably have to be raised significantly.

That was when the idea of Homer driving the rig had come up. For one thing, Homer had been an over-the-road tractor-trailer driver immediately after leaving the service. For another, Homer and his wife had finally had enough of each other, and it wouldn't be much of a hardship for him to spend a week or ten days away from Vegas.

And other benefits came to mind. If there was a motor vehicle in Saint Louis, say, of interest to Las Vegas Classic Motor Cars, Inc., and Homer was there—or near there—with the truck, he could both have a good look at it— without the cost of an airplane ticket to get there and back—make a recommendation to the partners, and if they decided to make the deal, just load the new acquisition on the truck right then and there.

And then there was the restoration business. Homer could look at a car someone wanted to have Las Vegas Classic Motor Cars, Inc., restore, quote the owner a price, and if a deal was struck, just load the car right then and there and haul it back to Vegas.

The original trailer, of course, was shot. They bought another, and really customized it. The new trailer was heated and air-conditioned, and would hold three cars, instead of two—five, if they were all Porsches, which happened several times. In addition, cabinets were built for tools, and there was what looked very much like an old-timey railroad sleeper compartment, which held a toilet, a bed, a shower, a tiny desk for Homer's computer, and a closet for Homer's clothes.

When Homer was trying to make a deal for, say, a 1940 Buick Limited spares-in-the-fenders convertible touring sedan worth, say, 150 large, he should look like a businessman, not a truck driver. And if he was going coast-to-coast—for that matter, anywhere overnight—and needed some sleep, he could just pull into a truck stop, go in the back, get a couple of hours of shut-eye, and then get back on the road without the hassle of having to find a motel where he could park the rig, and then pay fifty, sixty bucks—sometimes more—for just using the bed for a couple of hours.

The whole arrangement—traveling all over the country included—had proven ideal for Homer's hobby, which was to find some young bitch who looked like the bitch he had wasted ten years of his life on, who lived by herself, and then being very careful about it, when everything fell into place, get into her apartment, scare the living shit out of her—a man in a black ski mask waving a Jim Bowie replica knife with a polished, shiny twelve-inch blade in her face did that very nicely—cut her clothes off with the knife, tie her to her bed, and take before-during-and-after slipping the salami to her pictures with his digital camera.

This was the fourth time Homer had stood in the shadow of a tree looking up at the apartment of Miss Cheryl Anne Williamson, who at twenty-three looked very much like Mrs. Bonnie Dawson Daniels had looked when she was that age. That is to say, she was tall, slender, blonde, had very fair skin, and even, Homer thought, that deceptive look of sweetness and innocence that Bonnie had.

Deceptive because Bonnie the Bitch was anything but sweet and innocent.

The first time Homer had stood in the shadow of the tree, he had followed Cheryl home from Halligan's Pub, where he had seen her cock-teasing the guys at the bar. It had been immediately apparent to Homer that Cheryl had not gone to the bar to maybe meet somebody she could get to know really well, maybe even someday marry, much less to get laid.

She had gone to the bar to cock-tease some dummy, get him all worked up, and then let him know she wasn't at all interested in fucking him. What she got her kicks from—just like Bonnie the Bitch—was humiliating some poor bastard, letting him know he wasn't good enough for her.

The first night when Cheryl had left Halligan's Pub, he had followed her home. That time he was driving a year-old Cadillac DeVille, used as a loaner by Willow Grove Automotive, where he had parked the rig. Las Vegas Classic Motor Cars did a lot of business with Willow Grove—on that trip, he had dropped off two Porsches from California, and would leave with a really nice Rolls Royce—and the guy who ran it always loaned him a car overnight when he was in town.

That first time, Homer had watched her park her Chrysler Sebring, watched as she entered the apartment building, and then stood in the shadow of the tree until lights went on in a second-floor apartment. Then he went to the Sebring—Homer had once spent six months working for Las Vegas Towing and Repossession, and getting into the Sebring was no problem—and got Cheryl's name, address, and phone and social security numbers from documents in her glove compartment.

Then he got back in the DeVille and went back to Willow Grove Automotive, parked the DeVille, gave the keys to the security guy, went to the rig, made sure the current had been plugged in, and then went to the compartment in the trailer, locking it from the inside.

He took off all his clothes and sat down in front of the computer, turned it on, took one of the good CDs from its hiding place, slipped it in the drive, looked at the index, thought a moment, and then decided St. Louis was what he wanted, transferred the Folder STL to the computer, decrypted it, then ran Photo-Eaze, which allowed him to run a slide show of the digital images in STL.

The girl in St. Louis—Karen—didn't look as much like Bonnie the Bitch as the one tonight did, but he'd had his good times with her. As the slide show ran, he dropped his hand to his groin and played with himself. He ran the slide again—there were twelve pictures—and then pushed Hold on Number 11, which showed Karen tied to the bed immediately after he'd slipped her the salami. He'd really shown her she wasn't as high and mighty as she thought. She looked soiled and humiliated.

It'll really be great to get this new one, this Cheryl, like that!

That thought had been so exciting that he ejaculated before he intended to.

Couldn't be helped. Goddamn, this Cheryl's really going to be a good one!

He cleaned himself up with Kleenex, then took the CD from the drive and put it back in the hiding place, erased Folder STL from the hard drive, and then started the U.S. Government Approved Slack Wipe Program. That would run for a couple of hours. What the program did was overwrite and overwrite and overwrite again the slack space on the hard drive, so there would be no chance of anybody ever being able to recover the images of Karen he had just looked at.

Then he took a shower and went to bed.

At seven the next morning, he got behind the wheel of the Peterbilt, got on the Pennsylvania Turnpike, and headed west. There was a guy in Grosse Pointe, Michigan, who collected Rollses, and there was a good chance he'd be interested in some kind of a deal with the one now in the rig.

Three weeks, more or less, later, Homer had again stood in the shadow of the tree outside Cheryl Williamson's apartment. He had gone to Halligan's Pub in hopes of seeing her there, and when she hadn't shown, he'd gone to the apartment complex.

By then, primarily because of a credit check he had run on her, he knew a good deal about her. He knew where she worked, for one thing, and where she had gone to school, and that she had never been married, and that she owed fifteen payments of $139.50 on the Chrysler Sebring, and thirty-three payments of $105.05 on the furniture in her apartment.

The lights were on in her apartment, which meant that she was there, and that he could probably take the coveralls and face mask and Jim Bowie knife from his briefcase and get the job done. It was a temptation. He'd thought of her a lot.

But it was also possible that she wasn't alone in the apartment, and there was no sense taking any chances. All things come to he who waits. He had decided to wait.

It was a month after that that he stood for the third time in the shadow of the tree looking up at her apartment. This time, Cheryl had been in the Harrison Lounge, cock-teasing some poor slob who had no idea what a bitch she was, and when she'd left—alone, of course—he'd followed her home again. That night, he was sure, was going to be the night. He even went back to his car—this time a Plymouth Voyager loaner from Willow Grove, there being nothing better on the lot—and changed into the costume.

When the lights went out in Cheryl's apartment, he decided he would wait five minutes before climbing the back stairs to her apartment. Thirty seconds later, Cheryl came out of the building, got into the Sebring, and drove off.

There was no way of telling, of course, where the bitch was going. Or when—even if—she was coming back. If he continued to wait in the shadow of the tree, somebody might see him. And if he went back and waited in the

Voyager, the cops might drive by and wonder what someone was doing sitting in a car at quarter to three in the morning.

When he got back to Willow Grove and the rig, he loaded DEN into the computer, and watched the sixteen pictures he'd taken three months before of an arrogant bitch named Delores in Denver. A not-so-arrogant bitch anymore, which was nice to look at and remember. But Delores was not nearly as pretty as Cheryl, and Delores didn't look nearly as much like Bonnie the Bitch as Cheryl did.

Tonight, Homer had the feeling everything was going to fall into place. Willow Grove Automotive had loaned him a dark gray DeVille—not the one he'd had before—and when he got to the Halligan's, the minute he pulled into the parking lot, he saw Cheryl's Sebring, and didn't even have to go into the lounge.

He just sat in the DeVille and waited for her to come out. When she did, a guy came out after her, and they had a little argument in the doorway. The bitch was obviously telling the guy she'd been cock-teasing for the last hour, at least, that he had it wrong, that not only was she not that kind of girl, but even if she was, she wouldn't give any to a jerk like him.

The guy went back in Halligan's Pub, Cheryl got in her Sebring, and when she was out of sight, Homer started the DeVille. He knew where she lived and he didn't even have to follow her. And when he got near Independence Street, he saw—on Sixty-seventh Avenue, North—a dark place where he could park the DeVille where it wouldn't attract attention, and where he could change into the costume without being seen.

And when he got to the tree and looked up at Cheryl's apartment, the lights were on. He figured she had been there no more than four, five minutes at most.

The light came on a minute or so later in a little window he was sure was the bathroom, and he thought about what Cheryl would look like in the shower while he waited for the light to go out.

Ten minutes later, it went out, and no more than a minute after that, so did the lights in her bedroom.

Homer checked the pockets of the coveralls to make sure he had the Jim Bowie replica knife, the camera, and the plastic thingamajigs he would use to tie her spread-eagled on her bed.

As he pulled on a pair of disposable rubber gloves, Homer started to get a hard-on thinking about what he was going to do, and told himself to cool it. He didn't want it to be over too soon.

Outside wooden stairs, with a narrow platform, had been added to the old building to provide a rear entrance to the second-floor apartments.

He went up them quickly, putting his feet on the outside of each step. If you stepped in the middle, sometimes the stairs would squeak, and the last thing he wanted to do was to have some yapping dog hear him and start barking.

When he got to the platform and her back door, he pulled the black ski mask from his pocket and pulled it over his head, then took a close look at the door. There were actually two doors, an outer combination screen and winter door. The screen thing was in place.

He put the blade of the Jim Bowie replica in the crack between the screen and the frame, and carefully pried it open wide enough so that he could get his hand inside to unlatch it. Then he very carefully pulled it open. It came easy, without squeaking.

Once he had the screen door open, he made sure that the screen was back in place. He was pleased when he saw that he hadn't even scratched the sonofabitch.

The inner door wasn't much more trouble. There was a pretty good lock, but the construction was cheesy, and all it took to pop the lock was to force the blade of the Jim Bowie replica into the frame and lean on it a little.

Homer opened the door wide enough to get the blade inside and ran it up and down, checking for a chain or whatever, and when there was none, opened the door all the way, stepped into the kitchen, and then closed it behind him.

After a minute, there was enough light for him to see pretty good. He was glad he'd waited. There was a little table in the kitchen he probably would have bumped into.

This was the hairy part of the operation, making it from just being inside into the bedroom and to the bed itself without making any kind of racket.

Homer made his way slowly and carefully through the kitchen, into the living room, and then to a door he was pretty sure was the bedroom door. This sometimes was a problem; if there was a lock on the bedroom door and it had to be popped, it sometimes woke the bitches up.

No lock.

The door opened smoothly inward.

There was more light in the room, two of those go-to-the-bathroom little lights plugged into sockets near the floor.

Cheryl was in bed, lying on her stomach. She was wearing pajamas.

Homer walked to the bed, very carefully reached out for Cheryl's shoulder, and then suddenly grabbed it, jerked her over on her back, then pushed her hard down on the bed with his hand on her throat.

"One fucking sound and you get your throat cut!" he said, waving the Jim Bowie replica in front of her face.

Cheryl whimpered.

"Please don't hurt me," she said. Scared shitless.

"I'm going to fuck you, bitch," Homer said. "It's up to you whether you get hurt or not."

He grabbed Cheryl's left wrist, put a plastic tie on it, jerked it tight, and then tied it to the bed.

The headboard was wrought iron. Sometimes when the headboard was material—or there was no headboard at all; that had happened twice—there was a problem. You had to tie the bitch to the springs, which meant tying a couple of the ties together to make one long enough.

No problem like that tonight. He tied the left tie to a curve in the wrought iron, then reached across the bitch for her right hand.

Cheryl started to sob.

Homer slapped her, hard.

"Not a sound, bitch!" he said.

Once he had the second plastic tie in place, he jerked on it to make sure it wouldn't come loose, then jerked on the other one.

Then he knelt on the bed, sat back on his heels, and ran the blade of the Jim Bowie replica down Cheryl's body, from the neck between her boobs to her crotch.

She whimpered again.

He tied her right ankle to the wrought iron at the foot of the bed, and then the left ankle. Then he ran the blade up her body again.

"Not a peep, you fucking bitch!"

He went to the light switch by the door and flipped it on.

Cheryl's eyes were wide with terror.

He leaned over the bed and put the blade of the Jim Bowie replica under her pajama top, and one by one cut the buttons off so that it could be easily opened when it came time for that.

He took the digital camera from the coveralls and took Cheryl's picture.

Then he leaned over her and pushed the left side of her pajama top off her breast and took a picture of that.

Very nice. Her nipples had become erect.

Homer became aware that he had a hard-on. A real hard-on.

He reached into the coveralls and took it out and waved it at her.

"This is for you, bitch!" he said.

He walked to the bed and pushed Cheryl's pajamas off her right breast, and then took a picture of her like that.

Then he went and knelt on the bed so that he could rub the head of his penis on her nipples.

That was very exciting, so exciting that he knew he was going to have an orgasm, and since that was the case, he might as well have a good one, so he put his hand on it and pumped rapidly until he ejaculated onto her breasts and face.

She turned her head and whimpered.

As fast as the camera would permit, Homer took three pictures of that, and then had an artistic inspiration. He took the Jim Bowie replica and carefully scraped some of the semen from Cheryl's breast on it, and then laid it between her breasts, with the tip just under her chin. And he took two pictures of that, looked at them in the camera's built-in viewer, and then put the camera on the bedside table.

"I'll be right back," Homer said. "We're just getting started."

He went into the bathroom, and first urinated, and then, standing over the washbasin, washed his genitals, toying with them, thinking that when he went back in the bedroom, he would be able to get a shot of his sperm on her breasts and face.

That was an exciting thought, so exciting that he felt himself begin to grow hard again, and he thought that's what he would do, get it up again, so that when he went back in the bedroom, she would see it and get a hint of what was in store for her.

When he went back in the bedroom, the goddamn bitch had somehow got her right hand free from the plastic tie. That had given her enough movement to twist onto her side, and to pull her telephone from the bedside table. She was punching in a number.

"You goddamn fucking bitch!" Homer said, angrily. "What the fuck do you think you're doing?"

He moved quickly to the bed, made a fist, and punched her as hard as he could in the face. He turned her on her back again and punched her again. He reached for the telephone, to pull the line free from the socket. It wouldn't come at first and he pulled harder, and then the line snapped, and the phone came out of his hand and flew across the room and smashed into the mirror mounted on the wall. The mirror broke into three large pieces, and two of them fell to the floor, where they shattered into small pieces.

Jesus Christ, that made enough noise to wake the fucking dead!

"That's going to cost you, bitch!" he said, menacingly.

He realized he was breathing heavily and took a moment to calm down.

Then he looked down at Cheryl.

There was a little blood on her face, running down over her lips, and she was looking at something on the ceiling.

He looked up to see what she was looking at. There was nothing but the ceiling and the light fixture. He looked back down at her, and she was still looking at the ceiling.

He waved his hand in front of her eyes. There was no reaction.

"Jesus Christ!" Homer said, softly.

He reached down and slapped Cheryl on both cheeks.

"Goddamn you, wake up!" he said.

There was no reaction.

"Oh, shit," Homer said, softly, and waved his hand in front of her open eyes again.

"Shit, shit, shit," Homer said.

Then he went to the door, turned the lights in the bedroom off, and made his way back through the apartment to the kitchen, and let himself out, taking care to make sure the screen door's latch had automatically locked after he pushed it shut.

He went quickly to the DeVille, and was halfway down the block before he remembered to take the black ski mask off.

And then Homer had an at first chilling thought.

I don't have the fucking camera!

He patted his pockets to make sure.

Shit, shit, shit!

Oh, fuck it! I never took the rubber gloves off, so there won't be any fingerprints, and they can't trace it to me. I bought it in that store with the Arabs in Times Square in New York, the time I picked up the silver-gray Bentley. I paid cash. I'll just have to get another one. It was getting pretty old, anyway.

CHAPTER 7

[ONE]

On the other side of Cheryl Anne Williamson's bedroom wall in her second-floor apartment on Independence Street was the bedroom wall of the apartment occupied by Mr. and Mrs. Herbert McGrory.

There was a mirror on that wall, too—the apartments were roughly mirror images of each other—and when Cheryl's bedside telephone slipped out of Homer C. Daniels's hand and flew with sufficient velocity into her mirror to cause it to shatter, it also struck the plasterboard behind the mirror.

At that point on the wall, behind the plasterboard, was one of the two-by-four-inch vertical studs, arranged at sixteen-inch intervals along the wall. Between each stud, insulation material had been installed, more to deaden sounds between the two apartments than for thermal purposes.

Technically, this was a violation of the Philadelphia building code, which requires that living areas be separated by a firewall, either of concrete or cement blocks. The building inspector somehow missed this violation. Over the years, a number of Philadelphia building inspectors have been found guilty of accepting donations from building contractors for overlooking violations of the building code.

Many—perhaps most—of these corrupt civil servants have been found guilty and fined or sentenced to prison, or both, but it was obviously difficult for the city to reinspect every structure examined and passed by the inspector caught not looking, and it wasn't done.

The stud moved, not far, but far enough to strike the back of the mirror on the McGrorys' wall. The mirror bent, then cracked, and then a large, roughly triangular piece of it slid out of the frame and crashed onto the floor.

The noise woke Mrs. Joanne McGrory, a short, rather plump thirty-six-year-old, who was in bed with her husband, who was tall, rather plump, and thirty-eight years old.

She sat up in the bed and exclaimed, "Jesus, Mary, and Joseph!"

She looked around the dark room, and then down at Mr. McGrory, who was asleep on his stomach.

"Herb!"

After a moment, without moving, Herb replied, "What?"

"Get up, for God's sake!"

"Why? What's happened?"

"Get up, Herb, damn you!"

Mrs. McGrory turned on the lamp on her bedside table as Mr. McGrory sat up.

The first thing Mr. McGrory noticed was the shattered mirror.

"Jesus, what happened to the mirror?"

"How would I know?"

"It's busted."

"I can see that. What happened?"

Mr. McGrory ran over the possibilities.

"It could have been a sonic boom," he theorized.

"Sonic boom?"

"You know, when an airplane goes faster than sound."

"Oh, God, Herb! Sometimes . . ."

"Well, you tell me," he said.

"Get up and see if anything else is wrong," she said. "Don't cut your feet on the broken glass."

"Jesus!"

"Do it now, Herb!"

Two minutes later, after taking a cautious tour of their apartment, Mr. McGrory returned to announce that the only thing that seemed to be wrong was the mirror.

"You didn't hear anything?" Joanne asked, significantly, nodding toward the wall with the broken mirror.

Several times, the McGrorys had heard the sounds of Cheryl Williamson entertaining gentleman callers in her bedroom. Once they had had to bang on the wall to request less enthusiasm.

Mr. McGrory smiled and said, "Could be . . ." and then made a circle with the thumb and index finger of his left hand, into which he then inserted, with a pumping motion, the index finger of his right hand.

"You're disgusting," Joanne said, and then added: "This time, it's too much. The mirror is busted. I'm going to go over there and read the riot act to her."

"No, you're not," he said.

"Yes, I am."

"No, you're not."

"Then I'm going to call the cops. I won't have this!"

"Call the cops? What are you going to say, 'The lady next door's boyfriend screwed her so hard the mirror fell off our wall'?"

"Unless we do something about it, we're going to have to pay for that mirror," Joanne argued.

"Okay," Herb said after a moment's thought. "Go tell her what happened."

"If I go over there, what she's going to say is that she doesn't have any idea what I'm talking about. Would you?"

"Would I what?"

"Say, 'Gee, I'm sorry my scre . . . lovemaking broke your mirror, and I'll write you a check'?"

"And what good do you think calling the cops is going to do?"

"It can't do any harm, can it?" Joanne asked reasonably. "Maybe something is wrong next door—with her. And I don't want us to have to pay for the mirror."

Joanne went to the telephone on the bedside table and punched 911.

At 1:57 A.M., a call went out from Police Radio:

"Disturbance, house, 600 Independence Street, second-floor left apartment."

Officer James Hyde, a tall, thin, dark-haired young man of twenty-four, reached for his microphone in his patrol car, pushed the button, and replied:

"Thirty-five twelve, got it."

A moment later, there was another response, this one from Officer Haywood L. Cubellis, a 210-pound, six-foot-seven, twenty-five-year-old African-American from his patrol car:

"Thirty-five seventeen, I'll back him up."

Whenever possible—in other words, usually—two cars will respond to a "Disturbance, House" call. Such calls usually involve a difference of opinion between two people of opposite—or the same—sex sharing living accommodations. By the time the cops are called, tempers are at—or over—the boiling point.

If two officers are present, each can listen sympathetically to the complaints of one abused party vis-à-vis the other, which also serves to keep the parties separated. One lonely police officer can be overwhelmed.

Both cars arrived at 600 Independence Street a few minutes after 2 A.M., although neither—there was little traffic—had used either siren or flashing lights.

While it might be argued that neither Officer Hyde nor Officer Cubellis was a highly experienced police officer—Hyde had been on the job three years and Cubellis four—they had enough experience to know that it was better for officers responding to a "Disturbance, House" call to bring with them calm, reason, and order, rather than the heightened excitement that howling sirens, flashing lights, and screaming tires produce.

"Hey, Wood," Jim Hyde called as both got out of their cars and started into the apartment complex.

Officer Haywood Cubellis waved but did not respond.

He followed Hyde to the second-floor door of apartment 12B, and stood to one side as Hyde both knocked with his nightstick and pushed the doorbell.

Mrs. McGrory answered the door, in her bathrobe, with Herb standing behind her in trousers and a sleeveless undershirt, looking a little uncomfortable.

Both Hyde and Cubellis made a quick analysis.

Nice people. Looked sober. No bruises or signs of anything having been thrown or overturned in the apartment.

"You called the police, ma'am?" Hyde asked.

"Yes, I did."

"What seems to be the trouble?"

"I like to think of myself as a reasonable person," Joanne said. "Live and let live, as they say. But this is just too much."

"What is it, ma'am?"

"Come in and I'll show you," Joanne said, and motioned the two policemen into the apartment. Both nodded at Herb, and Herb nodded back.

Officer Hyde looked at the broken mirror.

"What happened?"

"That's what we would like to know," Joanne said. "That's why we called you."

"You don't know what happened to the mirror?" Hyde asked.

"Herb, my husband, and I were sound asleep when it happened."

"I told her I thought it was probably a sonic boom," Herb said.

"That's nonsense," Joanne said. "It came from in there."

She pointed at the wall.

"What's in there?"

"The next apartment," Joanne said.

"What do you think came from in there that broke your mirror?"

"You tell the officers, Herb."

"This was your idea. You tell them," Herb said.

"Sometimes you make me sick," Joanne said. "You really do."

"Why don't you tell us what you think happened, ma'am?" Officer Cubellis suggested.

"Well, all right, I will. So far as I know, she's a very nice girl. Her name is Cheryl Williamson. But she . . . every once in a while she *entertains* in there, if you know what I mean. Most of the time, there's absolutely no problem, but once or twice—more than once or twice—she, they have gotten sort of carried away with what they're doing, and it gets a little noisy, if you take my meaning."

"What's that got to do with your mirror?" Officer Hyde asked.

"It broke," Joanne said, as if surprised by the question.

"And you think the people next door are responsible?"

"Well, Herb and I certainly aren't," Joanne said.

"Jim, why don't I talk to the lady next door?" Officer Cubellis suggested.

"Why not?" Hyde said.

"Maybe something happened to her," Joanne said.

Officer Cubellis left the McGrory bedroom.

"I don't know how much it will cost to replace that mirror, but it won't be cheap, and I don't see why we should pay for it," Joanne said.

"Yes, ma'am," Officer Hyde said.

Five minutes later, Officer Cubellis returned and reported that it didn't appear anyone was home in the next apartment. He had both rung the bell and knocked at Cheryl Williamson's front door, and then gone outside the house, up the side stairs, and knocked at her back door. There was no doorbell button there that he could find. There was no response from either place, and he could hear no sounds from inside the apartment, or see any lights.

"I know she came in," Joanne said. "I woke up when she came in. Her screen door squeaks. It was a little after midnight."

"Possibly she went out again," Officer Cubellis said.

"Or maybe she knows the cops are here and doesn't want to answer her door."

"Why would she want to do that?"

"The mirror, of course," Joanne said. "Somebody's going to have to pay for it."

"Ma'am, you'll just have to take that up with her yourself in the morning," Officer Hyde said.

"Can't you just go in and see if she's there or not?" Joanne asked.

"No, ma'am, we can't do that."

"For all we know, she's in there lying in a pool of blood," Joanne said.

"Ma'am, why would you say that? Did you hear any noises, anything like that?"

Joanne thought it over before replying.

"No," she said finally, with some reluctance. "But that doesn't mean anything. The mirror *did* get busted."

"Yes, ma'am," Officer Cubellis said, patiently. "But that doesn't give us the right to break into that apartment. Think about this: You and Mr. McGrory are in here, watching a Stan Colt movie on TV. Lots of shooting, women screaming, explosions. Particularly at the end. The lady in the next apartment hears this and gets worried and calls 911. When the movie is over, you and Mr. McGrory go out for a hamburger. So when the police get here, there's no answer. And they break in. And then you come home, and find the police in your apartment, and the door broken in."

"Who would have to pay for the broken door if something like that happened?" Joanne inquired.

"The police . . ." Officer Cubellis began, and then changed his mind about the ending, ". . . would have to make the lady next door pay for the broken door," he said. "Because she was the one who wanted the police to break in."

"Jesus Christ, Joanne!" Herb McGrory said. "Officers, I'm sorry we put you to all this trouble."

"No trouble at all, sir. That's what we're here for," Officer Hyde said.

"I'm sure you'll be able to work things out about the mirror," Officer Cubellis said.

Officers Cubellis and Hyde left the McGrory apartment, got into their patrol cars, and put themselves back into service. Officer Hyde filled out a Form 75–48, an initial report form for almost all police incidents. On it he stated that the McGrory mirror had been broken, and that Mrs. McGrory believed the occupant of the adjacent apartment was somehow responsible. An initial investigation of the adjacent apartment revealed that there was no response at that location and the premises was locked and secured.

[TWO]

When it was 2:23 A.M. in Philadelphia—the time that Officers Hyde and Cubellis reported to Police Radio that they were back in service after the "Disturbance, House" call—it was 8:23 A.M. in the village of Cognac-Boeuf, a small village in the southwest of France, not far from Bordeaux.

Despite the name, no cognac was distilled in the area, and the local farmers raised only enough milk cows for local consumption. Although sheep were still grown in the area, even that business had suffered from the ability of Australian and Argentine sheep growers to produce a higher grade of wool and a better quality of lamb at a lower price.

What once had been a bustling small village was now just a small, out-of-the-way village catering to what small farmers were left and to retirees, both French and from as far away as England, Sweden, and even the United States of America.

The retirees sold their houses or apartments in Hamburg or Copenhagen, and spent the money to buy—at very low prices; nobody but retirees had use for them—ancient farmhouses with a hectare or two of land, spent enough money to make them livable, and then settled down to watching the grass grow.

The Piaf Mill, for example, which sat on a small stream a kilometer from Cognac-Boeuf, had been purchased, with 1.7 hectares of land, six years before by a Swedish woman, Inge Pfarr Stillman, and her husband, Walter, an American, using the money—about $80,000—Inge had gotten from the sale of her apartment in Uppsala, near Stockholm.

It had gradually become believed that Walter Stillman, a burly man who wore a sloppy goatee as white as what was left of his hair, was a retired academic. He was obviously well-educated, and it was thought he was writing a book.

The mill, now converted into a comfortable home, was full of books, and every day the postman on his bicycle delivered yesterday's *International Herald-Tribune* from Paris, and once a week, the international editions of *Time* and *Newsweek*.

Most afternoons, Stillman could be found in Le Relais, the better of Cognac-Boeuf's two eating establishments—neither of which had won even one of Michelin's stars—often playing chess with Père Marcel, the parish priest, and drinking the local *vin ordinaire*.

The people of Cognac-Boeuf—in particular the shopkeepers—had come to call Stillman, respectfully, "M'sieu Le Professeur."

His name was actually Isaac David Festung, and he was a fugitive from justice, having been convicted of violation of Paragraph 2501(a) of the Criminal Code of the Commonwealth of Pennsylvania, for having intentionally and knowingly caused the death of Mary Elizabeth Shattuck, a human being, by beating and/or strangling her by the neck until she was dead.

M'sieu Le Professeur's true identity had come to light two years before when, at sunrise, a dozen members of France's Gendarmerie Nationale had appeared, pistols drawn at the Piaf Mill's door. When Madame Stillman opened it to them, the gendarmes had burst in and rushed across the Mill's ground floor to the stairs, then up the stairs to the loft. There they found—naked under a goose-down comforter in bed—a man who, although he insisted indignantly that he had never even heard of anyone named Isaac Festung, they arrested and placed in handcuffs.

After a brief stop at the constabulary office in Cognac-Boeuf to report the suspect was in custody—there was no telephone in Piaf Mill, and the radios in the gendarmes' Peugeots were out of range of their headquarters—the man, still denying he had ever even heard of Isaac Festung, was taken in a gendarmerie car to Gradnignan Prison in Bordeaux, fingerprinted, and placed in a cell.

Forty-five minutes after that, a technician of the French Sureté, sent from Paris, after comparing "Stillman's" just-taken prints with a set of prints of one Isaac David Festung, furnished via Interpol by the office of the Philadelphia District Attorney, declared that it was his professional opinion that they matched beyond any reasonable doubt.

When confronted with this announcement, Isaac Festung shrugged his shoulders and said that it was sad but he wasn't surprised, that it had been inevitable that the American CIA would finally gain control of Interpol and finally be able to silence him.

Madame "Stillman," meanwhile, back at the Piaf Mill, had gotten dressed and then driven to the telephone office in Cognac-Boeuf. There she had made several telephone calls, and had then come out to repeat more or less what her husband had said in Bordeaux: He was being persecuted by the American FBI and CIA both for being a peace activist and "for what he knew." What he knew was not specified.

He had fled the United States, they both said, after he was arrested on a preposterous charge of murder. Furious that he had escaped their clutches, the CIA and FBI had arranged for a kangaroo trial *in absentia,* which had predictably found him guilty and sentenced him to death.

One of the telephone calls Madame Stillman/Mrs. Festung made was to a lawyer in Paris, who promptly called a press conference to make public what outrageous violations of law—and common decency—the barbaric American government was attempting to perpetrate.

The next day, the newspapers of France—and elsewhere in Europe—carried the story, often accompanied by outraged editorials.

For one thing, the European Convention on Human Rights had declared that an accused criminal was entitled to his day in court, which meant that he had the absolute right to be physically present in the courtroom to refute witnesses making, for example, preposterous charges that he had beaten and/or strangled his girlfriend and then stuffed her body into a trunk, which he then stored in a closet in his apartment, until the odor from there had caused his neighbors to call the police, asking them to investigate.

As astonishing an outrage as that was, the Americans had the incredibly barbaric arrogance to sentence the man illegally tried to an illegal sentence, that of being put to death by electrocution.

The death penalty was not permitted under French law. Extradition of someone sentenced to death, even in a trial at which he was present when a jury of his peers had found him guilty, was absolutely forbidden.

Many of the editorials demanded both that Mr. Festung be immediately set free and that the French government make, in the strongest possible language, their outrage known to the United States government.

The government of France wasn't willing to go that far, possibly because the United States government suggested that if it did, the United States government would no longer honor requests of France passed to them via Interpol.

The matter would be decided, the French government announced, as soon as humanly possible, in a French court. France being France, that took six months, during which Mr. Festung remained confined in Gradnignan Prison in Bordeaux.

Mrs. Festung visited him frequently, sometimes daily, while they waited for the wheels of French judicial bureaucracy to grind inexorably.

The United States government then contracted for the services of a French law firm to represent it at the appeal hearing. There was a legal counsel, with a large support staff—more than forty people, it was said—attached to the United States Embassy in Paris, but it turned out that before he had become the legal counsel of the United States, he—and most of the members of his staff—had been special agents of the Federal Bureau of Investigation, and were not allowed to practice law, even in the United States.

This revelation produced a plethora of editorials in the French press, on the theme that it was a gross violation of French sovereignty to have American secret policemen operating under diplomatic cover on the sacred soil of La Belle France. What was next, some editorials demanded, the CIA operating in France?

When the case—actually the appeal—was finally heard, the French lawyers representing the United States very politely made the following points:

(1) Trials *in absentia* are permitted under the laws of the Commonwealth of Pennsylvania, the immediate jurisdiction, when the accused has not shown up as promised after being released on bail, and his whereabouts are unknown and undeterminable.

(2) In the case of Mr. Festung, there was no sentence of death by electrocution. At the time of his trial, the Commonwealth of Pennsylvania had no provision in its laws to execute anyone, by electrocution or any other means. Mr. Festung had been sentenced to life imprisonment.

(3) The government of the Commonwealth of Pennsylvania, on learning that Mr. Festung had been located in France, and understanding the French distaste for trials *in absentia,* had passed special legislation applying specifically to Mr. Festung, guaranteeing his right to a new trial if he should wish one.

(4) Inasmuch as Mr. Festung had entered France illegally, on a false passport, in a false name, he was not entitled, under French law, to the protection of French law, and furthermore, French law stated that someone apprehended in France who had entered the country illegally would be immediately deported.

The three-judge bank of appeals justices considered the case for almost three-quarters of an hour before deciding to deny the request of the United States government for the extradition of Isaac David Festung, now known as Walter Stillman, resident of Cognac-Boeuf.

Isaac David Festung was free to go.

A cheering crowd greeted the Festungs both outside the court building and when they returned to their home in Cognac-Boeuf.

The United States ambassador to the French Republic decided to appeal the decision of the Court of Appeals. It was whispered that he did so somewhat reluctantly, and only at the insistence of the secretary of state personally. The story went that the secretary had been approached by the Hon. Carl Feldman, the senior senator from the state of Pennsylvania, at the urging of the Hon. Eileen McNamara Solomon, the Philadelphia district attorney.

The story whispered about went on to say that Mrs. Solomon had told Senator Feldman that she could see no way to keep out of the newspapers the fact that Senator Feldman had been this slimy sonofabitch's lawyer and had gotten him released on $40,000 bail—a ridiculous figure for someone facing a Murder Two charge—which he had then jumped, and offered the suggestion that if the senator hoped to get reelected, it might well behoove him to also get it into the papers that, having recognized the error of his ways, he was doing everything in his power to have the murdering sonofabitch extradited.

Neither Senator Feldman nor District Attorney Solomon would comment on this story, but it was soon announced by the French Ministry of Justice that what the Court of Appeals had *really* meant to say when it had released Mr. Festung was that he was to be released only to Cognac-Boeuf, and there he would be under the surveillance of the Gendarmerie National, pending the results of the appeal of the U.S. Embassy of their decision to the Supreme Court of France.

When Isaac Festung woke in his bed at just about the time Officers Cubellis and Hyde were reporting themselves back in service in Philadelphia—and six months after the Ministry of Justice's announcement—he was not at all worried about what the French Supreme Court would decide best served the interests of justice.

Not only had his lawyers told him he had nothing to be worried about, but based on his own analysis of the situation—by which he meant his analysis of France and the French mentality, intellectual and political—he did not see much—indeed, any—cause for concern.

The French, Fort Festung had concluded, had an identity problem, and an enormous capacity for self-deception. At the same time, they professed France to be a world power equal to any. They knew this wasn't true.

They were about as important in the world, Fort Festung had concluded, as the Italians, perhaps even less important. The difference was, the Italians knew what they were, and acted accordingly, and the French refused to admit what they were, and acted accordingly.

The most important factor in the equation was that the French really hated America and Americans. The Italians were grateful that the Americans had run the Germans, and the native fascists, out of Italy in the Second World War, and grateful again for the American relief effort after the war, and for American help in keeping the Communists from taking any real power in Italy.

The French were privately shamed that the Americans had twice been responsible for chasing the Boche from French soil. American aid to France after the war had made France resentful, not grateful, and France had been relieved when the Americans took a whipping in what had been French Indochina. It would have been almost too much for the French to bear if the Yankees had beaten the Vietnamese into submission after they had failed.

Dien Bien Phu was just one more name on a very long list of battles that the proud French Army had lost, something one would never suspect watching them strut down the Champs Elysées on Bastille Day with flags flying.

Fort saw proof of his theory in French automobiles. Most of them, he thought, in addition to being notoriously unreliable, were spectacularly ugly. And they had yellow headlights. No other country in Europe put yellow headlights on their cars. So far as Fort could tell, the only advantage of the yellow headlights was that they immediately identified a car as having been made in France.

They couldn't even sell French cars in the United States. They didn't meet American safety standards. Automobiles made, for example, in Korea did. And that was not even getting into the comparisons that could be made between Peugeots and Citroëns and the Mercedes-Benzes and Porsches made by the hated Boche on the other side of the Rhine and which were highly regarded around the world.

There were, when he had time to think about it, literally hundreds of other proofs of France's general inferiority and the French unwillingness—perhaps inability—to accept it.

What this all added up to was that when a Frenchman found himself in a position where he could tell the United States to go fuck itself, he could count on hearty cheers from the great majority of his countrymen.

The issue, in other words, no longer had anything to do with what happened in Philadelphia so many years ago, or with Fort Festung.

It had become a question of the French Republic proving its sovereignty and independence before the world. France, the world's center of culture and civilization, was not about to bow to the will of the goddamned uncultured, uncivilized, and despicable United States of America.

Vive La France!

In the meantime, living in Cognac-Boeuf wasn't at all bad. He admitted he missed the excitement of Philadelphia, and obviously, he could never go back there. But with this business all out in the open, when the Supreme Court issued its decision, he would be able to travel all over France, which meant Paris.

And in the meantime, Fort Festung thought, as he got out of bed and put on a loosely fitting shirt and baggy cotton trousers, and slipped his sockless feet into thong sandals, life here in Cognac-Boeuf wasn't at all bad.

He could, for example, get on his bicycle, ride into Cognac-Boeuf, take a table at La Relais, have rolls fresh from the oven, locally made butter, coffee, and a hooker of cognac placed before him, and consume them while he explained to the locals what the stories in *Time* and the *Trib really* meant.

And that was exactly what Isaac David Festung did, while Officers Hyde and Cubellis remained on patrol in Philadelphia, maintaining as well as they could peace and domestic tranquillity in the City of Brotherly Love.

[THREE]

When Captain Henry C. Quaire walked into Homicide a few minutes after eight the same morning, he saw Sergeant Matthew M. Payne sitting on a chair outside the chief of Homicide's office. Sergeant Payne rose when he saw Captain Quaire.

"Good morning, *Sergeant*," Quaire said, smiling, and then waved his hand toward the door of his office. "Come on in."

Matt Payne followed him into the office.

"One of your major responsibilities, Sergeant," Quaire said, pointing to his coffee machine, "is to make sure that one of your subordinates makes sure that machine is tended and ready for service by the time I walk in here."

"Yes, sir," Matt said.

Quaire poured an Emerald Society cup full, and turned to Payne.

"Help yourself, Matt, and then pull up a chair."

"Yes, sir. Thank you."

Privately, Henry Quaire was not overjoyed at the assignment of Sergeant Payne to Homicide. For one thing, he'd had nothing to do with it. Almost traditionally, the chief of Homicide had been able to select his men, and there were a number of sergeants—three, in particular, who wanted the assignment—whom Quaire considered to be far better qualified to be a sergeant in Homicide than Sergeant Payne.

But the commissioner had had his off-the-wall idea of giving the top five guys on the sergeant's list their choice of assignment, so Payne's assignment was a done deal, and there was no way he could fight it.

Not that he really wanted to, he decided. For one thing, he was off the hook about picking one of the other sergeants. If he had had to make a choice between them, two of them would not have gotten the assignment, and they—and their rabbis—would have been disappointed, and their rabbis probably pissed.

Now they could be pissed at the commissioner.

And it wasn't as if Payne was an absolute incompetent getting shoved down his throat. He was, in fact, a pretty good cop, who would probably do a good job in Homicide before moving onward and upward in the police hierarchy. Like his rabbi, Inspector Peter Wohl, he was one of those people who seemed predestined for ever-greater responsibility and the rank that went with it.

Nor was there going to be, so far as Quaire sensed, much—if any—resentment from the Homicide guys about having a brand-new sergeant with just over five years on the job as a Homicide supervisor.

For one thing, Payne was close to the two most respected people in Homicide, Lieutenant Jason Washington and Detective Tony Harris. Washington had no problem with Payne's assignment, and when Quaire had asked Tony Harris, Harris had been almost enthusiastic.

"I've worked with him, Captain," Harris said. "He's smart as hell. And this place can use a little class. Unless I'm wrong, he's going to be dynamite on the witness stand."

Smart as hell and being dynamite on the witness stand were two desirable characteristics for anybody in Homicide.

And then there was the fact that everybody in Homicide knew that Payne had had two good shootings. The first had been the serial rapist in Northwest Philadelphia who'd tried to run Payne down in his van. That bastard had already had his next intended victim trussed up like a Christmas turkey in the back of his van when Payne had interrupted his plans with a bullet in his head.

The second was when they were rounding up the doers in the Goldblatt & Sons Furniture job, and Wohl had put Payne and Mickey O'Hara in an alley to keep them out of the line of fire, while Highway and Special Operations uniforms went in the front. One of the doers had appeared in the alley with a .45 semiautomatic. Payne had taken a hit in the leg, but he'd downed the bad guy anyway.

And then there was the third incident, just six months ago. Payne had run down—good detective work—a lunatic terrorist we wanted. The FBI had been looking for him without coming close for years. Payne knew the critter was going to be in the parking lot of a diner in Doylestown. He had no authority in Doylestown, and didn't think the Doylestown cops would know how to handle the terrorist, so he'd called an FBI guy he knew—one of the good ones, for a change—and the FBI guy had gone to Doylestown.

When they'd tried to put the collar on the lunatic, he'd let loose with an automatic carbine, wounding a bystander woman and killing the woman who'd led Payne to the lunatic.

There'd been a hell of an exchange of gunfire, handguns against an automatic carbine. The FBI guy had actually put the critter down, but Payne had been involved up to his eyeballs and hadn't blinked.

If things were perfect, a cop would never have to take his pistol out of his holster, but things aren't perfect, and all cops—including homicide detectives—admire the cops who do it right when they have to take out their weapons.

And then finally Captain Quaire was aware that at Dave Pekach's wife's party for Payne last night, Payne had sat at a table with Deputy Commissioner Coughlin, District Attorney Eileen McNamara Solomon, Chief Inspector of Detectives Matthew Lowenstein, and Inspector Wohl, making it clear he had friends in high places.

"Welcome aboard, Matt," Quaire said.

"Thank you, sir."

"Would you have any objection to being assigned to Lieutenant Washington's squad?"

"No, sir."

"So be it," Quaire said. "You're a bright young man. Do I have to remind you that you're the new kid on the block, and that most of the people here have been in Homicide longer than you've been on the job?"

"I don't mean to sound flippant, sir, but that's not the first time that's been pointed out to me."

"And in a situation like that, what are you going to do?"

"Keep my eyes open and my mouth shut, sir."

"Don't go too far, Matt, with the mouth shut. You're a sergeant, and you'll be expected to act like one."

"Yes, sir. I understand."

What I'm doing here is wasting my time, and his. Before he walked in here this morning, he was coached on what to expect and how to behave by Peter Wohl, who was a very young detective here. Or by Denny Coughlin. Or by the Black Buddha. Maybe even by Matt Lowenstein. Or Tony Harris. Or, more likely, all of the above.

"When is this business with Stan Colt going to happen?" Quaire asked.

"I think he's coming on Friday, sir. I haven't had the time to check with Lieutenant McGuire."

"You better check with him soon, for the obvious reasons."

"I'll do it right now, sir."

"And let me know."

"Yes, sir."

"Okay, Matt. Go to work," Captain Quaire said. "Glad you're going to be with us."

"Thank you, sir."

[FOUR]

At 9:25 A.M., as Jack Williamson drove his Chrysler 300M northward on I-95 toward Bucks County—coincidentally, just beyond and to the left of the Industrial Correction Center, and just shy of the Philadelphia Police Academy—his cellular telephone buzzed.

Williamson was a tall, rather good-looking, well-dressed twenty-nine-year-old whose business card identified him as Senior Sales Consultant for Overbrook Estates, which offered custom-built executive homes on quarter-acre lots in Overbrook Estates, a new gated community in Beautiful Bucks County starting in the mid-$250Ks.

He cursed—for having forgot to do so earlier—as he reached for the earphone and jammed it in place, and then pushed the button on the microphone, which he was supposed to have clipped to his jacket, but now held somewhat awkwardly in his right hand.

"Jack Williamson," he said.

"This is your mother."

Oh, shit. Now what does she want?

"What can I do for you, Mother? On my way to work, where I'm already twenty-five minutes late?"

"I'm worried about Cheryl."

"Can we talk about this later?"

"She doesn't answer her phone . . ."

Probably because she knows it's you calling.

". . . and not even the answering machine answers."

"Maybe it's full."

"And she's not at work. I called there, too."

And just possibly, Mother Dear, she told them to tell you she was out.

"Mother, she probably had car trouble or something."

"No. She doesn't answer her cell phone, either. Jack, I'm really worried."

"Mother, what exactly is it you'd like me to do?"

"I want you to go by her apartment and see if she's all right."

"Mother, I'm on my way to work, and I'm already late."

"Jack, she's your sister. Your only sister."

He didn't reply.

"If only your father were still alive . . ." Mrs. Williamson began.

"Okay, okay. Don't start that. I'll go."

"You'll call me?" his mother asked.

Jack detected a triumphal tone in her voice.

Score another one for Momma Dear.

"I'll call."

He looked for, found, and took the next exit ramp—Exit 23—and a block onto Willets Road pulled to the side, clipped the cellular's hands-off microphone to his shirt, then picked the phone up and held down the 5 key, which caused the cellular to automatically dial Cheryl's number.

There was no answer, which meant she wasn't there. He hung up, then held down the 6 key, which caused the cellular to automatically dial Cheryl's cellular number. After five rings, a recorded female voice announced that the party he was attempting to reach was either not available at this time or out of the local calling area.

He cursed again, dropped the phone onto the seat, put the 300M in gear, and headed down Willets, deciding the best way to get to Cheryl's—all the fucking way across North Philly—was to take Roosevelt Boulevard and then Adams Avenue, into the East Oak Lane section of Philadelphia.

When he got to Cheryl's door, he could hear the chimes inside playing the first few bars of "Be It Ever So Humble," but there was no answer. Which meant that Cheryl was already probably at work.

He decided that when he got back to the car, he would call her at her office, and turned to leave.

Then nature called, and he was a long way from Overbrook Estates.

He felt around the top of the door frame for her spare key, and when he didn't find it, turned over the floor mat in front of the door, and when it wasn't there either, took a last shot and, standing on his toes, ran his hands over the trim above the windows next to Cheryl's door. He knocked a key off, failed to catch it, and it bounced off the floor and went over the edge of the walkway.

"Jesus H. Christ!" he said, and went down the stairs and two minutes later managed to find the key in the grass.

He unlocked the door and entered the apartment. There were, he remembered, two toilets, one with a bathtub off Cheryl's room, and another, just a water closet and a washbasin, off the kitchen. He went to the latter and relieved himself.

He was on the walkway checking to make sure the door was locked when a female voice asked, "Is everything all right?"

Now what the hell?

Jack found himself facing Mrs. Joanne McGrory.

"I'm Cheryl's brother," he said. "Jack Williamson."

And as soon as you satisfy your goddamn curiosity and go away, so you can't see what I'm doing, I will put the goddamn key back where it belongs.

"I'm Joanne McGrory. Next door."

"I'm pleased to meet you," Jack said.

"I'm pleased that everything is all right," Joanne McGrory said. "After the mirror, I was worried."

"Excuse me?"

"Our mirror came crashing off the wall, and I thought maybe something happened in there, too."

"Everything's fine in there."

"I called the cops, but they wouldn't go inside."

"You called the cops? Why?"

"Well, if you were in bed in the middle of the night and your mirror came crashing down off the wall, what would you do?"

"Mrs. McGrory, you're telling me the police were here last night?"

"Yes, they were," Joanne McGrory said. "I called them, thinking that something might have happened to Cheryl."

"And what did they do? Say?"

"They said they couldn't go into her apartment."

Jesus H. Christ, is my imagination running away with me? Is something really wrong here?

Jack Williamson put the key back in the lock and reentered the apartment. He'd already been in Cheryl's kitchen and living room, so he went to her bedroom and opened the door.

Oh, my God!

Holy Christ, what happened in here?

She's buck fucking naked and she's tied to the bed!

He walked to the bed and looked down at Cheryl. Her eyes were open, but sightless.

Oh, my God, she's dead!

He turned. Mrs. McGrory was coming into the bedroom.

"I think you'd better get out of here," he said.

"Well, excuse me. I'm just trying to be neighborly."

"Get the fuck out of here, goddamn it!" Jack said, waited until she had fled, and then looked for Cheryl's telephone.

It wasn't on her bedside table. It was on the floor, and he could see the cord had been broken.

Jesus, I'll have to use the cell phone in the car.

What the hell am I going to tell Mother?

As he went through the living room, he remembered that Cheryl had a second phone, mounted on the kitchen wall. He went to it, then stopped.

Maybe it's got fingerprints on it.

I better use my cell phone in the car.

Fuck it!

He took the handset from its cradle with his handkerchief and, using his ballpoint pen, punched in 911.

"Police department, operator 178," a male voice answered on the second ring.

"Jesus!"

"May I help you, sir?"

"I'm . . . my sister's apparently been murdered," Jack Williamson said.

"And where are you, sir?"

"In her apartment. Second floor, right, 600 Independence Street. I let myself in, and found her—"

"And your name, sir?"

"Williamson, Jack Williamson."

"You just stay where you are, please, Mr. Williamson. I'll get police officers over there right away."

"Jesus Christ, she's tied to the goddamn bed!"

"Help will be there very shortly, Mr. Williamson."

Officer Roland Stone was twelve blocks from Cheryl's apartment—near the intersection of Godfrey Avenue and Howard Street—when his radio went off.

"3514."

"3514," Stone replied.

"3514, take 600 Independence Street, second-floor apartment, right. Meet the complainant, report of a 5292. Use caution—the complainant is on the scene and states it is a possible homicide."

"3514, I have it," Stone said, and flipped on the light bar on the roof and the siren, as he turned left onto Water Street.

"35A-Andy," police radio called next, to alert the supervisor—a sergeant—in the area.

"35A, I copied. I'm en route," Sgt. John J. Haley responded. He was three blocks away from Cheryl Williamson's apartment. This meant Haley had heard the initial call to 3514, and there was no need for the police radio operator to repeat the information.

Without really thinking about it, Sergeant Haley oriented himself with regard to where he was—at Franklin Street and Sixty-fifth Avenue North—and where he was going, took a quick look, made a U-turn, and stepped hard on the accelerator. He used neither the light bar nor the siren. They wouldn't be necessary.

When he got out of his car at the curb in front of 600 Independence and started inside, a white, middle-aged woman was standing on the walkway just off the porch.

"Up there," she said, gesturing inside. "Second floor, on the right."

Haley took the porch stairs, and then the interior stairs, two at a time.

The door to Cheryl Williamson's apartment was ajar.

There was a white, late twenties male sitting on a couch, his head bent.

"Police," Sergeant Haley said.

"In there," the man on the couch said, gesturing toward an interior door.

"What's happened here?"

"Some fucking perverted cocksucker killed my sister, that's what happened here."

Sergeant Haley went into Cheryl's bedroom, stayed only long enough to determine that the naked female in the bed was dead—he had seen enough bodies to make that determination with certainty; he didn't feel for a pulse—and then stepped backward into the corridor and then went into the living room.

Looking at the guy who said he was the brother, Sergeant Haley squeezed the transmit switch on his lapel microphone.

"35A."

"35A," Police Radio responded.

"35A, notify Northwest Detectives, and Homicide. We have an apparent homicide. White female, no obvious cause of death, but there are signs of a possible rape. Hold myself and '14 car out at the scene."

Jack Williamson looked up at Sergeant Haley.

"She is dead, right?"

"I'm afraid so."

They both could hear the growing scream of Officer Stone's patrol car approaching.

CHAPTER 8

[ONE]

In the radio room—"room" doesn't do justice to the large area in which Police Radio is housed—in the Roundhouse, the radio operator who had taken Sergeant Haley's call then pressed a button on his console that automatically dialed the number of the deskman at the Northwest Detectives Division.

Detective units operate on what is known as "The Wheel." It's actually a roster of the names of the detectives on duty at the moment, and it's designed to equitably distribute the workload. In most detective divisions, there is a detective assigned to "man the desk." The "desk man" answers the telephone. When a job comes in, the desk man assigns it to the detective "next up" on the wheel.

When the phone rang in the Northwest Detectives Division, it was answered by Detective O. A. Lassiter, who was not the desk man but was filling in for Detective Len Ford, who was in the men's room "taking a personal," as a bathroom break is referred to on Police Radio. It also happened that Detective Lassiter was next up on the wheel.

Detective Lassiter was twenty-five years old, with 115 pounds distributed attractively around her five-foot-seven-inch frame. She had dark black hair, green eyes, long attractive legs, and had what her fellow detectives agreed—privately, very privately—were a magnificent ass and bosom.

"This is Police Radio, operator number 178," the Police Radio operator began, then went into the details of the call he'd received from Sergeant Haley.

Detective Lassiter wrote them down on a lined tablet and finally said, "Okay, we got it," then raised her voice to call out to Lieutenant Fred C. Vincent, "Hey, Lieutenant, we got one."

"What kind of job is it, Lassiter?" Vincent asked.

"Homicide, possible rape, white female, twenty-three years old. Her brother found her inside her apartment, tied to the bed. He's still at the scene."

"You better take somebody with you," Vincent said. "I'll get over there as soon as I can."

"Yes, sir," Detective Lassiter said, and then, raising her voice, called out, "Charley, you loose enough to go with me?"

"What's the job?" Detective Charley Touma, a plump forty-four-year-old, asked.

"That's not an answer, Charley, that's another question," Lieutenant Vincent answered for Detective Lassiter.

"I am at your disposal, Detective Lassiter," Touma said. "What's the job?"

"Homicide, possible rape, young white female," Detective Lassiter said, as she opened the drawer of her desk, took from it her Glock 9-mm semiautomatic pistol, and slipped it into its holster.

Lieutenant Vincent was pleased that Detective Touma would be working with Detective Lassiter. Touma was a good man, a gentle man. The job was probably going to be messy, and although he knew he wasn't supposed to let feelings like this intrude in any way in official business, the truth was that Lieutenant Vincent looked upon Detective Lassiter as, if not a daughter, then as a little sister.

Immediately after talking to the desk man at Northwest Detectives, the Police Radio operator pushed the button that automatically dialed the number of the man on the desk in the Homicide Unit, which was, physically, almost directly under him in the Roundhouse.

Detective Joe D'Amata, a slightly built, natty, olive-skinned forty-year-old, who was next up on the Homicide wheel, answered the phone: "Homicide, D'Amata."

"This is Radio," the operator said, and then proceeded to repeat almost verbatim what he'd reported to Detective Lassiter at Northwest Detectives. And Detective D'Amata, as Detective Lassiter had done, carefully wrote everything down, then said, "Got it, thanks."

He looked around for Lieutenant Jason Washington and saw that he was in his office talking with—almost certainly telling him the way things worked—Sergeant Matt Payne.

The only problem Joe D'Amata had with Payne as a sergeant in Homicide was that it made him reconsider the decision he'd made years before, when he'd been in Homicide a year, and there was a sergeant's exam coming up, and he had decided not to take it.

It was pretty clear by then that he'd cut the mustard and wouldn't be asked to "consider a transfer." He realized that he would much rather be a homicide detective than a sergeant, or a lieutenant, or even a captain, somewhere else. For one thing, with all the overtime, he was taking home as much—or more—dough as an inspector. But the money wasn't all of it. He liked Homicide.

Homicide was special, and it paid well. Who needs to be a sergeant?

So he hadn't taken the exam, and hadn't thought about getting promoted since. And he knew that many—perhaps most—of the homicide detectives had made the same decision at some time in their careers.

Another trouble with taking the exam and making sergeant was that he'd have to leave Homicide, the personnel theory there being it was bad policy to have somebody who last week was one of the boys this week be their supervisor. Even if he went to a regular detective district—South, for example—as a sergeant, he wouldn't be doing any investigations himself, just supervising detectives who were investigating retail thefts, stolen autos, and the occasional more exciting aggravated assaults, or bank robberies. And, if you turned up a good suspect on a bank job, the FBI would immediately take over. If he were sent to a uniform district, a very distinct possibility in today's "career-development-minded" department, then he would be devoting his investigatory skills to "Disturbance, House" calls.

There were exceptions, of course. There were exceptions to everything. Jason Washington had taken the lieutenant's exam with the understanding that if he made it, he would stay in Homicide. And the word was out that with a couple of belts in him, after he'd heard Payne was coming to Homicide, Tony Harris had gone to Washington and asked if he couldn't do the same thing, and Washington said he would work on it.

There was something else, too. The reason Payne was the new sergeant was the nutty "First Five Get Their Choice of Assignment" decision Commissioner Mariani had come up with.

That could have come out worse. Payne was a youngster, but he was a good cop. He'd been doing in critters from the time he'd come on the job. Denny Coughlin had gotten him assigned as Peter Wohl's administrative assistant to keep him out of trouble until he realized that rich kids from the Main Line really shouldn't be cops just because their father and uncle got blown away as cops.

He had been working for Wohl hardly any time at all when he'd popped the Northwest serial rapist and taken him permanently off the streets without putting the Commonwealth to the expense of a trial.

Maybe it was in his blood. Who the hell knew? But the point was Payne was a good cop. What if the Number One guy had been somebody else? Some dickhead out of Community Relations, some other candyass good at taking exams but who, on the street, couldn't find his butt with both hands and who would piss his pants if he had to stare down some critter? What then?

Joe D'Amata pushed himself out of his chair and walked to Lieutenant Washington's door. He waited until he had Washington's attention.

"We got one, Jason," he said. "White female, twenty-three, probably involved with a rape."

"Dare I hope the culprit is in custody?" Washington asked.

D'Amata shook his head, "no."

"No. Thirty-fifth District uniform is holding the scene," he said.

"Sergeant Payne will accompany you to the scene," Washington said, smiling broadly, "checking to make sure everything you know has to be done is done. You will explain each step in the procedure to him, so that he will be assured you know what you're doing."

In other words, show the rookie the ropes.

"Anytime you're ready, Sergeant," Joe said.

"Let me know what happens, Sergeant," Washington said.

"Yes, sir."

Matt got up and followed D'Amata into the outer room.

"What I usually do first, Sergeant," D'Amata said, "is secure my replacement on the wheel."

Matt nodded.

D'Amata raised his voice.

"Kramer, put the *Hustler* down and take the phone."

Detective Alonzo Kramer, who appeared to be reading a large ledger at his desk, waved his hand to indicate he understood he was now up on the wheel.

Matt Payne wondered if he really had a copy of *Hustler* magazine hidden behind the green ledger. And decided he didn't want to know.

"What I will do now, Sergeant," Joe D'Amata said, punching numbers on a telephone, "is inform the very clever technicians assigned to the Mobile Crime Lab that their services are going to be required."

Other detectives—who, Matt did not need to be told, were the squad who would work the case—began to gather around D'Amata's desk.

D'Amata put the telephone handset in its cradle.

"With your permission, Sergeant, I will designate Detectives Reeves and Grose to remain behind. Reeves, who went to night school and now reads almost at the sixth-grade level, will research the victim, see what he can find out about her in the files—does she have a rap sheet, outstanding warrants, et cetera, et cetera. Grose, who can't read at all, will seek out a judge to get us a search warrant for the premises."

Detectives Grose and Reeves, having picked up on what was happening, were smiling.

"I'm sure you're aware, Sergeant," D'Amata went on, "that our beloved Lieutenant Washington is picky-picky about getting a search warrant before we even start rooting in garbage cans in search of evidence, and photographing the deceased."

"He has made that point, Detective," Matt said.

"Something to do, I believe, with slimeball lawyers getting critters off because the evidence was gained unlawfully."

"So I was led to believe," Matt said.

"And I think, with your permission, Sergeant, that I will designate Detective Slayberg—that's the fat one in the cheap suit— . . ."

"Screw you, Joe," Detective Slayberg said, but he was smiling.

". . . as the recorder. He's very good at describing premises."

"So I usually get stuck with that, Sergeant," Slayberg said.

"Many years ago," Matt said mock seriously, "when I was a young police officer, I made the mistake of letting my sergeant know I could type with all the fingers on both hands."

The others chuckled.

"Boy," Slayberg said, "with all possible respect, Sergeant, that was a dumb fucking thing to do."

"So I learned," Matt said.

There were more chuckles.

"So now, these little details out of the way, and with your permission, Sergeant, I think we should proceed to the scene."

"Absolutely."

"With just about everybody working the Roy Rogers job, Matt, we're a little short of wheels. You mind if Slayberg and I ride out there with you? Or did Quaire beat you out of that new car you brought with you?"

"Not yet," Matt said. "But then, I haven't been here very long."

I wonder why Quaire didn't grab the car?

He watched as all the detectives who would be going to the scene went to filing cabinets, unlocked them, and then took from them their personal equipment, which included their weapons, surgical rubber gloves, and leather- or vinyl-covered folders holding legal tablets.

He followed D'Amata out of Homicide, at the last moment picking up his briefcase, with his laptop inside, from atop a filing cabinet near the door.

[TWO]

When Matt got out of the unmarked Ford, he saw that yellow-and-black tape reading Police Line Do Not Cross had been strung along both sides of the path into the apartment complex to prohibit access to one of the buildings.

Two uniformed white shirts, a captain and a lieutenant, were standing talking to two detectives, one of them a woman, on the concrete path in front of what was obviously the crime scene.

"Captain Alex Smith, the district commander," Joe D'Amata said. "Good guy. I don't make the lieutenant."

"Lew Sawyer," Slayberg furnished. "He's a prick. The broad is from Special Victims, and she's a real bitch."

"What the fuck is she doing here?" Slayberg asked. "Special Victims Unit doesn't have anything to do with homicide investigations, even when the victim has been raped."

"Smile nicely at her, Matt," D'Amata said.

Captain Smith saw the three of them coming and smiled.

"Hello, Joe," he said, putting out his hand.

"Good morning, sir. I know you know Harry, but . . . Sergeant Payne?"

"Yeah, sure, how are you, Harry?" He shook Slayberg's hand. "I know who you are, Sergeant, but I don't think we've ever actually met."

"I don't think so, sir," Matt said, reaching for Smith's outstretched hand.

"This is Lieutenant Sawyer," Smith said. "And Detectives Domenico and Ellis, of Special Victims."

"I think I used to see you around the Arsenal, didn't I?" Detective Domenico asked.

There was something about her smile Matt didn't like, and he remembered what Slayberg had said.

"I used to be out there with Special Operations," Matt said.

Everybody nodded at each other, but no hands were shaken.

"What have we got, Captain?" Joe asked.

"A dead girl, the doer is probably a sicko, and maybe a problem."

"What kind of a problem?"

"There was a 'Disturbance, House' call here last night. Two cars responded. The lady next door said her mirror fell off the wall. She said the trouble came from the Williamson apartment, and wanted them to check it out. There was no response when the officers rang the bell, no lights, no sounds, and no signs of a break-in. So they couldn't take the door."

"Uh-oh," D'Amata said. "I think I know what's coming."

Captain Smith nodded.

"So they left," he said. "And then the brother let himself in this morning, found his sister, and the lady next door told him what had happened last night. Actually, early this morning. And the brother is pretty upset with the police department for not taking the door the first time we were here."

"Ouch," D'Amata said.

Slayberg's cellular buzzed.

He said his name, listened, then said, "Thanks. We just got here. Wait." He turned to Matt.

"Sergeant, the search warrant is on the way. Grose will bring it. Reeves said there's nothing but a couple of driving violations on either the victim or her brother, and wants to know what you want him to do."

"Tell Grose to tell Reeves to come out with him and the warrant," Matt said, forgetting that he had promised himself to keep his eyes open and his mouth shut.

He stole a quick glance at D'Amata, and saw nothing on his face to suggest he thought Matt had ordered the wrong thing. And he remembered what Quaire had said about his being expected to act like a sergeant.

"Why don't we go have a quick look?" Matt said to D'Amata and Slayberg. "The search warrant's on the way."

He started to walk toward the stairs, and became aware that everybody started to follow him.

I'm not about to tell the district captain he can't have a look at the scene, but that doesn't apply to the lieutenant and certainly not to the smiling lady from Special Victims.

"It's your job, Sergeant, but I would like a look."

"After you, sir," he said, waving Captain Smith ahead of him.

"Lieutenant, would you mind waiting until the Crime Lab people do their thing?" Matt asked.

"I just wanted a quick look, but you're right," Lieutenant Sawyer said.

"You understand," Matt said to Detective Domenico.

The ice in your eyes, Detective Domenico, Sergeant Payne thought, *would freeze the balls off a brass monkey. What's your problem? You're not even supposed to be here. This isn't a rape, a child molestation, it's a homicide.*

The uniform in front of Cheryl Williamson's door stepped aside when he saw Captain Smith and the others.

Once they got inside, Captain Smith touched Matt's arm.

"I know Sex Crimes," he said, using the old name for the Special Victims Unit, "doesn't have anything to do with a homicide investigation, even when a sexual assault is involved. They just happened to be in my office talking to me about an unsolved rape when this job came out."

"Yes, sir," Matt said. And then he saw in Joe D'Amata's eyes that he found this interesting. After a moment, so did Matt.

An unsolved rape and they just happened to be here at a homicide rape scene? Is there something else we're not being told? I think I'll have to send a team over to the Special Victims Unit to see what their files may have.

Without a word Joe D'Amata opened his leather-bound notepad, turned to the last page of the tablet, and scrawled a note for himself: *Sex Crimes, unsolved rape in area, Lt. Sawyer, Det. Domenico, Ellis.*

There was another female detective in the apartment, sitting on the couch beside a well-dressed, somewhat distraught-looking man.

She stood up when she saw them.

Sergeant Payne had an unprofessional thought: *Now, that's a very interesting member of the opposite sex.*

"Captain, I'd rather not have anybody in there until we get the search warrant and the Crime Lab," the very interesting member of the opposite sex said.

"The warrant's on the way," Matt said. "And we're just going to stand in the door for a quick look."

"Take a good long look," the man on the couch said, as he stood up. "If you cops did what you're supposed to do, my sister would probably still be alive."

"I'm very sorry for your loss, sir," D'Amata said.

"You're sorry? That does Cheryl a lot of fucking good."

"Who are you?" Detective Olivia Lassiter asked, almost a challenge.

"Joe D'Amata, Homicide," D'Amata said. "I've got the job. This is Harry Slayberg, and Sergeant Payne."

D'Amata and Slayberg nodded at Detective Lassiter as they walked around Matt to the bedroom door.

"Who are you?" Matt asked.

"Lassiter, Northwest Detectives," she said.

D'Amata and Slayberg stood in the doorway of Cheryl Williamson's bedroom and looked around—without entering—for about sixty seconds. Then they stepped away from the bedroom door and started looking around the living room. Captain Smith went to the bedroom door.

"Jesus," he said, softly.

Matt saw that D'Amata and Slayberg had rubber gloves on their hands, wondered why he hadn't seen them put them on, and pulled a pair of his own from his pocket.

He was about to walk to the door when the apartment door opened again and two men entered. Payne knew one of them, a balding, rumpled man in a well-worn suit, Dr. Howard Mitchell of the medical examiner's office. He had with him a photographer, a young man Matt could not remember ever having seen before.

Matt found it interesting that Dr. Mitchell had come to the scene personally. Usually technicians from the M.E.'s office worked a death scene, and the M.E. did not; he either supervised the autopsy or did it himself.

Probably, Matt decided, Mitchell's appearance had something to do with a Special Operations job he'd heard about, one that had almost been assigned to him, although in the end it had been assigned to Detectives Jesus Martinez and Charles T. McFadden.

It had begun when a highly indignant citizen, the nephew of a woman who'd fallen down her cellar stairs and broken her neck, had gone to his district and told the desk sergeant to report that he'd just gotten Aunt Myrtle's last Visa bill. Aunt Myrtle didn't drink, couldn't drive, and there was no way she could have charged $355 worth of booze at Mickey's Liquor Store in Camden, New Jersey, on the day of her death.

The report had worked its way through the bureaucracy to the Roundhouse, where it had been discussed by Deputy Commissioner Coughlin and Chief Inspector of Detectives Lowenstein.

They agreed there was something about it that made it seem more than a simple case of credit-card fraud. And since it crosse1d state lines, it became a federal offense, which meant it was in the province of the FBI. Although both Coughlin and Lowenstein held the FBI in the highest possible respect, they also suspected that a credit card fraud involving only $355 would not get the FBI's full attention.

"Give it to Peter Wohl," Lowenstein said. "Not this job. Get him to see if there have been other reports of other things missing from other recently deceased citizens."

Coughlin had—unnecessarily—told Peter Wohl that if somebody at funeral homes, cops at the scene, or maybe even from the M.E.'s office were taking things they shouldn't, he would rather learn this from Special Operations than from the FBI.

Charley McFadden and Hay-zus Martinez had been given the job because they had less on their plates when the job came in than Matt did. It hadn't taken McFadden and Martinez long to discover—Matt couldn't remember ever before having seen Charley so personally indignant—that a lot of stuff had disappeared over the past six months, and that it was pretty clear it had disappeared into the pockets of some of the M.E.'s technicians. They had apparently decided that since the deceased had no further need for rings, watches, other jewelry and cash, they might as well put the same to good use—their own.

Four of them had been arrested, tried, and convicted.

"Good morning, Doctor," Captain Smith said from the bedroom door.

"Hey, Smitty," Dr. Mitchell said, and then spotted Matt. "Hey, Payne. I saw your picture in the paper."

"Good morning, Doctor," Matt said. "The search warrant's en route."

Dr. Mitchell winked at D'Amata and Slayberg, then walked to the bedroom door, pulling on rubber gloves as he did so. The photographer followed him. Mitchell gestured with his hand for the photographer to stop at the door, then went inside.

The medical examiner needed no one's permission to enter the crime scene. It belonged to him until he released it to Homicide.

Matt walked to the bedroom door.

Dr. Mitchell bent over Cheryl Williamson's body, took a quick look, put his fingers on her carotid artery, looked at his watch, and announced, "I pronounce her dead as of ten fifty-five."

He looked over his shoulder at Matt.

"Unofficially, it looks like her neck is broken, and to judge from the lividity of the body, I'd guess she's been dead eight, nine hours or so."

He signaled to the photographer that it was all right for him to enter the room, and started for the bedroom door.

Matt got his first look at the victim.

She was naked, with her legs spread apart by plastic ties tied to the foot-board. Her upper body was twisted to the left. Her left hand was tied to the headboard, and Matt could see another tie hanging loose from her right wrist.

She looked at him out of sightless eyes, and his mind was instantly filled with Susan Reynolds's sightless eyes looking at him in the parking lot of the Crossroads Diner.

He felt the knot in his stomach and the cold sweat forming on his back, and stepped quickly away from the door.

Jesus, not now! Dear God, don't let me get sick to my stomach and make an ass of myself on my first Homicide job!

He bumped into something, somebody, and saw that it was Detective Olivia Lassiter, and that he had almost knocked her over.

She looked at him with what he thought was annoyance.

He started to say "Sorry," but was interrupted by Jack Williamson, bitterly asking, "You got a good look, I hope?"

He turned his back to Williamson and touched Detective Lassiter's arm.

"You get anything out of him?" and then, before she could reply, asked, "Why didn't you get him out of here?"

"I was just getting him calmed down enough to talk when you walked in," she said. "He doesn't want to leave, and I didn't want to push him."

"Come with me," Matt said.

"That sounds like an order," she said.

"Okay," Matt said. "It was a request, a suggestion, but I want you to come with me."

She met his eyes defiantly for a moment, then shrugged and turned away from the open door.

Matt walked to the couch. Jack Williamson looked up at him with cold contempt.

"Mr. Williamson, I'm Sergeant Payne. I'm the Homicide supervisor, and I need to talk to you, and we can't do that in here. In just a few minutes, there will be technicians all over the place, and we can't be in their way. I want you to come with Detective Lassiter and me to someplace where we can talk. Okay?"

"The lady next door offered anything we need," Olivia said. "What about her kitchen? She had said she would put a pot of coffee on."

"We'll just sit around and have a friendly cup of coffee, right? And maybe a Big Mac? With my sister like that in there?"

"We have to talk someplace, Mr. Williamson, and we have to get out of the way of the technicians, and sitting down over a cup of coffee seems a better idea to me than standing on the sidewalk," Matt said. "What do you say?"

Williamson shrugged, a gesture of surrender, and stood up.

"Mrs. McGrory, this is Sergeant Payne of Homicide. We have to talk, privately, to Mr. Williamson," Olivia said when Mrs. McGrory answered her knock. "Could we use your kitchen?"

"Certainly."

"Thank you very much," Matt said, as she led them in her kitchen.

"Anything I can do to help. There's a fresh pot in the Mr. Coffee. Just help yourself."

"That's very kind of you," Matt said.

"I feel just terrible about this, especially with the cops being outside while it was happening."

"We don't know for sure that's what happened, Mrs. McGrory," Matt said.

"Of course, that's what happened. I was here, wasn't I?"

"Thank you very much, Mrs. McGrory," Olivia said, easing her out of the kitchen and then closing the door.

"Why don't you sit down?" Matt suggested to Williamson. "I'll get the coffee. How do you take yours, Mr. Williamson?"

"Black," Williamson said.

"Black," Olivia said.

Olivia and Williamson sat down at the kitchen table while Matt took the glass decanter and poured coffee into ceramic mugs. He walked to the table and set the mugs on it.

"Okay," Matt said. "Let's get a couple of things understood between us, Mr. Williamson. I don't know what happened last night, when Mrs. McGrory called the police, and I don't care."

"You don't fucking care?" Williamson asked, disgusted and incredulous.

"My job is to find the person, or persons, who killed your sister, and see that when they're brought to trial they won't walk out of the courtroom because some legal 't' wasn't crossed or some legal 'i' didn't have a dot. I understand that you're unhappy with what you think happened last night."

"What happened last night was that the fucking cops didn't do a goddamn thing to help my sister."

"If you believe the police did something they shouldn't have, or didn't do something they should have, you have every right to make an official complaint—"

"Fucking-A right, I do. And I will."

"But I think you'll agree, Mr. Williamson, that right now the priority is to find out who did this thing, and the sooner the better. Would you agree with that?"

"Jesus, of course I 'agree with that.' All I'm saying is that if those fucking cops had done what they were supposed to do last night, my sister would still be alive."

"There's one more thing, Mr. Williamson," Matt said. "Your language is beginning to offend me. I hope you'll watch your mouth. I would really rather not have you transported to Homicide and placed in an interview room until you get your emotions under control."

Williamson glared at him but didn't say anything.

Matt opened his briefcase and took out his laptop.

"What's that for?"

"I'm one of those guys who can't read his own writing," Matt said. "I take notes this way. Are you objecting to it?"

"If I did?"

"Then I'll take out a notebook and ballpoint, and waste a lot of time trying to make sense of my notes when I finally have to type them up. All right?"

Williamson shrugged. Matt turned the laptop on and began to type.

"Is it 'Jack,' Mr. Williamson?"

"John J. For Joseph."

"What's your first name and badge number, Lassiter?"

"Olivia, 582," she furnished.

"Okay, Mr. Williamson, let's start with your personal data," Matt said. "Residence?"

Twenty minutes later, Matt said, "I think that'll be enough for the time being, Mr. Williamson."

"Okay."

"You know how to work a laptop?"

Williamson nodded.

Matt slid the laptop in front of him.

"Would you take a look at that, please, and see if I've got it right?"

Williamson read the several pages Matt had typed and then nodded his head, "okay."

Matt turned the laptop off, closed the cover, and put it back in his briefcase.

"When I get that printed, Mr. Williamson, I'll have a detective—most likely Detective Lassiter—bring it to you for your signature."

"When?" Williamson asked.

"It'll wait until tomorrow," Matt said. "I know that you're going to be busy today. I'll call you tomorrow to see when it will be convenient."

"I have to tell you this," Williamson said. "When my mother hears about what happened last night, this morning, with the cops . . . God!"

"I'm not trying to talk you out of filing a formal complaint," Matt said, "honestly, I'm not. But for what it's worth, from what I've heard, the officers who responded to the 'Disturbance, House' call were just going by the book. If they had *any* indication that something—anything—was going wrong, had gone wrong, in the apartment, they *would* have taken action."

Williamson looked at him but didn't respond directly.

"What am I supposed to do if my mother wants to come here?"

"Well, right now she can't have access to the apartment. Not today, and probably not tomorrow, either. Tell her that."

"Jesus Christ!" Williamson said.

"I'd be happy to go with you, Mr. Williamson," Detective Lassiter said. "If you think it would make things any easier. And I'd like to talk to her, too. That doesn't have to be right now. Your call."

"It couldn't do any harm," Williamson said. "And maybe, if you were there . . ."

"If you'll give me your cellular number, Sergeant, I'll call and let you know how things went," Detective Lassiter said.

Matt wrote the number on a small sheet of notepaper and handed it to her. She tore it in half and wrote two numbers on it.

"I guess you have the Northwest number, right?" she asked. Matt nodded. "My cellular and apartment," she said.

"Thank you," Matt said.

Under other circumstances, Olivia, my lovely, I would be overjoyed that you shared your telephone numbers with me.

Come to think of it, Olivia, despite the circumstances, I am overjoyed that you have shared your telephone numbers with me.

Mrs. McGrory was not in her living room as they passed through, but Matt could hear her voice in the next room. Only her voice, which suggested she was on the telephone.

162 · W. E. B. GRIFFIN

He decided he had already thanked her and it would be better not to disturb her when she was on the phone.

When they went downstairs and through the front door, he saw that the press was gathered behind the POLICE LINE DO NOT CROSS tape, and that the moment they saw them—two detectives, with badges showing, escorting a so-far-unidentified white male—video cameras rose with their red RECORDING lights glowing, and still camera flashbulbs went off.

"Where's your car?" Matt asked.

"Halfway down the street," she said, and pointed.

Matt touched the arm of one of the uniforms.

"I want to get Detective Lassiter and this gentleman to her car, down the street, and I don't want the press to get in the way."

"No problem," the uniform said, raised his voice, and called, "Dick!"

Dick was a very large police officer of African-American heritage.

He and the other uniform led the way through the assembled journalists, one on each side of Detective Lassiter and Mr. Williamson.

Sergeant Payne brought up the rear, which gave him a chance to decide that Detective Lassiter had a very nice muscular structure of the lower half of the rear of her body.

As he walked back to 600 Independence, ignoring questions from the press about the identity of Mr. Williamson, he realized he didn't really have much of an idea of what he was supposed to do now.

He remembered something he had been taught at the Marine Base, Quantico, while in the platoon leaders program: *reconnoiter the terrain.*

He spent perhaps ten minutes walking around the outside of the big old house, even going up the rear stairs, and then into the basement. He saw nothing of particular interest.

[THREE]

When Matt returned to the front of the house, two uniforms were carrying a stretcher with Cheryl Williamson's body on it down the pathway to a Thirty-Fifth District wagon.

Well, I won't have to look at the sightless eyes again—not that I'm liable to forget them.

When they had moved past him, Matt went up the stairs and into the Williamson apartment.

"What happened to that very pretty detective from Northwest?" Joe D'Amata greeted him.

"She went with the brother to tell the mother."

"This is our job, Matt," D'Amata said. There was a slight tone of reproof in his voice.

"She calmed the brother down. He liked her . . ."

"I can't imagine why," D'Amata said.

". . . and (a) I thought that would make things easier with the mother. The brother suggested his mother was going to blow her cork when she found out that there was a 'Disturbance, House' call here and the uniforms didn't take the door. And (b) somebody had to talk to the mother, and I think she can do that as well as we could, which means that we can be here."

"Your call," D'Amata said. "Two things, Matt: You want a look at the rear door?"

"I saw the outside from the stairs," Matt said, as he followed D'Amata into the kitchen and to the door. "I didn't see any signs of forced entry. Did you?"

"Those scratches might be an indication that somebody pried it open," Joe said, pointing. "Operative word 'might.' The door was latched, locked, like that, but if you leave the lever in the up position like that, it locks automatically."

"What do the crime lab guys say?"

"What I just told you. No signs at all on the front door. So we don't know if the doer broke in, or whether she let him in. Could be either way. If she knew the doer, let him in . . ."

Matt grunted. Most murders are committed by people known to the victim.

"You said two things," Matt said.

"*This* is interesting," D'Amata said, taking a plastic evidence bag from his pocket. It held a digital camera.

"It may be, of course—and probably is—hers. But it was under the bed, which is a strange place to store an expensive camera like this. Even stranger, there are no fingerprints on it. Not even a smudge."

"Why don't we see what pictures are in it?"

"It doesn't work," D'Amata said, his tone suggesting that Matt should have known he could come up with a brilliant idea like seeing what pictures were in the camera all by himself. "Which might be because it got knocked off the bedside table when the doer jerked the telephone out of the wall and threw it at the mirror."

"No prints on the phone, either?" Matt asked.

D'Amata held up his rubber-surgical-gloved hands.

"I'm getting the idea the doer is a very careful guy," he said. "Which also suggests he knows how to get through a door without making a mess, and which suggests that although they are lifting a lot of prints in here—so far, they've done both doors, the bedroom and her bathroom—I would be pleasantly surprised if they came up with something useful."

"Yeah," Matt agreed.

"So, I was just about to call you to ask if I should take the camera to the crime lab and see if there are any pictures in it."

"As opposed to having a District car run it down there, which would put a uniform in the evidence chain?"

"That, too," D'Amata said. "I was thinking that if there are pictures in there, I could get a look at them a lot quicker if I was there when the lab took them out of the camera, then wait for the lab to print them."

"The camera's been fingerprinted?"

"I told you, there's nothing on it. Not even a smudge."

Matt set his briefcase on the kitchen table, opened it, rummaged around, and closed it again.

"We're in luck," he said. "I've got the gizmo."

"What gizmo?"

Matt walked to the door leading from the kitchen to the living room and motioned to one of the uniforms in the living room.

"Don't let anybody come in here until I tell you, okay?"

The uniform nodded and stood in the center of the doorjamb. Matt closed the door.

"Who's in the bedroom?" he asked.

"Harry, making the sketch," D'Amata said. "A uniform's keeping people out of there, too. What are you doing?"

Matt went back to the kitchen table and took out his laptop, then a small plastic object with a connecting cord. He plugged it into the laptop, then turned it on.

"You can look at them here?" Joe asked.

"And store them in the laptop," Matt said.

D'Amata handed him the evidence bag. Matt took the flash memory cartridge from it and saw that D'Amata had initialed it. If there were evidentiary photos in the camera, a defense attorney could not raise doubts in the jurors' minds that the pictures they were being shown had actually come from this camera.

He put the memory card into the transfer device, then copied the JPEG images from it to the laptop's hard disk.

"There's eight images," Matt said. "Let's see what they are."

The first picture was obviously evidentiary. It showed Cheryl tied to the bed, staring with horror at the camera.

D'Amata went to the door and called Harry Slayberg.

Matt waited until Slayberg came, then displayed the other seven pictures.

"This critter is a real psychopath," Slayberg said, softly.

"You can see, in the first one," D'Amata said, "that the phone's still on the bedside table."

"And both of her wrists—run the last couple back again, please, Matt, so I'm sure—are still tied to the headboard," Slayberg said.

Matt displayed the entire series of pictures again.

"So what might have happened was that she got one wrist free . . . ," Slayberg said.

"And he struggled with her . . . ," D'Amata picked up. "And that's when the camera got knocked under the bed."

"Or," Matt offered, "he went into the bathroom to take a leak, or clean himself up, and while he was in there, she got the hand loose, and tried to call 911 . . ."

"And Dudley Do-Right came out and caught her," Slayberg picked up, "hit her—probably harder than he intended—and jerked the phone out of the wall and threw it at the mirror."

"He was probably scared or in a rage or both," D'Amata said, "and didn't think that throwing the phone at the mirror was going to make a lot of noise."

Matt picked up the camera.

"It's an expensive camera," he said. "Kodak. I gave one almost like it to my sister for her birthday. Which triggers a couple of thoughts."

"Dudley Do-Right is either well-heeled or he stole the camera," Slayberg said.

"They are serially numbered," Matt said. "And come with a program that if it won't work, or you break it, you call them and they FedEx you a new one overnight. I think we should be able to find out who bought this. With a lot of luck, it will be the doer. But even if he stole it, he might have stolen it while doing another rape. That might tell us something."

"I don't think so, Matt," D'Amata said. "Dudley's a very careful guy, and, I suspect, smart. Smart enough not to take anything that could tie him to one of his escapades."

"And the second thought is that I'd like to show these pictures to my sister."

"Did you just say what I thought I heard you say?" Slayberg asked. "The sister at Dave Pekach's party?"

D'Amata laughed.

"One and the same," he said. "She's a shrink, Harry, a very good one."

"I didn't know," Slayberg said. "That's a thought, but the book says a department shrink and/or Special Victims, not a civilian."

"Maybe that rule could be bent," D'Amata said, smiling. "I heard Dr. Payne call Commissioner Coughlin 'Uncle Denny,' and Inspector Wohl 'Honey.'"

"That was at the party," Matt said, chuckling. "And subject to change. But she's worked with us before, Harry. I don't think there would be a problem."

"What I think we should do now," D'Amata said, "is seek the wise guidance of the Black Buddha. He's a white shirt—they get paid to make decisions."

Matt caused the screen of his laptop to go blank, then took out his cell phone and held down the number that caused the phone to automatically dial the cell phone of Lieutenant Jason Washington.

"Washington."

"Payne, sir."

"I was just about to call you, Sergeant Payne."

"Yes, sir?"

"Where are you, Matthew?"

"At the scene, sir."

"Stay there, and make sure D'Amata and Slayberg stay there. Commissioner Coughlin, Chief Lowenstein, Captain Quaire, and I will be there shortly, to exhort you vis-à-vis the rapid solution of that case."

"Yes, sir."

Washington turned off his cell phone.

CHAPTER 9

[ONE]

Matt pushed the End button on his cellular.

"Washington's on his way here," he announced. "And so are Coughlin, Lowenstein, and Quaire."

"What's that all about?" D'Amata asked.

Matt shrugged. "He wants the three of us here."

"Was he in the office?" D'Amata asked.

"He didn't say."

"Then we have to go on the premise that he—they—may be two minutes away," D'Amata said. "'Jesus is coming, look busy.' How can we best do that?"

"I don't know about you two, but I'm going back to doing the scene," Slayberg said, and walked out of the kitchen.

"Emperors and people like that like to be welcomed when they go someplace," D'Amata said. "Matt, why don't you and I go outside and wait?"

They left the apartment by the rear door. There was a uniform standing at the foot of the stairway, and other uniforms were standing just inside the POLICE LINE DO NOT CROSS tape. On the other side of the tape there were not only more spectators than Matt expected—Cheryl Williamson's body had been taken away; the show was over—but more than a dozen representatives of the print, radio, and television press.

He didn't see Mickey O'Hara, and wondered where he was. Mickey was usually the first press guy at the scene of a murder.

The answer to that came when—ignoring questions several of the journalists called out—they walked around the end of the building to the front. There, behind the yellow-and-black POLICE LINE tape were even more spectators and representatives of the press, and Mickey O'Hara was among them. To make sure they didn't cross the tape, two uniforms stood directly in front of the press, one male, one female, both looking as if they had left the Academy as long as two weeks ago.

On the inside of the tape, there were a number of police officers, in uniform, and others with badges visible on their civilian clothing. Captain Alex Smith, the Thirty-fifth District commander, and Lieutenant Lew Sawyer were talking to a woman with a badge on her dress, whom Matt remembered after a moment to be Captain Helene Durwinsky, the commanding officer of the Special Victims Unit, and a man with a lieutenant's badge hanging on his suit jacket. He saw Detectives Domenico and Ellis, of Special Victims, standing a few feet from the white shirts, with several other detectives Matt didn't recognize.

"You got the word?" Captain Smith said.

There was no question what "the word" was, but Matt didn't know if Smith was speaking to him or Joe D'Amata.

"With no explanation, sir," D'Amata replied.

"It may have something to do with *Phil's Philly*," Captain Smith said dryly. "On which—according to my wife, one of Phil's most devoted listeners— about forty-five minutes ago, Mrs. McGrory spoke at some length about Miss Williamson being raped and tortured while the police stood not caring outside her door."

"Oh, shit!" D'Amata said.

"I just talked to her," Matt said. "I used her kitchen to talk to the brother. She didn't say anything about talking to that ass . . . *Phil's Philly*."

Phil's Philly was a very popular radio talk show. Philadelphians dissatisfied with something in the City of Brotherly Love could call the number, and be reasonably sure both of a sympathetic ear on the part of Phil Donaldson, and that Mr. Donaldson would then call—on the air—whoever had wronged the caller, to indignantly demand an explanation, an apology, and immediate corrective action.

"Well, she did," Captain Smith went on. "My wife said that Phil's first call was to Commissioner Mariani, and when Commissioner Mariani 'was not available' to take the call, Phil called the mayor. Who made the mistake of taking the call."

Three unmarked cars pulled up shortly thereafter, within moments of each other. Television and still cameras recorded Deputy Commissioner Dennis V. Coughlin and Captain F. X. Hollaran as they walked into the apartment complex, ducked under the POLICE LINE tape, and walked up to Captain Smith's group. Smith and Sawyer, who were in uniform, saluted.

The press then recorded the same out-of-the-car-and-under-the-tape movement of Captain Henry C. Quaire and Lieutenant Jason Washington, and then turned their attention to Chief Inspector of Detectives Matthew Lowenstein.

Lowenstein ducked under the tape and then spoke, while the cameras rolled, to the two young uniformed officers standing in front of the assembled press.

"Do you know who I am?" Lowenstein demanded, firmly, as flashbulbs went off and television cameras followed his movements.

"Yes, sir," both young officers replied, in unison.

"Most of the ladies and gentlemen of the press will respect this crime scene tape," Lowenstein said, pointing to it. "That one"—he pointed to Mickey O'Hara—"will more than likely try to sneak under it. If he does, use whatever force you feel is appropriate. Like breaking his arms and legs."

"Yes, sir," both young officers said, earnestly, in unison.

Mickey O'Hara laughed with delight.

Chief Lowenstein then walked up to the group around Deputy Commissioner Coughlin. The uniformed officers saluted him.

"I can't believe you did that!" Coughlin said, not quite able to restrain a smile. "What the hell was that about?"

Chief Lowenstein was one of a tiny group of senior police officers who was not awed by either Deputy Commissioner Coughlin's rank or his persona, possibly because they had graduated from the Police Academy together and had been close personal friends ever since.

"You all looked guilty as hell," Lowenstein said. "Playing right into Philadelphia Phil's hand. I decided a little levity was in order."

"I hope Mickey doesn't try to get past the tape," Captain Hollaran said. "That female uniform's got her eye on him."

Deputy Commissioner Coughlin followed the nod of Hollaran's head, saw a very determined, very slight, very young female police officer, her baton in her hands, glowering at Mickey O'Hara, who outweighed her by fifty pounds. Coughlin had a very difficult time not laughing out loud.

He returned his attention to the group and settled his eyes on Matt.

"Sergeant," he ordered, "take us someplace where we can talk privately."

"Yes, sir," Matt said. "Will you follow me, please, Commissioner?"

He led the procession to the front stairs of the building and up them to Cheryl Williamson's apartment. This was not the time, he decided, to take further advantage of Mrs. McGrory's hospitality.

He led the procession into Cheryl Williamson's kitchen. It was crowded with all of them in it.

"This will all seem a lot less amusing if that little scene is on the six o'clock news, and the mayor sees it," Coughlin said. "Jesus, Matt!"

"I'd rather have that on the tube," Lowenstein said, "than poor Smitty here on it trying to explain the law that kept his uniforms from taking the door when—maybe, just maybe—the doer was inside raping and murdering the young woman."

"You don't think he was inside when the uniforms were here?" Coughlin asked.

"We don't know, Denny. Maybe he was already gone when the uniforms arrived, but if Smitty says that, in addition to explaining the law, it'll look as if he's loyally covering for his men."

Coughlin grunted.

"If, however," Lowenstein said, "some very senior officer, after half an hour personally investigating the facts, went down there and said the same thing . . ."

"You don't mean me?" Coughlin snorted.

". . . we could almost count on Mickey doing a thoughtful piece for the *Bulletin* explaining when the cops can and cannot take a door," Lowenstein finished, "and probably getting into how hard we're working, routinely, to get this guy."

"Routinely?" Coughlin said. "Matt, you weren't in the mayor's office with the commissioner and me. The mayor doesn't want this solved in due time, he wants it solved in time for the six o'clock news."

"Who's the lead detective, you, Joe?" Lowenstein asked.

"Yes, sir," D'Amata said.

"What are the chances for that?"

"Not good, sir," D'Amata said.

Lowenstein gestured with both his hands: *Give me more.*

"We have no idea who he is, other than he's a four-star psychopath," D'Amata said. "We have only one thing that might lead us to him."

"Which is?"

"He left his camera behind, and Matt Payne—"

"How do you know it's his camera?" Lowenstein interrupted.

"He took pictures of the victim, sir."

"How do you know that?"

"It's a digital camera, sir," Matt Payne said. "I downloaded the images from the flash memory card into my laptop."

"I don't know what the hell you're talking about. You're saying you have pictures the doer took of the victim?"

"Yes, sir," Matt said, and pushed his way through everybody jammed into the kitchen, and brought the pictures up on the screen of the laptop.

"My God," Dennis V. Coughlin said.

"How long have you had these?" Lowenstein demanded.

"Not long, sir," Matt said. "I was calling Lieutenant Washington to tell him when he said you were all headed here."

"And how can you locate the doer by his camera?" Lowenstein challenged.

"I'm not sure I can, sir. But I know that type camera. It comes with a program that . . ." He stopped, trying to think of a way to explain simply the Kodak camera replacement program.

"That what?"

"The camera has a serial number," Matt said. "If we can get Kodak to tell us where they shipped it—"

"Who the hell are you?" Lowenstein demanded, nastily, interrupting him.

"Detective Lassiter, sir. Northwest."

Matt turned and saw her standing in the doorway. She looked a little stunned by Lowenstein's greeting.

"And what is so important that you felt you could just barge in here like this?"

"I just left the victim's mother," Olivia said. "She understands why the uniforms couldn't take the door. I thought I should tell Sergeant Payne. I heard about Philadelphia Phil—or whatever his name is—on my way back here."

"The victim's mother understands why the uniforms couldn't take the door?" Dennis V. Coughlin asked, and then, before she could answer, asked another question. "What were you doing with the victim's mother?"

"I sent her with the victim's brother when he went to tell the mother," Matt said.

Matt happened to be looking at Washington, whose expressive eyebrows rose in surprise.

"You *sent* her?" challenged the lieutenant who had been standing with Smith and others when they first had gone outside.

"Yes, sir."

"You gave one of my detectives orders?"

"Not now," Lowenstein said, sharply, then turned his attention to Detective Lassiter. "You're sure the victim's mother understands about the door?"

"Yes, sir. I told her how that works," Olivia said. "She seemed to understand.

She even calmed the brother down about it. All she wants is for us to catch the doer."

"What's in the envelope?"

"A picture of the victim, sir," Olivia said, and handed it to him. "I borrowed it from the mother."

Lowenstein looked at it, then handed it to Coughlin.

"It'll come in handy," Lowenstein said. "You know about the doers' camera?"

"No, sir."

"You ever been on television, Detective?" Lowenstein asked.

"No, sir."

"Well, unless I'm mistaken, when Commissioner Coughlin goes outside in a couple of minutes, to tell the press why the officers couldn't take the door, he's going to want you to go with him, to repeat what you just said about the mother understanding. Could you handle that?"

"I'd rather not—"

"That's not what I asked," Lowenstein snapped.

"Yes, sir, I can handle that."

"I haven't said I'm going outside to talk to the press," Coughlin said.

"Oh, excuse me, Commissioner, I thought you had."

"I just had a brilliant idea, Chief Lowenstein," Coughlin said. "Since you're so good at it, I'll reassign you to Public Relations."

"Unless we do something, we'll all look as stupid as the mayor thinks we are," Lowenstein replied, unabashed. "You got a better idea, Denny?"

"No," Coughlin said. "As a matter of fact, I was trying to think of a way to thank you that wouldn't go directly to your head."

"You're welcome," Lowenstein said. "Can I make another suggestion?"

"How can I stop you?"

"Detective Lassiter has dealt very well with the mother and the brother. We don't know that possible problem has gone away permanently. . . ."

"And you want to detail her to Homicide for this job so she can sit on them?" Coughlin asked.

"That, too, but what I was thinking was that you could say, 'Detective Lassiter, who has been detailed to Homicide for this investigation, has spoken to Miss Williamson's brother and her mother. They have found no fault with police procedures, isn't that right, Detective?' "

"I don't know," Coughlin said, doubtfully.

"You have any problems with Northwest detailing Detective Lassiter to Homicide for this job, Captain Quaire?" Lowenstein asked.

"No, sir," Quaire said.

"Lieutenant Washington?"

"No, sir."

"You, Lieutenant?"

"No, sir," the lieutenant from Northwest Detectives said.

"Okay, done," Lowenstein said.

He gestured toward the kitchen door.

"You're on, Commissioner," he said.

Coughlin exhaled audibly, straightened his shoulders, and marched through it. Captain Frank Hollaran and Detective Lassiter followed him.

"There's a TV in the living room," D'Amata said. "There's a *Channel Six Live* camera out there."

D'Amata got it turned on and tuned to Channel Six by the time Coughlin, Hollaran, and Lassiter appeared on the screen as they came out of the walkway between the two buildings.

Coughlin marched to the massed press, with Olivia Lassiter following him. When he stopped, just inside the crime scene tape, she moved to his side.

There were shouted questions from a dozen reporters, to which Coughlin, his arms folded on his stomach, paid no attention whatever. Finally, almost in confusion, the questions died out.

"I'm Deputy Commissioner Coughlin," he said, finally. "I will take a few questions, one at a time."

Most of the reporters raised their hands; several shouted questions.

Coughlin pointed at one of the reporters who had raised her hand.

"If you can get these *gentlemen* to behave, I'll take your question."

One of the reporters who had been shouting a question said, disgustedly, "Oh, for Christ's sake!"

Another voice, female, very clearly answered her colleague with, "Why don't you shut the fuck up, you asshole? Some of us have deadlines."

Coughlin pointed to a reporter holding a microphone with a *Channel Six Live* sign on it.

"I don't want to tell you your business," he said, very politely, "but I really hope someone bleeped *that* question before it got on the air."

That brought laughter. When it died down, he pointed to the reporter he had selected before.

"Commissioner, what's happened here?"

"A murder," Coughlin said, "of a young woman named Cheryl Williamson."

"Not a rape and murder?"

"We don't know that yet. The medical examiner will make that determination."

"Is it true that somebody called 911, the cops came, and then refused to enter the apartment, while the murderer was inside?"

"A few minutes before two this morning, Miss Williamson's neighbor called 911, reporting that her mirror had fallen off the wall. Two patrol cars—not just one—of the Thirty-fifth District responded, and were here in just under four minutes. They listened to what the neighbor said, that she suspected that something had happened in Miss Williamson's apartment that had caused her mirror to fall off the wall. The officers rang Miss Williamson's doorbell and knocked at the door. They did that at both the front and rear doors. And they looked for signs of a forced entry and found none. There were no lights on in the apartment, and they could hear no sounds. They concluded there was no one in the apartment."

"And left?"

"And left."

"Why didn't they go in the apartment?"

"Because that would be against the law," Coughlin said. "Without sufficient cause, police have no right to break into anyone's home."

"The neighbor said, you said, that she thought something had happened in the apartment. That's not sufficient cause?"

"If there had been any sound, even any lights burning, any indication of forced entry, I'm sure they would have entered the apartment. There wasn't, and they didn't."

"And how do you think her family will react to that explanation?"

"This is Detective Lassiter," Coughlin said. "She can answer that better than I can."

"I've spoken to Miss Williamson's mother and brother," Olivia said. "They both told me they understand why the police did not break into the apartment. Mrs. Williamson said all that she wants is for the police to find whoever did this to her daughter before the same sort of thing happens to someone else."

"And what exactly did this guy do to her?"

"At this point, we don't even know it was a guy," Olivia said. "We just started the investigation. Commissioner, may I be excused?"

"Yes, you can, Detective, and I am about to excuse myself," Coughlin said. "Whenever we learn more, we will make it available to the press. Thank you."

. . .

"He's very good at that," Lowenstein said, in the apartment. "We look a lot better than we did five minutes ago."

Everyone agreed, but no one said anything.

Lowenstein looked around and found Jason Washington.

"You know O'Hara's cell phone number?"

"Yes, sir."

"I think it would be a very good idea for you to meet with him, now. Take Payne and Lassiter with you."

"Yes, sir."

"As for the rest of you, one or two at a time, not all at once, get out of here and let the Homicide people do their job."

There were nods of understanding and a few "Yes, sir"s.

Chief Inspector of Detectives Lowenstein had two more thoughts:

"If you don't mind a suggestion, Sergeant Payne," he said. "I think that you personally should try to run down connecting the camera with the doer."

"Yes, sir."

"And I think it might be useful if you asked Dr. Payne to look at those pictures. Do you think she would be willing to do that?"

"I'm sure she would, sir."

"Chief," Captain Durwinsky said, "I'd like to have copies of those pictures as soon as I can have them. We may be dealing with the same doer."

"How can that be done, Payne?"

"All I need is access to a computer with a digital photo program and a color printer," Matt said.

"We've got one at Special Victims," Durwinsky said. "That's not far."

"Okay," Lowenstein said. "There it is. O'Hara, Special Victims, your sister and running down the doer via the camera. Got it?"

"Yes, sir," Matt said.

"O'Hara first, Chief?" Captain Durwinsky asked.

"Yeah, Helene," Lowenstein said. "O'Hara first. I would like to see at least one story in the newspapers that doesn't gleefully point out our many failures and all-around stupidity. Okay?"

"Yes, sir."

"Okay. Now everybody get to work."

Lowenstein walked out of the apartment.

[TWO]

In the hope that it wouldn't be seen, Michael J. O'Hara of the *Philadelphia Bulletin* parked his Buick Rendezvous behind the Oak Lane Diner at Broad and Old York Road. The Rendezvous, with its array of antennae, was known to other members of the Philadelphia press corps, and some of his colleagues were even bright enough to be able to spot an unmarked car, and wonder what O'Hara was up to with the cops.

Mickey entered the diner and, after looking around, found Lieutenant Jason Washington, Sergeant Matt Payne, and that good-looking detective who'd come out of the crime scene with Denny Coughlin to face the press, at a banquette in the rear, drinking coffee.

He walked to them and slid in beside Washington.

"Well, isn't this a *coincidence*!" O'Hara said. "Mind if I sit down?"

"I hoped you parked that conspicuous vehicle of yours where it will not attract the attention of the Fourth Estate?" Washington asked.

"Jesus!" Mickey said, his tone suggesting that Washington should have known the question was unnecessary. He smiled at Detective Lassiter. "I'm Mickey O'Hara."

"Yes, sir, I know who you are," Olivia said.

Mickey shook his head sadly, gave out a long sigh, and turned to Matt.

"You're in luck, Matthew," O'Hara said. "This beauty—this young beauty—calls me 'sir,' which means she has decided I am too old to merit her interest."

"As obviously you are," Washington said.

"Then, speaking with the wisdom of a senior citizen, my beauty, let me advise you to beware of this young man. While some think of him as the Wyatt Earp of the Main Line, others more accurately describe him as the Casanova of Center City."

"That's not funny, Mick," Matt flared.

"Which part?"

"The Wyatt Earp part," Matt said. "As a matter of fact, both parts."

"One day, my beauty . . ."

"My name is Lassiter," Olivia said.

"One day, *Lassiter*, my beauty," O'Hara went on, "not so long ago, in an alley of our fair city, Wyatt Earp here put down a very bad guy who was shooting at both of us with a .45. I meant nothing but respect in dubbing him Wyatt Earp."

"As disassociated as I am from the realities of life," Washington said, "I actually thought you would be interested in learning what has transpired at 600 Independence."

"I *know* what happened at 600 Independence. A citizen called 911 when she heard strange noises in the next apartment. Two uniforms responded, and they all stood around chatting and not taking the door while the doer worked his wicked way on the victim. What else do I need to know?"

"You know why they didn't—couldn't—take the door?"

"This is not at all what I expected when you called, Jason, my oversized old pal," Mickey said.

"Excuse me?" Washington said.

"When you summoned me, I expected to find you, Tony Harris, and that black kid from the Roy Rogers—you do recall asking if I would mind going over the whole thing from Step One once again with the aforementioned?"

"That's at five o'clock this afternoon. That's when you said you'd be free and when the kid gets off work," Washington said.

"Then you called again, Jason, twenty minutes ago, and asked if I was free to come here now, and I said yes, and I walk in here, and not only do I get Wyatt Earp and the beauty here, instead of the expected aforementioned, but you ask me the really dumb question 'do I know why Hyde and Cubellis didn't take the victim's door?'"

"How'd you know their names?" Olivia blurted.

"I wouldn't want this to get around, my beauty, but some of my friends are cops."

"And?" Washington asked.

"What you've got are two nice young cops who are sick about maybe being outside doing nothing while this critter was doing what he did to the girl— that's their first reaction—and second, they are naturally a little worried that the mayor is going to hang them out to turn in the wind. I don't intend to let that happen. I'm going to do one of my famous think pieces. My working slug is 'A tough call, but the right one.'"

"Thanks, Mick," Washington said. "That's what I was hoping to hear."

"It would help if I knew a little about the doer, or maybe what he did to her."

"All we really know about him is that he is unquestionably a psychopath," Washington said.

"Isn't that a given with a rapist?"

"This guy is sick, Mick," Washington said.

"How do you know that?"

Washington hesitated just perceptibly.

"Not for publication?"

"Agreed."

"Show him the pictures, Matt," Washington ordered, and added: "He left his camera behind."

Matt took his laptop from his briefcase and slid it across the table.

"You know how to work Photo Smart?"

"Another unnecessary question."

"The pictures are in 'Wilifoto,' " Matt said.

O'Hara turned the laptop on and started the Photo Smart program.

"This fellow *is* a bit odd, isn't he?" Mickey said, looking at the first picture, and then, as he ran through the images, twice added: "Jesus H. Christ!"

"May I see those?" Olivia asked.

"No," Mickey said. "You really don't want to see them."

"I'm a cop, Mr. O'Hara," she said.

"Of that I have no doubt, my beauty," O'Hara said, as he turned the computer off and closed the lid, "but you are also indisputably a very nice young woman. My sainted mother would never forgive me if I showed those images to a very nice young woman."

He slid the laptop back across the table.

"You going to get him?" he asked.

"Still off the record?" Washington asked. O'Hara nodded. "All we have right now is the camera. They're serially numbered, and we're going to try that."

"Good luck," O'Hara said, getting to his feet. "This guy needs bagging, and soon."

"I'll keep you posted, Mick," Washington said.

"I'm counting on that," O'Hara said. He looked at Olivia. "Remember what I said about the Casanova of Center City, my beauty."

"Oh, for Christ's sake, Mickey!" Matt said.

"Parting is such sweet sorrow," O'Hara proclaimed, and walked out of the diner.

"We have a transportation problem," Washington said. "I rode out here with Captain Quaire. I have to get back. . . ."

Matt reached into his pocket and handed him the keys to his unmarked car.

"I'll ride with Lassiter," he said.

"I'm going to have to give my car back to Northwest," she said.

"You are very bright youngsters," Washington said. "I'm sure you'll be able to sort this out." He slid across the banquette and stood up, and added: "You can have your car back later—sometime after I meet with Tony, O'Hara, and the kid from the Roy Rogers. Okay if I leave it at the Roundhouse, the keys with the uniform in the lobby?"

"Fine," Matt said.

"Welcome to Homicide, Detective Lassiter," Washington said. "And I wouldn't worry too much about Sergeant Payne. His Lothario reputation is really far darker than the facts justify."

He walked away from the table.

After a moment, Olivia asked, "Special Victims?"

"I'm thinking," Matt said. "Sometimes that takes a little time."

"And I'd like to see those pictures."

He didn't reply.

"I'll be right back," he said.

She watched as he walked to a pay telephone booth in the front of the diner and looked in the yellow pages telephone book. He punched at the keys of his cellular for a moment, then returned to the table.

"What?" Olivia asked.

"Watch," he said, and pushed the Call button on his cellular phone.

"Center City Photo? I need to talk to someone about Kodak digital cameras."

Getting the correct number at Kodak from Center City Photo was like pulling teeth. The Eastman Kodak Company in Rochester, New York—once Matt had identified himself as Sergeant Payne of the Philadelphia police department Homicide Unit—was very cooperative. It would take them a little time to run the serial number down—was there a number where he could be reached?

Their call came as Olivia was pulling up before the Special Victims building at the Frankford Arsenal.

Their records indicated that a digital camera with that serial number had been shipped, as part of an order for a dozen identical cameras, five months before, to Times Square Photo & Electronics, 17 West Forty-second Street, New York City.

"That camera comes with an overnight FedEx replacement, right?"

"That's right, Sergeant, it does. And I checked to see if that program had been activated for that camera. It hadn't."

Oh, shit. But what did I expect? That this critter was going to leave a trail for me?

"But that sometimes happens," the lady from Kodak went on. "People some-times don't activate the program until they have problems with the camera."

Am I going to get lucky?

"You don't have a phone number of Times Square Photo, by any chance, do you?"

She gave it to him.

"Thank you very much," Sergeant Payne said. "I really appreciate your cooperation."

The two people at Times Square Photo with whom Sergeant Payne spoke on his cellular were not nearly so cooperative. The first person, a male, spoke only a few words of English, and the second, a female he finally managed to get on the line, had only a few more words of English than did her male colleague.

These were sufficient, however, to make Sergeant Payne understand that she couldn't do nothing like consult her records of sale for just anybody, that she was trying to run a business, for Christ's sake, and at that moment she had customers she had to take care of. For Christ's sake.

"Did you understand me when I said this is Sergeant Payne of the Homi-cide Unit of the Philadelphia police department?"

"No shit? Good for you. Good luck. Have a nice day."

And at that point she hung up.

"Sonofabitch!" Matt said, then, to Olivia, "Sorry."

"I have heard the expression before," Detective Lassiter said.

Matt held the key that automatically dialed the office of Amelia S. Payne, M.D. He was informed that Dr. Payne was with a patient.

"This is Sergeant Payne. This is official police business. Get her on the phone, please."

Dr. Payne came on the line thirty seconds later.

"Matt, this had better really be police business."

"It is. I'm working a murder."

"Not the one where the cops stood around outside her apartment shooting the breeze while the girl was murdered and raped?"

"I didn't know you listened to Philadelphia Phil, Amy."

"My secretary does. And it's *Phil's Philly*."

"That's not exactly the way it happened, Amy."

"Of course not," she said, sarcastically.

"Are you scrapping with Peter again, or is there some other reason you're being such a bitch?"

"What do you want, Matthew?"

"The doer left his digital camera at the scene. With pictures of the act. Chief Lowenstein wants you to look at them."

"Just Chief Lowenstein?"

"Me, too, Amy, okay?"

"Okay. Bring them by. I'll take a look."

"I'm about to print them. I'll be there in thirty, thirty-five minutes."

"Okay," Amy said, and hung up.

[THREE]

The Special Victims Unit did not have a color printer the quality of the one Mickey O'Hara had had the *Bulletin* buy for him. It was slow, there were eight images, and Matt made what he quickly realized was an error when he pushed the button that caused the printer to make three prints of each image.

He needed a set for Amy, of course. And the price of using their printer was a set for Special Victims, and a third set was necessary for Jason Washington, both for his edification and to make sure there was no screwup when the Forensics lab finally got the flash memory card and made the official prints.

The result of this was that it took thirty-six minutes for the printer to do the job, and as they came slowly out of the printer Detectives Lassiter and Domenico had the opportunity to take good, long looks at all of them. Matt didn't give a damn about Domenico, but he was made uneasy by Detective Lassiter's reaction. Her face made it evident that she was trying and failing to examine the photographs with calm professionalism.

When they were finally outside, in Detective Lassiter's more than a little beat-up unmarked car, she looked at him for orders.

"We're a little pressed for time— What do I call you? 'Olivia' all right?"

"Fine, Sergeant."

"We're a little pressed for time, Olivia. I think you should meet my sister; you'll probably have to see her again, so we'll go to the university first. Then, since Washington grabbed my car, we'll go to my place so I can pick up my car.

I'm going to New York. Then I want you to drop a set of pictures off at Homicide. If Lieutenant Washington is there—or Captain Quaire—give them to one of them. If not, seal the envelope and give it to the man on the wheel for Washington. Then I think you'd better go call on the Williamsons again. Get their statements."

"What do I do about getting this car back to Northwest Detectives?"

"We'll deal with that later," Matt said. "The priorities right now, I think, are to see if I can run this critter down through the camera store, and to keep the Williamsons happy."

"Happy?" she asked, sarcastically.

"You know what I mean."

[FOUR]

"Well, what did you think of my sister?" Matt asked when they were back in the unmarked car outside the University of Pennsylvania Hospital.

"She's nice," Olivia said. "And she's a professor of psychiatry?'

"Too young, you mean?" Matt asked, and Olivia nodded. "She got her M.D. at twenty-four. I wouldn't want you to quote me, but she's smart as hell. And she really can get into the minds of psychopaths. This isn't the first time she's helped. She'll probably give us a pretty good picture of how this guy thinks."

"Where to now?" Olivia asked.

"The Delaware Valley Cancer Society Building, South Rittenhouse Square."

"What are we going to do there?"

"I live there," Matt said, and waited for her curiosity to overwhelm him. It didn't.

When she pulled to the curb in front of the Cancer Society Building, Matt said, "You've got my cellular number?"

"And you've got mine," Olivia said.

"See you later," Matt said.

"Right," Olivia said.

He got the Porsche out of the basement garage and headed for New York. When he was out of Center City traffic—on I-95 North—he slipped his cellular into a dash-mounted rack, which permitted hands-off operation, and punched in Joe D'Amata's number.

"D'Amata."

"Payne. I'm on my way to New York, unless you need me there."

"There's not much you can do here," D'Amata said. "The crime lab folks are just about finished. Slayberg's done the scene. We got statements from both McGrorys. What I'd like to do is get the Williamsons' statements."

"I got a statement from the brother," Matt said.

"Then just the mother, then."

"Olivia's on her way to the Roundhouse to deliver the pictures to Washington—"

"He's not there," D'Amata interrupted. "He called to say if I needed him, if we needed him, he's going to take another look at the Roy Rogers."

"He's going to meet with O'Hara, Harris, and the black kid witness at five o'clock, to start all over again."

"So he told me."

"Olivia's going from the Roundhouse to see the Williamsons."

"*Olivia* is, is she?"

"Fuck you, Joe."

"I think that's what they call 'verbal abuse of a subordinate,' Sergeant. You'll be hearing from the FOP."

"Then fuck you twice, Joe," Matt said.

D'Amata laughed.

"You have the Williamson mother's address?" Matt asked.

"No, but I probably can get it from Detective Lassiter."

"I've got her cell number. You need it?"

"Yeah."

Matt gave it to him, then said, "Tell her that I said I want her to introduce you to the Williamsons as the lead detective on the case. Maybe 'senior homicide investigator' would be better."

There was a pause while D'Amata considered that.

"Lassiter's got them calmed down, and we want to show them how hard we're working, right?"

"Yeah. Make sense to you?"

"Yeah. That *Philly Phil* asshole business is still dangerous. My *wife* called and asked me what the hell was wrong with the uniforms, they didn't take the door."

"Well, let's keep the Williamsons stroked."

"Consider it done," D'Amata said. "If anything comes up, I'll call you."

"Same here."

"That digital camera's a long shot, Matt. But let's hope we get lucky."

"Amen, Brother."

[FIVE]

Sergeant Zachary Hobbs, a stocky, ruddy-faced forty-four-year-old, was holding down the desk in Homicide when Detective Lassiter walked through the outer door.

Detective Kenneth J. Summers, who should have been working the desk, was meeting a lengthy call of nature, which he blamed on something he must have eaten at the church supper of St. Paul's Lutheran Church the previous evening.

"Can I help you?" Hobbs asked. He was not immune to Detective Lassiter's looks.

"Lieutenant Washington?"

"I'm sorry, he's not here."

"Captain Quaire?"

"He's not here either. Can I do something for you?"

"Would you give whichever of them comes in first this envelope, please?" She handed it to him.

"Sure." He weighed it in his hands. "What is it?"

"It's from Sergeant Payne," Olivia said.

Hobbs looked at her, waiting for her to go on. After a moment's hesitation, she did.

"It's photographs of the victim in the Independence Street job."

Sergeant Hobbs immediately tore the envelope open and looked at the eight photographs.

"Where the hell did Payne get these?" Hobbs asked.

"The doer forgot his digital camera at the scene. Sergeant Payne downloaded the images to his laptop, and Special Victims printed them for us."

"Next question: Who are you, Detective? How did you get them?"

"My name is Lassiter," Olivia said. "Northwest. I've been detailed to Homicide. Sergeant Payne told me to bring them here."

"Detailed? By who?"

"Chief Lowenstein," Olivia said.

"Well, so long as you're with us, Detective, you're certainly going to bring a little class to the premises," Hobbs said. "Where's the camera?"

"Detective D'Amata has it," Olivia said.

"Okay. As soon as either the boss or the Black Buddha comes in, I'll see they get these. They may want to talk to you. . . ."

"I'll give you my cell phone number," she said, and did.

"Where will you be?"

"I'm going to take the victim's mother's statement," she said.

"Sergeant Payne told you to?"

"Yes, he did."

He looked at her a moment, then said, "Welcome, welcome. Would you be offended if I said you're the best-looking detective to come in here in my memory?"

"Not at all," Olivia said, and smiled at him. "Thanks."

"My pleasure," Hobbs said. "See you around."

In the best of all possible worlds, Olivia thought, as she left Homicide and the Roundhouse and got in her unmarked car, the encounter between herself and Sergeant Hobbs of Homicide would have been entirely professional and gender-neutral.

But the Philadelphia police department was not the best of all possible worlds, and Sergeant Hobbs had made it clear that he found her to be an attractive member of the female gender.

So what was wrong with that?

He wondered who the hell I was, which was natural, and he really wondered, which was even more natural, who had detailed me, even temporarily, to Homicide. Once I told him Lowenstein, that was the end of it.

It really couldn't have gone any better.

When Olivia Lassiter, then just shy of her twenty-first birthday, and a junior at Temple University, majoring in mass market communications, had told her parents that she had taken, and passed, the entrance application for the Philadelphia police department, and that she intended to drop out of college to enter the Police Academy, their reaction had been the opposite of unbridled joy.

Her father, a midlevel executive with an insurance company, had spoken his mind. "You're crazy. You have gone over the edge! You should be locked up for your own protection."

Her mother, a buyer for John Wanamaker & Company, had said more or less the same thing, then tried tears approaching hysteria, and said she was throwing her life and "the advantages Daddy and I have given to you" away.

Olivia had dropped out of Temple and entered the Police Academy and graduated and did a year working a van in the Ninth District, and then a second year in the Central City Business District. Truth to tell, she hadn't liked either job, and there had been a strong temptation to accept her father's offer to go back to college, get her degree, and make something of herself.

But that would have been admitting she'd made a mistake. And she hadn't been quite prepared to do that. She had been on the job just over a year when a detective's examination was announced. She took it, and passed it, ranking just high enough to get promoted—among the last few promoted from that list—eighteen months later.

That had put her in Northwest Detectives. From the first day, she'd liked being a detective, even though she was aware she was conducting a lot of investigations—of recovered stolen automobiles, in particular—that none of her new colleagues on the squad wanted to do.

It took her several years to pay off her car note and the furniture note, but that happened, too, about the time she realized she was no longer regarded by the squad as the "rookie broad," but as one of them.

She knew that she was not very popular with some of the wives and girlfriends of the guys on the squad—they seemed to suspect that the first order of business every day was to jump Detective Lassiter's bones—but there was nothing she could do about that, even if it was unfair as hell, and untrue. She had no interest, that way, in any of the guys.

She had taken the sergeant's exam, placing so low on the list that her chances of promotion were about as good as those of her being taken bodily into heaven. Her ego had been a little damaged—she hadn't thought she would do *that* badly—but it really hadn't bothered her. She liked the squad, she liked Northwest Detectives, and a promotion would have meant not only leaving the Detective Bureau but almost certainly being put back in uniform. Since she had been on the job, she had compiled a long list of uniform sergeant's jobs she really would have hated.

The bottom line there was that she liked what she was doing and had no reason to feel sorry for herself. She had wondered idly about going someplace else as a detective, and had snooped around Special Victims and Major Crimes and Intelligence enough to know that she was better off with Northwest Detectives. The District Attorney's Squad was a possibility to think of, and so was Special Operations, and for that matter even Homicide.

Olivia thought of herself as a realist, and understood that her chances of getting assigned to Homicide—even in ten years—were practically nonexistent.

But now this had been dumped in her lap, this detail—however long it lasted—to Homicide. There was no question at all that Opportunity Had Knocked, but there was a big question about how to deal with it. If she played it right, there was a chance—slim, but a chance—that it would help her get into Homicide. Maybe not now. But later.

And if she screwed up somehow, in any way, she knew she could kiss any chances of getting into Homicide farewell forever.

Olivia had just turned onto North Broad Street when her cell phone buzzed. She fumbled in her purse for it and finally pushed Answer.

"Lassiter."

"D'Amata. You know who I am?"

"Yeah, sure."

"I want you to start thinking of me as the senior homicide investigator on this case," D'Amata said. "Not just some ordinary Homicide schmuck."

"Okay. You want to tell me why?"

"Because when I told our beloved leader, Sergeant Payne, that I wanted to go with you to take the Williamson mother's statement, he said sure, but tell her to introduce you as 'the senior homicide investigator on the case.'"

"He say why?"

"Our orders, Detective Lassiter, are to keep the Williamsons stroked. I think it's a good idea. Our leader is as smart as a whip."

"Okay. Whatever you say. I'm on North Broad, six blocks from City Hall, en route to Mother Williamson's. You need the address?"

"Yeah."

"404 Rockland. It's just south of Roosevelt Boulevard."

"I know where it is. I'll meet you there. On the street. Either I wait or you wait, okay? Payne wants us together."

"See you there."

Olivia pushed the End button and dropped the phone back into her purse.

Sergeant Matthew Payne, she thought, was very likely going to cause some sort of problems for her vis-à-vis making the best of her opportunity to try to get into Homicide.

She had known who Detective Payne was before he walked into Cheryl Williamson's living room. She had seen him on television when there had been the shooting in Doylestown, covered with that poor girl's blood, tears running down his cheeks. It had made her cry.

And, purely as a matter of female curiosity, when she finally got her hands on the new sergeants list, she had looked to see who had scored well.

Detective Payne of Special Operations had scored number one.

The first time she had seen him in the flesh was when he walked into Cheryl Williamson's living room. The first thing she'd thought was that he was even better looking than he'd looked on television, and the second thing was *Christ, not now. I have never before been physically attracted to anyone on the job. Not now, please God, and not a hotshot like this one.*

The one thing I could do for sure that would screw up my chances of getting into Homicide would be for me to get involved with their fair-haired boy. And I will not. Not. Not.

CHAPTER 10

[ONE]

Matt more or less obeyed the speed limits crossing New Jersey. It was a temptation not to, but he was driving the Porsche, and from painful experience he had come to believe that so far as the New Jersey State Police were concerned, ticketing a Porsche often was the high point of their tour, giving them great joy and satisfaction.

As he came out of the Lincoln Tunnel, he looked at his watch. It was half past two, which explained why his stomach was telling him he was hungry. He turned downtown, and ten minutes later turned onto West Forty-second Street toward Times Square. Just before he got there, he saw Times Square Photo.

Now the question was finding someplace to park, someplace where the parking attendants might not find great joy and satisfaction in seeing how deeply they could scratch the glistening silver paint of a Porsche.

He moved through the crowded streets, and a few minutes later found himself entering Times Square again from the north. The only parking places he had found had SORRY, FULL signs in front of them.

He noticed, at first idly and then with great interest, an automobile—a somewhat battered black Ford Crown Victoria—parked on the right curb between Forty-third and Forty-fourth Streets, right beside a sign reading NO PARKING NO STOPPING AT ANY TIME. There were several antennae mounted on it, and it rode on black heavy-duty tires. The fenders were battered, and there were no wheel covers.

If that's not an unmarked car, my name is not Sherlock Holmes.

Matt pulled the Porsche to the curb in front of the Ford, then backed up until their bumpers almost touched.

The Ford's horn blew imperiously, and the driver put his arm out the window and gestured for him to move on.

Matt instead got out of the car.

Now he could see the driver and the man sitting behind him. The driver was heavyset and looked to be in his forties. His ample abdomen held his tweed sports coat apart and strained the buttons of his shirt. The man beside him was younger. He was wearing a leather jacket and a black turtleneck sweater. Matt thought he was in his mid-twenties.

Matt found his leather wallet with the badge and photo ID and took it out. He decided that standing on the sidewalk and speaking to the young man in the passenger seat would be safer than speaking to the driver, and went to that side of the car. The other choice would most likely have seen him rolled through Times Square under the wheels of a bus.

The young man rolled the window down.

"I'm Sergeant Payne, and—"

"Get in," the older man said, pointing to the rear seat.

Matt got in.

"Let me see that," the older man said, and Matt handed him his badge and photo ID.

"What can we do for you, Sergeant Payne?" the older man said, and then passed the ID to the younger one.

"I'm on the job, working a homicide," Matt said.

"You're not trying to tell me they *kill* people in the City of Brotherly Love?" the younger one said.

The older one chuckled.

"The doer left his camera at the scene," Matt said. "Kodak tells me they shipped it to Times Square Photo."

"Take the next right. It's right around the corner," the older one said.

"I called them before I came here," Matt said. "They spoke just enough English to make it clear they are not very cooperative."

"Welcome to New York," the younger one said. "Only a few of us speak English, and even fewer are cooperative."

The older one chuckled.

"The doer—"

"By 'doer,' you mean 'the suspected perpetrator'?" the younger one interrupted.

"Right. He's a real sicko—"

"By which you mean he's 'psychiatrically challenged,' right?" the younger one asked. "Has difficulty accepting the common concept of right and wrong as the *modus operandi* for his life?"

"Yeah, you could put it that way," Matt said. "I want to get this guy before he does it to another young woman."

"A noble thought," the young one said. "How could we be of assistance?"

"It would help me a hell of a lot if one of you would go into the store with me. I really need to have a look at their sales records."

"Presumably, Sergeant," the young one said, "this fishing expedition of yours has been cleared by the New York police department's Office of Inter-Agency Cooperation?"

Oh, shit!

"No. I haven't cleared anything with anybody. I just got in my car and drove here. This happened early today, and right now this is our best lead. I just acted on my urge."

The young man considered this a moment.

"Charley, take us out of service for ten minutes. I'm going to take a little walk with Sergeant Payne."

"Right, Lieutenant," the older one said, reaching for an under-the-dash microphone.

Lieutenant?

The young one got out of the passenger seat, then opened the rear door and motioned Matt out. Then he walked to the Porsche and got in.

Matt carefully watched the traffic and then quickly got behind the wheel.

"Do all the sergeants in Philadelphia get wheels like this?" the young man asked. Before Matt could reply, he ordered, "Two blocks down and make a right."

Matt got into the flow of traffic.

"I usually say it's something we took away from the drug industry," Matt said. "But the truth is, it's mine."

"They must pay better, one way or another, in Philadelphia," the young man said.

"My lieutenant borrowed my brand-new unmarked car," Matt said. "So I drove this, instead of taking the train."

"If one of my sergeants had a brand-new unmarked, I'd do the same," the young man said. "There's a parking garage on the left."

Okay, that makes you a lieutenant. What's a lieutenant doing sitting in an unmarked in the middle of Times Square?

"It says full."

"Some of us can read," the young man said. "Although I will admit we do have a number of people on the job who are literacy-challenged."

Matt pulled into the parking lot, nose to nose with a Mercedes. There was no room. He was blocking half the sidewalk.

The attendant came out, waving his hands, "no." He was wearing a beard and a turban.

"I think sign language is going to be necessary," the young lieutenant said, "and not because this fellow is *aurally* challenged."

He got out of the Porsche, took his badge from his pocket, and held it two inches from the bearded man's face. Then he signaled with arm gestures that the attendant was to move the Mercedes elsewhere so the Porsche could take its space.

The attendant waved his arms excitedly for a few moments, but then got into the Mercedes.

The lieutenant signaled, like a traffic officer, for Matt to back the Porsche up far enough to give the Mercedes room to pass. The Mercedes went around him, onto the street, and the lieutenant signaled for Matt to pull in.

Then he stood on the sidewalk waiting for Matt to get out of the car.

They walked back up Broadway to West Forty-second Street and into Times Square Photo.

Three people—two of them bearded and in turbans, the third a stout young woman whose flowing, ankle-length dress and gaudily painted wooden bead jewelry made Matt think of gypsies—descended, smiling broadly on them.

What they lacked in language skills they made up for with enthusiasm, offering Matt and the lieutenant cameras, tape recorders, and other items for sale, cheap.

"Get Whatshisname," the lieutenant ordered.

The three looked at him without comprehension.

"Get Whatshisname!" the lieutenant ordered, considerably louder.

Still no comprehension showed on the faces of the trio.

The lieutenant put his fingers in his mouth and whistled shrilly.

Almost immediately, another man in a neat turban and immaculately trimmed beard appeared. His suit and shirt were well-fitting, and he also wore a red vest with embroidered ducks in flight pattern.

He hurried up to them.

"Lieutenant Lacey," he said in British-accented English, "what a pleasant surprise! How may I be of service to you or this gentleman?"

"Tell him," Lieutenant Lacey said to Matt.

"Five months ago, you received a shipment of a dozen cameras from Kodak," Matt began.

"We receive shipments from Kodak virtually weekly," the man said. "They make a splendid product, and because we sell so many of them, we are in a position to offer them at the lowest possible prices. And in your case, of course, as a friend of Lieutenant Lacey, there will be a substantial additional discount. Permit me to show you—"

"I don't want to buy a camera, I want to know who you sold it to," Matt said, aware that Lieutenant Lacey was smiling at him.

"I will make you an offer you cannot refuse!"

"I have the serial number," Matt said.

"I gather this is an official visit, Lieutenant Lacey?" the man asked.

Lacey nodded.

"Sergeant Payne needs to know to whom you sold a particular camera."

"We are, of course, willing—I'll say eager—to cooperate with the police in every way."

"Is there a problem?" Lieutenant Lacey asked.

The man looked at Matt.

"You say the camera was shipped to us five months ago?"

Matt nodded.

"You know the model?"

Goddamn it, I don't.

"It's a rather expensive digital," Matt said.

"That only narrows the field down a smidgen, I fear," the man said.

"If I saw one, I'd know it."

"That sort of item is updated as often as the sun rises," the man said. "I rather doubt if it would still be in our inventory. You did say you have the serial number?"

"Yes, I do."

"Then it will be a simple matter to go through our sales records and find it. We assiduously record the serial numbers of all our better merchandise."

"Then we have no problem here?" Lieutenant Lacey asked.

"None whatever. I am delighted to be of service. I will return momentarily."

He headed for the back of the store.

"Good luck, Sergeant," Lacey said.

"Thanks very much, Lieutenant," Matt said.

"No thanks are required. I wasn't in here with you. I never ever saw you. I would never act in a case like this without the full authority—in writing—of the New York Police Department's Office of Inter-Agency Cooperation to do so."

He turned and walked out the door.

The turbaned man who spoke the Queen's English returned to where Matt stood a few minutes later, trailed by two turbaned men, each of whom held two large cardboard boxes in his arms.

He gestured rather imperiously for the men to place the boxes on a glass display case.

"The sales records are filed, Sergeant, to comply with IRS requirements, sequentially, or perhaps I should say chronologically. I have brought you the records for the last six months. If there is anything else I can do for you, please do not hesitate to ask."

Not quite an hour and a half later, Sergeant Payne found the sales slip he was looking for, near the top of the left stack of sales slips in Box Three.

The sales slips had been stored in the manner in which they had come out of the sales registry machines—that is to say, fan-folded. Each stack contained 250 sales slips. They had been placed in the storage boxes eight stacks high, six stacks to a box.

By the time Matt found what he was looking for, his feet hurt from standing, his stomach was in audible protest for being unfed, and his eyes watered.

And what he found wasn't much.

A Kodak Digital Science DC 410, Serial Number EKK84240087, had been sold for cash three and a half months previously to Mr. H. Ford, 400 Lincoln Lane, Detroit, Michigan. Mr. Ford's signature, at the bottom, acknowledging receipt of the camera in good working condition, was barely legible.

He then had a very hard time making the previously charming English-speaking proprietor understand that he would like, at the very least, a photocopy of the sales slip and would really like to have the sales slip itself.

Then he had an inspiration.

"What I really would like to have are several digital images of you. First in the act of separating that sales slip from the fanfold," Matt said. "And then another of you initialing the sales slip."

"And you have a camera?"

"No. But I thought if I bought one . . ."

"How interesting! I just happen to have a splendid, latest-model, state-of-the-art Kodak—a DC910 with fast-charge lithium batteries—that I could let you have at a substantial discount."

"The pictures, you understand, would be useless to me unless I had the actual sales slip itself?"

"You do have a credit card?"

"Of course."

"Of course you do. And nothing would give me greater pleasure than to cooperate with the police in this investigation."

A total of $967.50 and fifteen minutes later, Matt put a Ziploc bag in his briefcase. It held the original sales slip and a flash memory card holding images of the proprietor tearing the sales slip free from the others in the fanfold stack; initialing the sales slip; of himself initialing the sales slip; of himself and the proprietor each holding a corner of the sales slip; and a final shot of himself putting the sales slip in the Ziploc bag.

Counsel for the defense, he thought, would, considering the pictures, have a hard time raising doubt in the minds of a jury that he had acquired the real sales slip.

And he could give the Kodak DC910, with fast-charge lithium batteries, to his mother. She had expressed admiration for the camera he had given Amy, and it seemed only just that his mother get one that cost twice as much as Amy's.

Now all he had to do was find Mr. H. Ford, of 400 Lincoln Lane, Detroit, Michigan.

He walked back down through Times Square to the parking lot, and got into the Porsche. On his cellular telephone, he established contact with a Detroit directory assistance operator, who regretted to inform him they had no listing for a Mr. H. Ford at 400 Lincoln Lane in Detroit.

Matt had been prepared to be disappointed.

"Have you got a special listing for the Homicide Bureau, maybe Homicide Unit, something like that, of the Detroit police department?"

"Just the basic police department number."

"Give me that, please."

"Homicide, Sergeant Whaley."

"Sergeant, my name is Payne. I'm a sergeant in Homicide in Philadelphia."

"What can we do for Philadelphia?"

"I'm working a job where the doer left his camera at the scene. I traced it to the store where it was sold. According to their records, it was sold to a Mr. H. Ford of Lincoln Road in Detroit."

"And you're beginning to suspect there is maybe something a little fishy about the name and address, right?"

"To tell you the truth, yes, I am."

"Okay. So?"

"Maybe he once went to Detroit," Matt said. "Have you got any open cases of murder, or rape, or murder/rape where the doer tied the victim to a bed and then cut the victim's clothes off with a large knife?'

"Nice fellow, huh? That all you got?"

"This happened last night."

"You do know about the NCIC in Philadelphia?"

"We have inside plumbing and everything," Matt said. "And I don't mean to in any way undermine your faith in the FBI, but sometimes we suspect they don't give us everything out of their databases, including stuff we've put in."

"I can't think of any job like that offhand," Sergeant Whaley said. "But I'll ask around. You said your name was Payne?"

Matt spelled it for him and gave him Jason Washington's unlisted private number in the Roundhouse.

"I'll ask around, and if I turn up anything, I'll give you a call."

"Thank you very much," Matt said.

He pushed the End button, put the key in the ignition, and started to drive out of the parking lot.

The attendant jumped in front of the car, waving his arms.

It was necessary for Matt to dig out the credit card again, and sign a sales slip for $35.00 worth of parking before he could put the Porsche in gear and head uptown toward the Lincoln Tunnel.

He looked at his watch; it was quarter past five.

When he came out of the New Jersey exit of the Lincoln Tunnel, it looked very familiar and he wondered why. He rarely went to New York City, and when he did, he almost never drove, preferring the Metroliner, a really comfortable train on which one did not have to keep one eye open for the New Jersey State Police for being in violation of speeding and/or drinking laws.

It was a moment before he understood.

He saw it at least once a week, on television. The opening shot on *The Sopranos* was from the inside of New Jersey mob boss Tony Soprano's GMC Suburban as he came out of the tunnel.

Another segment of the TV show came to his mind. A New Jersey detective on the pad from the mob got caught at it, and jumped off a bridge.

That made him think of Captain Patrick Cassidy, whose sudden affluence—including his new Suburban—he had found to be completely legitimate.

If it had gone the other way, would Cassidy have taken a dive off the Benjamin Franklin Bridge? And would I have been at least tangentially responsible?

His reverie was interrupted by the tinkling of his cell phone.

"Payne."

"Where are you, Matthew?" Lieutenant Jason Washington's deep, rich voice demanded.

"I just came out of the Lincoln Tunnel on my way back."

"And what developed in New York?"

"The camera was sold to an H. Ford of Lincoln Road in Detroit," Matt said.

"Well, one never knows. There is a credible legend that Jack the Ripper was the King's brother."

"So I have heard. I've got the original sales slip, with a signature on it, in a Ziploc."

"How did you get that?"

"I explained how important it was to the proprietor, and then bought a nine-hundred-dollar camera, after which he gave it to me."

"There's a slim chance, if he signed it, we might get a print."

"Yeah."

Shit, I didn't even think about that. Oh, Jesus! If there are prints on there, they'll be the proprietor's and mine. There's no excuse for such stupidity.

"You're going to have to come to the office anyway, to get a property receipt for the sales slip, so I'll leave the keys to your car in the FOP mug on my desk," Washington said.

"You mean I'm getting it back?"

"You had doubts? I'm your lieutenant, Matthew. You can trust me," Washington said, and added, "I'm driving Martha's car, less because of spousal generosity than because she wanted to ensure my presence at a cultural event at the Fine Arts at seven-thirty."

"Have fun."

"If fortune smiles upon me, I may even be afforded the privilege of physical proximity to our beloved mayor."

Matt chuckled.

"I am at the moment en route to meet with Tony, Mickey, and the witness from the Roy Rogers," Washington went on. "If there are developments, call me between now and seven-thirty."

"Yes, sir."

"Otherwise, after ten, call me to report your progress or lack thereof. But do not call me while I am at the Fine Arts unless what you have to say is really important."

"Yes, sir."

"And drive carefully, always adhering to the posted speed limits of the Garden State, Matthew."

"Yes, sir."

The line went dead.

[TWO]

Detective Tony Harris, Amal al Zaid, and Michael J. O'Hara were sitting in the rearmost banquette of the Roy Rogers restaurant at Broad and Snyder Streets when Amal saw an automobile pull to the curb outside.

"Get those wheels," he blurted in something close to awe. "That's an SL600!"

"What's an SL600?" Tony Harris asked, looking. "You mean the Mercedes?"

"V-12 engine," Amal al Zaid said. "Six liters!"

A large black man in a dinner jacket got out of the Mercedes SL600.

"V-12?" Tony asked. "No shit? What's one of those worth?"

"V-12," Amal al Zaid confirmed. "That's worth at least a *hundred thousand* bucks!"

"Jesus," Tony said.

"More like a hundred and a quarter, kid," Mickey O'Hara said. "Well, I guess that's his coming-out present to himself."

"Excuse me?" Amal al Zaid asked.

"What did he get, Tony? Ten to fifteen?" Mickey asked.

Tony Harris shrugged.

"Or was it fifteen to twenty?" Mickey mused. "Well, whatever, he's out, obviously. Who said 'crime doesn't pay'?"

Tony Harris raised his eyebrows but said nothing.

Amal al Zaid nearly turned around on the banquette to follow the guy in the tuxedo who had gotten out of the Mercedes-Benz SL600.

"It looks like he's coming in here!" Amal al Zaid said.

"Why would a heavy hitter hood like that come in a dump like this?" O'Hara asked rhetorically.

Lieutenant Jason Washington walked through the restaurant, slid onto the banquette seat beside O'Hara, quickly shook hands with O'Hara and Harris, and then smiled cordially at Amal al Zaid.

"Thank you for coming," he said. "I really appreciate your time."

Amal al Zaid said nothing.

"I'm Lieutenant Washington," Jason said, oozing charm.

He had told Tony Harris to ask the witness to meet them in the Roy Rogers in the belief he would be more comfortable there than he would have been, for example, in the Homicide unit in the Roundhouse.

Amal al Zaid said nothing.

"Actually, I'm Detective Harris's—Tony's—supervisor."

"You're a cop?" Amal al Zaid asked, incredulously.

"I realize that dressed like this—I'm going to sort of a party with my wife. . . ." He paused, and then asked, "What did Mr. O'Hara tell you about me?"

"He said you just got out," Amal al Zaid said.

"Actually, sir," Tony Harris said. "The phrases Mr. O'Hara used were 'fifteen to twenty' and 'heavy hitter hood.'"

Washington came out with his badge and photo ID, and showed it to Amal al Zaid.

"Mr. O'Hara is an old friend," he said. "Despite a well-earned reputation for a really weird sense of humor."

"*I'm* weird?" O'Hara asked. "You're the first man in recorded history to walk into a Roy Rogers in a waiter suit."

"It's not a waiter suit, you ignoramus."

"It looks like a waiter suit to me," Mickey said. "What about you—Double-A Zee?"

Amal al Zaid giggled and nodded his head in agreement.

"Are you going to take our order, or is there something else Double-A Zee and I can do for the cops?" Mickey asked.

Amal al Zaid giggled again.

"Do you mind if he calls you that?" Washington asked.

Amal al Zaid shook his head, "no."

"Can I call you that?"

"Sure."

"Thank you," Washington said. "Okay, Double-A Zee, let me tell you where we are in finding the people who murdered Mrs. Martinez and Officer Charlton." He paused.

Amal al Zaid looked at him expectantly.

"Just about nowhere," Washington said, finally.

"How come?" Amal al Zaid asked.

Washington shrugged.

"We've done—and are still doing—everything we can think of. We're going to get them eventually. But the sooner we do, the sooner we can get them off the streets, the sooner they won't be able to do the same sort of thing again. We don't want any more people to die."

Amal al Zaid nodded his understanding.

"An investigation is something like taking an automobile trip," Washington said. "You can make a wrong turn and wind up in Hoboken when you really want to be in Harrisburg. I'm beginning to suspect that we've made a wrong turn, early on, and this is what this is all about.

"What we have here, where this trip began, are the only two witnesses who seem to know what they're talking about; the only two who kept their cool in terrifying circumstances—"

"I was scared shitless," Amal al Zaid corrected him.

"Make that two of us," O'Hara said.

Amal al Zaid looked at him with gratitude.

"Who kept their cool in terrifying circumstances," Washington repeated, "the proof of which, Double-A Zee, is your behavior in this from the beginning. And Mr. O'Hara's attempt to take a photograph when they came out of the restaurant—"

"Attempt's the right word," Mickey said. "All I got is an artsy fartsy silhouette."

Washington ignored the comment.

"So what we're going to do now," he went on, "is start from the beginning, once again, to see where we took the wrong turn. We're going to do this very slowly, to see where what you saw agrees with what Mickey saw, or where it disagrees. Detective Harris"—he pointed to a huge salesman's case on the banquette seat beside Harris—"has brought with him records and reports that he and others have compiled that he thinks will be useful. We're going to see if what you and Mickey saw agrees or disagrees with what other people saw, or thought they saw, and if it disagrees, how it disagrees. You still with me, Double-A Zee?"

"Yeah, I got it."

"If either you or Mickey thinks of something—anything—or if you have a question while we're doing this, speak up. I'll do the same. Okay?"

O'Hara and Amal al Zaid nodded their understanding.

"Let's get some more coffee," Washington said, waving for the attention of the shift manager, who was hovering nearby to see what he could see, "and then Tony can begin."

Tony Harris took a sheaf of paper from the salesman's case, took off a paper clip, and divided it into four.

"This is the chronology as I understand it," he said, as he slid copies to Washington, O'Hara, and Amal al Zaid.

"We know for sure that Mrs. Martinez called 911 at eleven-twenty P.M. We have that from Police Radio. And we know that at eleven-twenty-one, Police Radio dispatched Officer Charlton. So I sort of guessed the time of the events before that."

He waited until the shift manager had delivered a tray with coffee.

"If I get *any* of these details wrong, Double-A Zee, even if it doesn't seem important," Harris said, "speak up. Same for you, Mickey."

Both nodded again.

"Okay. Sequence of events," Harris said. "Double-A Zee was standing, there"—he pointed—"mopping the floor, when he saw the doers come into the restaurant. How long had you been there, Double-A Zee, when they came in?"

"A couple of minutes."

"A couple is two. Maybe several?"

"I keep the mop bucket right inside the kitchen door," Amal al Zaid said. "What happened was when I cleaned the table—"

"This table?" Harris interrupted.

"Yeah. I see that the people who'd left had knocked a cup of coffee—what was left of one—on the floor. So I went in the kitchen, got the mop and bucket, and come back. It wasn't a big spill, but it was right in front of the kitchen door—"

"The one on the left?" Harris interrupted.

"Yeah. The Out one, they come through with full trays and they couldn't see the spill."

"I understand," Harris said.

"So I figured I better clean it up quick, and I did."

"And you'd been there a couple, like two, minutes and the doers came in?"

"Right."

"Why did you notice, Double-A Zee?" Washington asked.

"Excuse me?"

"You were mopping the floor, paying attention to doing that. Why did you notice these two?"

Amal al Zaid thought that over carefully before replying: "I looked at the clock over the door. They was standing under it."

"And why did you pay attention to them?" Washington asked, softly.

"I could tell they was bad news," Amal al Zaid said.

"How?"

"The way they was standing, looking around. Nervous, you know? And the . . . I dunno. I just didn't like the look of them."

"Okay. So then what happened?"

"Then they split up. The one stayed in front, and the short fat guy came toward the back, toward here. That was funny."

"You had finished mopping the spill by then?" Harris asked.

"Yeah. Right. So I pushed the bucket back into the kitchen. And then I looked through the window and saw . . ."

"The window in the right door, the In door?" Harris asked, pointing.

"Yeah," Amal al Zaid said. "And I saw him take off his shade—"

"His glasses?" Harris interrupted. "Double-A Zee, I don't remember you saying anything before about him wearing glasses."

"Not glasses, his *shade*."

When he saw the lack of understanding on Harris's face, Amal al Zaid explained patiently, almost tolerantly: "You know, like a baseball cap, without a top."

"Oh," Harris said, understanding.

"The shade part was in the back," Amal al Zaid went on. He pointed at his neck. "I guess it got in his way."

"How was that?" Washington asked, softly.

"The wall," Amal al Zaid said. "He was sitting where you are. That cushion is against the wall." He pointed. "I guess when he sat down, his shade bumped into the wall. Anyway, he took it off."

"Okay," Harris said. "I'm a little dense. Then what happened?"

"Tony, would you hand me Mickey's pictures?" Washington asked.

"Any particular one?"

"Better let me have all of them."

"I thought," Amal al Zaid said, "the last time, you *told* me he took only one picture of these guys."

"There was only one image, Double-A Zee," Washington explained. "But they made a number of different prints, trying to see if they could come up with something useful. You know, they blew up different parts of the picture."

"Oh, yeah," Amal al Zaid said.

"I tried that myself," O'Hara said, "and got nowhere."

"What are you looking for, Jason?" Harris asked.

"I want to see if this fellow left the scene wearing his shade," Washington said. "Maybe Mickey's pictures will at least show that."

Tony Harris rummaged through the salesman's case and came out with a manila envelope stuffed with prints. There were, in all, about twenty prints of the one digital image Mickey O'Hara had made as he walked up to the Roy Rogers restaurant. Most were eight by ten inches, and most of them concentrated on the heads and shoulders of the doers, although the process had failed to overcome the bad quality and bring out more details than in the original print.

Washington began to examine each print carefully. After looking at perhaps ten of them, he set one aside.

"You got something?" Mickey asked.

Washington didn't reply.

After a moment, Mickey took the pictures Washington was finished with and started looking at them. As he finished the first one, he slid it across the table to Amal al Zaid, who looked at it and slid it to Harris. When Washington finished, he had set two more prints aside. He slid the rest to Mickey, then patiently waited until they were all through, before handing Mickey the three prints he had set aside.

"So far as I can determine from these," Washington said, "neither of these gentlemen was wearing anything on his cranium as they left the scene."

"I don't think a jury would fall in love with these," Mickey said. "But I do see silhouetted heads, and there ain't nothing on either of them."

Washington again waited until both Amal al Zaid and Tony Harris had examined all three prints.

"So what?" Amal al Zaid asked.

"This poses the question, Double-A Zee," Washington said. "If this fellow came into the restaurant wearing a shade, where is it now?"

Harris went back into the salesman's case.

He came out with a typewritten list.

"Here it is," he said. "On the unclaimed property list. Number fifteen. 'One black sun visor, make unknown, gray cotton-covered visor, plastic headband.'

They found it under the table. So far as prints are concerned. . . . 'One partially smudged print, possibly index finger, on rear of headband.'"

"That won't be enough, will it?" O'Hara asked.

"Oh, ye of little faith," Washington said.

He took out his cellular telephone and pushed an autodial key.

"Has Captain Quaire gone for the day?" he asked, and then a moment later, "Would you switch me to him, please?"

There was a brief pause.

"Lieutenant Washington, sir," he said, "with a request."

There was another pause.

"On the list of unclaimed property found in the Roy Rogers, as item fifteen, there is 'One black sun visor, make unknown, gray cotton-covered visor, plastic headband.' We have reason to believe it was left behind by one of the doers. The lab reports one partially smudged print, possibly index finger. I would like to inspire them to greater effort. This might be possible if you took the item down there personally, sir. . . ."

There was another brief pause.

"Thank you very much. And may I suggest that you tell them I will be in later tonight to check on their progress?" Pause. "Thanks, Henry. It's all that we have right now."

He pushed the End key and turned to Amal al Zaid.

"Double-A Zee, I think we're at the point where the doer took off his shade. What happened next?"

[THREE]

At twenty after six, just as he turned onto I-95 South, Matt's cellular rang.

"Payne."

"Sergeant, this is Lassiter."

"I have a surfeit of bad news, Detective Lassiter. With that caveat, you may proceed."

He thought he heard her giggle, and found it charming.

"No bad news. I just left the Williamsons' . . ."

"And?"

"Everything's under control. Their minister is there. I don't think she's going to change her mind about the uniforms being right in not taking the door. And I'm going back in the morning—she asked me to."

"You get a gold star to take home to Mommy, Detective Lassiter," Matt said.

"Sergeant," she said, a tone of exasperation in her voice, "Northwest wants their car back, that's one thing. The second thing is, Mrs. Williamson told me Cheryl used to hang out in a bar called Halligan's Pub. I'd like a look, but thought I'd better check with you first."

"Do they serve food in Halligan's Pub?"

"I don't know. I suppose so."

Matt looked at his watch.

"I'll meet you at Northwest in twenty-five, thirty minutes," he said. "You can give them their car back. Where is this Halligan's Pub?"

"In Flourtown."

"Okay. Then we will go together to Halligan's Pub. And after that, we'll see. Washington called. I can pick up my car at the Roundhouse."

"Fine," she said. "Anything else?"

"Call Joe D'Amata and tell him we're going to check out the saloon."

"Right."

A uniform sergeant put out his hand to stop the silver Porsche as it rolled into the POLICE VEHICLES ONLY parking lot at the Thirty-fifth District Building. Except for a few rooms used by the Inspector for the North Police Division, Northwest Detectives occupied most of the second floor of the building.

The driver of the Porsche rolled down the window.

"I think it'll be all right, Officer," he said. "I'm just here to pick up my date."

He pointed toward Detective Olivia Lassiter, who was leaning against the wall by the entrance.

The uniform sergeant whistled shrilly, attracting Detective Lassiter's attention.

"You know this guy, Lassiter?"

She looked, and then nodded.

"Yeah."

She walked to the Porsche.

"Next time, find some other place to park," the sergeant said.

"Yes, sir," Matt said.

Olivia got in the Porsche.

Where the hell did he get this car? A Porsche on a detective's pay?

"Have a good time, Lassiter," the sergeant said.

Matt grinned, but didn't say anything as he turned the Porsche around.

"What was that all about? 'Have a good time'?" Olivia asked.

Matt shrugged.

"What did you say to him?" Olivia challenged.

"Nothing," Matt said.

The hell you didn't. You're really a smart-ass. "You get a gold star for Mommy!" Jesus!

"Did you get anything from the Williamsons besides the name of this saloon?" Matt asked.

"The names of half a dozen guys Cheryl dated," she said. "And of a couple of her girlfriends."

"You'll have to give them to Joe."

"I already did."

"Where exactly is this saloon?"

"It's called Halligan's Pub. At Bethlehem Pike and College Avenue in Flourtown. I've been there. Sort of a neighborhood bar for the young and unattached."

"Spend a lot of time in places like that, do you?" Matt asked, innocently. "Looking for a little action?"

You sonofabitch!

She glared at him but said nothing.

If he thinks I'm looking for action, and so much as lays a hand on my hand, I'll knock him into next week.

"Hey, I'm kidding!" Matt said.

"I haven't been amused," Olivia snapped.

"Look, this is my first time," Matt said.

"First time for what? Working with a female detective, you mean?"

"Yeah. Or at least a good-looking one."

"Can we keep this professional?"

"I worked a couple of jobs with an Intelligence detective, a female," Matt said. "But she was old enough to be my mother. We got to be friends. So I asked her—we were having a couple of drinks—how I should behave with a younger female cop. And she said treat her like you would any other cop. That's what I was doing. Making a little joke."

Why do I believe him?

"What kind of a little joke were you making with Sergeant Pinski?"

"The uniform in the parking lot?"

"Yeah. What did you say to him?"

"I told him I was just picking up my date."

"You thought that was funny?"

"He believed it. And my other choice was to tell him I was on the job and show him my badge. Thirty minutes later, every uniform in the Thirty-fifth, and all your pals in Northwest Detectives, would have heard about the Homicide sergeant driving a Porsche picking up Northwest's good-looking Detective Lassiter."

He's right. That's exactly what would have happened.

"Where did you get this car, anyway?"

"When I finished college. It was my graduation present."

"It looks brand-new."

"It's five years old. I take pretty good care of it."

"It's beautiful," she said in genuine appreciation.

That was dumb. What's the matter with me?

"They're nice," Matt said. "Look, let's spell this out. I was not making a pass at you. I will not make a pass at you. I just got promoted, and I just transferred to Homicide. The last thing I want is for somebody to say Payne walked in, hung up his hat, and started hitting on Lassiter. That's the truth."

"Okay. Just so we understand each other."

"So what were you doing in Halligan's Pub? Looking for a little action?"

"You sonofabitch!" Olivia said, but she laughed.

And they found themselves looking at each other. And both looked quickly away.

"What can I get you?" the bartender at Halligan's Pub asked when they had taken stools at the bar.

"I don't know about Mother, but I would like a Famous Grouse on the rocks and a menu."

"You want to eat at the bar?" the bartender asked.

"I want to talk to you, and you're here," Matt said.

"And what for you, honey?" the bartender asked.

I will not ask what a famous whatever is.

"The same, please," Olivia said.

"You've been in here before, right?"

"Indeed she has," Matt said. "Mother tells me this is where the action is. Presumably there will be a shill's fee for her?"

The bartender chuckled, then turned to make their drinks. He put them on the bar and then laid two plastic covered menus on it.

Olivia picked up her glass and sipped it.

Scotch. Probably one of those very chic, very in, single malts or whatever they call them that the in people drink.

"Hot roast beef sandwich, please," Matt ordered after a ten-second perusal of the menu. "French fries, green beans. What about you, Mother?"

What the hell is that Mother business?

Damn it, a hot roast beef sandwich sounds good. But I'll sound like his echo.

To hell with it.

"The same, hold the fries," Olivia said.

"Coming right up," the bartender said, and walked down the bar to a computer.

Matt picked up his glass and raised it to Olivia.

"Mud in your eye, Mother."

"What's with 'Mother'?" Olivia asked.

"Even the Casanova of Center City does not make a pass at a mother," Matt replied.

"Oh, Jesus!" Olivia said.

"I'm just ensuring that I will not get carried away," Matt said.

"I won't let that happen," Olivia said.

"Good. I invariably falter in the face of temptation."

"You're out of your mind, you know that?"

"You sound just like my sister, Mother."

She shook her head, but she smiled.

"This is nice booze," she said. "I'm afraid to ask what it costs."

"Fear not, Mother, that was my round. But actually it's not very expensive. Not like twelve-year-old or single malts. I found it in Scotland. It was the bar whiskey."

"In Scotland?"

"My father and I, and my father's buddy and his-son-my-buddy, were shooting driven birds over there."

What the hell does that mean?

"I don't know what that means," Olivia confessed.

"They raise pheasants," Matt explained, "and charge people to shoot them.

They call it a 'drive.' The shooters form a line, and then the beaters drive the birds—hence 'driven birds'—toward the line of shooters. Great shooting."

"It sounds barbaric," Olivia said.

"You're a vegetarian?"

"No."

"Where do you think your roast beef came from? A steer that died of old age?"

Olivia didn't reply.

"The pheasants are raised to be eaten, just like chickens and turkey. I suppose you could argue that wringing their necks would be kinder than shooting them, but I don't see the difference. And three hours after they're shot, they're cleaned, plucked, packed in ice, and on the way to a gourmet restaurant."

"And you get your kicks by slaughtering the pheasants, right? You get a real kick out of killing things, right?"

"You got it, Mother," Matt said. "Once you understand that, everything falls in place."

She could tell by both the bitter tone of his voice and his eyes that she had really angered him.

He shook his head in disgust, turned away, and picked up his glass.

What made him so angry?

Oh, God! When Mickey O'Hara called him Wyatt Earp, he blew up. And then O'Hara told me about the bad guy Matt "put down"—by which he meant killed. I didn't mean to suggest he liked killing people! But I guess it sounded like I did.

So what do I do now, apologize?

The waiter slid plates holding hot roast beef sandwiches across the bar to them.

"I think you probably have just saved my life," Matt said, sniffing appreciatively and picking up a French fry. "But just to make sure, you'd better give me another of these."

Olivia saw that he had drained his glass.

The bartender chuckled and looked at Olivia.

"Why not?" she said.

Matt looked at her in surprise.

"I'm sorry," she said.

"Sorry for what, Mother?"

"I was out of line," she said.

Matt met her eyes. It made her uncomfortable, but she couldn't look away.

After a long moment, he said, "I guess that makes us even."

And then he looked away, and unwrapped his knife and fork from its napkin wrap and attacked the sandwich.

Olivia took a healthy swallow of her drink, and when the bartender delivered the second round, emptied what was left of hers into the new glass.

She was astonished at the speed with which Matt emptied his plate of the roast beef, the potatoes, and the beans. She had taken only her third bite when she saw him lay his knife and fork on the empty plate and slide it across the bar toward the bartender.

"Very nice," Matt said.

"Glad you liked it."

"Did you know Cheryl Williamson?" Matt asked the bartender.

"I guess you heard?" the bartender replied.

Matt nodded.

"Goddamned cops," the bartender said. "I guess you heard what those bastards did? Or didn't do. Pardon the French."

"What did you say your name was?" Matt asked.

"Charley," the bartender said.

"Mother, show Charley your badge," Matt said.

She looked at him in surprise.

"Detective Lassiter, show Charley your badge," Matt ordered.

Olivia pulled her oversweater far enough to one side so the bartender could see her badge, which she had pinned to the waistband of her skirt.

"Sorry, I didn't know . . . ," Charley the bartender said, uncomfortably.

"No problem," Matt said. "The reason we don't wear uniforms is so people can't spot us as cops right off. By the way, I'm Sergeant Payne. My friends call me 'Matt.'"

He extended his hand across the bar until Charley the bartender took it.

"Tell me, Charley," Matt said, as he slipped back onto his stool. "Have you made up your mind for all eternity, or would you be interested in the facts about what those goddamned bastard cops did or didn't do?"

"Hey, Sergeant, I said I was sorry. . . ."

"If we're going to be friends, call me Matt," Matt said. "And that wasn't the question, Charley. Are you interested in the facts, or have you made up your mind, and don't want the facts to get in the way?"

"Okay. Let's have the facts," Charley said.

"Mother, give Charley the facts," Matt said.

"Is that your name?" Charley blurted.

"I call her that to remind myself not to make a pass at her," Matt said.

"Really?"

"Really," Matt said. "Tell Charley what really happened, Mother."

"Okay. From the top . . . ," Olivia began.

". . . so at the end, what you have are two decent young cops who feel guilty as hell for not breaking into her apartment," Olivia finished. "Even though they did exactly what they were supposed to do."

"Jesus," Charley the bartender said, and turned away, to return in a moment with the bottle of Famous Grouse.

"On me," he said, as he started pouring. "Not on the house, on me. I feel bad about what I said before."

"That's absolutely unnecessary and we shouldn't," Matt said. "But we will."

"Are they going to catch this guy?" Charley asked.

"We're going to get him," Matt said. "The question is when. The sooner they get him, the sooner they'll be able to be sure he won't be able to do something like this to somebody else."

"Maybe I get this from the movies," Charley said, "but those homicide detectives seem to know what they're doing."

"I know two that don't," Matt said. Charley looked at him in surprise. "These two," Matt finished.

"You're Homicide?"

Matt nodded.

"And that's what we're doing here. Trying to run this guy down. We understand Cheryl used to come in here."

"Who told you that?" Charley asked.

"Her mother," Olivia said. "And she gave me a list of people Cheryl hung out with." She handed him the list. "Do you know any of these people?"

"Most of them," Charley reported after a minute.

"Any of them in here right now?"

Charley looked down the bar, then looked through the doors of two adjacent rooms and came back to report that none of them were.

"Well, we'll run them down," Matt said.

"It would help if you could tell us anything about Cheryl," Olivia said. "What kind of a girl was she?"

"Let me say something unpleasant," Matt said. "It's okay to say unkind things about the dead if the purpose is to find out who killed them."

212 · W. E. B. GRIFFIN

Charley considered that a moment.

"I take the point," he said. "Okay, so far as I know, she was really a nice girl. If she were a bimbo, I'd say so, okay? You want my gut feeling?"

"Please," Olivia said.

"I think she came in here hoping that Mr. Right, the guy on the white horse, you know what I mean, would walk in and make eyes at her. And I don't think he ever did. She was good-looking. Guys hit on her. But she wasn't looking for a one-night stand, and I never saw her leave here with a guy. Sometimes, when she was in here with her girlfriends, a couple of them would leave together with a couple of guys. Never alone. You know what I mean?"

"I get the picture," Matt said.

Matt's cell phone went off.

"Payne."

"D'Amata, Matt. Where are you?"

"Halligan's Pub."

"Yeah. Lassiter said you'd be going there. She with you?"

"Yeah."

"You eat yet?"

"Just finished."

"I'm in Liberties," D'Amata said. "I figured you might want to compare notes."

He's taking care of me. That's nice.

"Okay."

"The Black Buddha's going to want to know what's going on, and he'll be finished with that artsy thing pretty soon. If you don't want to come to Center City, I could meet you someplace."

"I'll come there. I've got to pick up my car at the Roundhouse anyway. Thirty minutes?"

"Thirty minutes," D'Amata said, and hung up.

Matt looked at Olivia.

"We have to meet D'Amata, Mother," he said.

She nodded.

"Can I ask you a favor?" Matt asked the bartender.

"Name it."

"I'm going to give you a card—a bunch of cards—with my number on it. If any of the people on the list Mother gave you come in, would you hand them one and ask them to call?"

"Sure."

"Give one to anybody who might have an idea," Matt said. "Okay?"

"You got it."

Matt took a small, stuffed-to-capacity card case from his pocket.

"These are old," Matt said. "They say Special Operations. But the number I write on them will be Homicide. Okay?"

"Okay."

"Tell them to ask for me or Detective Lassiter, but if neither of us is there, to talk to any Homicide detective, and leave a phone number and an address."

"Got it."

It took Matt and Olivia about five minutes to write her name and the Homicide number on all of the cards.

Then Matt asked for the check.

"On me," Charley the bartender said.

"No," Matt said, firmly, handing over his American Express card. "The one drink—between friends—we'll take with thanks. The rest we pay for."

Charley shrugged, but took the card.

Matt signed the receipt, looked at it, and said, "Mother, your half comes to fifteen-fifty, with tip."

She dug in her purse and came up with a five and a ten and handed it to him.

"I owe you fifty cents."

"I'll remember," he said.

He put out his hand to Charley.

"Thanks a lot," he said. "You've been more helpful than I think you understand. I'll probably come by again tomorrow, or Mother will. Okay?"

"Any time," Charley said.

"What we'll do, Mother, is go by the Roundhouse. I've got to get a property receipt for the sales slip I got in New York, and I want to pick up my car," Matt said when they were in the Porsche. "You can take it home after we meet with Joe D'Amata."

"I'm not so sure that's a good idea," Olivia said.

"Why not?"

"Because I'm not sure I should be driving. I'm not used to three drinks of scotch in forty-five minutes, and that third drink was really a double."

He looked at her and smiled.

"Mother, are you plastered?" he asked, amused.

"Tiddly, not plastered," Olivia said. "And I'm not your mother."

His eyebrows rose.

"I didn't mean that the way it sounded," she said, and he saw that she was blushing.

"*In vino veritas,*" Matt said, softly.

"What the hell does that mean?"

"It doesn't matter," Matt said, and moved his head the six or eight inches necessary to kiss her.

She didn't pull away.

"I really didn't want that to happen," she said, softly a moment later.

"Are you sorry?"

"Just drive the goddamn car, will you, please?"

He put the Porsche in gear and started off.

CHAPTER
11

As Matt approached Liberties Bar on North Second Street, he saw Martha Washington's Mercedes parked in front, beside Peter Wohl's Jaguar and a half-dozen unmarked cars.

Well, so much for Joe D'Amata's noble attempt to bring me up to speed before Washington asks what I've been doing on my first day as a Homicide sergeant.

He pulled the Porsche to the curb beside one of the unmarked cars, turned off the key, and turned to Olivia.

"You all right, Mother?" he asked.

"Of course I'm all right," she snapped.

"Hey, you're the one who admitted she was too . . . 'tiddly' . . . to drive."

"You're an arrogant sonofabitch, you know that?"

He looked at her a moment.

"I owe you that one," he said. "But that ends it. I am not going to burn for my sin through all eternity. You could have turned your head."

"You bastard!"

"What I'm doing right now—fully aware that no good deed ever goes unpunished—is trying to be a nice guy."

"How?" she asked, thickly sarcastic.

"You go in there and they see you're plastered and bitchy, you'll be back at Northwest in the morning."

"Who's 'they'?"

Why can't I keep my mouth shut?

Why did I have to call him an arrogant sonofabitch? And a bastard?

Because I'm bitchy and plastered, that's why.

Shit!

"The Mercedes belongs to Lieutenant Washington—or his wife, same thing—and the Jaguar to Inspector Wohl. There's a new unmarked, which probably means Captain Quaire. . . . You getting the picture?"

"Got it," Olivia said. "Thanks."

"Just sit there, pay attention, and speak only when spoken to, smile, and lay off the booze. Got it?"

"Got it."

Matt got out of the car and stood impatiently, waiting for Olivia to figure out the seat belt and get out of it. He did not hold the door to the bar open for her, but once he was through it, he did hold it open long enough so that it didn't close in her face.

Matt walked to the table holding Jason Washington, Peter Wohl, Joe D'Amata, Harry Slayberg, and—surprising him—Deputy Commissioner Dennis V. Coughlin and Captain Francis X. Hollaran; the new unmarked car was the commissioner's. Matt stood there, sort of waiting for permission to sit down.

Coughlin smiled at Detective Lassiter.

"Matt been keeping you busy, Detective?"

"Yes, sir."

"Good work with the Williamsons, Detective," Coughlin said. "I think— between you and the story Mickey O'Hara had in the paper—that fire's now under control."

"Thank you, sir."

"Sit down, and help yourself," Coughlin ordered, nodding at the bottles on the table. "You, too, Matt."

"Could I get a Diet Coke?" Olivia called to the bartender.

"You don't drink?" Coughlin asked, making it a statement. "Sorry."

"Sometimes, sir, not now."

"Joe tells me you got the sales slip for the camera in New York?" Coughlin asked Matt.

"Yes, sir. Henry Ford of Detroit, Michigan, himself bought it."

"You might call out there and see if they have something similar. Maybe there is a Detroit connection."

"I've already done that, sir," Matt said, and added, to Washington, "I gave a Homicide sergeant there your number. I didn't have any other direct Homicide number."

Washington nodded.

"How did you do at Halligan's Pub?" he asked.

"The bartender said she was looking for Mr. Right to come riding in on a white horse," Matt replied. "That so far as he knew, she didn't play around. We left him cards to pass out to anybody who might know anything, specifically including the names of the guys Mother got from Mrs. Williamson."

"'Mother'?" Coughlin asked.

"I call Detective Lassiter that to remind myself this beautiful female *is* Detective Lassiter, and that sergeants aren't supposed to notice the beautiful part."

There was laughter and chuckles.

"Good thinking, Sergeant," Coughlin said, smiling broadly.

Goddamn him!

Does he really think I'm beautiful?

"What we're doing now, Lassiter," Wohl said, "is waiting for another beautiful woman—"

"You'll notice he used the word 'beautiful,'" Coughlin interrupted, "which suggests *that* war of the sexes is in the armistice mode."

Wohl flashed him an angry look. The others chuckled.

"—Dr. Payne," Wohl continued, "who has graciously agreed to provide her take on the Williamson doer."

"Where is she?" Matt said.

"Where else, Matt? At the hospital. We were on our way here when her phone buzzed."

What's going on here? Is Inspector Wohl in a relationship with Matt's sister? They had a fight, and everybody knows about it? That maybe they fight all the time?

"What did Amy give you so far?" Matt asked.

"Why don't we wait and get it from her?" Wohl said.

"In the meantime," Washington said, "we *may* have, using the term 'lead' in the broadest possible sense, finally come up with a lead in the Roy Rogers job."

"Jason looked under the rock under the rock again," Coughlin said, approvingly.

"The witness neglected to tell us," Washington went on, "that the miscreant presently known, for lack of more precise information, as 'the fat guy' was wearing a visor—a crownless baseball cap, so to speak—when he sat down at the booth by the kitchen door. He was not wearing it when he left the scene."

"How do we know that?" Olivia asked.

Washington's look showed that he did not like to be interrupted.

And Matt told me to keep my mouth shut!

"While O'Hara's digital image does not show the faces of the malefactors, Mother, it does offer rather sharp silhouettes of their heads. No visor—the witness said he was wearing the visor to the rear, over his neck—was visible fore or aft."

He called me "Mother." Goddamn it, now everybody will.

"I didn't mean to interrupt you, sir," Olivia said.

"Apology noted," Washington went on. "We have such a visor cap among the unclaimed items at the crime scene. On it the lab, on its first look, found a rather poor print of what may be an index finger. Detective Harris has gone to the lab asking them to exert greater effort. I have visited the lab myself with the same purpose. I am going to drop by again on my way home tonight."

"Would I do any good, do you think, Jason?" Coughlin asked.

"With all due respect, Commissioner, I think that would be counter-productive."

"Is that so?" Coughlin challenged.

"On the other hand, if Captain Hollaran could find a moment in his busy schedule to drop by the lab," Washington replied, "that would suggest great interest in their activities by someone in a high position without invoking the terror a visit by you personally would generate."

"Terror?" Coughlin chuckled. "Your call, Jason."

"When, Jason?" Hollaran asked.

"To preserve what little is left of my once-happy marriage, I am going home—via the lab—just as soon as we hear from Doctor Payne," Washington said. "How about immediately after you see the commissioner home?"

"Done," Hollaran said.

"Our finding a useful print is what the wagering fraternity would term a long shot," Washington went on. "But at the moment, it's all we have."

"Just before I came here, Matt," D'Amata said, "I checked the results of the door-to-door interviews. Zero. Nobody saw or heard a thing. So Harry and I are going to try that again in the morning."

There was the sound of tortured metal, as if a bumper had scraped the curbstone.

Wohl looked at Matt. They smiled.

"She must have missed the fire hydrant," Matt said.

"One of her good days," Wohl said.

Amy came through the door a moment later, holding a lined pad. A stethoscope stuck out of the side pocket of her suit jacket.

"Everybody's here," she said.

She bent over Coughlin to kiss his cheek, slid into a chair beside Wohl, and smiled at the people around the table.

"What did you just hit?" Wohl asked.

She looked at him in genuine surprise.

"Nothing," she said. "Why do you ask?"

They're all smiling. She really must be a lousy driver, Olivia thought.

And she really doesn't look old enough to be a doctor.

And she doesn't look at all like Matt.

"I appreciate your help, sweetheart," Coughlin said. "It's important to us."

"Sweetheart"? What's that all about?

"What have you got for us, honey?" Wohl asked.

"I'm not your honey, Peter," she said. "I'm doing this as a concerned citizen."

Good for you!

"Okay, Concerned Citizen," Wohl replied, smiling, "what have you got for us?"

"Can we get you a drink, sweetheart?" Coughlin asked.

"God knows I earned one," she said. "Yes, thank you, Uncle Denny."

"Uncle Denny"? What's that all about? Are they related?

"What?" Coughlin asked.

Amy looked at Olivia.

"What are you having?"

"Diet Coke."

"That's not going to do it," Amy said. "I'll have a Bushmills martini."

What the hell is a Bushmills martini?

"Jerry," Coughlin called to the bartender. "One of the Doctor's Irish Specials, please."

"Coming right up."

He knows what she means. Which means she comes in here often.

As Wohl's . . . what? Girlfriend? More than that? . . . But with him. *Not alone. Not like that poor Williamson girl, who went to Halligan's Pub alone looking for Mr. Right to ride in on a white horse and make eyes at her.*

Poor Williamson girl? Who am I kidding?

When Charley the bartender told us that Cheryl wasn't looking for a one-night stand, that he never saw her leave the place with any of the guys who hit on her, I thought, I understand. That description fits me.

That's how I spend my spare evenings, going to Manny's, where I don't think they know I'm a cop, which is important because if Mr. Right ever rides into Manny's on his white horse and makes eyes at me, I know he will gallop right out again the moment he hears the whispered words "she's a cop" from the bartender.

But what if Mr. Right has just ridden into my life in a silver Porsche? At least . . .

"You take Irish whiskey . . ." Commissioner Coughlin said.

He's talking to me!

". . . and you put it in a cocktail shaker with ice, and shake it well, and then you pour it into a martini glass. That way, you don't dilute the whiskey as the ice melts."

"Very interesting," Olivia said. "I've never heard of that."

"They're really pretty good," Amy Payne said.

"You want to try one?" Coughlin asked. "You really earned a drink today with the Williamsons."

"Why not?" Olivia said.

"Jerry!" Coughlin called. "Two Doctor's Irish Specials."

"*Two* Doctor's Specials coming up," Jerry called back.

Olivia looked at Matt.

He was rolling his eyes and shaking his head.

Yeah, I know. "Lay off the booze."

Fuck you!

You're not my father. You don't tell me when not to drink.

How dare you be exasperated, disgusted, whatever with me?

"Did you get a chance to talk to Dr. Mitchell, Amy?" Washington asked.

"Cause of death was a broken neck," Amy said, matter-of-factly. "There are contusions on the right side of the face, suggesting that she was thrown, or forced, against the bedside table with such force as to break the neck."

She jerked her head violently to one side in demonstration.

"Big guy, huh, Doc?" Slayberg asked.

Amy nodded.

"We're sure it's a male?" Olivia asked.

Detective Lassiter saw that Sergeant Payne was rolling his eyes again.

Why now? Why was that *a stupid question?*

Oh, God, the sperm on her breast!

That was a stupid question.

Keep your mouth shut!

"There was sperm on the body," Amy said.

Sergeant Payne was now shaking his head.

"*On* the body," Amy went on. "On her breast and face. None in the vagina, anus, or mouth. . . ."

The bartender set a martini glass before each of the women.

Amy took a sip.

Olivia reached for the glass and picked it up.

She glanced at Sergeant Payne. He was holding both his hands palms out-ward. The gesture was clear: *I wash my hands of you.*

Fuck you again.

I will drink this drink and I will keep my mouth shut.

The drink had a strange, heavy, but not unpleasant taste.

Something like a martini.

"What do you think, Lassiter?" Coughlin asked.

"Interesting," Olivia said.

"Don't take more than two at one sitting," Wohl said.

"I won't."

"I presume there were sufficient quantities of that bodily fluid for DNA?" Washington said.

"Plenty," Sergeant Payne and Detective D'Amata said at the same time.

"I asked Dr. Mitchell to see if there was any saliva," Amy said.

"You think he licked her, Doc?" Slayberg asked.

Was that a bona fide question, or homicide humor?

"I think he may have spat on her," Amy said. "If so, that would confirm my first guess about this man."

"Which is?" Washington asked, softly.

"That he gets his satisfaction from the humiliation of his victims."

"Victims, plural?" Wohl asked. "You think he's done this before?"

"I think he has. For one thing, with the exception of killing the victim, which may have been—probably was—accidental, I think things went as he wanted them to go, as he planned them to go."

"Why do you say that?" Wohl asked.

"Those plastic things he used to tie her to the bed. That and the knife. Peo-ple don't usually carry things like that around. He brought them to the apart-ment, intending to use them."

Wohl grunted agreement.

"Let me put it this way," Amy said. "Psychologically, this guy is the oppo-site of Isaac 'Fort' Festung."

Who the hell is that?

"Fort Festung?" Coughlin asked, visibly surprised. "What's his connection with this?"

"Bear with me, Uncle Denny," Amy said.

"Your show, sweetheart," Coughlin said. "Handle it any way you want."

"When I was at Martha Pekach's party, she told me that David was upset because he'd gotten another postcard from Festung. I guess he's been in my mind since then. He's another interesting character, psychologically speaking."

"Harry," D'Amata said, chuckling, "'interesting character, psychologically speaking' is doctor talk for miserable slimeball."

Wohl chuckled. Amy smiled at D'Amata.

Why do I know that if Inspector Wohl had said that, Amy would have snapped his head off?

"How, Joe, and why did Festung kill that girl?" Amy asked.

"Mary Elizabeth Shattack," Coughlin furnished.

"He beat her to death," D'Amata said. "With his fists."

"Why?"

"He didn't like her?" Wohl asked, mock serious.

"Screw you, Peter," Amy said.

"She left him," D'Amata said. "He couldn't take that."

"She was his possession," Amy said. "And when she misbehaved— announcing she had found someone else—that was unacceptable behavior, and he punished her. Like you whack a dog with a newspaper when he poops on the carpet."

"Sweetheart," Coughlin said, "you're losing me."

"And then he stuffed her body in a trunk and just left it there," Wohl said. "Where are you going with this, Amy?"

"I believe the phrase you policemen use is *modus operandi*," Amy said. "They're different here."

"Explain that to me. I'm a little dense this time of night," Wohl said.

"Let me have a shot, if I may, Amy," Washington said. "You are saying that Festung regarded Miss Shattack as something worthless that he could deal with—in this case, discard—in any way that pleased him at the moment. An empty cigarette package, so to speak."

"Right," Amy said.

"And the Williamson girl?" Matt asked.

Amy ignored him.

"Which suggests to me that Festung has an enormous ego," she said.

"Which would also explain the postcards," Wohl said. "Festung is making the point with his postcards that he can do whatever he wants to do, and there's nothing we can do about it. 'We' being the police, representing society."

She ignored him too.

"Are you suggesting, Amy," Washington asked, "that the Williamson girl was in some way important to her killer?"

"I think that as Festung had this pathologically enormous ego, the man who killed the Williamson girl has a pathologically *inadequate* ego, which he has to buttress. I don't think he intended to kill her or, possibly, even rape her. What he wanted, what he was driven to do, was humiliate her. He had to prove to himself that she was in his power."

No one responded.

"Rape, generally speaking," Amy went on, "is rarely to attain sexual gratification. The satisfaction comes from having the victim in your power, terrifying them, forcing them to do something they really don't want to do, something that will humiliate them."

"The sperm on the victim's face and breasts . . . ," Wohl said.

"Precisely, Peter," Amy said. "Breasts he exposed by cutting away her clothing with that enormous knife . . ."

". . . suggesting he masturbated, ejaculating on her face . . ."

". . . for the purpose of humiliation," Amy finished for him. "I can think of nothing more humiliating for a young woman . . ."

"Who was not a bimbo," Olivia said.

". . . he believed to be a, quote, nice girl, unquote," Amy said.

Olivia had a quick mental image of herself tied naked to a bed while some sicko . . . did that . . . in her face. She felt a chill.

She picked up her Doctor's Irish Special and took a deep swallow without knowing she had done so until the whiskey began to warm her body.

She sensed Matt's eyes on her and glanced at him. This time she thought she saw understanding—maybe even a little sympathy—in his eyes.

"You're saying this guy is a real sicko," D'Amata said. "I mean, we know he's sick to start with, but . . . ."

"This man is driven, Joe," Amy said. "And from the—what do I say?— *practiced* manner in which he did this—the plastic ties, the knife, the camera to capture the victim in her humiliation—I would be very surprised if this was his first victim."

"And you feel certain there will be others?" Washington asked.

"That opens another unpleasant avenue of thought," Amy said. "His reaction to her death. I don't think he intended to kill her. But he did. The question then becomes whether the knowledge that he has taken a life is going to frighten him, possibly to the point where he will at least try not to let something like that happen again, or whether killing the Williamson girl gave him greater satisfaction than the previous incidents of humiliation ever gave him. And thus make him want to do it again?"

"Jesus Christ!" Slayberg said.

"So who do we look for, Concerned Citizen?" Wohl asked. "How do we find this guy?"

"I don't think he knew her," Amy said. "I mean, I don't think you're going to find him by finding a rejected suitor. He may have known about her . . . as Detective Lassiter said. . . ." She paused and looked and smiled at Olivia. "Sorry, I've forgotten your first name."

"Olivia."

"As *Olivia* said, the Williamson girl was not a 'bimbo.' Maybe that's why this man selected her as his next victim. He may be a customer at some bar she went to . . ."

"Halligan's Pub," Matt furnished.

". . . or someone at work, at church. I was about to say car wash, grocery store, but I don't think so. I think this man is intelligent, which would tend to eliminate minimum-wage people. For that matter, he may be from Podunk, South Dakota, just passing through. . . . So, I have no idea where to look for him."

"Has anyone thought to ask Special Victims if they have jobs like this?" Coughlin asked.

"I did," Olivia said. "When Sergeant Payne and I were there printing the photographs. No, sir. They have had nothing like this."

"Accepting for the moment," Washington said, "the Doctor's premise that this is not the first time this fellow has done something like this, and I think she's right, and Sex Crimes—"

"Special Victims, Jason," Wohl interrupted.

"To be sure. *Special Victims,*" Washington said, his voice dripping with sarcasm. "Thank you, Inspector, for the correction. The proper terminology is now burned indelibly in my memory. May I proceed?"

"As long as you get the terminology right," Wohl said, smiling, unabashed. "Correct terminology, as you have so often pointed out to me in the past, is very nearly as important as turning over the stone under the stone."

Coughlin chuckled. Hollaran, D'Amata, Slayberg, and Matt smiled.

"A serpent's tooth causes no greater pain than an ungrateful child," Washington said, solemnly. "Or a once barely adequate homicide detective who, realizing his inadequacies, left Homicide for the far less challenging arena of supervision, and then mocks his mentor."

"Commissioner," Wohl said. "I think he's talking about you."

"I thought he was talking about Frank," Coughlin said.

Now the suppressed laughter could not be contained.

"Is there no one at this table except for Olivia and myself over the mental age of fourteen?" Amy demanded angrily.

"Probably not, Doctor," Washington said. "But I will nevertheless continue."

He waited until everyone was looking at him.

"Despite serious doubts that any or all of you has the mental capacity to follow this reasoning, I submit the following possible scenario: In the presumption that this fellow (a) is everything Dr. Payne believes him to be and (b) has done something like this—possibly, probably, without fatal results—several times before, and inasmuch as we have no record of a similar *modus operandi* here. . . . Were they positive about having nothing similar at Special Victims, Olivia?"

"Yes, sir."

He called me by my first name.

"The reasonable inference may be drawn that the previous incidents were in another large city."

"Why large city, Jason?" Coughlin asked.

"I have added to Amy's hypothesis (a) he is intelligent and (b) he was probably not known to the victim; that he stalked, so to speak, Miss Williamson because she represented the type of nice young female he wished to humiliate. His pool of potential victims would obviously be in proportion to the population of a city—"

"And he would not be known in—could hide easier in—a large city not his hometown," Wohl interjected.

"Perhaps you did learn something from your mentor after all, Peter," Washington said. "Say thank you."

"Thank you," Peter said. "Yes, I'd love another."

He signaled to the bartender for another round of drinks.

"I will not rise to that," Washington said. "You are not very bright, but you knew precisely what I meant."

"I want somebody here to be sober enough," Coughlin said, "to check the NCIC database tonight, and maybe to send wires to every large—"

"I've already checked with the FBI, Denny," Washington said. "They have nothing. And I have very little faith in the efficacy of a teletype message to other police departments. They probably pay as little attention to them as we pay to theirs."

He met Coughlin's eyes for a moment and then, when Coughlin said nothing, turned to Matt.

"Sergeant Payne, I suggest that starting first thing in the morning, whenever she is not occupied with the Williamson family, you have Detective Lassiter make two telephone calls to every major city police department in the country. One to their homicide bureau and the second to whatever they have elected to dub their sex crimes unit."

"Yes, sir."

"While you're at it, Olivia," Amy said, "get their fax numbers, and tell them you're going to fax them the DNA makeup of this guy. If they have any unidentified rapists where the only positive identification factor is the DNA, they can run theirs against ours to see if there is a match."

"I didn't know that really worked," Olivia said. "We can really do that?"

"Sure," Amy said. "DNA markers are a series of unique, really unique, identifiers, according to scientific standards used around the world. No two are alike; they're much more difficult—almost impossible—to challenge in court."

"And as my contribution to the general fund of knowledge," Washington said, "let me add that two months ago, in federal court right here in Philadelphia, a defense lawyer successfully challenged the scientific validity of fingerprints—the admission thereof as evidence—arguing that the standards for fingerprint identification vary from state to state, and even other countries. I'm really glad Amy brought that up."

"Good thinking, honey," Coughlin said.

"That's my big sister," Matt said with mock pride.

"And as for you, Sergeant Payne," Washington said quickly, to keep Amy from replying to the sarcasm, "whenever you can tear yourself from the supervision of the other detectives working this investigation it would be useful for you to lend Detective Lassiter a hand in that endeavor. Perhaps fortune will smile on us."

"Yes, sir."

What he's saying, Matt decided, *is that the two people least likely to make any other substantial contribution to this investigation, Mother and me, will spend all day tomorrow—or for however long it takes—with a telephone stuck in our ears.*

Well, what the hell, sergeant or not, I am the rookie in Homicide, and that's what rookies do, whatever jobs will release someone who knows what he's doing to do it.

Olivia thought: *Well, however politely put, that was a kick in the teeth, wasn't it, Sergeant Hotshot? You and the temporary employee from Northwest get to work the telephones, while the real detectives do their thing.*

And you really deserved a kick in the teeth to bring you down to size, so why do I feel sorry for you?

The bartender began distributing drinks, starting with Doctor's Specials for Dr. Payne and Detective Lassiter. She was surprised that the first martini glass was empty. She looked at the fresh one.

I don't need that. I don't want that. I'm going to make a fool of myself.

"How are you going to get home, Olivia?" Amy asked.

"I'm riding with Matt . . . Sergeant Payne."

Like just now.

"Are you all right to drive, Matt?" Amy asked.

"Hey, fight with Peter all you want, but lay off me."

"I was thinking of Olivia," Amy replied, "and what makes you think I'm fighting with Peter?"

"Your claws are showing."

Washington stood up, holding his glass.

"I am leaving before these adorable, loving siblings enter the violent stage," he said. "But not before I take aboard sufficient liquid courage to face the unsheathed claws I fear I will myself find at home."

He took a healthy swallow of his drink.

"You will drop by the lab, Frank?"

"Just as soon as I drop the boss off," Hollaran said.

"I was going to say Frank could take Lassiter home," Coughlin said, "but his going by the lab is important." He looked at Matt. "You drive very carefully, Matt. I don't want to hear on *Philadelphia Phil* that you ran into a school bus."

"I'm all right, Uncle Denny," Matt said.

"Okay, Frank," Coughlin said. "Let's call it a night."

He stood up, finished his drink, and walked to the door. Hollaran followed him. Washington finished his drink and followed them.

"What Slayberg and I are going to do tomorrow, Matt," D'Amata said, "is run down the known acquaintances and ring some doorbells. If anything turns up, we'll let you know."

"Fine," Matt said.

That was really nice of him, Olivia thought. *He picked up on Matt getting kicked in the teeth and was trying to make him feel better.*

D'Amata and Slayberg left.

"You want to go, Mother?" Matt asked.

She stood up, picked up her glass, met his eyes, and drained it.

He shook his head in resignation and gestured toward the door.

. . .

"You were lucky in there, Mother," Matt said when they were in the Porsche.

"I'm not your Mother, goddamn it!"

"You were lucky, Mother," Matt went on, "that your mouth didn't run away with you any more than it did. Nobody likes a drunken woman. Last warning."

"Fuck you!"

"With the additional warning to never say that to me again, the conversation is closed, Detective Lassiter," Matt said. "Now, where do you live?"

"Take me to City Hall. I'll take a taxi."

"Commissioner Coughlin ordered me to take you home. Answer the question, Detective Lassiter.'"

"The 100 Block of Orchard Lane," she said, icily, after a moment. "It's east of the North Philadelphia Airport. Take I-95, and get—"

"I know where the North Philadelphia airport is."

Matt put the Porsche in gear and backed away from the curb.

[TWO]

"Take the next left, onto Knight's Road," Olivia said, as they were headed down Woodhaven Road.

It was the first thing either of them had said since leaving Liberties.

Matt wordlessly made the turn.

Two minutes later, Olivia said, pointing across the median, "Orchard's over there. You can make a U-turn at the stoplight."

Matt saw that the stoplight at the intersection of Knight's Road and Red Lion Road was green and that a Dodge Caravan, headed his way on the other side of the median, was the only traffic. It had just passed the stoplight.

He touched the brake, flicked the turn signal lever, downshifted, and prepared to make the U-turn at the intersection, after the Caravan.

A Pontiac Grand Am came out of nowhere down Red Lion, ran the red light, flashed past the nose of the Porsche, and then slammed into the side of the Dodge Caravan.

Slammed hard into it. There was the sound of tearing metal as the Dodge was knocked, mostly sideward, across the street, coming to rest at an angle against the curb.

"That sonofabitch ran the light!" Matt said.

He braked sharply, stopped, turned on his flashers, and opened his door.

"Call Radio," he ordered, handing his cellular to Olivia.

The driver's door of the Grand Am opened and the driver got out. He was a young, tall, white male.

"You stupid sonofabitch!" Matt muttered.

"This is Detective Lassiter, badge 582. We are at Red Lion and Knights Road. We have a vehicular accident, auto-auto. Possible injuries, start in Fire Rescue, and a sector car."

There was a moment's hesitation, then Olivia added, "No. We are not involved."

Thank God! Matt thought. *Neither one of us could pass a Breathalyzer test right now.*

The young, tall, white male looked first at the Caravan and then at the Porsche stopped on Knight's Road with its warning flashers blinking. Then he sort of shrugged and took off at a lope down Orchard Lane.

"Check on the people in the van," Matt ordered, and jumped out of the Porsche and ran after the young, tall, white male.

Now it's leaving the scene of an accident, you dumb sonofabitch!

And that Grand Am is probably stolen.

"Stop!" he shouted. "I am a police officer."

The young, tall, white male kept running. Matt saw him turn off the street into a driveway.

When Matt reached the lawn of the next house, he cut across it diagonally and at a full run encountered with his foot a wire supporting an ornamental tree on the lawn.

He flew through the air and landed flat on the concrete driveway. He felt his face scrape against the concrete, and a stinging in both hands where they had struck the concrete.

He shook his head and got to his knees.

The young, tall, white male was running around the side of a garage.

Matt ran after him.

When he turned the corner of the garage, he saw the young, tall, white male about to top a five-foot hurricane fence.

"Stop, police officer!" Matt shouted.

The young, tall, white male looked right at him and then dropped to the ground on the far side of the fence.

"I'm going to get you, you sonofabitch!" Matt shouted, and ran toward the fence.

It was his intention to leap the fence gracefully by vaulting over it with the use of his left hand on the parallel pipe at the top of the fence.

Two problems arose. First, the parallel pipe at the top of the fence was perhaps an inch below the top of the fence itself. Second, the uppermost joints of the twisted wire of the fence were above it. One of them penetrated the heel of Matt's hand, which he had planned to use for leverage.

This caused (a) Matt's passage over the fence to be considerably less graceful than he intended; (b) a puncture wound in the heel of Matt's hand; and (c) Matt's trousers to be torn from just below the knee almost to the cuff as they became ensnared in the twisted wire at the top of the fence.

"Son of a bitch!" Matt cried, and got to his feet.

He saw that he was between two lines of hurricane fence running behind the houses. The young, tall, white male was running between them. Matt ran after him.

At the end of the parallel lines of hurricane fence there were a dozen garbage cans. The young, tall, white male leapt nimbly over the first two cans, but then his foot slipped between two of them and he sprawled onto the ground amid toppled garbage cans.

Matt, breathing heavily, shoved the garbage cans to one side, then fell to his knees beside the young, tall, white male and pulled his arm behind his back. Then he put his knee on the small of the young, tall, white male's back.

He tried to catch his breath. He became aware that blood was dripping from his chin onto the white sweatshirt of the young, tall, white male.

He heard the wail of a siren, and then the wail of a second siren.

Matt felt the small of his own back for his handcuffs.

I left the fucking things in the goddamn car!

"You gonna let me up now?" the young, tall, white male asked.

"Shut your fucking mouth!"

The sound of one of the sirens died, and then the other. After what seemed like two and a half years, Matt saw the beam of a sweeping flashlight.

"Over here!" he tried to shout, which told him he had not fully recovered his breath.

The flashlight beam came closer.

"My God, what happened to you?" Detective Lassiter asked.

"You got cuffs?"

Detective Lassiter sort of squatted on the ground, put her small flashlight in her mouth, opened her purse, and took from it a set of handcuffs.

She moved to place the handcuffs on the wrist Matt was holding. The young, tall, white male, realizing what was happening, resisted. Before he was adequately restrained again, Detective Lassiter's flashlight had been knocked from her mouth and had fallen to the ground, in such a position that it shone directly on the junction of her legs, which, covered with pale blue panties, was now, due to the displacement of her skirt, fully exposed.

He heard the sound of a third siren dying.

"Thanks," Sergeant Payne said.

"Happy to be of help," Detective Lassiter said.

"Put your foot on his neck," Sergeant Payne ordered.

Detective Lassiter complied, and Sergeant Payne got to his feet.

"You're bleeding," Detective Lassiter said.

"My, aren't we observant?" Matt said, and took a handkerchief from his pocket and mopped at his face.

Matt started to pull the young, tall, white man to his feet.

"Keeping in mind that there is nothing I would rather do right now than rub your face in the garbage, get up and behave," Matt said.

"Not quite 'make my day,' " Olivia said. "But not bad, Sergeant."

I'll be a sonofabitch, she's laughing at me!

Another flashlight beam appeared, and a moment later, another. One was held by a uniform, the other by a Highway Patrol sergeant. The latter flickered across Matt's face.

"Payne! What the hell happened to you?"

"What the hell does it look like?" Matt snapped. He pointed to the uniform. "Put this gentleman in a car," he ordered. "He has not been Mirandized."

"What did he do?" the Highway sergeant said as he stepped closer to Matt as if he thought he was going to need some help.

Then, when his back was to the uniform and he could not be seen, he put something into Matt's hand.

Matt saw what it was. Three round pellets of a very strong brand of English mints.

"Chew those slowly and try not to breathe on anybody. I already gave some to your friend."

"Thanks," Matt said. "I owe you."

"So what did this critter do?"

"For openers, first running a red light and then leaving the scene of an accident," Matt said. "Give me thirty seconds and I can think of a lot more. I wouldn't be surprised if the Grand Am is hot."

"You sure you're all right? You look like hell," the Highway sergeant said.

. . .

There were four city vehicles on Knight's Road: a highway car, a patrol car, a sergeant's car from the Eighth District, and a Fire Department fire-rescue vehicle.

Two paramedics were loading the passengers of the Caravan into the fire-rescue truck.

"I think the little boy's got a broken arm," the Eighth District sergeant said. "You're Detective Lassiter?"

"She's Lassiter. My name is Payne."

"You're on the job?"

No, you stupid fuck, I'm a concerned citizen who gets his rocks off chasing tall, young white males through people's backyards.

"Sergeant, Homicide," Matt said.

"You want to go in with them? Or in your own car?"

"Go where?"

"You look pretty beat up, Sergeant," the Eighth District sergeant said. "You better have a doctor look at your face."

"I'm all right," Matt said. "I scraped it, that's all."

"No, you're not," Detective Lassiter said. "Let the medics look at it."

It was the paramedic's professional judgment that while he had really done a job on his cheek, there wasn't much that could be done for it except clean it up and get some antiseptic on it.

"I live right around the corner," Detective Lassiter said. "And I've got alcohol and hydrogen peroxide."

"That'll do it," the paramedic said.

Matt met Olivia's eyes for a long moment.

"Thank you," he said.

"You're welcome."

"Can we find out if the Grand Am is hot?" Matt asked.

"He's running it now," the Eighth District sergeant said, nodding toward a uniform in a patrol car.

Less than a minute later, the uniform got out of the car and announced that the Grand Am had been reported stolen.

"Can you take him and hold him on that?" Matt asked. "I'll come by later and do the paper."

The District sergeant shook his head, "no."

"You know better than that, Sergeant. You're the arresting officer and you need to make the statement to the detective at Northeast."

The Highway sergeant stepped between them. "I'll get all of Sergeant Payne's necessary information and make sure the detective has it, Sergeant. Besides, we helped him to make the pinch back there, and I want to make sure Highway gets in on the paperwork. You know how it is."

The Eighth District sergeant looked at him for a moment, then walked away.

The Highway sergeant turned to Matt.

"Let me have your badge and payroll numbers. And I better have hers, too. Tell me what happened and how you hurt yourself so the Northeast Detective can document it if you need to go out IOD,* and make sure you touch base with the assigned detective so you agree with the statement before he puts it on the '49."

"Thanks a lot," Matt said. "I owe you two now."

"You better let me drive," Olivia said.

"Why?"

"It looks like you scratched your hand, too. You'll get blood all over your pretty leather gear shifter."

He walked around the rear and got in the passenger seat of the Porsche.

Detective Lassiter opened the door of her second-floor apartment, reached inside, flicked on the lights, and then motioned Sergeant Payne inside ahead of her.

"The first aid stuff's in the bathroom," she said. "The bedroom's just the other side of the living room."

He walked across the living room to the bedroom, noticing as he passed through it to the bathroom that it was not messy, and that a white comforter covered her bed.

Intimate feminine apparel was hanging from the shower curtain rod. When she came into the bathroom, she snatched it off and threw it behind the shower curtain.

She took bandages, swabs, Mercurochrome, and bottles of hydrogen per-

*Injured On Duty.

oxide and alcohol from a cabinet and then turned to him and started cleaning his face.

"That's pretty nasty," she said. "You sure you don't want to go to the emergency room?"

"I'm sure," he said.

Three minutes later, his scraped face had been cleaned with both hydrogen peroxide and alcohol. He had manfully tried, and failed, not to wince when the alcohol stung painfully.

"Let's look at the leg," she said.

"What's wrong with the leg?"

"The fence got that, too, I guess. In the car, I saw it. It's all bloody."

Three minutes after that, his leg had been treated with alcohol and hydrogen peroxide and painted with Mercurochrome, but not bandaged.

"Your trousers are ruined," Olivia said.

"I noticed."

"And let me see what you did to your hand."

"I guess I scratched it the same place I tore my pants, going over the fence."

She took his left hand in both of hers.

"That's a puncture wound," she said.

He didn't reply.

"You just can't leave it like that," she said.

He didn't reply.

She looked up at him. Their eyes met.

"What?" she asked.

"You know goddamn well what, Mother."

"I'm not your goddamn Mother."

"I know," he said, softly. "Your move."

She had not taken her eyes from his. She took her left hand from his and raised it to his unmarked cheek.

"Oh, God!" she said.

Ninety seconds later, atop the white comforter on her bed, while still partially clothed, Detective Lassiter and Sergeant Payne came to know each other, in the biblical sense of the term.

And in the next half hour, now completely devoid of clothing, and between the sheets, Detective Lassiter and Sergeant Payne twice came to know each other even better.

CHAPTER 12

Matt Payne awoke at five minutes to six. For a moment, he wondered why so damned early—he had two alarm clocks to make sure he was awakened at seven—and then he remembered some of what had happened the night before, and thought that might have something to do with it.

"Jesus Christ!" he said in wonderment, then went to his bathroom, which his father had described as being somewhat smaller than those found on old Pullman railroad cars.

He examined himself in the mirror over the toilet.

What the hell happened to my face?

He remembered.

Sliding along the concrete driveway in hot pursuit of the critter in the hot car who'd run the red light and slammed into the Caravan.

"Nevertheless, sir, minor facial blemishes aside, you look like the well-laid man of fame and legend!" he said aloud.

He smiled at the memories of other of the previous evening's activities.

However, a moment later, when in an habitual act he reached inside the shower stall to open the faucet that would long moments later bring hot water all the way from the basement to the garret apartment, his hand really hurt him.

Shit! The goddamn—what did she say?—"puncture wound."

When he came out of the shower, the damned thing still hurt, and it looked angry.

"Shit!"

He had two thoughts, one after the other.

Maybe Olivia would know what to do with it. Do I put a bandage on it? Soak it in hot water? What?

Maybe, if I called, she might say, "I'll come by on my way to work and have a look at it."

That's a very interesting prospect.

He went naked and dripping into his bedroom—which his father also compared unfavorably to a sleeping compartment on an old Pullman car—and picked up his cellular from the bedside table, where it lay beside his Colt Officer's Model .45.

Twenty seconds later, a sleepy female voice said, "Lassiter."

"Good morning."

"Oh, God!"

"I was calling to inquire whether your schedule is free for breakfast."

"Oh, God! What time is it?"

"A little after six."

There was no immediate response.

"For reasons I can't imagine, I'm ravenous," Matt said.

"I don't even want to think about breakfast," Olivia said. "My God, Matt!"

"My God, what, Olivia?"

"I haven't even had time to think, and you want breakfast?"

"Think about what?"

"Oh, for God's sake! Everything!"

"What is there to think about?"

"You know I didn't want that to happen."

Oh, shit!

"Do I detect a slight tone of regret?"

"I didn't say that, Matt," Olivia said. "Oh, God!"

"May I infer, then, that it was not an entirely disappointing experience for you?"

Olivia giggled.

"Not entirely," she said. "My God!"

"You keep saying 'My God.'"

"I keep remembering what happened," she said. "My God, I can't believe I behaved like that!"

"For my part, it was an entirely delightful experience."

"Was it?"

"Couldn't you tell?"

"Oh, Matt! What are we going to do?"

"That brings us back to breakfast."

"No. For one thing, I'm not hungry, and for another, I don't want anyone to see us together."

"Why not?"

"You know why not."

"I don't give a damn who sees us together. Anyway, we're working together."

"I do. I want to stay in Homicide."

"Oh."

"I need time to think, and if I see you, I won't be able to think clearly." She paused. "Matt, will you do me a big favor?"

"Name it."

"Forget what happened last night."

"How the hell am I supposed to do that? It happened, and at the risk of repeating myself, I found it to be an entirely delightful experience."

"I'm not saying it wasn't," she said. "My God, couldn't you tell? What I'm saying is that I don't want anybody even to guess about it until I can think about it, really think about it. Will you do that for me?"

"Whatever you say, Mother."

"Thank you."

"I suppose your having a look at my hand is entirely out of the question?"

"What's wrong with your hand?" she asked.

That's genuine concern in her voice.

"I believe you described it as a 'puncture wound.'"

"And I also told you to stop at an emergency room on your way home. You mean you didn't?"

"I seem to have forgotten that instruction. I must have had something else on my mind. Bleeding to death didn't seem important at the time."

"You're bleeding now?"

More genuine concern.

He looked at his hand.

"No, but it looks unhealthy."

"Matt, go to an emergency room, please. Right now. I'll see you at work."

"How about doing me a favor?"

"If you want me to come there, I will," she said after a moment.

"What I want you to do is tell me now if you're trying to . . . let me down gently."

"Oh, God! If I was trying to dump you, kindly or otherwise, I would not have offered to come there."

"You mean that?"

238 · W. E. B. GRIFFIN

"You think last night was a one-night stand for me?"

"Oh, God, I hope not," he said, and laughed.

"What's funny?"

"I seem to have acquired your penchant for 'Oh, God!'"

"Are you all right to drive with your hand?"

"Sure."

"Then go to an emergency room and I'll see you at work. Okay?"

"Okay."

"And we won't look in each other's eyes. Agreed?"

"With great reluctance."

"Oh, God!" she said, and then there was the hiss that told him she had pressed the End key on her cellular.

[TWO]

Matt pulled the Porsche into the Emergency Trauma Center of Hahnemann Hospital on North Broad Street and parked beside a Sixth District wagon in the area reserved for Police and Emergency Vehicles Only.

A man of about his age, wearing hospital greens and what looked like twenty-four hours of beard growth, stopped him as he was walking toward the hospital entrance.

He pointed wordlessly at the sign.

"I'm on the job," Matt said, and pushed his jacket away from the badge on his belt with his sore hand.

"What did you do to the hand?"

"Fell over a fence," Matt said.

The man waved his hand in a signal for Matt to follow him inside.

"You're a doctor?" Matt asked.

"No, I wear this stuff because I like pastel colors."

The paperwork didn't take long.

The doctor was waiting for him in a treatment room.

"That's nasty," the doctor said. "Puncture wounds can be bad news. How'd you do it?"

"Going over a fence," Matt said. "The top of the fence—the twisted ends of the wire?"

The doctor nodded. "Your tetanus up to date?"

"I suppose so."

"Suppose doesn't count," the doctor said, as he opened a glass door in a white cabinet.

"This is going to hurt," the doctor said.

It did.

And so did the injection of an antibiotic "as a precaution" in the other buttock.

"I hope you can shoot right-handed, Sherlock," the doctor said. "For the next three, four days, that paw is going to be tender."

"I'm right-handed. You going to put a bandage on it?"

"You *want* a bandage?"

"What I don't want is people asking, 'What did you do to your hand, it looks *ghastly*?' "

"I could paint the area with some lovely lavender antiseptic."

"Just a simple large Band-Aid, please."

"Okay. Why not?"

"Thank you."

"You mind if I ask a couple of questions, Sherlock?"

"Shoot."

"Why were you jumping over a fence?"

"I was chasing a guy who drove a stolen car through a red light and clobbered a family in a minivan."

"You get him?"

Matt nodded.

"Good for you."

"You said two questions."

"Why did the cops stand around with their thumbs up their ass while that girl was being raped and murdered?"

[THREE]

Matt's gluteus maximus began to ache as he got on the Roundhouse elevator. The doctor had said that both the tetanus booster and the antibiotic would probably cause "mild discomfort."

The mild discomfort left his mind when he walked into Homicide and found that Detective Lassiter had already reported for duty. She was sitting at a desk with a telephone to her ear.

She was wearing a skirt and a double sweater. It didn't matter. Her naked form was engraved forever in Matt's mind.

She looked at him, then away.

"Already at it, Mother?" he said.

She looked at him, nodded, and then quickly looked away again.

"Captain wants to see you, Sergeant," Detective Alonzo Kramer, a stocky, ruddy-faced, forty-three-year-old, said, pointing to Captain Quaire's office.

Matt could see through the glass enclosure that Lieutenant Gerry McGuire, the commanding officer of Dignitary Protection, was with Quaire.

I wonder what that's about?

Oh, shit! Stan Colt! I forgot all about that!

Quaire saw Matt coming and waved him into his office.

"Good morning," Matt said, politely.

"What happened to your face?" Quaire asked.

"I took a slide on a concrete driveway last night chasing a guy."

Quaire gestured *give me more* with both hands.

"I almost had Lassiter home. . . ."

"From where?" Quaire asked, smiling.

"From Liberties. Lieutenant Washington had us meet him there. And afterward, I took her home. She had to give her unmarked back to Northwest."

"And what happened? Detective Lassiter didn't do that to your face, did she, Sergeant?" Captain Quaire asked, mock seriously. He looked to see if Lieutenant McGuire shared his sense of humor. From his smile, it was obvious that he did.

"No, sir," Matt said. "As we came down Knight's Road, off Woodhaven, a fellow in a stolen Grand Am ran the Red Lion stoplight, rammed into a Dodge Caravan, and took off running."

"I saw that in the overnights," McGuire said. "I thought Highway bagged that guy. You got involved in that?"

"I saw it. I had to."

Quaire made another *give me more* gesture with his hands.

"It happened right in front of us. Lassiter called it in, then checked the people in the van, and I started chasing the guy."

"And he gave you trouble?" Quaire asked, now seriously. "The face?"

"No, sir. While I was chasing him, I took a dive over a wire and scraped my face on a driveway. Then I tried going over a fence, and bruised my hand."

"But you got the guy?"

"Yes, sir. Eighth District locked him up. But I'm going to have to go to Northeast Detectives to give a Detective Coleman a full statement. He only got the initial details for the affidavit* last night."

"Why didn't you give your statement last night?" Quaire asked.

"I wanted to get some antiseptic on my face."

"So why didn't you do the paperwork last night, after you went to the emergency room and got some antiseptic on your face?"

"I didn't go to the emergency room last night. I went to Hahnemann this morning."

Quaire nodded.

"Consider yourself as of right now on temporary assignment to Dignitary Protection," he said, and added, to McGuire: "Getting Sergeant Payne to Northeast Detectives Division to give his statement is now your responsibility, Lieutenant."

"Thanks a lot," McGuire said.

"Captain, can't I get out of that?" Matt asked.

"Ask Lieutenant McGuire," Quaire said. "You are now working for him."

"I'm working the Williamson job," Matt said.

"You are now working the Stan Colt job, Sergeant Payne," McGuire said. "Mr. Colt, who will arrive at approximately three-fifteen, told Monsignor Schneider, who told the cardinal, who told the commissioner, who told me, that he's really looking forward to working with you."

"What does that mean?"

Quaire and McGuire smiled at each other.

"I think," McGuire explained, smiling broadly, "that when the monsignor—who apparently is one of your biggest fans—spoke with Mr. Colt, he told him about your many heroic exploits. I think Mr. Colt heard that when Harrison Ford was preparing to make the movie *Witness* he came here to spend time with a real, live Philadelphia homicide detective . . ."

"Jesus Christ!" Matt said.

---

*Affidavit of Probable Cause for Arrest. It is filled out by the assigned detective in a case, who then submits it to the District Attorney's office, where an assistant district attorney on duty approves or disapproves the charges against the person in custody.

". . . and has apparently decided that what was good enough for Harrison Ford is good enough for him."

"Harrison Ford is an actor. Colt is a goddamn joke!"

"Don't let the monsignor hear you say that," Quaire said. "Much less the commissioner."

"And for that matter, I have one day on the job in Homicide. I am hardly an experienced—"

"Lie down, shut up, and take this like a man, Matt," Quaire said. "You're dead. The commissioner has spoken."

"It's a dirty job, Sergeant, but someone has to do it," McGuire said, smiling broadly.

Quaire chuckled. Matt glared at McGuire, who didn't seem to notice.

"Mr. Colt," McGuire went on, "will arrive by private jet at North Philadelphia Airport at three-fifteen. He will be met by the commissioner—or possibly the mayor, if he can get free; or both—Monsignor Schneider, myself, four Highway Patrol bikes, two of my people, representatives of the media, and of course you. Following what that good-looking press agent— What's her name?"

"Terry Davis," Matt furnished, automatically.

Jesus, Terry! She certainly dropped off my radar screen in a hurry after Olivia, didn't she?

"—what Miss *Terry Davis*," McGuire went on, "refers to as a 'photo op,' Mr. Colt and party will proceed—escorted by the Highway bikes—to the office of the cardinal, where there will be another photo op as the cardinal welcomes Mr. Colt back to Philadelphia . . ."

"He's just a movie actor," Matt said, shaking his head. "A *lousy* movie actor!"

"Who is about to raise several million dollars for West Catholic High School," Captain Quaire said. "Which pleases the cardinal, and whatever pleases the cardinal pleases the commissioner."

". . . following which," McGuire went on, "we will proceed to the Ritz-Carlton. Highway's responsibility—the bikes—will end there. They'll provide bikes to escort his limo to the events, but aside from that, it's up to me to protect Mr. Colt from his hordes of fans, and you to keep him happy."

"What makes him happy is young girls," Matt said.

"Excuse me, Sergeant?" Quaire asked, coldly.

"Mr. Colt apparently likes young girls," Matt said. "Very young girls."

"Did you get that from one of the magazines in a supermarket checkout lane, or do you have another source of information?" Quaire asked, sarcastically.

"Terry Davis told me," Matt said. "I think she wants us to be prepared for that."

"Oh, God!" Quaire said. "She wasn't pulling your leg, Matt?"

"No, sir. I'm sure she was serious."

"That should make this interesting for you, Gerry," Quaire said.

"I don't know how to handle something like that," Matt said.

"We'll just have to sit on him around the clock," McGuire said. "If something like that gets in the papers, we'll be held responsible."

"He wants to see how real cops work," Quaire said. "Show him. Everything from school crossing guards up. Keep him busy."

"He's going to want to see what he thinks is interesting," Matt said. "Narcotics, Major Crimes, Homicide . . ."

"Vice," McGuire said, chuckling.

"I wouldn't be laughing if I were you, Gerry," Quaire said. "And I don't want him around here."

"With all respect, sir, how do I tell him no?" Matt said.

Quaire thought that over before replying.

"If it happens, Matt, it happens. You know how I feel about it."

"Yes, sir."

"We're going to get some help from Special Operations?" Matt asked.

McGuire nodded.

"Sure."

"Do we know who?"

"Somebody special you wanted?"

"Detectives McFadden and Martinez," Matt said.

"Mutt and Jeff?" Quaire asked. "Dignitary Protection isn't quite their specialty, is it?"

Detective Jesus Martinez, who was of Puerto Rican ancestry, and who was five feet eight inches tall and weighed just over one hundred thirty pounds, and Detective Charles T. McFadden, who was six feet two and outweighed Martinez by a hundred pounds, had been partners since they had graduated from the Police Academy.

The first assignment for nearly all Academy graduates was to a district, and there almost always to a district wagon, where for their first year or so on the job, they learned the nuts and bolts of being a police officer on the street by responding with the wagon to assist other officers in everything from hauling

Aunt Alice to the hospital after she'd fallen in her bathtub, to hauling drunks and other violators of the peace and dignity of the City of Brotherly Love to the district lockup.

Almost routinely, however, two brand-new police officers were assigned to work undercover in the Narcotics Division. McFadden and Martinez were chosen for the assignment in the hope that few drug dealers would suspect either the small, intense Latino or the large, open-faced South Philadelphia Irishman of being police officers when they tried to make a buy of controlled substances.

McFadden and Martinez quickly proved themselves to be very adept at what they were assigned to do. But their superiors realized it was only going to be a matter of time until they became known to the drug trade generally—in other words, their appearance in court to testify against the drug dealers—and would lose their usefulness.

At this point, it was expected the young officers would be assigned to a district and start driving the district wagon.

Something else happened: McFadden and Martinez had—on their own, off-duty—joined the citywide search for the junkie who had shot Captain Dutch Moffitt, of Highway Patrol, to death. In the belief that Gerald Vincent Gallagher would be somewhere in the area, they staked out the Bridge and Pratt Street terminal of the subway.

When Gallagher had finally shown up, he refused to obey their order to halt and had run off down the subway tracks. McFadden and Martinez—already known as "Mutt and Jeff," after the cartoon characters—had chased him, ignoring the danger, down the tracks until Gallagher fell against the third rail and then got himself run over by a subway train.

In the movies, or in a cops-and-robbers program on TV, with the mayor and assorted big shots beaming in the background, the commissioner would have handed them detective badges and congratulations for a job well done. But this was real life, and promotions to detective in the Philadelphia police department came only after you had taken, and passed, the civil service examination. Martinez and McFadden hadn't been on the job long enough even to be eligible to take the examination.

And their sudden celebrity—their faces had been on the front pages of every newspaper in Philadelphia, and on every TV screen—had of course completely destroyed their usefulness as undercover Narcotics officers.

It had looked as if their reward for catching the junkie who'd shot Captain Dutch Moffitt—something the rest of the police department hadn't been able to do for an embarrassingly long period—was going to be reassignment to driving a wagon in a district.

It didn't seem fair, but who said a cop's life was fair? Life's a bitch, and then you die.

At the same time, Cadet Matthew M. Payne, Captain Moffitt's nephew, had been about to graduate from the Police Academy. In the opinion of (then) Chief of Patrol Chief Inspector Dennis V. Coughlin, the chances that Matt Payne would last six months on the job—much less that the police department would be his career—ranged from zero to zilch.

Coughlin believed that Matt—whom he had known from the day of his birth—had reacted to (a) the death of his uncle and (b) his failure of the U.S. Marine Corps' Pre Commissioning Physical Examination by applying for the police department to (a) avenge his uncle and (b) prove his manhood.

It was understandable, of course, but the bottom line was that a *summa cum laude* graduate of the University of Pennsylvania, who had been raised not only in wealth but as the adopted son of a Philadelphia Brahmin, was very unlikely to find happiness walking a police beat. Worse, he was liable to get hurt.

Sergeant Dennis V. Coughlin had knocked at the door of his best friend's pregnant wife to tell her that Sergeant Jack Moffitt had been killed responding to a silent alarm at a gas station in West Philadelphia.

Chief Inspector Coughlin had no intention of knocking at the door of Mrs. Patricia Moffitt Payne to tell her that her son—Jack's son, his godson—Matt, had been killed in the line of duty.

And all of this had coincided with the formation, at the "suggestion" of the then-mayor of the City of Philadelphia, the Hon. Jerome H. "Jerry" Carlucci, of the Special Operations Division of the police department.

Mayor Carlucci, who boasted that he had held every rank in the Philadelphia police department except for policewoman, had not been at all bashful about making suggestions about the department to then–Police Commissioner Taddeus Czernich.

Mayor Carlucci had also "suggested" to Commissioner Czernich that he consider Staff Inspector Peter F. Wohl, then assigned to Internal Affairs, to be the commanding officer of the new Special Operations Division. Commissioner Czernich had immediately seen the wisdom of the suggestions, and issued the appropriate orders.

Peter Wohl was then the youngest staff inspector—ever—in the department. It was well-known that his father, Chief Inspector (Retired) August Wohl, had been Jerry Carlucci's rabbi as the mayor had risen through the ranks. But it was also well-known that Peter Wohl was a hell of a good cop, an absolutely straight arrow, and smarter than hell, so the cries of nepotism were not as loud as they might have been.

Coughlin, the then–chief inspector, had solved the problem of what to do with Officers Martinez, McFadden, and Payne by ordering their assignment to Special Operations.

In a private chat with then–Staff Inspector Wohl, he suggested that in his new command Wohl would probably be able to find places where Officers Martinez and McFadden could be useful in plainclothes, and that Officer Payne could probably make himself useful as Wohl's administrative assistant, until he realized the mistake he had made by coming on the job, and quit and got on with his life.

Wohl had accepted Coughlin's suggestions with as much alacrity as the commissioner had accepted the mayor's suggestions. He was wise enough to know that he had very little choice in the matter. His rabbi had spoken.

Finding useful employment for Martinez and McFadden had posed no problem. Wohl had been pleasantly surprised how well they had performed in interviews with suspects. Between them, they had seemed to know when they were not being told the truth, the whole truth, and nothing but the truth, and then one or the other of them had been able to get it.

When they played Good Cop/Bad Cop, Martinez had been very effective as the frightening arm of the law, and McFadden, despite his size, as the kindly young Irishman who understood what had happened and wanted only to help.

Officer Payne had, not surprising Wohl, been an efficient administrative assistant—sort of a male secretary—from the first day. Wohl, who agreed with Chief Coughlin that Payne would leave the job just as soon as he realized that he really belonged in law school, as the next step on the ladder to an eventual partnership in Mawson, Payne, Stockton, McAdoo & Lester, arguably Philadelphia's most prestigious law firm, was surprised to realize that he was actually going to miss him when he was gone.

When a serial rapist began to operate in the Northwest, and Northwest Detectives had difficulty finding him—and this difficulty was gleefully reported daily in the press—Mayor Carlucci had been very unhappy. When the rapist killed one of his victims, triggering even more scornful journalistic comment, Mayor Carlucci called a press conference and announced that henceforth the investigation would be handled by the newly formed Special Operations Division.

It was good press, but the reality was that Wohl's Special Operations Division was less qualified to conduct the investigation than Homicide was, and Wohl, who had been a homicide detective, knew it.

Homicide had assigned the two best homicide detectives, Jason Washington and his partner, Tony Harris, to the job. Wohl, with the assistance of Chief Coughlin, arranged—over their bitter objections—the transfer of Washington and Harris to Special Operations. Once they had reported for duty, Wohl assigned Officer Payne to the job. Payne was told that his duties were to relieve Washington and Harris of as many administrative details as possible, and to report to Wohl at least once a day—more often if necessary—of how the investigation was proceeding.

It was, Wohl thought, a really useful thing for Payne to be doing before he left the job.

It never occurred to Wohl, Washington, or Harris that Payne would do anything but run errands. Everyone understood that despite the badge on his belt and the .38 "Detective's Special" snub-nosed revolver in his shoulder holster, he wasn't really on the job.

He was a really nice college boy, and Denny Coughlin's godson, and Coughlin had given him to Peter Wohl to sit on, out of harm's way, until he realized he wasn't cut out to be a cop.

When Wohl told Coughlin that he had given Payne to Washington and Harris as a gofer, Coughlin had smiled.

"Twenty years from now, he will fondly remember his days as a homicide officer," Coughlin said.

Four days after Officer Payne went to work as Washington's and Harris's gofer, the following story appeared on page one of the Philadelphia *Bulletin*:

NORTHWEST SERIAL RAPIST-MURDERER KILLED BY "HANDSOME" SPECIAL OPERATIONS COP AS HE RESCUES KIDNAPPED WOMAN

BY MICHAEL J. O'HARA
BULLETIN STAFF WRITER

Officer Matthew Payne, 22, in what Mayor Jerry Carlucci described as an act of "great personal heroism," rescued Mrs. Naomi Schneider, 34, of the 8800 block of Norwood Street in Chestnut Hill, minutes after she had been abducted at knifepoint from her home by a man the mayor said he is positive is the man dubbed the Northwest Serial Rapist.

The man, tentatively identified as Warren K. Fletcher, 31, of Germantown, had, according to Mrs. Schneider, broken into her luxury apartment as she was preparing for bed. Mrs. Schneider said he was masked and armed with a large butcher knife. She said he forced her to disrobe, then draped her in a blanket and forced her into the rear of his Ford van and covered her with a tarpaulin.

"The next thing I knew," Mrs. Schneider said, "there was shots, and then breaking glass, and then the van crashed. Then this handsome young cop was looking down at me and smiling and telling me everything was all right, he was a police officer."

Moments before Officer Payne shot the kidnapper and believed rapist-murderer, according to Mayor Carlucci, the man had attempted to run Payne down with the van, slightly injuring Payne and doing several thousand dollars' worth of damage to Payne's personal automobile.

"Payne then, reluctantly," Mayor Carlucci said, "concluded there was no choice but for him to use deadly force, and he proceeded to do so. Mrs. Schneider's life was in grave danger and he knew it. I'm proud of him."

Mayor Carlucci, whose limousine is equipped with police short-wave radios, was en route to his Chestnut Hill home from a Sons of Italy dinner in South Philadelphia when the rescue occurred.

"We were the first car to respond to the 'shots fired' call," the mayor said. "Officer Payne was still helping Mrs. Schneider out of the wrecked van when we got there."

Payne, who is special assistant to Staff Inspector Peter Wohl, commanding officer of the newly formed Special Operations Division, had spent most of the day in Bucks County, where the mutilated body of Miss Elizabeth Woodham, 33, of 300 East Mermaid Lane, Roxborough, had been discovered by State Police in a summer country cottage.

Miss Woodham was abducted from her apartment three days ago by a masked, knife-wielding man. A Bucks County mail carrier had described a man meeting Mr. Warren K. Fletcher's description and driving a maroon Ford van, identical to the one in which Mrs. Schneider was abducted, as being at the cottage where her body was discovered. Police all over the Delaware Valley were looking for a similar van.

Payne, who had been assigned to work as liaison between ace homicide detectives Jason Washington and Anthony Harris and the Special Operations Division, had gone with Washington to the torture-murder scene in Bucks County.

He spotted the van in the early hours of this morning as he drove to the Chestnut Hill residence of Inspector Wohl to make his report before going off duty.

"He carefully appraised the situation before acting, and decided Mrs. Schneider's very life depended on his acting right then, and alone," Mayor Carlucci said. "She rather clearly owes her life to him. I like to think that Officer Payne is typical of the intelligent, well-educated young officers with which Commissioner Czernich and I intend to staff the Special Operations Division."

Payne, who is a bachelor, recently graduated from the University of Pennsylvania. He declined to answer questions from the press.

After that, Chief Coughlin was no longer quite so sure that Officer Payne would soon resign from the police department. And he didn't.

"Captain," Sergeant Payne said now, "those two can do anything they're asked to do." He looked at Lieutenant McGuire. "I'd really like to have them."

"Wohl said 'anything we think we need,'" McGuire said. "Let's see if he meant it."

He asked permission with his eyes to use Captain Quaire's telephone. Quaire nodded. McGuire punched in numbers.

"Lieutenant McGuire for Inspector Wohl, please."

Then he reached to Quaire's phone and pushed the Speaker button.

Peter Wohl's voice came somewhat metallically over the speaker:

"Hey, Gerry, what can I do for you?"

"Inspector, you said I could ask for anything for the Stan Colt job."

"My toothbrush excepted, ask away."

"Mutt and Jeff. They on something that won't wait?"

"When and where do you want them, Jerry?"

"North Philadelphia Airport at three. Tell them to report to Sergeant Payne."

"They'll be there."

"Thank you, sir."

"Any time."

The line went dead.

"Why don't you take Lassiter to Northeast Detectives now, and get that over with?" Quaire said.

"Yes, sir."

"And then I'll see you at the airport at three," McGuire said.

"Yes, sir."

[TWO]

Matt stood patiently by Olivia's desk and waited until she finished talking on the telephone.

"I really appreciate that, Lieutenant," she said. "We really want to get this guy."

She put the handset in its cradle and looked up at Matt.

"Cincinnati Homicide," she said. "Nice guy. Nothing that he can think of offhand, but he's going to check around for me. What's up?"

"Let's go out to Northeast and get our statements out of the way," Matt said.

She didn't reply, but stood up, and took her purse from the desk drawer, and then waited for him to lead the way out of the office.

In the elevator, she asked, "What was going on in the captain's office?"

"That was Lieutenant McGuire of Dignitary Protection," Matt said. "He's about to protect Stan Colt from his horde of fans."

"And?"

"I'm going to help him," Matt said.

"What's that all about?"

The elevator door opened onto the lobby.

"I'll tell you later," he said, and held the keys to the Porsche out to her. "Follow me to my place, and I'll dump the car there."

It seemed for a moment as if she was going to object, but she finally took the keys without comment.

Matt drove the unmarked Crown Victoria into the basement garage first, pulled it into one of his slots, and got quickly out to show her where to park the Porsche.

When she opened the door, he was standing there. When she got to her feet, they were so close that he could feel her breath on his face.

He resisted the impulse to put his arms around her, but bent slightly, far enough down to kiss her.

"Oh, God!" she said. "I should have trusted my instincts."

"About what?"

"About what you had in mind when you handed me the keys."

"What I had in mind was getting the Porsche out of the Roundhouse lot before it got ticketed or boosted," he said.

Her face told him she did not believe this at all.

"All the way here, I thought of reasons why I shouldn't let you kiss me."

"Which are?"

"I can't remember," she said, and they kissed again.

She looked into his eyes.

"What are you thinking?" she asked.

"Which question would get the desired response," Matt said. "One, 'Would you like to see my etchings?' or two, 'You want to come upstairs for a minute?'"

"You really have etchings?" she asked.

He nodded.

"If we go to your apartment, you know what will happen."

"I hope I know what will happen."

"I mean it will take longer than a minute."

"The way I feel right now, I'm not sure it'll take as long as a minute."

"Oh, God!" Olivia said.

Olivia came out of Matt's bathroom wearing his terry-cloth robe. He thought she looked adorable.

"Well, now we know, don't we?" she asked.

"Know what?"

"That just beneath my nice girl surface there is a lewd, lascivious, and shameless slut."

"Come on!"

She walked to the door and began picking her clothing up from the floor.

"I don't suppose you'd believe me if I said I never have behaved like this in my life."

"Yeah, I would," he said.

"I don't believe you, but thank you anyway."

Matt's cellular buzzed.

"Don't answer it!" Olivia ordered.

Matt picked it up.

"Payne," he said, then, a moment later, "Hold one."

He shoved the telephone under a pillow on the bed.

"I asked you not to answer that," Olivia said.

"It was more like an order, but I have worked for Peter Wohl for five years, and have developed an uncontrollable Pavlovian response to my phone ringing: Answer it immediately."

"That's Inspector Wohl?"

"No. It's my regular girlfriend."

He could tell by her face that she could not quite make up her mind whether to believe him or not.

"You want me to go in the bathroom and give you a little privacy?"

"No. Come and eavesdrop," he said. "You'll probably find it interesting."

She headed for the bathroom.

"Hey!" Matt called. "Here!"

He pointed to the bed.

She didn't move.

He took the cellular out.

"Detective McFadden," he said. "It warms the cockles of my heart to hear your voice."

He pointed to the bed again, and Olivia came and sat gingerly on the edge. He moved the cellular away from his ear so that she could hear.

"Matt, what the fuck's going on?" Detective McFadden demanded.

"You mean right now?"

"Yeah."

"I'm in bed with a beautiful, almost naked woman."

Olivia pinched Matt painfully on his inner thigh.

"I wouldn't put it past you, you bastard." McFadden chuckled. "I mean, Dignitary Protection at the North Philly Airport at three o'clock. Wohl just told me."

Matt responded to the pinch of his thigh by reaching into Olivia's robe and taking her nipple between his fingers.

"You wouldn't dare!" she whispered furiously.

"You and Man Mountain Martinez have been selected to assist Lieutenant McGuire and his staff, and me, in the protection of Mr. Stan Colt, the movie star. . . ."

"What?" McFadden challenged incredulously.

Matt let go of Olivia's nipple, then kissed the fingers that had held it with appreciation. Olivia shook her head in resignation.

"With particular emphasis on protecting Mr. Colt from himself."

"What the hell does that mean?"

"He likes very young girls, Charley. We are going to see that he doesn't get any while he's in town."

"You're not pulling my chain, are you?" McFadden asked, seriously.

"No. If there is an . . . incident, we are all up that famous creek without a paddle."

"How the hell did you get involved in this?"

Matt started to push his robe from Olivia's shoulders. She stiffened, but then relaxed and then shrugged out of it.

"Colt is here to raise money for West Catholic High—"

"I saw that in the paper," McFadden interrupted.

Matt raised his head and kissed Olivia's nipple.

She sighed. When he lay back down, she shook her head, tolerantly.

"—Monsignor Schneider, who's the cardinal's man for the visit, is a cop groupie. When Colt told him he would like to see real cops at work, Schneider thought of me and went to the commissioner, and I got stuck with it."

"But why you?"

"Schneider thinks I was a real heroic cop in Doylestown," Matt said after a perceptible pause.

"Oh, shit!" McFadden said, sympathetically.

Susan Reynolds's sightless eyes came to Matt's mind.

"Shit!" Matt said.

"What?" McFadden asked.

Olivia looked at him with concern, then touched his cheek to turn his head so that she could look in his eyes. Her eyes asked, "What?"

"Nothing," Matt said. "Charley, I have to go. . . ."

"The naked broad's horny?"

"Absolutely. I'll see you and Hay-zus at the airport at three."

"Yeah," Detective McFadden said, and hung up.

Matt tossed the telephone aside and looked up at Olivia.

"A lot of people thought you acted heroically in Doylestown," she said.

"That's a joke. I didn't even do the job right. If I had, Susan would still be alive."

"'Susan'? You were friends?"

"More than friends," Matt said.

"I saw you crying on TV," she said. "I wondered."

He looked at her but didn't say anything.

"You know what I feel like doing to you right now?" she said.

"I'm yours! And I love your imagination."

"I feel like putting my arms around you and holding you and telling you that everything's going to be all right."

"That isn't exactly what I thought you had in mind."

"Can I?" Olivia asked.

"Yeah," he said after a moment.

She leaned toward him and he half sat up, and she put her arms around him and held him to her breast.

They stayed that way for perhaps three minutes, and then Olivia glanced down at the sheet covering his groin.

"You horny sonofabitch," she said, wonderingly.

"Is that a complaint?"

She pushed him away from her breast and back onto the bed and looked down at him for a moment before shaking her head, "no."

Fifteen minutes later, they got into the unmarked Crown Victoria and rode out to the Northeast Detectives Division and gave their statements.

CHAPTER 13

[ONE]

J. Richard Candelle, a squat, gray-haired fifty-year-old black man who wore his frameless spectacles low on his nose, looked over them at Detective Tony Harris, backed against a laboratory table, shook his head, and announced,

"Tony, I'm sorry, that's the best I can do. There's just not enough points."

The reality of identification through fingerprints is not nearly as simple, or as easy, as a thousand cops-and-robbers movies have made the public—and, in fact, a surprising number of law enforcement officers—think it is.

Fingerprints are identified—and compared with others—through a system of point location, and the classification of these points. The more points on a print, the better. The more prints—prints of more than one finger, of the heel of the hand, or ten fingers and both heels—and the more classified points on each print, the easier it is to find similarly classified prints in the files.

Presupposing having *both* to compare, comparing the print found on the visor hat left behind by the doer at the Roy Rogers restaurant with the print of the doer himself would be relatively simple and would just about positively identify the suspect.

But establishing the identity of the doer by finding a match of his index-finger print among the hundreds of thousands of index-finger prints in the files of the Philadelphia police department, or the millions in the FBI's files, was a practical impossibility.

Except, if a print could be obtained with many "good" points, that could be point classified.

J. Richard Candelle, Philadelphia's fingerprint expert, had just not been able to detect enough points on the single index finger print he had to offer even a slight chance of matching it with a print in the files.

"Fuck, that's not good enough," Harris said, bitterly.

"I will elect not to consider that a personal criticism, and under these circumstances forgive your vulgarity." Candelle, whose forensic laboratory skills were legendary, was a dignified man, befitting his part-time status as an adjunct professor of chemistry at Temple University.

"It wasn't a shot at you, Dick, and you know it," Harris said.

Candelle waited until he saw what he thought was a genuine look of regret on Harris's face, and then went on:

"I was here all fucking night, Tony. I had two fucking doughnuts for breakfast, my fucking feet hurt, and I have had every fucking white shirt in the Roundhouse in here making sure I was really doing my fucking best."

Harris looked at him.

"Well, in that case, you fucking overworked old fart, I guess I better buy you some fucking lunch before you fucking expire of starvation, old age, and self-pity right here in the fucking lab."

"I think that would be an appropriate gesture of your gratitude," Candelle replied, smiled, and started to replace his laboratory coat with a sports coat.

Using tweezers, Candelle picked up the crownless visor cap the doer had left behind in the Roy Rogers and replaced it in the plastic evidence bag.

"You want me to hang on to this, Tony?"

"No. Give it to me. Maybe I'll take it to a psychic."

Candelle chuckled.

"I really am sorry, Tony," he said.

Harris punched him affectionately on the arm.

"We both are, Dick," he said. "What do you feel like eating?"

They went to DiNic's in the Reading Terminal Market on Twelfth Street and sat on stools at a counter. Both ordered roast pork sandwiches with sharp provolone cheese and roasted hot peppers and washed them down with beer.

"I hate to reopen a wound," Candelle said, "but I just had another unpleasant thought."

"Which is?"

"It's really a shame Luther Stecker retired."

"Who's he?"

"The State Police guy, in Harrisburg. Lieutenant."

"Oh, yeah. I don't think he could have done anything you couldn't," Harris said. "I hadn't heard he'd retired."

Candelle looked at his watch.

"Today," he said. "I was invited to his retirement party. Tonight. I decided Harrisburg was too far to drive for free beer."

"What makes you think he could have helped?"

"He's got a new machine, AFIS. It stands for Automated Fingerprint Identification System."

"And?"

"It's supposed to be able to get points off a week-old print on a dry falling leaf in a high wind."

"You're serious?"

Candelle nodded.

"Harrisburg, here I come," Tony said.

"I told you, Stecker's retiring today."

"Well, there ought to be somebody else out there who knows how to operate this wonder machine."

"Tony, if I thought there was, I'd suggest you go out there."

"Well, won't the FBI have one?" Harris asked. "As a last desperate move, I'm going to send the goddamn hat to them."

"They probably have a half-dozen of them. But whether they have anybody who knows how to use one, get all that it is capable of from it, is another question." He paused, then added, "There's a question of experience, even art, in this."

"So we're dead, huh?"

Candelle shrugged.

"It looks that way. I'm sorry. So what are you going to do now?"

"We're down to showing the artist's sketches to everybody again. And we both know that's not going to work. Everybody in the place saw somebody else."

"At the risk of repeating myself, Tony, I'm really sorry I couldn't do more. Maybe the FBI'll be able to."

"You're sure nobody in the State Police could do us any good? Who's taking Stecker's place?"

"I met the gentleman," Candelle said. "He left me with the impression he would have trouble finding his posterior with both hands."

"Great!"

Harris drove his Crown Victoria to the rear door of the Roundhouse.

"You're not coming in?" Candelle asked.

"No. I'm going to go somewhere to try to figure out what to tell the Black Buddha," he said.

"I'll do that for you, Tony," Candelle said, "before I go home. I don't want him calling me at the house to have one more shot at it."

" 'Turn over the stone under the stone'?"

"We're out of stones on this hat, Tony," Candelle said. "And I think the Black Buddha's more likely to accept that from me than you."

"Good luck!" Harris said. He held out his hand to Candelle. "Thanks a lot, Dick. I really appreciate all the effort."

"I'm just sorry it didn't get us anywhere," Candelle said, nodded, closed the car door, and walked toward the Roundhouse entrance.

Tony started to drive out of the parking lot, but at the last moment pulled into a vacant space, took out his cellular telephone, and punched the key that automatically dialed directory information.

"What city, please?"

"Fuck it," Tony said, and punched the End key.

He backed out of the parking space, then left the parking lot, wondering what was the best way to get onto Interstate 76 this time of day.

"Jason," he said, aloud, "if you want the last goddamn stone under the stone turned over, I'll damned well turn the sonofabitch over."

Ten minutes later, just as he turned onto I-76 West, his cellular buzzed.

"Harris."

"Presumably you are aware of Professor Candelle's—" Lieutenant Jason Washington's unmistakable dulcet voice said.

"I was there."

"And what are your plans now?"

"I'm thinking, Jason."

"And may I inquire about what?"

"No. Not now."

"May I dare to hope that when you feel comfortable in telling me, you will call?"

"Don't hold your breath, Jason. This is probably one more blind alley."

"Sometimes at the end of a blind alley, one finds a stone—" Washington began.

"Thank you for sharing that with me, Lieutenant," Tony interrupted. "I'll write it down so that I won't forget it."

"Good afternoon, Detective Harris," Washington said, and the hiss that followed told Harris Washington had hung up.

He tossed the cellular onto the seat.

So he's a little pissed that I won't tell him.

Better that than to tell him, get his hopes up, and then get kicked in the teeth again when this doesn't work.

[TWO]

Matt arrived at the North Philadelphia Airport at half past two, to find that he was ahead of Lieutenant McGuire, but not of the Eighth District captain, who was supervising more than a dozen of his uniforms in setting up barriers to keep what looked like sixty or seventy—maybe more—of Stan Colt's fans under control.

Matt looked closer and saw that there were two barriers, one for the fans a surprising number of whom were gray-haired adults—and a second for the press.

He was wondering if he should at least identify himself to the Eighth District captain when Lieutenant McGuire arrived, got out of his car, waved at Matt, and then went to talk to the captain.

Four Highway bikes arrived next, in a roar of engines, under a sergeant. McGuire pointed out where they should park, and when they had, the Highway sergeant took off his helmet and hung it on his handlebar. Matt then recognized him as the sergeant who had been on Knight's Road the night before.

The night before? That seems like two weeks ago.

He walked over to Matt.

"How's the face?" he asked.

"It's sore, and I went to Hahnemann this morning and they gave me shots and now my ass hurts."

The sergeant chuckled.

"You did get to see Detective Coleman at Northeast, right?"

"Just came from there. I appreciate the help last night. All of it."

"I know guys on the job wouldn't have done what you did," the sergeant said. "They'd say, Fuck it, I've had a couple of drinks, why take the chance of getting my ass in a crack?"

"I wasn't being noble. I just did it."

"You were being a good cop," the sergeant said. "Good cops take care of each other."

Detective Charley McFadden walked up to them.

"What happened to your face?" he asked.

"Where's Man Mountain Martinez?" Matt asked, ignoring the question.

260 · W. E. B. GRIFFIN

"He took a dive onto a concrete driveway running down the guy in the hot Grand Am who smacked the van on Knight's Road," the Highway sergeant offered, helpfully.

"That was you?" Charley asked.

"Where's Martinez?" Matt asked again.

"He'll be here in a minute."

"What have Mutt and Jeff got to do with this nonsense?" the Highway sergeant asked.

"Sergeant," Charley said, "that's what I've been trying to get Sergeant Payne to explain."

A white Lincoln stretch limousine rolled up. McGuire signaled to the driver to put it behind the Highway bikes.

"Our hero's chariot, I guess," the Highway sergeant said.

"That's a Classic Livery limo," Matt said. "I wonder if we should tell our hero he's being ferried around by the mob?"

The Highway sergeant and McFadden, who knew that Classic Livery was one of Philadelphia mob boss Vincenzo Savarese's legitimate businesses, chuckled.

A black Cadillac, a black Crown Victoria, and a black Buick Park Avenue rolled onto the tarmac.

"The mayor and the commissioner," the Highway sergeant said. "I think that's one of the cardinal's cars, but there's no one in it."

That mystery was immediately explained when both the Hon. Alvin W. Martin, mayor of the City of Philadelphia, and Monsignor Schneider climbed out of the Cadillac. Police Commissioner Ralph J. Mariani got quickly out of the passenger's front seat of the Crown Victoria and walked up to them.

"I guess I better start looking busy," the Highway sergeant said, and started to walk back to the Highway bikes. As he passed the mayor and party, he saluted. Commissioner Mariani waved him over.

A moment later, the Highway sergeant pointed to Matt, and a moment after that, started to walk quickly—almost trot—back to where Matt and McFadden were standing.

"The commissioner wants to see you," the Highway sergeant said.

"Oh, shit," Matt muttered, and walked over.

"Good morning, Mr. Mayor, Commissioner, Monsignor," Matt said.

"My goodness," Monsignor Schneider said, "what happened to your face?"

"I lost my footing chasing a fellow last night, Monsignor."

"How was that, Sergeant?" the mayor asked.

"I was chasing a car thief, sir."

"The one on Knight's Road?" Commissioner Mariani asked.

"Yes, sir."

"Correct me if I'm wrong, Sergeant," the commissioner said. "But it was a little more than that, wasn't it? The fellow ran a light, slammed into a family in a van, and sent them all to the hospital? And then left the scene?"

"Yes, sir."

"I saw that in the paper," the mayor said.

"Did you catch him?" Monsignor Schneider asked.

"Yes, sir."

"You really do get around, don't you, Sergeant?" the monsignor said, admiringly.

"What's with the hand?" the commissioner asked.

"I bruised it on the driveway, sir."

"And still managed to catch this fellow?" the monsignor asked.

"Yes, sir."

"What did you do, walk up on it, Sergeant?" Mariani asked.

"Yes, sir. I was taking . . . a detective—we were working on the Williamson job—home. And it happened right in front of us."

"And how is that going?" Schneider asked. "The Williamson 'job,' I think you said?"

"Well, sir, we have a pretty good psychological profile of the doer that should help us find him, and we have some pretty good evidence to put him away once we do—"

"For example?" the monsignor interrupted.

"With all respect, Monsignor, I'm not supposed to talk about details of an ongoing investigation."

"And that's a good rule, and I'm pleased to see you're paying attention to it," Commissioner Mariani said. "But I'd like to know, and I think the mayor would, and neither the mayor nor me is about to ask Monsignor Schneider to give us a moment alone. I'm sure he understands why."

"My lips are sealed, Sergeant," the monsignor said.

"Yes, sir," Matt said. "There was sperm at the scene, sir. They are already doing the DNA. Once we catch this fellow, get another DNA sample from him, and match it, it'll prove conclusively that he was at the scene."

"The certainty of a DNA match is on the order of several million to one, Monsignor," Commissioner Mariani pronounced.

"Absolutely fascinating," the monsignor said. "I was just telling the commissioner and the mayor, Sergeant, that when I last spoke with Stan, he made it pretty clear that while he's here—and we don't have him occupied— he'd like to spend some time watching the police—specifically you, Sergeant— at work. I confess I hadn't thought about what you just said about your having to be closemouthed about details of an ongoing investigation."

"I don't think that would be any problem with Mr. Colt," the mayor said. "Do you, Commissioner?"

"The problem, Mr. Mayor," Mariani replied, "would be making sure that Mr. Colt understood that whatever he saw, or heard, when he was with Sergeant Payne couldn't go any further."

"I don't think that would be a problem at all," Monsignor Schneider said. "I'm sure Stan would understand. After all, he's played a detective on the screen so often."

The commissioner smiled. A little wanly, Matt thought.

A Traffic Unit sergeant walked up to them, saluted, and said, "Commissioner, Mr. Colt's airplane's about to land."

[THREE]

Lieutenant Ross J. Mueller of the Forensic Laboratory of the Pennsylvania State Police in Harrisburg rose to his feet and extended his hand when Tony Harris was shown into his office.

"What can we do for you, Detective?" he asked, smiling cordially.

Mueller was a very large, muscular man who wore a tight-fitting uniform and his hair in a crew cut. Tony remembered what Dick Candelle had said about him probably having trouble finding his ass with both hands.

"Thank you for seeing me, sir," Tony said, "but I really hoped I could see Lieutenant Stecker."

Mueller looked at his watch.

"At the end of this tour—in other words, in an hour and five minutes— Lieutenant Stecker will hang up his uniform hat for the last time, and enter a well-deserved retirement. I'm taking his place. Now, how can Headquarters help Philadelphia?"

"Sir, I'm working a homicide. . . ."

"In what capacity?"

"Sir?"

"As the lead detective? One of the investigators? In what capacity?"

"I'm the lead detective on the job, sir."

"And you're here officially?"

"Yes, sir, I'm here officially."

"I thought perhaps that was the case. I don't recall hearing that you were coming."

"Sir, I just got in the car and came out here."

"You didn't check with your supervisor so that he could make an appointment for you?"

"No, sir, I did not."

"And who is your supervisor?"

"Lieutenant Jason Washington, sir."

"I don't believe I've had the pleasure," Lieutenant Mueller said, writing Washington's name on a lined pad.

If you don't know who Jason Washington is, Herr Storm Trooper, you really can't find your ass with both hands.

"Could you give me his phone number, please?" Lieutenant Mueller asked.

Tony gave him, from memory, the number of the commanding officer of the K-9 Unit of the Philadelphia police department. It was in his memory because he had noticed that it was identical, except for the last two digits, which were reversed, to that of the Homicide Unit.

He had made the quick judgment that despite his implied offer to help, Lieutenant Mueller was going to be part of the problem, not a solution.

"I'm going to call your Lieutenant and introduce myself," Lieutenant Mueller said, "and suggest the next time he thinks we can help Philadelphia, he call and set up an appointment."

"Yes, sir. Sir, I wasn't aware that was necessary, and I don't think Lieutenant Washington is, either."

"Probably not," Mueller said, smiling. "But you've heard, I'm sure, Detective . . . Harris, was it?"

"Yes, sir."

"That a new broom sweeps clean."

"Yes, sir, I've heard that."

"I'm the new broom around here."

"Yes, sir."

"But you're here. So how may we be of assistance?"

"Sir, as I said, I'm working a homicide. We have a visor hat . . . like a baseball cap, without a crown, that the doer left at the scene. Our lab, specifically Mr. Richard Candelle, has been able to lift only a partial that's probably an index finger."

"Candelle, you say?"

"Yes, sir."

"I believe I have met your Mr. Candelle. African-American, isn't he?"

"Yes, sir. He is."

"Go on, Detective Harris."

"I was hoping that you could have a look at it, and see if you couldn't find more than we have."

"We have, as you might not be aware, an Automated Fingerprint Identification System."

"Yes, sir. I've heard that."

"It's state-of-the-art technology. In the hands of an expert—I've been certified in its use myself—it sometimes can do remarkable things."

"Yes, sir."

"Well, we'll have a look at it for you, Detective. And get word back to you within, possibly, seventy-two hours."

"Sir, I'd sort of hoped to stick around until you . . ."

"Take a hotel room, you mean? Well, if that's all right with your supervisor, it's fine with me. As I say, we're talking about three days, if things go well."

"I meant today, sir."

"That's out of the question, I'm afraid. You just leave the evidence item with me, and we'll get to it as soon as possible."

"The thing is, Lieutenant, my supervisor, Lieutenant Washington—you're sure you don't know him?"

"Quite sure. I'd remember a name like that."

"Well, sir, Lieutenant Washington wants to ship the hat—the *evidence item*—to the FBI lab first thing in the morning."

"Well, that solves our problem then, doesn't it? The FBI really knows how to handle this sort of thing."

"Thank you for seeing me, sir. And I'm sorry I didn't have an appointment."

"Just don't do it again in the future, Detective."

"No, sir, I won't."

[FOUR]

The airplane, a Cessna Citation, came in from over Bucks County, touched down smoothly, and began to taxi to the terminal.

Nesfoods International had a Citation either identical to this one or very nearly identical to it. Matt's father had told him he had to spend an inordinate amount of time trying to convince the Internal Revenue Service that when the Nesbitts (father and/or son) and their families rode it to Kentucky or Florida the purpose was business, not to watch the Kentucky Derby or lie on the sands of Palm Beach.

The Citation stopped two hundred feet from them, and ground handlers went quickly to it to chock the wheels.

The mayor, the commissioner and the monsignor started to walk toward it. The commissioner turned and signaled for Matt to come with them.

The door rotated open, revealing stairs, as they—and a gaggle of photographers and reporters holding microphones—approached the airplane.

What at first—until Matt saw that it was wearing a goatee—looked like a fat woman in a dirty blonde pageboy haircut wearing pajamas came quickly out of the door and down the stairs. The man held one 35-mm camera with an enormous lens in his hand, and another, with a slightly smaller lens, hung from his neck.

He knelt to the right and aimed his camera at the door.

Stan Colt appeared in the doorway, smiling and ducking his head.

"Go down a couple of steps!" the fat photographer ordered.

Colt obeyed. He carefully went down two steps, then waved and flashed a wide smile. He was wearing blue jeans, a knit polo shirt, and a Philadelphia 76ers jacket. His fans applauded. Some whistled.

Colt came down the rest of the stairs and walked to Monsignor Schneider, who enthusiastically shook his hand and introduced him to the mayor and the commissioner, who both enthusiastically shook his hand.

Jesus, he's a hell of a lot smaller and shorter than he looks in the movies!

Photographs were taken, and the momentous occasion was both recorded on videotape and flashed via satellite to at least two of Philadelphia's TV stations, which interrupted their regular programming to bring—live—to their viewers images of Mr. Colt's arrival.

Matt saw that a young man his age and a prematurely gray-haired woman Matt guessed was probably in her late thirties had begun to take luggage from both the cabin and the baggage compartment. Both were stylishly dressed. Matt had no idea who they were, but presumed they had been on the airplane.

When they had all the luggage off the plane, they began to carry it to a black GMC Yukon XL, on the doors of which was a neat sign reading "Classic Livery."

The side windows of the truck were covered with dark translucent plastic. Matt knew that the truck—there were several just like it—was usually used to move cadavers from hospitals to funeral homes that rented their funeral limousines from Classic Livery. He wondered if the truck was going to be able to haul all the luggage.

The commissioner indicated the white limousine. Colt nodded, then sort of trotted over to the fans behind their barriers, shook hands, kissed two of the younger females, and then, waving, sort of trotted to the white limousine and ducked inside.

The fat photographer got in the front seat. The mayor and the commissioner got in the back.

"Hi!" Terry Davis said.

He hadn't seen her get off the Citation.

Jesus, she looks good!

"Hi!"

"You're going wherever they go from here?"

"I'm afraid so," he said.

"Got room for me?"

"Absolutely."

He saw that she had two large pieces of what he thought of as "limp" luggage and a squarish item he thought was probably a makeup kit. Plus an enormous purse.

"My car's over there," he said, gesturing in the general direction.

"Will all this stuff fit in a Porsche?"

"The *city's* car," he said. "It's a Ford."

When he picked up her limp luggage, his left hand hurt.

"What did you do to your face?" Terry asked, as she picked up her own bag.

"I fell down," Matt said, as he started to walk to the Crown Victoria.

He saw that Detective Jesus Martinez had finally shown up; he was standing with McFadden, and they did, he thought, indeed look like Mutt and Jeff.

"You better follow me," Matt said, and his voice was drowned out by the roar of the Highway bikes starting up.

"You better follow me," Matt repeated.

His hand hurt again when he loaded Terry's luggage into the backseat.

By the time Terry'd gotten in and he'd gotten the engine started, McFadden and Martinez had pulled their identical unmarked Crown Victorias in behind him.

And the convoy had left. He could see the GMC and four assorted vehicles bearing the press bringing up the end of it, disappearing around the corner of the administration building.

Discretion forbade racing to catch up with the convoy. He knew where it was going; he could probably catch up with it on I-95.

But when he reached the airport exit, it was barred by a line of cars stopped by two Eighth District uniforms and a sergeant apparently charged with seeing that Mr. Colt's fans did not join the convoy.

Matt drove to the side of the line of cars, and when he reached the head of it, reached under the dash and pushed the button that caused the blue lights under the grille to flash and the siren to start to growl.

The uniform sergeant waved the first fan's car through the gate, then waved Matt through the space he had occupied, with McFadden and Martinez following.

"So tell me about the face," Terry said when he had caught up with the convoy and was driving a stately fifty-five miles per hour down I-95 at the end of it.

"I was trying to stop a homicidal maniac from detonating an atom bomb and ending life as we know it on our planet."

Terry giggled. It was an accurate synopsis of Stan Colt's last opus.

"And in so doing, I fell down."

"And landed on your face?"

"Correct."

"But you caught the bad guy?"

"Yeah."

"What did he do?"

"Stole a car, ran a red light, and slammed into a family in their van."

"That's awful. But what did it have to do with you?"

"I saw the crash. That made it my business."

"Stan will love that story," Terry said.

"Please don't tell him," Matt said.

She looked at him strangely.

"Okay. If you don't want me to."

[FIVE]

Lieutenant Luther Stecker of the Pennsylvania State Police had obviously just finished shaving when his doorbell rang, for he answered the door in a sleeveless undershirt, with a towel hanging from his neck, and with vestiges of shaving cream under his chin and near his left ear.

He was a small and wiry man who wore what was left of his gray hair in a crew cut.

He waited wordlessly for his caller to announce his purpose.

"Lieutenant Stecker?" Tony Harris asked.

Stecker nodded.

"Sir, I'm Detective Harris from Philadelphia Homicide."

Stecker nodded and waited for Harris to go on.

"I'm working a job, and I really need your help."

"This is my last day on the job. Why'd you come here?"

"I went by the lab, sir. And saw Lieutenant Mueller."

And again Stecker waited expressionlessly for him to go on.

"Lieutenant, Dick Candelle said if anybody can come up with enough points from what I've got, it's you."

"You know Candelle?"

"Yes, sir. We go back a while."

"And he couldn't develop enough points from what you've got?"

"No, sir. But all he had to work with was a partial, sir. Probably an index finger."

A plump, pleasant-looking woman appeared behind Stecker.

"What?" she asked.

"This is Detective Harris from Homicide in Philadelphia."

"Did you tell him this is your last day on the job, and that . . ." She looked at her watch. ". . . in an hour and ten minutes, you're having your retirement party at the Penn-Harris?"

"Tell me about the job," Stecker said.

"Two black guys held up a Roy Rogers," Harris said. "They killed a Puerto Rican lady."

"That's terrible," the gray haired lady said, sucking in her breath.

"And then when a uniform—a friend of mine, nice guy, Kenny Charlton, eighteen years on the job, two kids—responded to the robbery in progress, one of the doers—who was wearing the visor hat, cap, I've got—stuck a .38 under his vest and blew him away."

Stecker didn't say anything.

"The only tie we have to these critters is this," Tony said. He held up the plastic evidence bag containing the crownless visor cap.

"That's all? No witnesses?"

"Nothing's worked."

"Grace, why don't you get Detective Harris a cup of coffee and a piece of cake while I put my shirt on."

"Luther, your party starts in an hour and ten minutes."

"You told me," Lieutenant Stecker said.

[SIX]

The chancellery of the Archdiocese of Philadelphia was prepared for the "photo op" presented by Mr. Stan Colt paying a courtesy call upon the cardinal.

The cardinal "just happened" to be on the ground floor of the chancellery as the Highway bikes, Lieutenant McGuire's unmarked car, the white Lincoln limousine, and the mayoral Cadillac limo rolled up it. That permitted the recording for posterity of images of the cardinal warmly greeting Mr. Colt as he got out of the limo.

The Hon. Alvin W. Martin had to move quickly to get in that shot, but he made it.

The cardinal, the mayor, and Mr. Colt, preceded by the fat photographer in the pageboy haircut, then entered the building. Lieutenant McGuire trotted after them, turned at the door, spotted Matt getting out of his car, and signaled for him to come along.

"Are you going in there?" Matt asked Terry Davis.

"That's what I get paid for," she said.

When they reached the cardinal's office, there was a delegation of faculty from West Catholic High School lined up to shake Mr. Colt's hand and to welcome him back to his alma mater. The mayor didn't manage to get in that shot, but he did manage to get in another shot in front of the cardinal's desk, of the cardinal, the principal of West Catholic, Monsignor Schneider, and Mr. Colt.

Then, after shaking hands a final time, Mr. Colt, again preceded by the fat photographer moving backward and frantically snapping pictures, left the cardinal's office.

Mr. Colt stopped when he saw Terry Davis.

"Where's the homicide detective?" he demanded.

Terry pointed at Matt.

Mr. Colt's eyebrows rose in surprise, or disbelief, and then he moved on.

As the procession went back through the lobby, Matt heard the engines of the Highway bikes roar to life.

The mayor of Philadelphia shook Mr. Colt's hand a final time, said he looked forward to seeing him a little later, and then walked back to the mayoral limousine.

Mr. Colt paused as he was about to enter the limousine, spotted Terry Davis, and called: "He's going to be at the hotel, right?"

"Right, Stan," Terry called back.

Mr. Colt nodded, then got in the white limousine.

The fans who had somehow learned that Mr. Colt would be staying at the Ritz-Carlton and had waited there in hopes of seeing him, and perhaps even getting his autograph, touching him, or perhaps coming away with a piece of his clothing, were disappointed.

All they got was a smile and a wave, as—preceded yet again by the fat photographer running backward—Colt went quickly into the hotel and through the lobby to a waiting elevator.

Stan Colt was sprawled on a couch in the sitting room of his suite, taking a pull from a bottle of beer from the Dock Street Brewery, when Lieutenant McGuire, Sergeant Payne, and Miss Terry Davis were ushered into his presence by the gray-haired, stylishly dressed woman Matt had seen carrying luggage from the Citation.

The stylishly dressed young man from the airport was talking on a telephone on a sideboard.

"With that out of the way, Terry, what's next?" Stan Colt greeted them.

"There's a cocktail party at the Bellvue-Stratford—it's right around the corner . . ."

"I know where it is, sweetheart. I'm from here."

". . . at six-thirty. Black tie. The limo will be here at six-fifteen."

"Where the hell did that virginal white one come from?"

"You want another color?" Terry asked.

Colt pointed to the young man on the telephone.

"That's what Lex is doing," he said. "Getting a black one."

"The cocktail party will be over at seven-thirty, which leaves the question of dinner open. I think you can count on at least one invitation."

"Let me think about that," he said.

He recognized Lieutenant McGuire for the first time.

"You're the security guy, right?"

"I'm Lieutenant McGuire of Dignitary Protection, Mr. Colt."

Mr. Colt's somewhat contemptuous shrug indicated he considered that a distinction without a difference.

"And you're the homicide detective, right?"

"I'm Sergeant Payne."

"But Homicide, right? You're the guy that was in the gun battle in Doylestown Monsignor Schneider told me about?"

Matt nodded.

"No offense, but you don't look the part."

"Perhaps that's because I'm not an actor," Matt said.

"You look—and for that matter sound like—you're a WASP from the Main Line."

"Do I really? Maybe that's because I am indeed a White Anglo-Saxon Protestant who was raised in Wallingford; that's not the Main Line, but I take your point."

Matt saw that Lieutenant McGuire was being made very uncomfortable by the exchange.

"Why am I getting the feeling, Sergeant," Colt asked, "that you would rather be somewhere else?"

"You're perceptive?"

Colt chuckled.

"You want to tell me what you'd rather be doing?"

"I was working a homicide before the commissioner assigned me to sit on you."

"'Sit on' me? That sounds a little erotic. Kinky. You know?"

"It means that my orders are to see that you don't do anything while you're here that will embarrass in any way anybody connected with this charitable gesture of yours."

"For example?"

"Payne!" Lieutenant McGuire said, warningly.

"Let me put it this way, Mr. Colt," Matt said. "As long as you're in Philadelphia, the virtue of chastity will have to be its own reward for you."

Terry Davis giggled.

"You telling me, I think, that I don't get to fool around?" Colt asked.

"That's right."

"Not even a little?"

"Not even a little."

"You understand who I am?"

"That's why you don't get to fool around, even a little."

Colt turned to Terry Davis.

"You think this is funny, don't you?"

"You're the one who said you wanted to hang out with a real, live homicide cop."

"And I do. I do. And I really like this guy! This is better than I hoped for." He turned to Matt. "I am going to get to watch you work, right?"

"The commissioner said I was to show you as much about how Homicide works as I think I can."

"Which means what?"

"I will show you everything I can, so long as doing so doesn't interfere with an investigation."

"And you make that call?"

"Right."

"And what if I complain to him?" Colt asked, pointing to McGuire. "He's a lieutenant, right? And you're a sergeant?"

"The lieutenant's job is to protect you," Matt said. "Mine is to ensure your chastity."

Colt was now smiling.

"That may be harder than you think," he said. "You think you can stay awake twenty-four hours a day?"

"No. But there's two detectives in the corridor who've also been assigned to the Chastity Detail."

Colt glanced at the stylishly dressed young man who had just hung up the telephone.

"Well?" he asked, curtly.

"You'll have a black limo in the morning, Stan, but not tonight. It's the best I could do."

"Not good enough, Alex," Colt snapped. "Call somebody else, for Christ's sake. I don't want to arrive at this place looking like Tinkerbell." Then he had another thought. "You going to the cocktail party, Sergeant Payne?"

Matt looked at McGuire, who nodded, and then nodded himself.

"You must have a police car. Any reason I can't ride with you?"

"No."

"Will there be room for everybody?" Alex asked.

"Who's everybody?" Matt asked.

"Me, Jeanette, Terry, and Eddie."

Jeanette, Matt decided, must be the gray-haired woman.

"Eddie's the character with the pageboy?" he asked.

"My personal photographer," Colt furnished.

"No," Matt said.

"Eddie goes everywhere with me," Colt said. "They all do."

"They don't go everywhere with you when you're with me," Matt said. "Your call, Mr. Colt."

"You're a real hardass, Payne," Colt said, admiringly. "I'm going with Payne. The rest of you can go in the wedding limo." He turned to Matt. "And after this party thing, you'll show me stuff, right?"

"If you like," Matt said.

[SEVEN]

"We're here," Sergeant Payne said to Mr. Colt after they had rolled up to the Broad Street entrance of the Bellvue-Stratford Hotel, third in line behind Lieutenant McGuire's unmarked and the white Lincoln limo. Behind them were three unmarked cars, one belonging to Dignitary Protection and the other two to Detectives Martinez and McFadden.

Matt had taken a leaf from the uniforms who had kept Colt's fans from leaving the North Philadelphia Airport and had ordered McFadden and Martinez to keep Eddie the photographer, and anybody else, from following Matt's car when it left the hotel.

"Don't get your balls in an uproar. I'm waiting for Eddie to get out of the limo."

Eddie the photographer got quickly out of the limo, sort of knelt, and prepared to photograph Mr. Colt's arrival at the Bellvue-Stratford.

"Come on, Payne," Colt said.

"I'll catch up with you inside," Matt said. "I've got to park the car."

"No, first you let Eddie take our picture, and then you park the car."

"I don't think so," Matt said.

"If you don't let him take our picture now, I'll tell him I changed my mind, and he gets to go with us when we leave here."

"That'll be hard to do after McFadden handcuffs him to that brass rail."

"Hey . . . It's Matt, right?"

"Right."

"I'm meeting you halfway, Matt. He's shot two hundred pictures since we got here, and the only one that'll do me any good is this one."

"Excuse me?"

"The real press doesn't give a shit about one more picture of me shaking hands with a mayor, or even a cardinal. But Stan Colt with a *real* homicide sergeant, that's news. Come on. Get out and smile."

"I don't want my picture in the goddamn newspapers."

"Tough shit. Either now, or he follows us around all night." He paused, then did a very creditable mimicry of Matt: "Your call, Sergeant Payne."

Matt got out of the car.

"Look serious, but think of pussy," Mr. Colt whispered to Sergeant Payne as, following Eddie the photographer's hand signals, he moved Matt where Eddie wanted them.

Inside the Grand Ballroom of the Bellvue-Stratford, Sergeant Payne hurried to answer Commissioner Mariani's summons, a crooked finger.

"Yes, sir?"

"Colt just told the mayor how grateful he is for the opportunity to, quote, hang out, unquote, with you."

"Yes, sir?"

"What are you going to do with him?"

"I thought I'd show him Liberties Bar and, if nobody from Homicide is there, take him to Homicide."

"And if somebody from Homicide is in Liberties?"

"Hope I can get them talking about closed cases."

Commissioner Mariani nodded.

When they saw that Sergeant Payne and Mr. Colt had gotten into the Crown Victoria, two white-capped Traffic Unit uniforms stopped traffic moving in both directions on South Broad Street, and then one of them gestured to Sergeant Payne, who then made a U-turn that saw him headed toward City Hall.

The traffic uniforms then blew their whistles and gestured, restoring traffic to its normal flow, and incidentally effectively preventing anyone from following Matt's unmarked car.

"Thanks, guys!" Detective McFadden called to the uniforms, and gave a thumbs-up gesture.

Detectives McFadden and Martinez then got into their unmarked cars and drove off. The members of the press who were cleverly prepared to follow them, did so. They followed Martinez to the Ritz-Carlton front door, where he parked his car and went inside to await the return of Sergeant Payne and Mr. Colt, or the arrival at midnight of Detective McFadden, whichever came first.

The members of the press who followed Detective McFadden drove deep into South Philadelphia, where he pulled the unmarked half onto the curb in front of a row house on Fitzgerald Street, then went inside to catch a couple of hours' sleep before relieving Hay-zus at the Ritz-Carlton.

"Aren't I going to stand out like a sore thumb in this?" Mr. Colt inquired of Sergeant Payne, indicating his dinner jacket. "Maybe we could stop by the hotel and let me change?"

"Not at all," Matt said. "We're going to Liberties Bar, and the last time I was there, my boss was there, dressed just like that."

"You're bullshitting me, right?"

"Boy Scout's Honor," Matt said.

"Were you a Boy Scout?"

"Yes, as a matter of fact, I was."

"Me, too," Colt said. "Well, what the hell."

He pulled open his black bow tie.

There were no members of the Homicide Division in Liberties Bar.

"We can wait a couple of minutes and see if somebody shows up," Matt said.

"I will have one of three drinks I allow myself a day," Colt said. "This will be number two; I had a beer at the hotel."

"You *allow* yourself three drinks a day?" Matt asked.

"If I have more than that, I get in trouble," Colt said. "Sometimes, I have four, if like I have one at lunch and a beer in the afternoon, then I might have two at night, but never any more than that."

They had a drink. Matt ordered a scotch on the rocks, Colt—at Matt's suggestion—a Bushmills martini, aka an Irish Doctor's Special.

When the bartender delivered them, he looked closely at Colt.

"Anybody ever tell you you look a lot like Stan Colt?"

"Yeah. Lots of people."

"Any of the guys from Homicide been in?" Matt asked.

"Earlier," the bartender said.

Colt looked at Matt.

"You get stuck with the tab," he said. "Alex has my dough, and you didn't want him to come."

Matt laid a bill on the bar.

"I'll get that back to you."

"My pleasure," Matt said. "Alex is not here."

Colt took a sip of his drink.

"I like this," he said.

"Good."

"So what's the plan now? You 'sit on' me here? Nobody from Homicide shows up? Eventually I get sleepy? And—"

"Finish your drink, we'll take a run past Homicide," Matt said.

"Good," Stan Colt said.

"Nice," Stan Colt said, vis-à-vis Detective Olivia Lassiter, who was sitting at a desk with a phone to her ear.

"Very," Matt agreed.

He saw that Captain Quaire and Lieutenant Jason Washington were in Quaire's office.

"Detective Lassiter, this is Mr. Colt," Matt said.

Olivia gave him her hand and a smile, but didn't say anything.

"What's going on in there?" Matt asked.

Olivia shrugged. "They both came in about an hour ago."

She started to add something to that, but then directed her attention to the telephone: "Good evening, Lieutenant. Thank you for taking my call. My name is Lassiter, Philadelphia Homicide, and I'm working a job. . . ."

Matt took Colt's arm and propelled him toward the coffee machine.

"And she's a homicide detective, too?" Colt asked.

Matt nodded.

"She's been on that phone most of day," Matt said. "Calling every police department in the country, looking for a similar job to one we're working on here."

"The one you were working on before you were told to sit on me?"

Matt nodded. "It's a rape murder. Real sicko. Ties young women up, cuts off their clothes with a large knife, and then . . . jerks off . . . onto them."

"Jesus!"

"And then takes their picture. This time, he killed the victim."

"And you don't know who he is?"

"We haven't a clue. If we ever find him—that's what Lassiter is doing on the phone; other detectives are looking down other streets—we can probably get a conviction. But first we have to find him."

Colt's face was serious as he absorbed this.

"I have to check in with my boss," Matt said, pointing at Quaire's glass-walled office. "I'll be right back."

"I'll talk to her," Colt said. "Take your time."

And then he saw something on Matt's face.

"Do I detect that your interest in the lady detective is not entirely professional?"

"I'll be right back," Matt said, and walked to Captain Quaire's office and knocked on the door.

Quaire waved him in.

"I've got Stan Colt out there, sir."

"I can see. Now, can you get him out of here?"

"I'll try. . . ."

"Tony went to Harrisburg," Washington explained, "and talked Lieutenant Stecker, their print expert, into going late to his retirement party. He and Tony are still at the State Police lab running the print through the AFIS. Presuming the doer's prints are on file, and we get a match from the machine, Tony will contact us."

"So get Mr. Colt out of here, and the sooner the better," Captain Quaire ordered. "If there's a match, everybody and his brother will be in here, and he shouldn't."

"He seems to be stricken with Detective Lassiter," Washington said. "May I suggest you take both of them someplace while she at great length explains how we are working the Williamson job?"

"Can I send her in here so you can tell her that?"

278 · W. E. B. GRIFFIN

"Make it quick," Quaire said.

"Yes, sir."

Matt walked to Olivia and told her the boss wanted to see her.

When she was out of earshot, Colt asked, "What was that all about?"

"I just got permission from the captain for her to tell you what's going on with the Williamson job."

"That's the guy who . . . ?" Colt asked, moving his hand in a pumping motion.

"Cheryl Ann Williamson is the victim," Matt said. "But yeah."

Olivia came out of Quaire's office looking more than a little unhappy.

"Where are we going to do this?"

"Could we do it over dinner?" Stan Colt asked in his most charming manner.

"You mean in a restaurant?"

"I was thinking of my place," Colt said. "At the Ritz-Carlton. We could be alone, and get room service."

"You were planning to come along, Sergeant?" Olivia asked.

"Absolutely," Matt said.

"I haven't had my dinner," Olivia said.

"Then it's settled," Stan Colt said. He punched Matt affectionately on the shoulder. "I really appreciate this, Matt."

CHAPTER 14

[ONE]

It was either a light rain or a heavy drizzle, and Deputy Commissioner Dennis V. Coughlin, holding an umbrella over his head with his right hand, stood at the gas charcoal grill in the backyard of 8231 Jeanes Street in Northwest Philadelphia wondering if he could trust the brand-new, state-of-the-art $129.95 electronic thermometer stuck in one of the two rolled-and-tied tenderloins of beef on the grill.

It indicated that the interior temperature of the meat was 145 degrees Fahrenheit, which in turn meant, according to the instruction manual, that when permitted to rest for five minutes, the meat should be just a little more done than rare.

Denny Coughlin didn't think so. It didn't look nearly that done to him.

"To hell with it," Coughlin muttered, and reached for the very long-handled, stainless-steel knife, part of a $79.95 Master Griller's Kit—knife, fork, and grill-scraper—that had been another gift from Coughlin to Chief Inspector (Retired) August and Mrs. Olga Wohl, at whose grill he was standing.

When he tried to cut the loin that was not electronically connected to the Interior Temperature Gauge, the perfectly tied-and-rolled meat rolled across the grill but remained uncut.

"Shit," Chief Inspector Coughlin muttered, laid the umbrella upside down on the grass, picked up the extra-long-handled fork from the Master Griller's Kit, impaled the tenderloin with the sensor in it, sliced it halfway through, and examined it carefully.

"I'll be damned," he said.

The thermometer was telling the truth.

He looked up in annoyance at the sky. It had suddenly begun to rain harder. Much harder.

He looked back at the tenderloins. The flexible metal cord connecting the sensor impaled precisely in the center of one of them would have to be removed before he could move the meat to the platter.

He touched it gingerly, and it didn't seem to be *that* hot. He got a decent grip on it and gave it a tug. It remained impaled. He picked up the fork again, and using the fork to hold the meat in place, tugged harder. The sensor came free, suddenly, which caused Coughlin, in the moment in which he realized the goddamn thing was burning his fingers and let go of it, to throw both the sensor, the metal cord, and the Stainless Steel Easy-To-Read, Dishwasher-Safe Interior Temperature Indicating Device into the grass of Chief Wohl's backyard.

There were cheers, whistles, and applause from Chief Wohl's back porch, where Chief Wohl, Chief Inspector of Detectives Matthew Lowenstein, Inspector Peter Wohl, Captain Frank Hollaran, and Mr. Michael J. O'Hara were standing—out of the rain—watching the Master Chef at work.

After glancing momentarily at the porch, Commissioner Coughlin impaled the tenderloins, one after the other, and placed them on the platter—a stainless-steel plate with blood grooves resting in a depression in a wooden plate with handles; yet another culinary gift to the Wohls. Then he balanced the platter on his right hand, like a waiter, and sort of squatted to pick up the umbrella.

Then he marched toward the porch under the umbrella and somewhat unsteadily climbed the stairs, to further whistles, cheers, and applause from the men standing on it.

"You can all kiss my royal Irish ass," Commissioner Coughlin announced.

Five minutes later, Commissioner Coughlin, fresh from drying his face and hair, sat down to table with everybody, which now included Mrs. Olga Wohl, Mrs. Sarah Lowenstein, and Mrs. Barbara Hollaran, at a table heavily laden with what else they were going to eat.

"I've got to get one of those little digital cameras and carry it with me," Chief Lowenstein said. "I'd love to have pictures of the Master Chef at work."

"I already told you what you can do," Coughlin said. "And, yes, Augie, thank you for asking, I will have a glass of that wine."

"I've got mine," Mickey O'Hara said, holding up his camera. "But I've seen that Angry Irishman look in his eyes before and didn't think I'd better."

Twenty minutes after that, as Sarah Lowenstein poured coffee and appropriate comments of approval were being offered vis-à-vis the chocolate cake Barbara

Hollaran had prepared for the nearly ritual once-every-other-week supper at the Wohls', Commissioner Coughlin's cellular phone buzzed.

He took it from his shirt pocket, said, "Hold one" before his caller had a chance to say anything, and handed the cellular to Hollaran, who quickly went into the kitchen.

Hollaran returned almost immediately.

"Commissioner, it's Captain Quaire," he said, formally.

Coughlin nodded, and reached for the phone.

"What's up?" he asked, listened, and said, "I'll get right back to you. Don't do anything until I do."

He pushed the End button and, holding the cellular in his palm, looked thoughtfully at it a moment.

"Mickey, this is out of school, okay?"

"Sure," O'Hara said.

"What is it, Denny?" Chief Wohl asked.

"We've identified one of the doers in the Roy Rogers job," he said. "Tony Harris went to the State Police fingerprint guy, Lieutenant Stecker, who worked some kind of magic with their new AFIS machine and was able to get enough points to let us run them, and . . ."

He stopped in midsentence, and forestalled any other questions by punching his way through the stored numbers on the cellular until he found what he wanted, and then pressing Call.

"Ben, Denny Coughlin. I apologize for calling you at home. . . ."

He stopped and laughed.

"What, Denny?" Chief Wohl asked.

"Ben Solomon told me to take two aspirin and call him in the morning," Coughlin said, and then his voice suddenly grew serious, as Mrs. Solomon, aka the district attorney of Philadelphia, came on the line.

"Eileen, we've identified one of the doers in the Roy Rogers homicide and now have a pretty good idea who the other one is," he said. "I thought I'd better let you know."

There was a pause, and then he continued.

"Tony Harris got the State Police, using some kind of a new machine they have, to get enough prints—points—from a hat, a visor, one of them left at the scene."

Pause.

"Yeah, that's it, Eileen. But, once we arrest them, I'm pretty sure some of the witnesses will be able to pick them out of a lineup. . . ."

Pause.

"No. Henry Quaire's getting the warrant as we speak. . . ."

Pause.

"Whatever you say, Eileen. Is Unger there? You want me to send a car?"

Pause.

"Okay. Thirty minutes, in my office."

Pause.

"Matt's here. We're at Augie Wohl's house."

Pause.

"Thirty minutes. Thanks, Eileen."

He took the phone from his ear and pushed End.

"The district attorney says she wants to make sure this is done right. She's going to meet us in my office in thirty minutes."

"Just you two?" Peter Wohl asked.

"That's what she said. What are you driving at?"

"The last I heard, this job was given to a Special Operations task force."

"Jesus, I forgot about that," Coughlin said. "Peter, why don't you just happen to be in Homicide in case Eileen wants to see you?"

Peter Wohl nodded.

"Yes, sir."

"Mickey, you didn't hear any of this," Coughlin said.

"When do I hear any of this?"

"I'll let you know what happens when we meet with Eileen, but that'll probably still be off the record."

"If you've identified these crumbs, what's all this about?"

"In the words of our beloved district attorney, we want to make goddamn sure these critters don't walk out of the courtroom because we did something stupid now that we finally know who they are," Coughlin said.

He rose to his feet.

"Eat Barbara's cake and drink your coffee first," Olga Wohl ordered firmly. "Five minutes one way or the other's not going to matter."

Five minutes later, the first radio call was made when Frank Hollaran took the microphone from beneath the dash and spoke into it: "Radio, C-2 en route to the Roundhouse from Chief Wohl's residence."

Immediately after that, there were two more calls, as D-1 (Chief Inspector of Detectives Lowenstein) and S-1 Inspector Wohl (Special Operations) reported that they, too, were on their way from Chief Wohl's house to the Roundhouse.

[TWO]

"I don't know what I'm doing here, Eileen," Police Commissioner Ralph J. Mariani said, as he walked into Deputy Commissioner Coughlin's conference room.

"You're the police commissioner, Ralph," the Hon. Eileen McNamara Solomon replied, matter-of-factly. "I thought you ought to be on this, so I asked Al Unger to call you."

There were several shadings to their relationship. The most important was that Commissioner Mariani served at the pleasure of the Hon. Alvin W. Martin, mayor of the City of Philadelphia. The mayor is one of the two senior officials in Philadelphia who have no one to answer to but the law and the voters. The other is the district attorney.

Almost as important, both the police commissioner and the district attorney felt—even if they never articulated this belief—that the burden of protecting the citizens of the City of Brotherly Love from the barbarians hung primarily from his/her shoulders alone, and that the function of the other was to assist them in this noble pursuit.

As a practical matter, both realized there had to be sort of a partnership arrangement to effectively keep the barbarians at the gate, since neither could issue orders to the other.

In the relationship between district attorneys and police commissioners there were also the factors of respect, trust, and admiration. In the past, district attorneys and police commissioners had sometimes not respected, trusted, or admired each other at all. Eileen Solomon and Ralph Mariani not only held each other in high professional regard, but were also friends.

But in this case, the truth was that Eileen hadn't even thought of Ralph when she asked Denny to meet her in the Roundhouse until she had called Al Unger to tell him she needed a ride, and he had brought the subject up.

Detective Albert Unger was the senior of the two members of the District Attorney's Squad who served as driver/bodyguard for the D.A. So far as he—and others—were concerned, the D.A. needed round-the-clock protection. Threats against her life had been made by a number of people he thought were perfectly capable of trying to whack her.

The D.A., however, firmly said she didn't want a cop in the lobby of her apartment building twenty-four hours a day, much less hanging around in her apartment.

So a deal was struck. A word was spoken into the ear of Wachenhut Security, who provided the unarmed doorman/concierge/security guard in the lobby of the luxury apartment building on the Parkway in which Dr. and Mrs. Solomon resided. Four new employees, all of them retired Philadelphia police officers, were shortly afterward engaged to work the lobby of the apartment building. All of them were licensed to carry firearms, and all of them shared Al Unger's belief that there were critters who would like to whack the D.A., whom all of the retired police officers held in very high regard.

The second part of the deal was a solemn promise by the D.A.—"What would you like me to do, Al, put one hand on a Bible and swear to God?" she had asked in exasperation—that she would never leave the apartment unless he knew where she was going and why.

This meant that Unger—or somebody else from the squad—would either drive the D.A. or follow her in an unmarked car, whether she was riding in the doctor's Caddy, or jogging along the Parkway on her thrice-weekly hour-long jaunts to keep her hips and thighs under control.

When the D.A. had called Al Unger to say that she was sorry, but she had to go to the Roundhouse and right now, he had naturally asked why, and she had told him.

"I didn't hear Mariani's name mentioned, boss."

"You think he should be there?"

"I think he ought to be asked."

If I don't ask him, Eileen had decided, *when he hears about it, Ralph will get his macho Italian ego bruised, and maybe decide Denny went behind his back.*

"Okay. Ask him," she said. "I'll be waiting downstairs in ten minutes."

Detective Unger had, en route to the apartment, made a radio call.

"DA-1 to C-1."

"Go."

"Can you tell the commissioner that DA-1 is en route to the Roundhouse, and would like him to be there if he has the time?"

There was a thirty-second delay, which Detective Unger had correctly presumed was how long it took to relay the message to the commissioner in the backseat and get a response.

"DA-1, the commissioner will be there in thirty minutes."

. . .

Commissioner Mariani nodded at Deputy Commissioner Coughlin and Chief of Detectives Lowenstein, and sat down in Coughlin's chair, left vacant for him at the head of the table.

"I didn't hear anything on the radio," he said. "What's going on?"

"We've positively identified one of the doers in the Roy Rogers job," Coughlin said. "And have a pretty good idea who the other one is. He fits the description, he's the other guy's cousin, and he's been in trouble with the doer before."

"Good. You could have told me that on the telephone. Who are they?"

"Two young guys from the Paschall Homes Housing Project," Coughlin said. "You know, Seventy-second and Elmwood in southwest Philly?"

Mariani nodded.

"Lawrence John Porter, twenty, the doer, the one we've been calling the 'fat guy,' and Ralph David Williams, nineteen," Coughlin went on. "Neither has ever been in bad trouble before."

"How'd you find them?"

"Tony Harris went to Harrisburg. The State Police've got a new machine, and they could lift more points from the print than Candelle could here," Lowenstein said.

"Good points?"

"It wouldn't matter if they were, Ralph," Eileen said.

"Excuse me?"

"A federal judge refused to admit fingerprints in a trial—a trial here—a couple of months back."

"I heard something about that."

"I'm not saying it'll happen, but we do have judges here who like to make law by following federal precedent. If the prints are inadmissible, all you've got is witnesses. . . ."

"Something wrong with that, Eileen?"

"All the defense has to do is create reasonable doubt in the mind of one juror," she said. "And we all know the jury pool always contains a number of people who are simply unable to believe that any black kid ever did anything wrong."

"You're not trying to tell me you think these two cop-killers are going to walk?"

"I'm trying to tell you, Ralph, that it's a possibility, which will become a certainty if we make any mistakes from here on in."

"God damn it!"

"That's the bad news, Ralph," Coughlin said. "The good news might, I say might, be that we can find the murder weapon. . . . It's a revolver and we have a bullet—"

"And can tie the weapon to either one of these two," Eileen interjected. "*Credibly* tie it to either one of them."

"Or really get lucky, and once they're arrested, they confess. They're just a couple of young punks," Coughlin went on.

"Which any public defender six months out of law school will contend was obtained by mental duress . . ." Eileen said.

"Jesus," Lowenstein said.

". . . or worse. And I don't think we can count on these two being defended by an incompetent from the Public Defender's Office. This is Murder Two, and they will assign the best man they've got. Or, worse than that, some really competent defense lawyer will take it *pro bono* because this trial's going to be all over the papers and TV."

"You've got their sheets?" Mariani asked.

Lowenstein shoved a folder across the conference table to him.

"There's not much," he said. "A couple of shoplifting charges, car burglaries, that sort of thing."

Mariani read the records of previous encounters with the law of the two suspects, shrugged, and then looked at Eileen Solomon.

"Okay, Eileen. What do you think we should do?"

"I don't think we should rush to arrest these two until we have a better case."

"Matt told me he was concerned that these two, having gotten away so far with the Roy Rogers job, and knowing you can only be executed once, might do the same sort of thing again, just as soon as they spend what they took from the Roy Rogers," Mariani said, but it was a question.

"That's a valid concern, and I share it," Eileen said.

"So you're suggesting we just sit on these two until we can make a really tight case?" he asked.

She nodded.

"Now that we know who they are, maybe we can get something from snitches," Lowenstein said. "For example, whether or not they still have the .38."

Mariani nodded.

"And we could run their mug shots before some of the witnesses and see if it jogs their memory," Coughlin said.

"Taking great care with that, so the defense can't claim we suggested whom the witnesses should pick out," Eileen said.

"How soon could you start surveillance of these two?" Mariani asked.

"I can have detectives from Southwest outside their door in however long it takes them to get there. I'd rather use undercover cars, which means I would have to have your permission to take a couple—five or six would be better—undercover cars away from the Impact Unit or Internal Affairs. With a little luck, I could have them in place in probably under an hour," Lowenstein said.

"You've got my permission, of course," Mariani said, then had a second thought. "No, you don't. Because you don't need it. Peter Wohl's already got the authority. The mayor ordered the formation of a Special Operations task force for this job, remember?"

"I remember," Lowenstein said.

"That's right," Coughlin said.

"He's already got authority to request support from everybody, right?" Mariani asked.

Coughlin and Lowenstein nodded.

"The mayor gave Wohl the job," Mariani said. "Let him do it. You better put the arm out for him."

"He's downstairs in Homicide with Quaire and Washington," Lowenstein said.

"You already called him?" Mariani asked.

"I didn't have to. We were all having dinner at Augie Wohl's house when Quaire called me," Coughlin said.

"Okay, then, Denny," Mariani said, and then his voice changed as he added, formally, "Under your supervision, Commissioner Coughlin, the Special Operations task force, paying cognizance to the suggestions of the district attorney, will proceed with the investigation. So inform Inspector Wohl."

"Yes, sir," Coughlin said.

"Then that's it," Mariani said. "Eileen, we all appreciate your support."

"Let's do this right," Eileen said. "We need to get those two off the street permanently."

[THREE]

When the district attorney of Philadelphia started to get off the Roundhouse elevator at the first floor, where the Homicide Division had its headquarters, she saw the surprise on the faces of Deputy Commissioner Coughlin and Chief Inspector Lowenstein.

"Why not?" she asked. "I'm here. And the last I heard, I was welcome in Homicide."

"The last I heard, there was no place in the department where you are not more than welcome at any time," Coughlin said, and waved her off the elevator. "But I thought I detected a tone of annoyance in Ben's voice."

"We have a deal," she said. "I keep my mouth shut when the hospital calls Ben, and he keeps his shut when I have to work." She chuckled.

"What?" Lowenstein asked.

"One time when the hospital called, I said, 'Oh, hell, Ben, not now,' and he replied, 'You knew what you were getting into when you married a doctor.'"

Coughlin looked confused.

"Isn't that what you cops tell your wives when they complain about the odd hours you have to keep?" the D.A. asked.

Lowenstein chuckled.

"I don't have a wife. I wouldn't know," Coughlin said.

They got off the elevator and walked down the corridor to Homicide.

Coughlin was not surprised that a lot of people would be in Homicide, but he was surprised at how many were actually there. The suite of offices was crowded with a number of non-Homicide white shirts, detectives, and uniforms.

In, or standing around the doorway of, Captain Quaire's office were Quaire, Inspector Peter Wohl; Lieutenant Jason Washington; Detective Tony Harris; Captains Frank Hollaran and Mike Sabara—Wohl's deputy—both in plainclothes; Captain Stuart Jenkins, the commanding officer of the Twelfth District, which covered the Paschall Homes Housing Project, where, according to the addresses on their last arrest sheets, both Lawrence John Porter and Ralph David Williams lived; and Captain Dave Pekach, the Highway Patrol commander. Jenkins and Pekach were in uniform.

In, or standing around the doorway of, the lieutenant's office—the three Homicide lieutenants, who were rarely on duty at the same time, shared an office—were Lieutenant Robert Natali, who was the tour lieutenant, and Sergeants Zachary Hobbs and Ed McCarthy.

Scattered around—in some cases, sitting on—the desks in the main area were Detective Al Unger; Sergeant Harry McElroy, Chief Lowenstein's driver; Sergeant Jerry O'Dowd, Pekach's driver; Sergeant Charley Lomax, Sabara's driver; and Sergeant Paul Kittinger, Captain Jenkins's driver.

Kittinger and O'Dowd were in uniform.

The term "driver" is somewhat misleading. Although all of these people did actually drive the cars assigned to their superiors, they were far more than chauffeurs. Their official job was to relieve their bosses of what administrative details they could, in addition to driving them around.

But it was actually more than that. They had all been recognized as having both the ambition and the ability to rise higher in the police hierarchy, and their assignment as drivers gave them a chance to see how their supervisors recognized and dealt with the problems that came their way. In many ways—except they never passed canapés—drivers were the police version of military aides-de-camp.

Coughlin marched across the outer office to Quaire's office and stood for a moment in the doorway.

"It looks," he said, smiling, "as if everybody's here but Homicide's newest sergeant. Where's Payne?"

"He was here, Commissioner," Captain Quaire said. "With Stan Colt."

"Oh, God!" Coughlin said.

"So I ran him off with the girl from Northwest. She is—I told her to do it thoroughly and slowly—bringing him up to speed on the Williamson job."

"Clever," Coughlin said, approvingly. "Give us a minute alone with Inspector Wohl, will you, please?"

Everybody filed out of Quaire's office. When only Coughlin, Lowenstein, Solomon, and Wohl were left, Coughlin closed the door.

"I've got a suggestion, Eileen," he said.

"Shoot."

"You tell Peter what your concerns are, I'll tell him what his orders from the commissioner are, and then the three of us leave."

She didn't reply, and waited for him to go on.

"The point will be made to everybody out there that there's a lot of interest in what's going on from us. That's all that's really necessary, and if we hang around it will look like we're all going to be looking over his shoulder. I don't want any question in anybody's mind about who has the responsibility and the authority in this."

The district attorney considered that for a full thirty seconds, which seemed longer.

"Peter," she said, finally, "I don't want these two to walk because we get enthusiastic or careless and do something stupid. Before we arrest them, I want a damned tight case against them. I don't think we can safely rely on their fingerprints—or, for that matter, a confession. Now that defense attorneys have got their foot in the door with the successful challenges to fingerprints and confessions, we need to add to what we have now. Tying them positively to the murder weapon, for example, would be nice."

Wohl nodded his understanding.

"I'll pass the word that you get what you want, when you want it," Chief Lowenstein said.

"Yes, sir," Wohl said. "Thank you."

"I've got an idea about that, too," Coughlin said. "Everybody out there is wondering what the hell we're talking about in here. So let's give them a little show. Matt, you open the door, and tell Sergeant McElroy to call Southwest Detectives, and get Captain Calmon down here, now, to report to Inspector Wohl."

"You're serious about that, aren't you, Denny?" Eileen asked.

"Yes, I'm serious. I want to make sure everybody knows who's in charge."

Lowenstein left the office, called his driver over, and told him what Coughlin had told him to tell him. Then he went back into the office.

Eileen started for the door.

"Where are you going, Eileen?"

"I'm going out there and tell Al Unger to call Steve Cohen and tell him to get right down here to advise Peter," she said. She turned to Wohl. "Steve's pretty bright, and I think he'll be useful. If he gets in your way, call me."

"I know Steve. We get along. But thanks, Eileen."

Steven J. Cohen was one of the best of the more than two hundred assistant district attorneys of Philadelphia.

Eileen McNamara Solomon left Quaire's office, spoke with Detective Al Unger, and then came back in.

Deputy Commissioner Coughlin then left the office, called Captain Hollaran over, and told him to call the Internal Affairs Division and the Impact Unit in his name, ordering them to get a senior officer to Homicide immediately to report to Inspector Wohl. Then he went back into the office.

"Can we go now, Denny?" Eileen asked.

"One more thing," Coughlin said. "Inspector Wohl, your orders from the commissioner are, 'The Special Operations task force, paying cognizance to the suggestions of the District Attorney, will proceed with the investigation.'"

"Yes, sir."

"Did I get that right, Eileen?"

"Verbatim," Eileen said. "And paying cognizance to my suggestions, Inspector, means before you arrest either of these two critters, you check with me."

"Steve Cohen won't do?"

"With me, Inspector."

"Yes, ma'am," Wohl said.

"Don't ma'am me, Peter. I'm not old enough to be your mother," the District Attorney said, and left Quaire's office. A moment later, Coughlin and Lowenstein followed her.

[FOUR]

Even as he was pulling the unmarked Crown Victoria into one of the spaces reserved for the hotel limousine and other important cars—over the indignant, both arms waving, objections of the Ritz-Carlton doorman—Matt saw eight, ten, maybe more members of the press start to rush toward it, brandishing cameras and microphones.

"Do they always follow you around like this?" Matt asked.

"It is the price of celebrity," Stan Colt said, solemnly, resignedly, and then added, in a normal voice, "And let me tell you, buddy, it gets to be a real pain in the ass."

The car's arrival, Stan Colt in the front seat, and the movement of the press had also been seen by Sergeant Al Nevins of Dignitary Protection, who had apparently stationed himself and two uniforms just inside the hotel's door. The three of them walked quickly to the car. Nevins opened the door, and when Colt got out, the three of them made a wedge and escorted Colt into the hotel. Once he was through the door, the uniforms barred the press from following him.

Matt and Olivia got out of the car and went into the hotel.

Nevins was standing by an open elevator door.

Matt made the introductions. "Sergeant Nevins, Detective Lassiter."

"How are you?" Nevins said, but his surprise that Olivia was a cop was evident on his face.

Stan Colt was in a rear corner of the elevator, hiding himself as best he could. Matt and Olivia got on the elevator and the door closed.

Detective Jesus Martinez was sitting on a chair outside the double doors of the Benjamin Franklin Suite, reading the Philadelphia *Daily News*. When he saw them, he stood up and knocked on the door.

"What the hell are you doing out here?" Matt asked.

"This is where the guy inside told me to wait," Jesus said.

"You had your dinner?"

Martinez shook his head, "no."

The suite door opened a crack, and Alex peered out, then saw Colt and opened the door all the way.

Matt signaled for Jesus to follow him into the room.

"Detective Martinez is not a rent-a-cop," Matt announced. "He doesn't sit in the corridor. Clear?"

Alex looked at Colt.

"What the hell is the matter with you, Alex?" Colt snapped.

"Sorry, Stan," Alex said.

"Stan, this is Jesus Martinez, a detective from Special Operations."

"I'm pleased to meet you," Colt said, sounding as if he meant it.

"He's half of your chastity squad," Matt said. "The other half will relieve him at midnight."

Colt chuckled, and held out his hand to Martinez.

"If you can get rid of these two," he said, "I've got some phone numbers and we could have a party."

Matt shook his head.

"Hay-zus," he said. "This is Olivia Lassiter from Northwest."

They briefly shook hands. It was obvious from the surprise on Alex's face that he had taken one look at Olivia and assumed Stan Colt's trolling for companionship had been successful.

Eddie the photographer and Jeannette the secretary were in the room.

"Have you made a decision about dinner?" Jeanette asked.

"Yeah. Here. You're not invited," Colt said. "Just me and the detectives. You've got a menu?"

She went to a sideboard and returned with a menu and handed it to him. He handed it to Olivia.

"Does Jesus get to stay?" Colt asked.

"Yes, he does," Matt said.

"Good. Okay. Thank you. That's all. I'll see you in the morning," Colt said.

They all filed out of the suite.

Matt noticed that they had not—except for the surprise on Alex's face—acknowledged the presence of him, Hay-zus, or Olivia at all.

"They're necessary," Colt said when they were gone. "And they do what they're supposed to do well, but sometimes, having them around my neck all the time is worse than the goddamn press."

Colt lay down on the couch and gestured for the others to sit down.

"I was about to ask you if they have a cheese steak sandwich on there, Olivia. But it has now occurred to me that if they do, it'll be a Ritz-Carlton cheese steak, not a real one. Like from D'Allesandro's on Henry Avenue?"

"I can't believe these prices," Olivia said.

"Well, don't worry about them, everything's on the studio," Colt said. "I wonder, could we send out for a cheese steak?"

"It would be cold by the time it got here," Matt said.

"Well, maybe later on," Colt said.

Olivia handed the menu to Matt.

"Inspire me," she said.

"I think you already do, baby," Colt said. "Give me the menu."

Matt handed him the menu.

He glanced at it quickly.

"Anybody doesn't like shrimp cocktails?"

No one spoke.

"Anybody morally or intellectually opposed to filet mignon?"

No one spoke.

"Anyone determined to ruin a good steak by cooking it well done?"

No one spoke, but Matt and Olivia chuckled.

"Well, that wasn't hard, was it?" Colt said, and walked to the sideboard and picked up the telephone.

"This is Mr. Colt in . . . I have no idea where I am, but I'll bet you can find out. What we need right away is four shrimp cocktails; four filet mignons, medium rare; all the appropriate side dishes; and a couple of nice bottles of cabernet sauvignon. Thank you very much."

He hung up.

"Okay," he said. "You can start now, pause while they set up the table, and then continue, okay, Detective Lassiter?"

"Fine," Olivia said.

"Can I call you Olivia, or will your boyfriend here think I'm making a pass at you?"

"I'm not her boyfriend," Matt said.

"He's not my boyfriend," Olivia said, simultaneously.

"Methinks thou dost protest too much," Colt said in a surprisingly credible British Shakespearean accent.

"Hay-zus," Matt said, quickly. "The commissioner wants Mr. Colt to see how—"

"Hey, I thought we were friends. What's this 'Mr. Colt' shit?"

"The commissioner wants *Stan* to see how Homicide works a job," Matt went on. "Lassiter was next up on the wheel at Northwest when the Thirty-fifth uniform called in what turned out to be the Williamson homicide. For a couple of reasons, she's been detailed to Homicide for the job, and Captain Quaire told her to bring *Stan* up to speed on the job."

"I wondered what was going on," Martinez said.

"I'm still wondering," Colt said. "You want to say that again, please, slowly, in English? What's the wheel, for example?"

When room service delivered the dinner—two rolling carts of it—in what Matt thought was an amazingly short time, Matt had just about finished explaining what the wheel was and how Olivia and then Homicide had become involved.

He interrupted his explanation as long as he could—the object of the exercise was to keep Colt out of the way of whatever was happening with the doers of the Roy Rogers job—and then when Colt insisted, halfway through the steaks, that he "keep talking, this is the sort of stuff I really want to hear," he explained everything in minute detail, hoping that Olivia would follow his lead when she began to relate what had happened when she had first gone to the Williamson apartment.

She did, but even stretching it, and even with Hay-zus kicking in with detailed explanations of why things were done, and done in certain ways, there was only so much to relate, and when Olivia had finished, it was far too early to hope that Colt would have had enough and want to go to bed.

He didn't have enough—despite his having asked a number of intelligent questions that had required long explanations—and he didn't want to go to bed.

"You know what I'd like to do now?" Colt asked, rhetorically, and went on without waiting for a reply. "It's only a little after ten. I'd like to take a ride. Maybe go back to that bar you took me to before, maybe go by this Special Operations place where Hay-zus works, maybe take a quick look at that warehouse where you said they keep the undercover cars. . . . And go out to D'Allesandro's for a real cheese steak."

"You just finished eating," Olivia blurted.

"I didn't each much," he said. "And I really want a cheese steak. We can get the cheese steak last before we call it a night, after we see the other stuff."

Although he sensed it was going to be futile, Matt offered objections.

"There's a couple of problems with that, Stan," he began.

"Like what?" Colt replied with a smile, but in a tone of voice that made it clear he was used to getting whatever he asked for.

"Well, for one thing, we'll have to run the gauntlet of the press waiting for you downstairs."

"The other security guys can handle that," Colt said.

"Stan, the people downstairs are police officers, members of the Dignitary Protection Unit. Not 'security guys.' Security guys are rent-a-cops."

"No offense, that's very interesting, good to know, and I won't make that mistake again. What else?"

"We can't go into the IAD warehouse if we go there in my unmarked car."

"But we could drive by it, right? If we didn't stop?"

"Yes, we could."

"Okay, that solves that. What the hell, if I went inside, all I'd see is a bunch of cars, right?"

"Right."

"Anything else?"

"If we go to D'Allesandro's, you're probably going to be recognized, and likely mobbed by your fans."

"Sergeant Payne," Colt said, switching voices again, "I have a deep, one might say profound, trust that you and Detective Lassiter can shield me from the enthusiasm of my fans. Anything else?"

"Not that I can think of."

"Stan," Olivia said. "I'm not working Dignitary Protection. I have to do one of two things: go back to the phone in Homicide, or go home, so I can start off first thing in the morning."

"You've already put a lot of hours in today," Matt said. "We'll take you home. . . ." And then he had a second thought. "Why don't we drop you at Homicide, and you see what the Captain or Washington wants you to do?"

It took her a moment to understand what he really meant.

"If anything interesting has come up, I could call you," she said.

"Great idea!" Colt said.

"Hay-zus, you got the number of the sergeant downstairs?" Matt asked.

Martinez took out his telephone, punched in numbers, and handed the phone to him.

"Sergeant Nevins."

"Matt Payne," Matt said. "Mr. Colt wants to ride around town a little. Is that going to pose any problems for you?"

"You want to take a couple of uniforms with you?"

"No. I was thinking about the press. They still there?"

"Yeah. We can handle them. Just give a couple of minutes' notice."

"We'll be down in five minutes," Matt said.

"I really appreciate this, buddy," Stan Colt said.

[FIVE]

When officers commanding, for example, the Impact Unit and Internal Affairs get an order directly from the first deputy commissioner, they tend to drop whatever they might have been doing and start to comply with the order. The same is true when the commanding officer of a detective division gets any kind of an order from the chief inspector of detectives.

This being the case, Inspector Wohl had been more than a little surprised that the first person to respond to the summons issued was Steven J. Cohen, Esq., head of the District Attorney's Homicide Unit, a dapper, tanned, well-dressed forty-year-old.

"That was quick, Steve," Wohl greeted him. "Thank you."

"I would say I heard my mistress's voice, but that would be subject to mis-interpretation," Cohen said. "I was in Center City. Please don't ask me why."

"Why were you in Center City, Steve?" Wohl asked.

"Would you believe my wife is a Stan Colt fan? And/or that I paid a hundred dollars each for two tickets entitling us to stand in a long line in the Bellvue-Stratford to shake his hand, and two very watery drinks? And that when Al called me, I was in the bar of the Ritz-Carlton, where he is staying, and where, my wife hoped, he would appear?"

"I believe you," Wohl said. "If you can't believe a lawyer, who can you believe?"

Cohen gave him the finger.

"What's up, Peter?"

"We've identified one of the doers in the Roy Rogers job," Peter began.

He had just about finished when Inspector Michael Weisbach of Internal Affairs walked into Homicide. Weisbach was a slightly built man who wore mock tortoise-frame glasses and always managed to look rumpled. Weisbach and Wohl were longtime friends.

He nodded at Cohen and looked expectantly at Wohl, but didn't say anything.

"So how's by you, Michael?" Wohl asked, finally, in a creditable mock-Yiddish accent.

Cohen chuckled.

"What the hell is this all about, Peter?" Weisbach asked, not able to resist a smile.

"I would deeply appreciate your patience, Inspector, until Captain Mikkles of Impact and Captain Calmon of Southwest Detectives get here," Wohl said. "I've just explained the whole thing to the shyster here, and I'd rather do it only once more, when everybody is here."

"How come the shyster gets special treatment?"

"Because I like him," Wohl said.

"Oh, Christ," Weisbach groaned.

Cohen pointed toward the door to Homicide. Captain Michael J. Mikkles, who commanded the Impact Task Force—a special antidrug unit—had just come in. He was a tall, very thin, bald-headed man in his fifties. He was halfway to Captain Quaire's office when Captain Calmon entered Homicide.

When he was in the office, and they had all shaken hands all around, Wohl closed the door.

"First things first," he said. "I need six undercover vehicles for an indefinite period, said vehicles suitable for a round-the-clock surveillance at the Paschall Homes Housing Project, and I need them right now."

"Who are we going to—" Weisbach started to ask.

"Indulge me, Mike," Wohl interrupted. "I'll explain everything in a minute. Right now, I want two undercover vehicles at Special Operations, two more within a couple of hours, and a total of six by morning. You two decide between you where they're coming from."

"You're just asking for vehicles, right? You don't want any of my detectives?" Captain Calmon asked.

298 · W. E. B. GRIFFIN

"Just the vehicles. We'll use Special Operations and Homicide detectives for surveillance until we run out of people."

"Inspector," Captain Mikkles said. "I don't have any undercover cars to spare. The only way I could give you vehicles is to take them off jobs."

"Then that's the way it'll have to be," Wohl said, "unless Inspector Weisbach can give me two right now."

Weisbach took out his cellular and punched an autodial number.

"This is Weisbach," he announced. "How many covert cars—anything suitable for surveillance in a project—can I get out of the warehouse right now?"

The Internal Affairs Division, which is engaged primarily in investigating policemen, had a fairly large fleet of bona fide "civilian" cars and other vehicles because very few policemen cannot spot an unmarked car in the first glance. The vehicles—many of them forfeitures in drug cases—were kept in a warehouse several blocks from the IAD offices on Dungan Road.

He waited and listened, and then turned to Wohl.

"I've got two pretty beat-up vans and a Chrysler, almost new, you can have right now. Maybe tomorrow we can do better."

"They're in the warehouse?" Wohl asked. Weisbach nodded. "Then we have to figure a way to get them out to Special Operations."

"I'm here in my car," Weisbach said. "I could run a couple of people by the warehouse."

The IAD warehouse had no identifying signs on it, and IAD tried to preserve its anonymity by never going near it in marked or unmarked cars.

"Can you carry four people?" Wohl asked.

Weisbach nodded.

"Then we'll do that," Wohl said.

"Do I get an explanation of what's going on?" Weisbach asked. "I'd kind of like to know."

"Well, if you're going to be difficult," Wohl said, and turned to Captain Mikkles. "Mick, I'm going to have to have two more cars in, say, two hours. If that means you have to call off a surveillance, so be it."

"Yes, sir," Mikkles said. It was obvious he did not like the order.

"Okay," Wohl said. "Then let's go out there, and I'll explain, for what I really hope is the last time, what's going on."

Just about everybody in the outer office stopped talking and directed their attention toward Captain Quaire's office as Wohl and the others filed out of it.

[SIX]

"For you, Inspector," Captain Michael J. Sabara said, handing Wohl one of the phones on Captain Quaire's desk. "It's Mickey O'Hara."

Sabara was sitting in Quaire's chair. Peter Wohl and Jason Washington were sitting on wooden chairs—Washington with his legs sprawled in front of him, Wohl sitting in his chair backward. Quaire had left five minutes earlier, at Wohl's pointed suggestion that since everybody had a lot to do in the morning, and he could think of nothing else they could do tonight, it might be a good idea to get some rest, it was already almost eleven.

Sabara, Wohl had just told him, was going to be responsible for providing what detectives Washington—to whom Wohl had given responsibility for the Paschall Homes Housing Project—decided he needed, and to make sure there were Highway Patrol cars always no farther than five minutes away from the surveillance site.

"And how is my all-time favorite journalist?" Wohl said into the phone.

"Pissed is how I am," O'Hara said. "Suspecting, as I do, that I am about to get another runaround."

"Another? Implying you have already been run around? By whom?"

"The Master Chef," O'Hara said. "You were there, Peter. Denny Coughlin promised to keep me informed. He didn't. And when I called him just now, he told me to call you, and you'd fill me in."

"Fill you in about what?" Wohl said, innocently.

"I knew it, I knew it. Be advised, Inspector, that my promise to have seen and heard nothing is now null and void."

"Where are you, Mick?"

"Liberties."

"Washington and I will be there in five minutes. We're just finishing up here."

"I'll trust you that far, Peter. But not sixty seconds longer."

"We'll be there in *about* five minutes. We're leaving right now. Okay?"

"You have ten minutes, Old Pal of Mine," O'Hara said, and the line went dead.

Washington's cellular buzzed as he and Inspector Peter Wohl walked out of the Roundhouse into the parking lot.

"Joe D'Amata, Lieutenant."

"Don't tell me, please, Joseph, that you have encountered a problem at the warehouse. I want that car in the project right now."

"It's an old Chevy van, not a car. And I don't know if it's a problem or not, but I thought I should tell you."

"Please do. The suspense is too much for my tired old heart."

"When I came out of the warehouse just now, there was a Ford parked halfway up the street. Lights out but people in it. When I got closer, I saw Payne was sitting in it."

"You refer to our Sergeant Payne?" Washington asked.

The question caught Wohl's attention.

"Yeah. And sitting beside him was either Stan Colt or somebody who looks a hell of a lot like Stan Colt. Is there something I don't know?"

"What were they doing?" Washington asked.

"Looking at the warehouse," D'Amata said.

"With their lights out?"

"With their lights out."

"Joseph," Washington said, looking at Wohl, "I have no explanation whatever for Sergeant Payne and Stan Colt being outside the IAD warehouse in an unmarked car with the lights out, but I will make inquiries and advise you. Thank you for bringing this to my attention."

Washington pushed the End button and looked at Wohl. Wohl took out his cellular and pushed an autodial number.

"Matt, is Mr. Colt with you?"

"Yes, sir."

"Meet me at Liberties. Now. Do not go inside."

"Yes, sir."

Inspector Wohl, Lieutenant Washington, and Sergeant Payne arrived at Liberties within thirty seconds of one another.

Lieutenant Washington went inside Liberties.

Mr. Michael J. O'Hara was sitting alone at the bar.

"You better be about to tell me that Peter's right on your heels," O'Hara greeted him.

"Peter's right on my heels."

"You want to tell me what's going on?"

"We've identified one of the miscreants in the Roy Rogers job, and have a good idea who the other one is."

"I heard that much at Augie Wohl's."

"Mrs. Solomon is very concerned that, unless we exercise great care, the malefactors may slip through the cracks in the floor of the criminal justice system."

"Which means what, exactly?"

"That an arrest will not be made until such time as Mrs. Solomon feels there is a stronger case than what we have now, which is identification of one of them by fingerprints."

Inspector Wohl went to Matt's unmarked Crown Victoria and got in the backseat.

"Mr. Colt, I'm Inspector Wohl," Wohl said.

Stan Colt reached over the back of the seat and enthusiastically shook Wohl's hand.

"Hey! Great! How are you? Matt's been telling me all about you!"

"You were seen outside the IAD warehouse, Sergeant Payne," Wohl said. "You want to tell me what that was all about?"

"Mr. Colt wanted to see it, so I showed it to him."

"Okay. Is there anything else Mr. Colt wants to see tonight?"

"We're going to D'Allesandro's for a cheese steak," Matt said.

"And we'd love to have you come along," Stan Colt said.

"That's very kind, but it's been a long day, and what I'm going to do is have a nightcap with Lieutenant Washington and go home."

"Tell you what, Inspector," Colt said. "Why don't we all go in there and have a nightcap, then Matt and I will go to D'Allesandro's, and then we'll all go home."

Mr. Colt put action to his words by getting out of the car, walking quickly to the door of Liberties, motioning cheerfully for Matt and Wohl to follow him, and disappearing inside.

"Jesus Christ!" Wohl said. "Mickey's in there, waiting for me to tell him what's going on."

"I saw the pressmobile," Matt said.

"This isn't funny, goddamn it!"

"What are you going to do?" Matt asked.

"Goddamn movie actor!"

"Actually, he's not really such a bad sort," Matt said. "He sort of grows on you."

CHAPTER 15

"I may have had more of these than I remember," Mickey O'Hara said, interrupting Washington, and holding up his Old Bushmills on the rocks, "because the guy in the door looks just like Stan Colt."

"Yes, he does, doesn't he?" Washington agreed.

Mr. Colt, smiling, his hand extended, marched up to them.

"Hi," he said. "You're Matt's boss, aren't you? Lieutenant Washington?"

"Yes, I am," Washington said. "And unless I err, you are Mr. Stan Colt?"

"Right!"

"I'm very pleased to meet you, Mr. Colt," Washington said, adding: "This is Mr. Michael J. O'Hara, of the *Bulletin*."

"No shit!" Mr. Colt exclaimed. "You're Mickey O'Hara? Goddamn! You're a goddamn legend!"

He enthusiastically pumped Mickey's hand.

"Mr. O'Hara is indeed one of our more prominent journalists," Washington said, as Wohl, trailed by Matt, came into the bar.

"When you and Bull Bolinski got caught running numbers for Frankie the Gut, you took the fall for him, got expelled, and the Bull got to graduate, got to be All-American . . . you know. The Bull told me all about you."

"You know Casimir?" Mickey asked.

"Hell, yeah, I know the Bull. We West Catholic guys got to stick together, you know. He always stays with me when he's on the Coast."

"I'll be damned," Mickey said. "I heard you were in town, raising money for West Catholic, but I didn't know you went there."

"You probably wouldn't remember me. I used to be Stanley Coleman, I was a freshman and you and the Bull were juniors when you got shit-canned, but I sure remember you."

"I'll be damned," Mickey said, and now returned Mr. Colt's enthusiastic hand-pumping.

Wohl walked up, smiling a little lamely.

"Well, I see you've met Mr. O'Hara, Mr. Colt," he said.

"Met him, shit! We go way back; we both got kicked out of West Catholic. Jesus, I'm glad you brought me in here!"

"Me, too," Mickey said.

"Hey, bartender," Mr. Colt called, and when he had his attention, made a circling motion with his hand, which the bartender correctly interpreted to mean that he should bring liquid refreshment to one and all.

"The usual, Inspector?" the bartender asked.

Wohl nodded.

"Detective?"

"Hey, he's a sergeant," Mr. Colt corrected him. "Give us both one of those Irish martinis."

"And if I don't want an Irish martini?" Matt asked, smiling.

"Drink it anyway, you're an outnumbered WASP," Colt said, and then frowned, remembering. "Hey, I still don't have any money. I'll pay you back."

"Sure."

"The *Bulletin* will pay," Mickey announced. "Why don't we get a table?"

They took a table. The bartender delivered a round of drinks.

"You hang out with these guys, right, Mickey?" Mr. Colt inquired.

"Yeah. What I want to know is what you're doing with them."

"Matt's showing me around the police department, and doing a goddamn good job of it."

"For a WASP," Mickey said, "Matty's a pretty good cop. I owe him big time."

"How come?"

"A couple of years back, we were in an alley, and a really bad guy comes down it shooting at us with a .45—"

"Jesus, Mickey!" Matt protested.

"—and Matty put him down," O'Hara went on. "Took a bullet in the leg, but the bottom line was one dead bad guy."

"No shit?"

"We call him the Wyatt Earp of the Main Line."

"My friends don't call me that," Matt said, coldly.

"Or sometimes the Casanova of Center City," O'Hara went blithely on.

"Yeah, I like his taste in women," Mr. Colt said. "You should have seen the one he had with him tonight."

"Curiosity overwhelms me," Washington said. "To whom does Mr. Colt refer, Matthew?"

"Captain Quaire assigned Detective Lassiter to explain the Williamson job to him," Matt said.

"You got something going with her, Matty?" O'Hara asked.

"No, I don't."

Mr. Colt winked broadly, held up his balled first with the thumb extended, and said, "Right."

Washington and Wohl smiled.

"So what's going on in here?" Mr. Colt inquired. "You're just hanging out, or what?"

O'Hara looked at Wohl.

"You tell him, Peter," he said.

Wohl's smile vanished. He looked thoughtful for a moment, then shrugged.

"Mr. Colt . . . ," he began.

"I can't get you to call me 'Stan'?"

"*Stan,* just about everybody in the department trusts Mickey to keep his mouth shut when he knows something we don't want to be public knowledge," Wohl said.

"There's usually a little you-scratch-my-back-and-I'll-scratch-yours in the deal, Stan," Mickey said. "You asked before if what we're doing here is hanging out. No. What I'm doing is waiting to see if, or how well, the inspector is going to scratch my back."

"Under the circumstances, Stan, I'm going to have to ask you not to repeat, to anyone, what I'm about to tell Mickey and you."

"You got it. My lips are sealed," Mr. Colt said. He looked at Matt, held up his right hand with the three center fingers extended, and added, "Boy Scout's Honor."

"Tony Harris went to Harrisburg," Wohl said. "The State Police were able to get a hit from the print on the visor cap using the AFIS."

"I'm terribly sorry to interrupt, old sport," Mr. Colt interrupted in his British accent, "but I haven't the foggiest fucking idea what you are talking about."

Wohl turned his head to look at Colt, and for a moment Matt thought Colt was about to be either frozen with a Wohl glance, or perhaps even treated to an example of Wohl sarcasm, but Wohl surprised him by smiling.

"Well, dear boy, we certainly can't have that, now can we?" Wohl said, in a British accent very nearly as good as the actor's. Then he dropped the accent

and added, "There was a double homicide in connection with an armed robbery of a Roy Rogers restaurant on South Broad, the guys who did it got away,
and we just found out, using a fingerprint we previously thought was useless,
who they are."

"You got a match?" Mickey asked. "I thought the lab—Candelle himself—
said there wasn't enough?"

"We've identified one of them. The fat guy. And in Known Associates on
his sheet is a guy who lives two doors away from him in the Paschall Homes
Project in Southwest Philly who fits the description of the other one."

He stopped and looked at Washington.

"You brought the pictures for Mick?"

Washington nodded and went into his suit jacket, coming out with two
Philadelphia Police mug shots. He handed them to O'Hara.

"Can you make either of them, Mick?" Wohl asked.

O'Hara looked carefully at both and then shook his head.

"As much as I'd like to, no," O'Hara said. "It was dark, and as you may
recall, the bastards took a shot at me."

"No shit?" Mr. Colt inquired, awe in his voice.

"Anyway, the D.A. doesn't think what we have is enough to convict them
for sure. We need more—the weapon, for example. So we're not going to arrest
them right now."

"Instead?"

"We're going to keep them under surveillance until we can develop more.
That's the reason that Jason and I were still in Homicide when you called. We
had everybody and his brother in there, setting up the surveillance. . . ."

"And that's why I was ever so politely booted out of there, right?" Mr. Colt
inquired.

"Excuse me?" Wohl asked.

"When that captain sent Matt's girlfriend to explain that other job to
me . . ." He paused and made a pumping motion with his fist. "That was to get
me out of Homicide, right?"

"I think one could reasonably draw that assumption, Mr. Colt," Washington said.

"I would have been in the way, right?"

"And been privy to things we would rather not be known to the public,"
Washington replied.

"Well, what the hell, we had a nice dinner, right?" Mr. Colt said.

"Very nice," Matt said.

"Can I ask you a question, Mickey?" Mr. Colt inquired, and then went on without waiting for an answer. "How come you was at this Roy Rogers? Just a coincidence? You went there for a hamburger or whatever?"

"No. I responded to a possible armed-robbery-in-progress call, and I got there just as these bastards were leaving."

"Explain that? You've got a police scanner? Right?"

"He has a battery of police scanners," Washington said. "With which he eavesdrops on police communications in the tristate area. You may have noticed all the antennae."

"That Buick Whatchamacallit outside is yours? I saw all the antennas."

"It's a Rendezvous," Mickey said. "Yeah, that's mine."

"If you want to really see the police department at work, Mr. Colt," Washington said, "perhaps Mr. O'Hara would be good enough to let you ride around with him. He responds to every interesting call, which usually means a call where violence is likely to be found."

"Be glad to have you, Stan," Mickey said.

"Jeez, I'd like that."

"Then we'll do it," Mickey said.

"There's a problem there," Wohl said. "We really have to make sure you have a police officer with you, Stan."

"Why, and what's wrong with Matt?"

"Because the commissioner says so," Wohl said. "And what's wrong with Matt is that he's been on the job all day and it's getting close to midnight."

"What about the other detective?" Mr. Colt asked. "The little one?"

He held out his hand to indicate Detective Martinez's diminutive stature.

"Who's he talking about?" Wohl asked Matt.

"Hay-zus," Matt said. "McFadden relieves him at midnight."

"Another Mick, Stan," O'Hara said. "Good guy. You'll like him."

"Inspector, I would venture to suggest that Mr. Colt would be safe in the capable Gaelic hands of Detective McFadden," Washington said.

"You mind if I ask if you always talk like that?" Mr. Colt asked.

"Always, I'm afraid," Wohl said, chuckling. He looked at his watch. "Put the arm out for him, Matt. Have him meet us here."

"Have him meet us at D'Allesandro's," Mr. Colt said. "This drink is my third and last one for the day, and I'm determined to have a cheese steak. You're all invited, of course."

Washington and Wohl looked at each other.

"Far be it from me to reject Mr. Colt's generous invitation," Washington said. "And not only because it will afford me a splendid answer to Martha's inevitable question when I finally get home."

"Where the hell have you been, what have you been doing, and with whom?" Wohl asked.

"'Actually, my precious, I was having a cheese steak at D'Allesandro's with Mr. Stan Colt, the movie star.' That should for once strike her dumb."

[TWO]

At five past one, Mr. Stanley Colt having had his cheese steak, and having been transferred into the capable hands of Detective Charles McFadden, Matt got in his unmarked Crown Victoria and started home.

He smiled at the memory of Mr. Colt's response to Inspector Wohl's instructions to Detective McFadden: "He is not to get out of Mickey's car without your permission. If he gives you any trouble, cuff him, and turn him over to Dignitary Protection at the Ritz-Carlton. Trouble is defined to include any gesture toward a member of the opposite sex beyond a friendly smile."

"That's not going to be a problem. I can get laid anytime. But doing this, wow!"

He had just turned onto Walnut Street and was headed west toward Rittenhouse Square when his cellular went off.

Jesus, now what?

"Payne."

"Can you talk?" Detective Olivia Lassiter inquired.

"Yeah."

"They have a positive ID on one of the doers in the Roy Rogers job—"

"I heard," Matt interrupted. "And they're running an around-the-clock surveillance, which is why they threw us out of Homicide."

There was a silence.

"How's your hand?" Olivia asked after a long moment.

He looked at it.

"Fine," he said. "I had just about forgotten about it."

"Oh."

Another silence.

"I thought maybe you needed the bandage changed," she said, finally.

"No. It looks fine."

"Oh."

Jesus Christ, Matthew, you are the dumbest sonofabitch in Philadelphia!!!

"Where are you, Mother?"

"I'm not your mother."

"Where are you, Not My Mother?"

"In the Starbucks at Twelfth and Market."

"What are you doing there? I thought you went to Homicide?"

"I hung around Homicide for a while, made a few more calls. Then I came here and waited until I thought you'd probably put Colt to bed. Then I called."

"I'm at Nineteenth and Walnut. I'll be there in ten minutes."

"No."

"For Christ's sake, I'll take you home."

"If you come here, somebody who knows one or both of us will see us."

"Then go stand in the dark around the corner on Twelfth and Filbert. I'll pick you up there and take you home."

There was a long pause again, before she asked,

"If I took a cab to Rittenhouse Square, how could I get in the building this time of night?"

Another pause, this one on Matt's part, and shorter.

"When you get out of the cab, I'll be waiting for you in the lobby."

And one final pause before she said,

"The way you were talking before, I thought you didn't want me to come over there."

"Oh, baby!"

[THREE]

The chiefs of police of Daphne and Fairhope, Alabama, were privately not at all happy with the Jackson's Oak Citizens' Community Watch, Inc.

Daphne and Fairhope are small, prosperous, primarily residential communities in Baldwin County on Mobile Bay in South Alabama. They lie across Mobile Bay from the city of Mobile, and about thirty miles from the Gulf of Mexico.

Baldwin County, which is larger than the state of Rhode Island, is similarly prosperous, both because of its fertile fields and its seashore on the Gulf of Mexico—known, despite the valiant efforts of the local chambers of commerce, as the Redneck Riviera—which is famous for its spectacular snow-white beaches, and which attracts affluent tourists throughout the year.

There is not much crime—certainly not as that term is interpreted in Philadelphia—in Baldwin County or in Daphne or Fairhope. But to fight what there is, there is a nice tax base to support law enforcement and the various fire departments.

The police cruisers of the Daphne and Fairhope police departments are state-of-the-art vehicles, equipped with the latest communication systems, television cameras, computers, and speed-detection radar. They are generally replaced annually, and the "old" vehicles sold to less prosperous communities.

The Daphne chief of police was not happy with the Jackson's Oak Citizens' Community Watch, Inc., because he thought it was unnecessary, potentially dangerous, and enjoyed the opposite of respect from his sworn officers. The Fairhope chief of police was not happy with JOCCWI (sometimes referred to privately within the law enforcement community as "Jabberwocky"), because he feared it would be contagious and Fairhope would get one like it.

JOCCWI had been formed by a group of concerned citizens as their response to what they regarded as the Daphne police department's inability to rid the community of drug addicts, petty thieves, Peeping Toms, and other disturbers of the domestic tranquillity.

There was a thread of justification in their complaints. So far as the chief knew, if there were those in Daphne using hard drugs, they did so in their homes and purchased them elsewhere. If a stranger appeared in either Fairhope or Daphne who looked remotely as if he might be using—much less selling—hard drugs, a cop trailed him until a search of his/her person was legally justified, or he/she left town, whichever came first.

There was cannabis sativa, of course. And on any given pleasant evening, the chief knew, the young and sometimes not-so-young might go to the beach and smoke a joint or two. Or they might go outside the clubhouse of the Lake Forest Golf and Country Club and take a couple of puffs. If his officers saw them, they were arrested.

There was more validity to the petty-theft charge. There were more than two hundred boats, power and sail, in the marina of the Lake Forest Yacht Club. Just about every one of them had something aboard—from radar sets and depth meters or "fish finders" on a forty-foot Hatteras to oars in a rowboat—that was both quickly removable and easily sold, no questions asked, in any one of a hundred places from Biloxi, Mississippi, in the west to Pensacola, Florida, in the east.

Most of these thefts could be prevented by the boats' owners taking reasonable measures. And the only way to stop the thefts completely would be to station officers not only at the marina but in boats guarding access to it. That was out of the question.

Easily removable things, from radar detectors to hubcaps to entire wheels, were stolen from cars, too, as the founders of JOCCWI contended. And sometimes expensive lawn furniture—or even a new garden hose—bought from Home Depot would vanish from a back lawn overnight.

Sometimes the thieves were caught, sometimes they were not. It was obviously impossible for the police to be everywhere all the time.

The Peeping Tom allegation also had some merit. There were a lot of good-looking young women, married and not, in the condominiums adjacent to the Yacht Club, and on the fringes of Lake Forest, a huge area of small to medium-sized homes. It was not a gated community. It was easily possible for someone with an interest in watching young women undress to go into Lake Forest and hide behind one of its many trees with binoculars. And hard as hell to catch them at it.

Among the other disturbers of the peace JOCCWI wished to control were high school kids racing around in Pop's—or their own—car in the middle of the night. The chief had his officers spend a lot of time trying to stop that—he had had more than his fill of picking up dead kids who'd missed a turn and hit a tree—but he knew he hadn't stopped it all.

On the surface, having a number of responsible citizens roaming through the area at night in their own cars, looking for something amiss, and when finding it, reporting it to the police by cell phone seemed at first—even to the chief—to be not so bad an idea.

And among the founders of JOCCWI were the pillars of the community. They were lawyers, executives, schoolteachers, businessmen, dentists, and retired members of the armed forces, including two full colonels, three lieutenant colonels (one of them a former Green Beret), a number of other commissioned officers, and nearly a dozen retired master chief petty officers, sergeants major, and other high-ranking former noncoms.

They showed the chief what they intended to do, and how they intended to do it, and he frankly had felt more than a little admiration for their plan.

The night the concerned citizens went into action, the chief and the mayor went to their headquarters, a rented former concession stand at the Yacht Club, to wish them well.

They learned that the organization now had a name, Jackson's Oak Citizens' Community Watch. It was taken from Jackson's Oak, a tree in Daphne under which Stonewell Jackson had allegedly stood shortly before moving west to fight the Battle of New Orleans.

That's when the chief and the mayor saw that the retired Green Beret, who would serve as watch commander that night, had a Colt .45 semiautomatic pistol in the small of his back. And so did Dr. Smiley, the dentist who would command the first four-hour tour. Other members of JOCCW (without the "I" for "Incorporated") were also armed, with everything from pistols to shotguns.

As tactfully as he could, the chief had suggested to the retired Green Beret that perhaps firearms weren't really such a good idea. All that JOCCW was supposed to do was keep an eye open and call the police if they saw something that looked suspicious.

"How the hell can you go on guard without a weapon? Jesus Christ, Charley!"

The next morning, the mayor, the chief, the (part-time) municipal judge, and the (part-time) city attorney conferred vis-à-vis the armed members of JOCCW patrolling the city.

Legally, there didn't seem much that could be done about it. Under the laws of Alabama, any law-abiding citizen over twenty-one could apply to the Baldwin County Sheriff for a permit to carry a handgun concealed about the person, on or in a vehicle. The permit could not be denied without good cause.

They agreed that the sheriff of Baldwin County, who is an elected official and wished to be re-elected *ad infinitum,* was not about to tell the pillars of the community who had organized JOCCW that he'd changed his mind, and they could no longer go about armed.

The laws regarding longarms were similarly not very comforting to the mayor et al. No licenses were required to own longarms. Citizens had to pass a firearms safety program to get a hunting license, unless they were veterans of an armed force, or over the age of sixty-five. Many, perhaps 75 percent, of the members of JOCCW met both of the latter two requirements.

Finally, the city attorney suggested that since the members of JOCCW were all reasonable men, if they were aware of the legal ramifications—primarily tort lawsuits for hundreds of thousands of dollars—for shooting someone without full justification, they might lose their enthusiasm for carrying weapons.

This was brought tactfully to the attention of one of the two retired full colonels—a Marine who'd fought all over the Orient from Guadalcanal to Khe

Sanh—who listened attentively, thanked the city attorney for his interest, and said it wasn't a problem.

"That potential difficulty occurred to Bob Skinner," the colonel said. J. Robert Skinner, Esq., one of the founders of JOCCW, was an attorney, specializing in corporate liability. "We expected to be incorporated within the week. If somebody sues JOCCWI—'I' for 'Incorporated'—the corporation treasury will be empty, or nearly so."

The chief, therefore, was concerned but not surprised when his bedside telephone rang at 1:30 A.M. (2:30 A.M. Philadelphia time) and the police dispatcher somewhat excitedly told him,

"Chief, we just got a call from Jabberwocky. Request assistance at the Yacht Club Condominiums. Shots fired."

"I'm on my way. Call the mayor."

Christ, it was inevitable. I'm only surprised that it didn't happen long before this.

Dear Jesus, please don't let them have shot some kid, or some guy trying to sneak into his own house.

When the chief turned off Highway 98 into the drive of the Lake Forest Yacht Club, he saw that three Daphne police cruisers and one each from the Fairhope police department, the Baldwin County sheriff's patrol, and the Alabama state troopers had beat him to the scene.

When he got out of the car, the wail of sirens he heard told him that additional law enforcement vehicles were on the way.

Then he saw there had been a vehicular collision just inside the brick gate posts. A Chevrolet Impala on its way out of the complex had slammed into the side of a Mercedes sports utility vehicle sitting sideward in the road. He recognized the Mercedes to be that of Chambers D. Galloway, retired chief executive officer of Galloway Carpets, Inc., and a founding member of JOCCWI, who lived in one of the big houses overlooking the beach and Mobile Bay.

The chief shouldered his way through the spectators and law enforcement officers.

"Who was shot?" he demanded, before he saw a very large man wearing black coveralls lying facedown on the ground, his wrists handcuffed behind him.

"Nobody was shot," the retired Green Beret said, just a little condescendingly.

"I was told 'shots fired'!"

"I didn't try to *hit* him, Charley. At that distance, I could have easily popped him. But I knew that Galloway could intercept him at the gate—I'd already alerted him and others—but I figured, what the hell, if I let off a couple of rounds into the air, he might give up back there."

He pointed into the condominium complex.

"Why? . . . What did he do to attract your attention?"

"He had a ski mask on and he was trying to pry open a window with a knife . . . great big sonofabitch. It's still in his car—I looked. . . . For some reason, I got a little suspicious. So I alerted the shift, told them to block the entrances, and then I shined my light on this clown and asked him, 'Excuse me, sir. May I ask what you're doing?' At that point, he took off running."

"Chambers Galloway stopped him?" the chief asked, just a little incredulously.

And then the chief saw Chambers Galloway. The tall, ascetic septuagenarian was standing beside the state trooper, chatting pleasantly, looking more than a little pleased with himself.

Mr. Galloway was wearing a tweed jacket with leather patches on the elbows and shoulder and a matching brimmed cap. He held a twelve-bore Belgian Browning over-and-under shotgun, the action open, crooked over his right arm. He could have been standing in a Scottish field, waiting for the beaters to start the pheasants flying.

As the chief looked, a flashbulb went off, and then a second and a third. The chief saw Charley Whelan, of the *Mobile Register,* standing atop his Jeep Cherokee in such a position that he could get Mr. Chambers D. Galloway; the prone, handcuffed man in black coveralls; and most of the police officers and their vehicles in his shot.

In a sense, Mr. Whelan was Mobile's Mickey O'Hara. He was considerably younger, and far less well paid, but he was the crime reporter for the *Register.*

And he had a police frequency scanner both on his desk in the city room of the *Register* and in his Cherokee. He had been in the city room—the *Register* had just gone to bed—when he heard the call announcing that shots had been fired at the Lake Forest Yacht Club.

He almost didn't go to the scene. No matter what he found at the Yacht Club, it was too late to get it in the morning's paper. But on the other hand, it might be an interesting story. Shots were rarely fired on the eastern shore of Mobile Bay, which was not true of other areas in Mobile.

So he got in the Cherokee and raced across the I-10 bridge, which connects Mobile with the eastern shore.

And when he saw what was happening, he was glad he'd come.

This was hilarious. Half the cops on the eastern shore had gathered at the scene of a captured Peeping Tom. And the actual capture of this dangerous lunatic had been made by an old fart with a shotgun, who looked as if he was about to bag a couple of quail.

Charley Whelan got off the roof of his Cherokee, tried and failed to get the Peeping Tom's name from the chief, got the old fart's name and another picture of him, and then drove back to Mobile, this time exceeding the speed limit by only fifteen miles per hour.

The city editor was still there, and Charley made quick prints of the images in his digital camera and showed them to him.

"Well, it's too late for today's rag," the city editor said. "Put it on the Atlanta wire; those big papers close later than we do. We'll run it tomorrow."

Charley sat down at his computer terminal and quickly typed,

Daphne, AL
Possible Peeping Tom Bagged By
Community Watcher, 72

Shown here with his shotgun and his as yet unidentified quarry hand-cuffed on the ground is retired business executive Chambers D. Galloway, 72, a member of Daphne's Jackson Oak Citizens' Community Watch, Inc., who made a middle-of-the-night citizen's arrest of the man after he was seen peeping into the windows of a resident of the Lake Forest Yacht Club Condominiums, whom police declined to identify.

Four Daphne police cars, two Fairhope police cars, a Baldwin County deputy sheriff, and an Alabama state trooper converged on the scene to take the suspect off Mr. Galloway's hands. The accused peeper will be held in the Daphne police jail while the investigation continues.

Mobile Register Photos By Charles E. Whelan

When the pictures and the story reached the Associated Press in Atlanta, the night man there also thought the yarn—and especially the pictures of the old guy with the shotgun—was funny, good human interest, and pushed the National button. This caused the photos and story to be instantly sent to newspapers all over the United States, which of course included those in Philadelphia.

[FOUR]

The device that electronically chimed "Be It Ever So Humble" when the door-bell of the residence of Sergeant Matthew Payne was pushed had two controls. One provided a selection of the numbers of bars of music to be played, from Six to All, and the other was a volume control.

Detective Payne, who had few visitors to his home, and used the device primarily as a backup alarm clock, had set both controls to the maximum choices offered.

A full rendition of "Be It Ever So Humble" played at maximum volume in the small confines of the apartment had so far never failed to wake Sergeant Payne from the deepest sleep.

And so it did the following morning at 6:05 A.M. when the Wachenhut security guard, a retired police officer who both liked the young cop in the attic and was grateful for the bottle of Wild Turkey he'd been given for Christmas, rode the elevator up, laid a copy of the just delivered *Bulletin* on the floor outside the door to the attic, and pushed the doorbell.

Half awake, Sergeant Payne had just identified the sound, glanced through half-opened eyes at the time displayed on the ceiling, and decided he had a good half hour to get leisurely out of bed, when a female voice quite close to him brought him suddenly to full wakefulness.

"What the *hell* is that?" Detective Olivia Lassiter had asked, as much in alarm as curiosity.

Matt opened his eyes fully.

Olivia had been so startled by the music that she had suddenly sat up on the bed and not thought about pulling the sheet up to modestly cover her exposed bosom.

Jesus, she has beautiful breasts!

"That's the newspaper," he said.

"The *newspaper*?"

"The security guy rings the doorbell when he brings the paper up," Matt explained.

Olivia saw where his eyes were directed and pulled the sheet up over her chest.

"The cow, so to speak, is already out of the barn," Matt said.

"What time is it?" Olivia asked, ignoring him.

Matt pointed at the ceiling. After a moment's confusion, Olivia looked at the ceiling.

"My God, I've got to get out of here!" she said.

"Why?"

"Because I have to go home and change my clothes," she said. "Something I didn't think about last night."

"Okay. I'll take you, and we can get some breakfast someplace."

"I'm going to take a cab," she said. "I should have taken one last night and gone home."

"So we won't be seen together, and someone will suspect what's going on?"

"Exactly."

"That cow, I have to tell you, is really out of the barn."

"What does that mean?"

"Mr. Colt somehow got the idea—you saw that—that you and I have become something more than professional associates . . ."

"And?"

". . . and decided to share this perception with Mickey O'Hara, Peter Wohl, and Jason Washington."

"My God, I hope you denied it!"

"Of course," Matt said, "whereupon Stan showed his acceptance of my denial in the following manner."

He winked broadly, mimicking Colt, and demonstrated the balled-fist, thumb-up gesture Colt had used.

"That sonofabitch!"

"Honey, he thought he was being funny."

"His being funny blew my chances of getting in Homicide," she said, bitterly.

"Realistically, honey, there doesn't seem to be much chance of that," Matt said.

"Thanks a lot!"

"Well, there doesn't," he insisted. "At least right now."

"I'm going to take a shower," she snapped. "And then a cab."

He watched her enter the bathroom.

After a moment, he reluctantly concluded that—however delightful an idea it was on the surface—there was not room in the shower for the both of them.

And besides, she's already pissed that our shameful secret has become public knowledge.

He swung his legs out of bed, got fresh underwear, and went down the stairs to get the newspaper.

He started to read it as he climbed the stairs back to his apartment, and just as he reached the top, he saw that the picture that Eddie the photographer had taken of him and Stan Colt outside the Bellvue-Stratford was on page one of the *Bulletin*.

There was a rather lengthy caption:

Stan Colt, movie detective, in Philadelphia to raise money for West Catholic High, found time in his busy schedule to meet with the real thing. He is shown here arriving at the Mayor's Reception at the Bellvue-Stratford with Sergeant M. M. Payne of the Phila. PD Homicide Unit. Payne will be showing Colt what police work is really like whenever Colt has a spare minute. (The full schedule of the Colt Fund-raising Visit can be found on page 2 of Section Four of today's *Bulletin*.)

Matt remembered that Colt had said that the picture was the only one that would get printed.

Olivia was toweling herself by the side of the bed, which he found to be an interesting sight.

"I'm famous," he said, showing her the newspaper.

Olivia glanced at it very quickly.

"Put your clothes on. You can drive me home," she said.

"Oh, thank you, thank you!"

"I have three choices: putting on wet underwear, getting in a cab without my underwear, or you."

"With or without underwear?"

"My God! Get dressed."

[FIVE]

The Swedish philosopher/theologian Emmanuel Swedenborg believed that there is sometimes an unspoken communication between loved ones. That one loved person knows what the other loved one is thinking.

This may or may not have had anything to do with what Detective Olivia Lassiter said to Sergeant Matthew Payne when he pulled to the curb in front of her apartment.

"You wait in the car. I know what you're thinking."

Sergeant Payne had in fact been thinking, all the way from Rittenhouse Square, that there was something wonderfully erotic having Olivia sitting beside him, with nothing beneath her dress but Olivia, and that with just a little bit of luck he might get lucky when they got to her apartment and they went inside while she changed clothing.

"What am I going to do out here?" he asked.

"That's up to you. You're not coming in," Detective Lassiter said, and got out of the car.

He watched her enter the apartment, shrugged, and then reached for the *Philadelphia Bulletin,* which had his picture on the front page, and which he had dropped onto the floor.

When he saw the picture, he smiled, remembering what Stan Colt had said when he got out of the car to pose for Eddie the photographer: "Look serious, but think of pussy!"

Then he started looking through the rest of the *Bulletin.* Ten minutes later, on page 4 of Section Three, "Living Today," he saw a picture of an old geezer with an over-and-under crooked over his arm standing with a bunch of cops and with half a dozen patrol cars of various law enforcement agencies in the background.

Then he read the caption, and then looked very carefully at the picture again, at the handcuffed man in black coveralls on the ground.

"Jesus Christ!" he said aloud, and reached for his cellular.

"Police department," a female voice with a thick southern accent announced.

"I'd like to speak to whoever's handling the case of that Peeping Tom you bagged last night."

"So would everybody else from New Orleans to Destin," the woman replied.

"My name is Matthew Payne. I'm a sergeant in Homicide in Philadelphia. . . ."

"Yeah, I bet you are."

"Excuse me?"

"How do I know that?"

"Because I just told you. Now get me some supervisor on the phone, and right now."

"You don't have to bite my head off!"

A male voice with an equally heavy accent next came on the line.

"Can I help you?"

"With whom am I speaking. Please?"

"I'm Sergeant Kenny."

"Sergeant, I'm Sergeant Payne. Philadelphia Homicide."

"So Barbara-Anne said. How can I help you?"

"That Peeping Tom you bagged last night? Was there a knife involved? A great big knife?"

There was no response.

"Hello?" Matt asked after what seemed like a long time.

"What can I do for you?" a new southern-accented male voice inquired.

"Was I just talking to you?"

"No. You were talking to Sergeant Kenny. I'm the chief. How can I help you?"

"Chief, my name is Payne. I'm a Philadelphia homicide sergeant."

"So Sergeant Kenny said. What can we do for you, Sergeant?"

"This a long shot, Chief, but that Peeping Tom you bagged last night may be a man we're looking for in connection with a homicide here."

"You don't say?"

"Can you tell me if there was a knife involved? Did your guy have a great big knife?"

"Sergeant, I don't know for sure you're who you say you are, and even if I did, I'm not sure if I could answer that question. This is an ongoing investigation, and there's some things we don't want to get out, you understand."

Which means, of course, that he did have a knife, otherwise you would have said "no."

"How about a camera? A digital camera? Could you tell me that?"

"What part of I'm-Not-Going-To-Answer-Any-Questions-About-This-Investigation don't you understand, Sergeant?" the chief asked.

"Certainly, Chief, I understand. But if you don't think it would interfere with your investigation, could you tell me if the window he was peeping through was that of a young woman? And was he just looking, or maybe trying to open the window?"

There was a long pause.

"No, I don't think I'd better get into that," the chief said, finally.

This sonofabitch isn't going to tell me a goddamn thing!

"Chief, I'll probably be in touch with you again," Matt said, politely. "In the meantime, if you'll give me your police teletype address, I'll have the department confirm who I am."

"That sounds like a good idea, Sergeant," the chief said, and gave it to him.

"I'll get that out as soon as I get to the Round . . . police headquarters," Matt said. "And thank you for taking the time to talk to me, Chief. I can imagine how busy you are."

"My pleasure," the chief said, and hung up.

[SIX]

"You don't look so happy, boss," Captain Frank Hollaran said as Deputy Commissioner Dennis V. Coughlin slipped beside him into the front seat of the car.

"Have you seen the *Bulletin*?" Coughlin asked.

"Yes, sir."

"And Matty's picture on the front page with Stan Colt?" Coughlin asked, and then went on without waiting for a reply. "I don't like it, Frank. I understand why Matty's showing that guy around, and from the perspective of Mariani and the mayor, it may be a great idea, but I don't think it belongs in the newspapers."

"I guess you haven't seen the *Ledger*?" Hollaran asked.

"Same picture?"

"And worse," Hollaran said, and indicated the newspaper on the seat between them. "The editorial page, Commissioner."

" 'Commissioner'? The editorial page? That sounds ominous," Coughlin said, as he flipped through the paper looking for the editorial page.

Ten seconds later, he said, "Oh, shit!"

And ten seconds after that, "Those bastards!"

NO WONDER MURDERERS REMAIN FREE

This newspaper received a publicity photo (below) of movie star Stan Colt and Homicide Sergeant M. M. Payne, getting out of a police car at the Mayor's Reception for Colt at the Bellvue-Stratford last night. The press release went on to say that while Colt is in town raising money for West Catholic High School, his alma mater, Sergeant Payne is showing him how things really are in the Philadelphia police department.

The way things really are in the police department are that there are two open unsolved recent cases of brutal murder, and one can only guess how many "old" unsolved murders on the books.

One of the new open cases is that of a young woman who very probably was raped and murdered in her apartment while police officers chatted with her neighbors.

The second is that of a single mother of three who was murdered in a fast-food restaurant during a robbery. When the police finally responded to that call for help, the murderers killed the responding officer.

At last report the Philadelphia police department doesn't have a clue as to the identity of the murderers.

Perhaps they would if Sergeant Payne were spending his time doing what the taxpayers hired him to do, investigate homicides, rather than spending it showing a movie star how things really are.

And it's not only Sergeant Payne. Earlier yesterday, Payne was seen taking into Colt's hotel an attractive young woman later identified as Detective Olivia Lassiter. Presumably, she was showing Colt how things really are in the Philadelphia police department.

And it's not only the junior officers. At midnight, Inspector Peter Wohl, Commanding Officer of the Special Operations Division, and who is supposed to be heading up the Mayor's Task Force to solve the murders at the fast-food restaurant, and Homicide Lieutenant Jason Washington were seen showing how things really are in the Philadelphia police department by feeding Stan Colt beer and cheese steak sandwiches at D'Allesandro's.

But maybe that's the way things really are in the police department.

And maybe it's time for a change in the police department, starting at the top with the commissioner, who permits this sort of thing to happen.

Or maybe in City Hall itself. After all, one of the primary responsibilities of Mayor Alvin W. Martin is the supervision of the police department.

And ten seconds after that, the radio went off.

"C-2, go," Halloran said to his microphone.

"C-2, meet the commissioner at the Roundhouse."

"Radio, we are en route. Estimate ten minutes."

"I guess somebody else has been reading the morning's papers," Deputy Commissioner Coughlin said.

CHAPTER 16

[ONE]

The editorial in the *Philadelphia Ledger* was brought to Mayor Alvin W. Martin's attention by Mr. Philip Donaldson, who decided the editorial was worth finally playing one of his aces in the hole, this one the mayor's unlisted and carefully guarded home telephone number.

After this call, Phil was sure, the number would go unanswered until another unlisted number could be obtained and the original one taken out of service.

"Yeah?" the mayor said, somewhat less than charmingly, into his kitchen telephone.

"Am I mistaken, or did the Honorable Alvin W. Martin, our mayor, answer his phone himself?"

The voice was familiar, but the mayor could not quite place it.

"This is Alvin Martin," he said, now far more pleasantly, "who not only answers his own phone, but whom you caught in the midst of making his own breakfast."

"The little woman didn't make it for you, Mr. Mayor?"

"No, she didn't. Who is this?"

"Phil Donaldson, Mr. Mayor, of *Phil's Philly*. And you're on the air!"

How the hell did you get this number?

Just in time, the mayor stopped himself from asking that thought aloud. Instead, mustering what charm he could under the circumstances, he said,

"Well, good morning, Phil."

"And good morning to you, Mr. Mayor."

"What can I do for you, Phil, so early in the morning?"

"Just a question or two, Mr. Mayor, and then you can go back to making your own breakfast. Do you always make your own breakfast?"

What business is that of yours?

"Is that one of your two questions?"

"Maybe it will be three questions. But what about breakfast?"

"I try, like every other husband, I suppose, to pitch in whenever my wife is tied up."

"Tied up?"

You flip sonofabitch!

"A figure of speech, Phil."

"Of course."

"The questions, Phil?"

If I ever find out who gave this bastard my number . . .

"Have you seen this morning's *Ledger*, Mr. Mayor?"

"I was just about to."

"After you finished your breakfast, you mean?"

"I thought I'd have a glance at it while I was eating my breakfast."

"That's probably a good idea, Mr. Mayor. The *Ledger* has some pretty startling, even unkind, things to say in an editorial about the police department generally, and you specifically."

Oh, shit!

"Oh, really?"

"Yes, they do, I'm sorry to tell you. And I—and all the good folks out there listening in *Phil's Philly*—would like to get your reaction to them."

What the hell's in this goddamn editorial?

"An editorial, you say, Phil?"

"That's right, Mr. Mayor. They just about called for you to resign, *after* you fire Police Commissioner Mariani."

Goddamn it! What the hell is the Ledger *onto now?*

"Did they say why, Phil? Or are they just still sore that I won the election?"

"No, it's a little more serious than that, I'm afraid, Mr. Mayor. Now, I don't want to put you on a spot, Mr. Mayor . . ."

The hell you don't! That's your stock-in-trade, you slimeball!

". . . and if you haven't read the *Ledger.* . . . So you read the *Bulletin* first, did you?"

You prick!

"Actually, Phil, I read both every day before I go to Center City, in no particular order, but I just haven't had a chance to look at either so far today."

"Well, what I'd like to do, Mr. Mayor, if you're willing . . ."

"Anything within reason, Phil."

"How about I call you at the office at eleven?" Mr. Donaldson asked, reasonably. "By then you'll have had plenty of time to read the editorial. . . ."

This is the last fucking time you're ever going to get me on the phone. How stupid do you think I am?

"I may not be in the office at eleven, Phil."

"Well, then, where will you be at eleven? Someplace without a telephone? I thought they were all over these days, like inside plumbing."

"I really don't know right now, Phil, where I'll be at eleven. You have to understand . . ."

"You wouldn't be trying to give me—and all the good folks out there listening in *Phil's Philly*—the runaround, would you, Mr. Mayor?"

"Now, Phil, why would you say something like that?"

"Because that's what it sounds like, Mr. Mayor."

You sonofabitch, you got me!

"You call my office at eleven, Phil, and I'll be happy to take your call."

"Cross your heart and hope to die?"

"I give you my word, Phil."

"I asked you to cross your heart and hope to die," Phil said, paused, and added, "Just a little joke. I'll take you at your word, Mr. Mayor, of course. And we'll look forward to talking to you at eleven."

"I look forward to it myself, Phil. It's always a pleasure."

"Have a nice breakfast, Mr. Mayor," Mr. Donaldson said.

He broke the connection and leaned into his microphone.

"Well, you heard it folks, the mayor gave his word that he'd take my call—which means he'll take *our* call—at eleven. That should be an interesting conversation. Make sure you tell all your friends to be tuned in. And now a word from the friendly folks at Dick Golden Ford on the Baltimore Pike. Be right back afterward."

He turned off his microphone.

"Gotcha, you bastard!" he said.

[TWO]

Lieutenant Jason Washington was in the lieutenant's office in Homicide when Matt and Olivia walked in. Matt was surprised; it was quarter to eight, and Washington usually showed up at ten or later.

As Matt walked toward the lieutenant's office, Washington looked up, saw them, and motioned for them to come in.

"Good morning, Detective Lassiter," he said.

"Good morning, sir," Olivia said.

"Is there some reason you chose to answer neither your radio nor your cellular, Matthew? Or you, Detective, your cellular?" Washington asked.

"I turned the radio off when I was ferrying Colt around," Matt said, "or he would have wanted to respond to anything that came over it. And obviously, I didn't turn it back on this morning." He took his cellular from his pocket. "And the battery is dead in this."

"And you, Detective?"

Olivia had her cellular in her hand.

"I guess I didn't turn it on this morning, sir," she said.

"Need I say that I would be both disappointed and more than a little annoyed if this ever—the operative word is 'ever'—happened again?"

"No, sir," they said, almost in unison.

"Then the incident is closed," Washington said.

"Have you seen the *Bulletin* this morning, Lieutenant?" Matt asked.

"With your image adorning page one? Indeed, I have. And so, I daresay, has most of the population of Philadelphia."

"I wasn't talking about my picture," Matt said. "I meant this."

He laid Section Three of the *Bulletin,* "Living Today," open to page four, on the desk.

"Then you stand out like a cork bobbing in the middle of the Atlantic Ocean, for everyone else in Philadelphia is talking of nothing else. . . . What am I being shown?"

"Look at the guy on the ground in the picture," Matt said.

Washington looked.

"You can doubtless imagine the odds against that fellow being our critter," he said after a moment. "But if you wish to turn over the stone under the stone, why don't you give them a call?"

"I already have."

Washington looked at him with interest.

"They wouldn't tell me whether or not this guy had a knife," Matt said. "Or whether he was just peeping in windows or trying to break in, or whether the window belonged to a young woman. . . ."

"And you have concluded, obviously, that this proves he did indeed have a knife, with which he was trying to break into the apartment of a young woman?"

"I think the possibility exists," Matt said, a little lamely.

One of the telephones on the desk rang, and Washington had it to his ear before it could ring again.

"Homicide, Lieutenant Washington," he said.

And a moment later,

"Yes, sir."

And a moment later,

"Yes, sir. They are both here with me."

And a final moment later,

"Yes, sir. We're on our way."

He put the handset in its cradle.

"Detective Lassiter, it is said that God takes care of fools and drunks. While you are certainly not a drunk, Sergeant Payne qualifies on both counts, and you have apparently been taken under his protective mantle."

"Sir?" Olivia asked.

"The reason I attempted—and failed, and we now know why, don't we?—to communicate with the both of you this morning was to relay the order of Deputy Commissioner Coughlin to get you both in here immediately, and keep you here until I had additional instructions from him."

"I don't understand," Matt said. "Is he pissed about the picture? Olivia had nothing to do with that."

Washington ignored the reply.

"Those were the additional instructions promised. We are to report to Commissioner Mariani forthwith."

He stood up and gestured for them to precede him out of the office.

"You're not going to tell me what's going on?" Matt asked.

"Obviously, you haven't had time to read the editorial page of the *Ledger,* have you?"

"No. What's on the editorial page?"

"Among many other things, your photograph."

Commissioner Mariani was sitting behind his desk. Deputy Commissioner Coughlin and Inspector Wohl were sitting side by side on a couch, and Captain Quaire was sitting on a straight-backed wooden chair just inside the door.

"Good morning, gentlemen," Washington said.

Matt and Olivia said nothing.

"I presume everyone has seen the *Ledger?*" Commissioner Mariani asked.

"No, sir," Matt and Olivia said, in duet.

Mariani gestured impatiently to Captain Quaire to hand the newspaper to them.

Matt took it, and Olivia stepped close to him and read it over his shoulder.

"My God!" Olivia said.

"I'm sure you will understand why I have to ask this question, Detective," Mariani said. "Did anything improper, or anything that could be construed as improper—say, by Philadelphia Phil—happen while you were in Mr. Colt's hotel room?"

"No, sir," Olivia replied, visibly shocked by the question.

"Were you ever alone with Mr. Colt at any time, for even a brief period?"

"No, sir. Matt . . . Sergeant Payne . . . was there all the time, and so was Detective . . . What's his name, Matt?"

"Detective Hay-zus Martinez," Matt furnished.

"I'm not surprised, but I had to ask," Mariani said. "And what you did was only—acting on orders from Captain Quaire—explain to Mr. Colt your involvement in the Williamson murder?"

"Yes, sir."

"And there was absolutely nothing social about your visit to Mr. Colt?"

"He bought us dinner, sir."

Mariani thought that over. It was obvious he hadn't liked to hear that.

"Philadelphia Phil somehow got the mayor's unlisted home number," Coughlin said. "He called him, and asked him to respond to the *Ledger* editorial. The mayor said he hadn't read it. Philadelphia Phil will call him at his office at eleven. The mayor's going to have to take that call. All of Philadelphia Phil's early-morning listeners heard him promise to take it."

"And so far, according to Lieutenant Pearson of Northwest Detectives, Mr. Philadelphia Phil—" Mariani began.

"The bastard's name is Donaldson," Coughlin furnished. "Phil Donaldson."

"Mr. *Donaldson* has called twice there asking to speak to Detective Lassiter," Mariani went on, "and twice to Homicide, according to Captain Quaire, where he asked to speak to either her or Payne."

Mariani let that sink in for a moment, then went on.

"Mr. *Donaldson,* as we all know, is a skilled interviewer. Moreover, it has been suggested to me that he is more than a little annoyed with Lassiter, for her having gotten Mrs. Williamson to say she understood why the uniforms couldn't take the Williamson girl's door, after he had painted the uniforms as . . . We all know what he said."

"Commissioner, may I go off at a tangent?" Washington asked.

Mariani glared at him but nodded.

"Make it quick, Jason."

"Just before we were all summoned here, sir, I was about to order Sergeant Payne and Detective Lassiter to immediately proceed to Daphne, Mississippi, to run down a lead in the Williamson case."

"Sir, that's Daphne, Alabama," Matt said.

"*Daphne, Alabama*?" Mariani parroted, incredulously.

"Yes, sir. I believe it's on the Gulf of Mexico," Washington said.

"Tell me about the lead, Jason," Coughlin said.

"Why don't you explain to the Commissioner what you think you may have, Sergeant Payne?" Washington said.

"Yes, sir. Sir, last night the Daphne police—actually it was a civilian from one of those community watch things—apprehended a man in what looked like the act of prying open the window of a young woman's apartment."

"So what?" Quaire snorted. "You're not suggesting it's the Williamson doer?"

"Let the sergeant continue, please, Captain," Peter Wohl said, softly. He added, wonderingly, "Daphne, Alabama? That's a long way from here, isn't it?"

"Yes, sir," Matt said. "When I heard about this—"

"How did you hear about this?" Mariani asked.

"It was in the newspaper, sir. The *Bulletin*."

"Go on, Sergeant," Wohl said.

"I called down there, sir, and from what I learned, there is enough of a similarity of *modus operandi* to merit further investigation."

"Over the years, I have come to appreciate Lieutenant Washington's belief that the stone under the stone sometimes has to be turned over," Wohl said. "Even if that stone is as far away as . . . Where is this place?"

"Daphne, Alabama, sir," Matt said.

"As far away as Daphne, Alabama, and that turning the stone over might take three, four days, perhaps even longer."

"I think that Lieutenant Washington was right in deciding to send Sergeant Payne and Detective Lassiter all the way down to Daphne, Alabama, for four or five days to run this lead down, wouldn't you agree, Captain Quaire?" Deputy Commissioner Coughlin said.

"Yes, sir, I certainly would," Captain Quaire, having just realized the all-around wisdom of getting Sergeant Payne and Detective Lassiter out of town for four or five days, quickly agreed.

"And under the circumstances," Wohl went on, "that sending them immediately, without waiting for the ordinary administrative procedures to take place, would be justified. Would you agree, Commissioner?"

Mariani thought that over for two seconds.

"Yes, I would agree, Inspector," he said.

"Have you got any cash, Matt?" Wohl asked.

"Some, and I've got credit cards," Matt said.

"Is there any compelling reason, Detective Lassiter, why you can't leave, right now, to pursue this investigation wherever it takes you?"

"I'd have to pack," Olivia said, practically.

"There might not be time for that," Wohl said. "Perhaps you could pick up whatever you need when you get there?"

"Yes, sir," Detective Lassiter said.

"In that case, I suggest that you and Sergeant Payne leave for the airport immediately," Inspector Wohl said. "Leave your car with the airport unit. I'm sure Lieutenant Washington will arrange to have someone pick it up."

"Indeed, I will," Lieutenant Washington said. "*Bon chasse,* Sergeant Payne."

[THREE]

"We want to go to Daphne, *Alabama,* not Florida," Sergeant Payne said to the lady at the Delta ticket counter in the Philadelphia International Airport.

"According to the computer, Daphne, Alabama, is served by both Mobile, Alabama, and Pensacola, Florida," the ticket agent said. "I can get you—first class only—on a flight connecting at eleven-twenty-five to Pensacola in Atlanta leaving in thirty-five minutes. If you want to go to Mobile, you'll have to wait until five-forty-five in Atlanta."

Matt handed her his American Express card.

"I never leave home without it," Matt said to the ticket agent.

"Oh, God!" Olivia said.

"Oh, shit, the guns!" Matt said.

The ticket agent looked at him with great interest.

"We're police officers," Matt said, which caused the ticket agent to look at him with even greater interest.

Olivia produced her badge and photo identification, which caused the ticket agent to look at her with great interest.

"You'll have to pack any firearms, unloaded, in your luggage," the ticket agent said.

"We don't have any luggage," Matt said.

The supervisory ticket agent was consulted.

Two metal lock-boxes were produced. Olivia's Glock and Matt's Colt were produced, which caused the people in line to look at them with great interest. The guns were then unloaded to the satisfaction of the supervisory ticket agent, the cartridges placed in small Ziploc plastic bags, and the bags, in padding, placed in one of the lock-boxes. Then the pistols were put in Ziploc bags and, with packing, placed in the other lock-box. Matt filled out an orange Unloaded Firearm Declaration card. It was placed inside with the pistols, then the boxes locked and placed on the baggage belt.

"You're not the first," the supervisory ticket agent said, handing Matt the keys and the claim checks to the boxes. "Have a nice flight."

"Can I get you a cup of coffee? Or something else?" the stewardess inquired of the cute young couple in seats 2A and 2B.

"No champagne?" Sergeant Payne replied. "I thought you got champagne in first class?"

"Oh, God!" Olivia said.

"We're celebrating," Matt said to the stewardess.

"Just married, maybe?" the stewardess asked.

Matt grabbed Olivia's hand with his left hand, and held the index finger of his right over his lips.

"Don't ask," he said.

"I'll get your champagne," the stewardess said, smiling warmly.

"You're insane," Olivia said when the stewardess had gone. "You're absolutely bonkers."

But she was smiling, and she did not attempt to free her hand.

Matt moved his champagne glass out of the way, took the in-flight telephone from its holder between the seats, fed it—with some difficulty—his American Express card, and then made two calls.

The first was to the Homicide Unit, where he left a message for either Captain Quaire or Lieutenant Washington that he and Detective Lassiter were airborne.

The second was to the law offices of Mawson, Payne, Stockton, McAdoo & Lester, where he asked to be connected with Mrs. Craig. Mrs. Irene Craig, a tall, silver-haired svelte lady in her fifties, was executive secretary to Mr. Brewster Cortland Payne II, a founding partner of the firm.

"Your dad's on his way in, Matty," Mrs. Craig greeted him. "I don't know if he's seen the *Ledger* or not, but the colonel's already in the library reading up on libel."

The colonel was Colonel J. Dunlop Mawson, another founding partner of the firm, whom Matt's father sometimes described as the firm's resident pit bull.

"That's not really what I called about, Mrs. Craig," Matt said. "I need a favor. . . ."

"Matty, what else did you do?"

Her tone was maternal. She had known Sergeant Payne since he wore diapers.

"Nothing," he protested. "I'm on a plane to Atlanta. Final destination, via Pensacola, Florida, Daphne, Alabama."

"I don't think I'm going to like this," Mrs. Craig said.

"What if I told you it's police business?"

"I'd have trouble believing you. Where did you say you were headed? *Alabama?*"

"Daphne, Alabama," he furnished. "And what I need is a rental car in Pensacola, and then someplace to stay—two rooms—in Daphne, Alabama."

"Somebody's with you?"

"Yeah. We're going to need two rooms."

"I'll need his name."

"It's a her. Olivia Lassiter. Two 's's."

"Oh?"

"*Detective* Lassiter."

"Oh. Her."

"Like I said, it's police business."

"I'm sure it is. How do I get in touch with you? Will your cellular work in Alabama?"

"We'll soon find out. We get to Atlanta at ten-fifty. Oh, wait a minute. My cellular battery's dead."

There was a slight delay as Matt got Olivia's cell phone number. He gave it to Mrs. Craig.

"Thanks, Mrs. Craig."

"You realize you've made your father's day, I hope. What do I tell him? I don't even want to think about your mother."

"The truth, the whole truth, and nothing but the truth."

"How do you spell Daphne?"

"I have no idea."

[FOUR]

"Good morning, Mr. Donaldson," the Hon. Alvin W. Martin said, charmingly. "I've been waiting for your call."

"It's Phil, Mr. Mayor. Calling for all the people out there in *Phil's Philly.*"

"All right then, *Phil.*"

"Thank you for taking my call."

"It's always a pleasure, Phil."

"I've been trying to call Detective Lassiter and Sergeant Payne, Mr. Mayor. They don't seem to be available."

"Is that so?"

"They seem to be out of town, Mr. Mayor."

"So I understand. Commissioner Mariani told me."

"You wouldn't want to tell me where and why, would you, Mr. Mayor?"

"I'll tell you why. They have a developing lead in the Williamson murder, one that looks very promising."

"Which just happens to make them unavailable to talk to me, right?"

"I'm afraid, Phil, that seems to be the case. But as soon as they get back in town, I'm sure they will be as delighted to talk to you—and all the people out there in *Phil's Philadelphia*—as I am."

"And when will that be?"

"In four or five days, possibly."

"And in the meantime, we don't get to hear what happened in Stan Colt's hotel room, right? That's a convenient coincidence, wouldn't you say?"

"I'd call it the press of duty, Phil. A matter of priorities. Solving that case takes precedence, as I'm sure you'll understand, over just about everything else."

"So what you're telling me, Mr. Mayor—correct me if I'm wrong—is that no one out there in *Phil's Philly* is going to hear what went on in Stan Colt's hotel room until Sergeant Payne and the beautiful lady detective come back to town?"

"I didn't say that, Phil. Would you like to talk to someone who was in Mr. Colt's hotel suite all the time Sergeant Payne and Detective Lassiter were there?"

"And who would that be?"

"Pick up the extension, please, Detective Martinez, and say hello to Mr. Donaldson."

"Hello."

"With whom am I speaking, please?"

"Detective Jesus Martinez."

"Good morning, Detective. Say hello to all the people out there in *Phil's Philly.*"

"Hello."

"And where are you assigned, Jesus . . . You don't mind if I call you 'Jesus,' do you?"

"Suit yourself."

"All right, Jesus. Could you tell me what you were doing in Stan Colt's hotel room all the time the mayor says Sergeant Payne and the lovely Detective Lassiter were in there?"

"I was on the Dignitary Protection Detail."

"Mr. Colt needed protection? From what, Jesus?"

"Excuse me?"

"What does Stan Colt need police protection from, Jesus? Pretty women?"

"You bet he does. They was all over the street outside the hotel."

"Who was?"

"His fans were. His lady fans."

"And they were all beautiful?"

"Not all of them. Some was dogs."

"Well, Phil," the mayor of Philadelphia said, "you asked for the truth."

"Yes, I did," Phil said. "Detective Martinez—Jesus—what I'm interested to hear—what all the folks out there in *Phil's Philly* want to hear—is what happened in Stan Colt's hotel room."

"Okay."

"You're going to tell me, right?"

"Lassiter told him what had gone down on the Williamson job."

"By which you mean the brutal murder of Cheryl Williamson? You call that a *job*?"

"That's what we call it."

"And why did Detective Lassiter feel she was equipped to tell him 'what had gone down'? And why was she telling him?"

"She was the first detective on the scene. And the Homicide captain told her to tell him."

"I see," Phil said. "And what you're telling me—correct me if I'm wrong— is that all that happened in Stan Colt's hotel room was that Detective Lassiter told him about the Williamson murder?"

"Yeah."

"She told him everything, right?"

"Probably not. She's a pretty good cop, from what I've seen, and I don't think she told him everything."

"Why not? What's everything?"

"You don't tell civilians some things about a job. I don't know what she didn't tell him, but I'm sure there was a lot."

"And what else happened?"

"He bought us a steak dinner. He's a pretty good guy."

"Phil," the mayor of Philadelphia said, "I really hate to break this up, but Detective Martinez has got to get back to his duty—Mr. Colt is having lunch with the cardinal in connection with his fund-raising for West Catholic High School, and Detective Martinez has to be with him. And I've got a pretty full plate myself. How about just one more question?"

"Well, let me think of one more question," Mr. Donaldson said, "to ask for all the folks out there in *Phil's Philly.*"

He paused a moment.

"Just tell me the first thing that pops into your mind, Jesus, please," he said. "Do you think assigning police officers to protect Mr. Colt is a good investment of the time of yourself and other detectives like you?"

"Hell, yes. Christ, he comes to town to raise money for West Catholic. It wouldn't be right if we let his fans get at him. They're nutty. What they would like to do is tear his clothes off for souvenirs."

"Thank you for calling, Phil," the mayor of Philadelphia said. "It's always a pleasure."

"Thank you for taking my call, Mr. Mayor."

The mayor put his phone in the cradle and signaled for Martinez to do the same thing.

"Gotcha, you bastard!" the mayor said, and extended his hand to Detective Martinez.

"Thank you very much, Detective. You did very well."

"Yes, sir."

In the studio, Mr. Donaldson turned off his microphone.

"Shit," he said aloud.

And then he had a second thought.

"Shit! I forgot to ask him about Wohl and Washington in D'Allesandro's!"

[FIVE]

A Pensacola, Florida, police officer watched the carousel delivering baggage and then stepped up to Matt when he saw him take the metal lock-boxes, which he recognized from previous use.

"That looks too small for a couple of shotguns," he said, pleasantly. "If that's handguns, why don't you wait until you're out of the airport before you open the box?"

"Sure," Matt said. "You use the term 'on the job' down here?"

"Sure."

"We're on the job, from Philadelphia. Had to leave in a hurry. What we need is someplace where we can buy clothing for a couple of days, and some nice place for lunch."

"Leave the airport, take a left at the second light. You'll see a shopping mall on the left. Then, when you leave there, get back on the same street, go the same way as far as you can, then make another left. McGuire's Irish Pub. Best place in town."

"Thanks. And then we're headed for Daphne, Alabama."

"When you leave McGuire's, you'll have to turn right. Get on I-110 until you hit I-10. Turn west. It's about forty miles."

"You get the car, Matt," Olivia said. "I have to—"

"Right the other side of the stairs," the officer said, pointing.

When Olivia had walked away, the officer said, "Her, too?"

"Detective Olivia Lassiter."

"Nice."

"Yeah," Matt agreed.

Hertz had a car waiting for them, a Ford Mustang convertible. And the clerk drew a Magic Marker route on a map showing how to reach the Marriott in Point Clear, Alabama. Matt saw that Point Clear was next to Fairhope, and Fairhope was next to Daphne, which was right on Interstate 10.

They found the shopping mall—a large one—without trouble, and went inside.

"Just what we're looking for," Matt said, happily, pointing to the entrance to Victoria's Secret.

"I'm not going in there with you," Olivia said. "I'm not going in there, period."

"You told me on the plane you maxed out your credit card," Matt said. "I have you in my power, Little Maiden."

"You sonofabitch!"

"I'll wait outside," Matt said. "See what they have in translucent black."

While he was waiting for Olivia, Matt found an ATM and withdrew a thousand dollars. When she appeared at the door to motion him in to sign the credit card charge, he handed her five hundred dollars.

"Thanks," she said. "I'll give you a check."

"When we get back to Philly," he said.

"It'll take months for the city to write a check, you know that?"

"You have an honest face. I can wait."

An hour later, having bought enough clothing and other necessities of life to last them four days, and suitcases to carry it in, they got back into the Mustang and went looking for McGuire's Irish Pub.

"I can't believe you ate the whole thing," Olivia said to Matt, making reference to the assorted sausage plate he had ordered for lunch. It looked to her more than adequate for the both of them, but by the time she had seen it, the waitress had delivered her Irish stew, which looked like it, too, had been intended for at least two people.

"I have to keep up my strength," he said, and looked around for the waitress to get the bill.

Then he looked at her.

"You know," he said, seriously, "there's only one person in the department who thinks this peeper may be our doer."

Olivia shook her head, "no."

"Two," she said.

"Why?"

"I've got a gut feeling, Matt," Olivia said. "You know?"

"Yeah," he said. "Washington says you should listen to your gut."

"What's next?" she asked.

"I've been thinking about that," he said. "Before we go to the police station, or wherever they have this guy, I'd like to know more than we read in the paper."

"How are you going to get that?"

"I think I'm going to start with the civilian—from the Citizens' Watch, or whatever the hell it's called—who saw him by the window."

"How are you going to find him?"

"When we get to the hotel, the first thing I'm going to do is plug in my brand-new cellular battery charger, then I'll ask, look in the phone book, whatever."

She nodded.

The waitress delivered the bill. Matt handed his credit card to the waitress and said, "Please add fifteen percent for yourself. Great meal."

Olivia shook her head as the waitress walked away.

"What?"

"You didn't even look at that check," she said. "And God knows how much we spent in the shopping center. And you got a lot of money from the ATM. Don't you worry about maxing out your card?"

"No, I don't," Matt said. "And I took the money from my bank. If you get money on a credit card, they charge you some outrageous interest."

"So you are rich? I heard something—"

"I'm *comfortable,* Olivia. So what?"

"It must be nice."

"It is."

It took them a little over an hour to drive from McGuire's Irish Pub to the Marriott in Point Clear, Alabama. Their route took them first through Daphne. There Olivia touched his arm and pointed out a sign identifying the entrance to the Lake Forest Yacht Club & Condominiums.

A mile or so away they saw the Joseph Hall Criminal Justice Center, which was obviously the police station, an attractive brick building that looked as if it had been built last year. As they went through Fairhope, they saw the Fairhope Police Station, another clean, attractive building that looked even newer.

The hotel was several miles the other side of Fairhope, down a tree-lined road along the shore of Mobile Bay. There were half a dozen fair-sized sailboats bobbing along in the bay.

"I don't know what I expected, but it wasn't this," Matt said.

Neither was the hotel what Matt had expected to find after Mrs. Craig had told him she'd reserved two rooms in his name at the Marriott.

It turned out to be more of a luxury resort than a hotel. Ancient oaks lined the drive to the entrance. There were signs indicating the direction of a golf course, and he could see both an enormous swimming pool and the masts of a fleet of sailboats.

A gray-jacketed bellman pulled their luggage from the backseat of the roof-down Mustang and said, "Welcome to the Grand Hotel."

There were two pleasant young men behind the reception desk.

"My name is Payne," Matt said, as he handed one of them his American Express card. "I'm supposed to have a reservation."

The young man consulted his computer.

"Yes, sir," he said. "Two 'nice' singles is what was requested. We think our bayside rooms are 'nice,' and we've put you into two of those. I'm afraid they're not adjacent . . ."

"That's fine," Detective Lassiter said.

". . . at $305 per day. Will that be satisfactory, Mr. Payne?"

"That's fine," Matt said.

They were handed brochures outlining all the hotel had to offer and electronic keys to the rooms. Two bellmen appeared.

"Call me when you're settled," Matt said. "I'm going to get on the phone."

"You want me to come there?" Olivia asked.

"Probably a good idea," Matt said.

Following the bellmen, they marched off through the lobby toward the elevators.

The young man who had handled their reservation turned to the other.

"What would you like to bet me that only one set of sheets will be mussed tonight?" he asked.

[SIX]

"Police department," a female voice with a thick southern accent announced.

"Good afternoon," Detective Olivia Lassiter said. "I'm hoping you can help me."

"Be happy to try, ma'am."

"Do you happen to have a phone number where I could call the Jackson's Oak Citizens' Community Watch?"

"You mind if I ask why you want to call them?"

"Well, we just moved into the area, and my husband wanted to ask about volunteering."

"Would you believe you're the sixth call we've had today, saying the same thing?"

"Is that so?"

"You got a pencil handy?"

"Yes, I do."

"The best person to call is Colonel Lacey Richards Jr.," the Daphne police operator said. "He's the one who really runs Jabberwocky. He lives on Captain O'Neal Drive. . . ."

Pause.

"Damn, I had his number here somewhere."

There was another pause.

"Here it is," the Daphne police operator said, and recited it.

Another female with a thick southern accent answered Sergeant Payne's call, and said that she was sorry, "but the colonel's out playing golf. He should be back about five."

"Thank you very much," Sergeant Payne replied. "I'll call again then."

He put the telephone down, leaned against the headboard of the king-size bed, and looked across the room at Detective Olivia Lassiter, who was sitting in an armchair.

"He's playing golf, but will be back at five. I still think we should see what he has to say before we talk to the cops."

"So do I," Olivia said.

"On the other hand, if all they've got him on is a Peeping Tom charge, which is a misdemeanor, he may post bail and be long gone."

"They won't let him post bail without knowing who he is. We can find him."

"Great minds run in similar paths," Matt said. He looked at his watch. "We have a little over an hour. What do you want to do?"

Detective Lassiter looked at him for a long moment, then stood up, and then looked at him a long moment again.

Then she reached down for the hem of the light blue cotton dress she'd bought in the shopping mall in Pensacola and pulled it off over her head.

"Jesus Christ!" Matt said.

"Well, you said to see what they had in translucent black," Olivia said.

. . .

"Hello?"

"Colonel Richards?"

"Right."

"Colonel, my name is Matthew Payne. . . ."

"Has this got something to do with the Jackson's Oak Citizens' Community Watch?"

"Yes, sir. It does."

"I'll tell you what I'm going to do. I'm going to give you my office number. You call there in the morning, and ask my secretary to mail you an application."

"Colonel, I'm a sergeant with the Homicide Unit of the Philadelphia police department. . . ."

"You're calling from Philadelphia?"

"No, sir. I'm in the Grand Hotel in Point Clear."

"You came all the way down here about that pervert I bagged last night. . . . Hey, you said Homicide, didn't you?"

"Yes, sir, I did."

"I knew that sonofabitch was up to more than peeping through windows," Colonel Richards said.

"Colonel, I'd like to talk to you."

"Sure. When?"

"At your earliest convenience, sir."

"How about right now? Let me tell you how to get here."

"Thank you very much, sir."

CHAPTER 17

It took some time for Sergeant Payne and Detective Lassiter to find the home of Lieutenant Colonel Lacey Richards Jr. on Captain O'Neal Drive in Daphne. Captain O'Neal Drive was a winding road in a heavily wooded area, and the house numbers were hard—or impossible—to find.

But they finally found it, a large home sitting under massive oaks between Captain O'Neal Drive and Mobile Bay. Colonel Richards, a short, totally bald, barrel-chested man wearing a yellow polo shirt and khaki pants, opened the door himself.

"You're the homicide guy from Philadelphia?" he asked.

"Yes, sir."

"Payne, right?"

"Yes, sir. Sergeant Matt Payne."

"You didn't tell me you were bringing the little lady. A pleasure to meet you, ma'am."

"This is Detective Lassiter, Colonel," Matt said.

"I'll be damned," Colonel Richards said. "Well, come on and tell me what you want to know. Can I offer you a little taste? I was about to have one myself."

"That's very kind of you, sir," Matt said.

"I didn't catch your name," Richards said to Olivia.

"Lassiter, sir."

"I meant your first name."

"Olivia, sir."

"Can I offer you a little something, Olivia?"

"Yes, thank you."

He led them through the house to a patio in the rear. There was a row of upholstered desk chairs and a well-stocked wet bar.

"You're just in time for sunset," he announced, pointing at the sun setting across the bay. "I like to come out here and watch and have a little taste."

"It's very nice," Olivia said.

A tanned, gray-haired woman at least a foot taller than Richards came onto the patio.

"I'm not sure you should be here, baby," Richards said.

"I live here, Lacey," she said, matter-of-factly. "Hi, I'm Bev Richards."

"This is sort of official, honey."

"Did he offer you something to drink?" she said, ignoring him.

"Yes, ma'am."

"Sir, I have no objection to Mrs. Richards hearing what I have to ask," Matt said.

"I surrender," Richards said. "This is Olivia Lassiter—*Detective* Olivia Lassiter—and this is Sergeant Payne."

They shook hands.

"My husband said you were here about that pervert he caught last night," Bev Richards said.

"Yes, ma'am."

"All the way from Philadelphia?"

"Yes, ma'am."

"I really want to hear about this," she said. "But will it wait until I make you something to drink?"

"Yes, ma'am," Matt said.

"What'll it be?" Richards asked.

"Whatever you're having will be fine, sir."

"You may want to reconsider," Bev said. "What he drinks is something he calls a scotch martini."

Matt and Olivia looked at each other and smiled.

He saw that Richards had seen the smile and didn't like it.

"You make a martini, except no vermouth, and with scotch?" Matt asked.

"Right."

"That would be fine with us, sir. I just taught Oliv . . . Detective Lassiter to drink those. Except with Irish."

"See, wiseass?" Colonel Richards said to his wife.

"They're the drink of choice at a bar where we go," Matt said.

"You mean you and her, or the other homicide cops?" Richards asked.

"She, and me, and the other homicide cops," Matt said.

"Oh, God, I'll never hear the end of that," Bev Richards said.

"You want me to make enough for you, or are you going to continue to be difficult?"

"Make the damn scotch martinis," Bev Richards said. "I can't wait to hear what he's going to ask you."

"I can make the drinks and talk at the same time, just like I can chew gum and walk at the same time. What do you want to know, Sergeant?"

"Actually, sir, I'd like to ask you what happened. And if you don't mind, I'd like to get our conversation on my tape recorder."

Richards frowned, and for a moment Matt thought he might say no.

"What the hell, why not?" Richards said, and began to pour scotch into a glass martini shaker full of ice.

He looked over his shoulder at Matt.

"Where should I begin?" he asked.

"When was the first time you saw this fellow?" Matt asked.

"Well, just before the whole thing went down was the first time I saw him," Richards said. "I was checking the guard, so to speak."

"I'm not sure I follow you, sir."

"Well, we run three roving patrols. Some of our guys are getting a little long in the tooth, and in the wee hours, they sort of pull off and catch a few winks. You can get yourself shot in the service for that, but this isn't the service, and all I can do is roam around and try to catch them. And then all I can do is wag my finger in their faces and tell them they're letting the side down."

"I understand," Matt said.

Colonel Richards interrupted himself to vigorously shake the martini mixer for a full sixty seconds, and then, with the precision of a chemist dealing with a known poisonous substance, to pour the mixture into oversized martini glasses.

"Welcome to our home," Bev said, raising her glass.

"Thank you," Matt and Olivia said, in duet.

The colonel took an appreciative sip and then went on,

"Well, I saw this guy—or thought I did—I saw what looked like somebody running between trees. You know what I mean?"

"Yes, sir."

"So I figured if I stopped, he'd see that, so I drove a couple of blocks away, and parked, and then came back on foot. My night vision's not what it used to be, but I can still move pretty good through the dark. I was in Special Forces for a long time."

"Were you really?" Olivia asked.

"Yes, ma'am, I was," Richards said. "So I see him doing this again. Moving from one tree to another, stopping a minute, and then running to the next. By the time he'd done that three, four times, I had a pretty good idea where he was running to, and while he was hiding behind a tree, I ran, and a little faster, and pretty soon I was ahead of him."

"Interesting," Matt said.

"And I was right about where he was going," Richards said. "Building 202. I got down on the ground when I saw him coming, and I saw him pull a mask— a black ski mask—over his head. Did I say he was wearing black coveralls?"

"No, sir. You did not. What about the mask?"

"You've seen them. One of our guys—I mean one of the Delta Force guys, not the guys in Jabberwocky—came up with the idea of using them—all they are is regular ski masks, except black, and without all that cutesy-poo reindeer stuff you see on some ski masks—for their psychological effect when you're hitting an objective. They scare hell out of people. They think they're being attacked by Darth Vader."

"I understand," Matt said.

"So, the first thing I thought was that I didn't have to be Sherlock Holmes to figure out that somebody running around dressed up like that wasn't selling Bibles door-to-door. And what I should do was shove my .45 up his left nostril. But you always think twice, or should, and I did. Then I thought maybe this was just some clown trying to scare his wife or girlfriend or, for that matter, boyfriend—you'd be surprised at the weirdos that collect in those condominiums. The things we've seen in Jabberwocky . . ."

"Disgusting," Bev Richards chimed in. "Absolutely disgusting!"

"Anyway, so I decided I better be sure this guy wasn't some kind of pervert—or if he was a pervert, he was playing with his own squeeze—before I did anything. So I kept him under surveillance. Then he goes to the kitchen window of 202B—there's two apartments to a floor in the condo buildings, four apartments to each one: 202B is the ground floor one to the left, if you're facing it from the front—and whips out this knife. Sword is more like it, it looks like something the bad guys carry in a Stan Colt movie, a great big sonofabitch—"

"Watch your mouth, Colonel!" Bev Richards said.

"This gentleman then begins to attempt to pry the kitchen window open with this knife, the blade of which I would estimate to be at least fourteen inches in length, as much as four inches in breadth at the widest point, and highly polished, perhaps even chromium plated," the colonel said, paused, and inquired, "Better?"

"Much better," Bev said.

"In other words, Sergeant, a great big sonofabitch," the colonel went on, visibly pleased with himself.

"You *saw* him, Colonel," Olivia asked, "attempt to pry open the window? You're sure that's what he was doing?"

"Well, he could have been attacking a column of ants with that sword, but it looked to me like what he was doing with it was trying to pry the window open."

"Yes, sir. Thank you."

"Well, I got out the ol' cellular, alerted the team, told them what was going down, and to block the exits. Unless you want to swim, there's only two ways out of there. Then I got up, put a round in the chamber, turned the flashlight on him, and said, 'Excuse me, sir. May I ask what you're doing?'"

"Those were your exact words?" Matt asked.

"Those were my exact words," Colonel Richards said.

"And then what happened?"

"For a moment, I thought he was going to attack me with the sword, and I hoped he wouldn't, because I never was any good at taking sharp objects away from people, and I didn't want to have to put him down with the .45 because that would really have opened a large can of worms, and then he just turned and ran off."

"Still wearing the mask?" Matt asked.

"I dunno. I suppose so. Anyway, I called 'Halt, or I'll fire' and let off a couple of rounds in the general direction of the moon, thinking that might scare him into stopping. It didn't. So I called the team and told them to block the exits, and to be careful because this guy had a knife. Then I called the cops. Then I started for my car. I saw headlights go on, and heard an engine start and tires squealing. So I got in my car. When I got to the Highway 98 exit, I saw that he'd run into Chambers Galloway's brand-damned-new Mercedes truck thing, and that the old guy had him spread-eagled on the ground with a twelve-bore shotgun pointed at him."

"Did he have the mask on then?" Matt asked.

"No. But I looked into his car just before the cops came, and it was in the car, that and the knife."

"Did the police find out who he is?" Olivia asked.

"Not right away," the colonel said, and looked at his wife. "At first, he wouldn't say anything, and he wasn't carrying any identification. Not even a driver's license. So Charley tossed him in the slam—"

"Charley?" Olivia asked.

"Charley Yancey, the chief of police. And a pretty good one," the colonel explained, and then went on: "I think Charley charged him with leaving the scene of an accident, which is heavier than being a Peeping Tom, which is like spitting on the sidewalk. Anyway, once he had him locked up, Charley began to try to identify him through the car."

"And did he?"

"Not until about ten o'clock this morning," the colonel said. "The car had Illinois plates, but when Charley called out there, they said the plates were not for the car this guy was driving, and they didn't have the VIN . . . the Vehicle Identification Number? . . ."

"Yes, sir. I'm familiar with the term," Matt said.

". . . in their data bank. So Charley checked with Montgomery—that's the state capital, where our data bank is—and neither did they. Nor did Florida or Mississippi."

"Interesting," Matt said.

"So Charley finally decided to make sure he was using the right VIN, and when he went out to the impound yard, he finally saw the Gambino Motor Cars chrome thing on the trunk. You know what I mean?"

"I'm not sure, sir."

"Next to where it says Chevrolet Impala or whatever, the dealers put their own name."

"Yes, sir. Now I understand. Colonel, can I ask you how you know all this?"

The question made Colonel Richards uncomfortable.

"The minute I started to tell you, I was afraid you'd ask that question," he said. "Would you be satisfied if I told you I have a source inside the police department? I do, and I don't want him getting in trouble with Charley because he's keeping me up to speed on this."

"You're talking about a police officer?"

"No, I'm talking about the guy who goes there once a week to wax the floors."

"Colonel, I can't see any reason why I should tell the chief of police that I even know who you are. I was just curious. . . ."

"That's probably a good idea. Don't tell him you talked to me."

"All right, sir, I won't. You were saying something about the car dealer?"

"Fats Gambino. Great big fat Italian guy. He takes a lot of heat with a name like that, as you can imagine."

"Yes, sir."

"Anyway—he's a friend of mine, by the way—Fats has the Mercedes franchise and the Porsche franchise and others. Volvo, for one. And he deals in classy cars, exotic cars, is that what they call them? Rolls Royces, old Packards, stuff like that."

"Exotic cars. Yes, sir, I understand."

"And he also does things like buy fleets of cars from people like Hertz and Dollar and Alamo. I think they get rid of them after forty thousand miles, or a year. Something like that. Anyway, Gambino buys them up north, brings them here, cleans them up, and puts them on his used-car lot. That's where the peeper got his car."

"He bought it from Gambino?"

"No. He borrowed it from Gambino. It turns out this guy is in the exotic-car business. He was in town to try to sell Fats a Rolls Royce and something else, I forget what, and to try to make a deal with Gambino for a couple of Porsches."

"I'm a little confused here, Colonel," Olivia asked. "You're saying this fellow drove here from someplace in a Rolls Royce, and then borrowed a Chevrolet from Mr. Gambino?"

"No. He drove here in a great big tractor-trailer rig with three, four, really fancy cars in it. Then he borrowed the Chevy from Gambino. Told him he was going to Biloxi to play blackjack. Fats is one pissed-off guy, let me tell you. . . ."

"There goes your mouth again," Mrs. Richards said.

"Mr. Gambino is apparently distressed at the prospect that his name will be associated in the public's mind with that of a chap charged by the police as a Peeping Tom. Better?"

"Sometimes, Lacey . . ."

"Let me see if I can get this in sequence, Colonel," Matt said. "When the chief of police couldn't identify the car by its VIN, he did so by tracing it to the Gambino dealership?"

"A little after ten this morning. Gambino goes to work late. When he finally came in, he said, yeah, he owned a car like that, he owned a dozen cars like that, and he had loaned one to a friend of his to go to Biloxi. Bingo. Mr. Peeper is identified."

"Okay. I think I've got it straight," Matt said. "Thank you."

"And now are you going to tell me why you're interested in this guy? Interested enough to come all the way down here from Philadelphia, P.A.?"

"Colonel, you've been very helpful, and I'm really grateful. But I would be in deep trouble if it ever got out I told you anything that could possibly jeopardize our investigation."

"Okay. I had twenty-seven years in uniform, and for most of that time I had a top-secret clearance. But okay."

"Would you be satisfied if I told you, Colonel, that from what you've told me, the way this Peeping Tom operates is unusually like the way a man we're looking for in connection with a homicide in Philadelphia operates?"

"Your guy is a pervert too?" Colonel Richards asked.

"Yes, Colonel," Olivia said. "He is."

"If our guy turns out to be your guy, will I have to read about in the newspaper? Or will you tell me first?"

"You'll hear about it long before it gets into the papers," Matt said. "I promise."

[TWO]

It was ten to seven when Matt pulled the rented Mustang into the Joseph Hall Criminal Justice Center in Daphne.

There was a large parking lot, and it was full. Matt wondered why, at this time of day.

"I'm getting hungry again," he said to Olivia.

"After all you had for lunch? I can't believe it."

"I don't know. I must have done something to work up an appetite."

"I can't imagine what," Olivia said. "When are you going to call Lieutenant Washington?"

"I don't have anything to tell him yet," Matt argued. "And if he had something to say to us, he would have called."

Inside a double glass door was a barren room with shiny tile walls. There were several metal doors and a small window in the walls. Next to the window was a buzzer button and a sign reading, RING BELL FOR SERVICE.

Matt pushed the button. There was a buzzing sound, and a moment later the small door opened inward, and the face of a plump middle-aged woman appeared in the opening. She had what looked like a police uniform on, but Matt saw neither badge nor weapon.

"Can I help you?"

"Good evening," Matt said, and showed her his identification. "I'm Sergeant Payne, this is Detective Lassiter, and we'd like to see Chief Yancey, please."

"Can't right now, he's in court."

She pointed to her left, to a single door in the shiny tile wall.

"Well, then, may I please speak to the supervisor on duty?"

"That'd be Sergeant Paul."

"Do you think I can see Sergeant Paul?"

"You want to *see* him, or just speak to him?"

"I'd really like to speak to him in person," Matt said.

"He's on patrol. I'll give him a call."

"Thank you very much."

Ninety seconds later, her face appeared again.

"He's still working a DUI. Says it will take him fifteen minutes to get here."

"Thank you. Should we wait here?"

"If you went in the courtroom, you could sit down," she said. "I'll tell him where you are."

"Thank you very much."

Matt opened the single steel door in the tiled wall for Olivia, then followed her in.

They found themselves at the head end of a fairly large courtroom, right by the judge, who, sitting on his bench a few feet above them, looked down at them in what was certainly curiosity and possibly annoyance.

"Go along the wall," Matt quickly ordered Olivia, and he followed her past a railing dividing the bench area—which had tables for the accused and their counsel—from the spectator area, which was furnished with benches not unlike church pews.

Behind the last row of benches was an open area, fairly crowded with people—Matt thought they looked like the accused and their counsel—and behind that a set of double doors.

They found seats in the next-to-the-last row and tried to look inconspicuous.

There were a number of police officers in the courtroom, most of them on the bench side of the barrier. Two of them stood out. One was a short, trim man in a neat, white shirt uniform. On each of his collar points was a colonel's eagle. In the Philadelphia police department, that was the uniform insignia of a chief inspector. Inspector Peter Wohl, on those rare occasions when he wore a uniform, wore a silver leaf, the same insignia as that of a lieutenant colonel.

When the man wearing the colonel's eagles looked at them with unabashed curiosity, Matt decided he had to be Chief Yancey, and had the unkind thought that the Homicide Unit of the Philadelphia police department probably out-numbered the Daphne police department, and that Captain Quaire only got to wear the insignia of a captain.

The second police officer who stood out looked, Matt thought, as if he could be Jason Washington's younger brother. He was an enormous, very black, sergeant. He was quietly talking on a cellular phone, which almost disappeared in his massive hand.

It didn't take either Matt or Olivia long to figure out what was going on. This was Municipal Court, primarily occupied with misdemeanor level violations of the law, primarily traffic offenses.

And it was a smooth-running operation. The clerk called a case number. The accused, sometimes accompanied by his counsel, or his mother and/or father, approached the bench. One of the uniforms then detached himself from the knot of fellow police officers and stood facing the bench. The clerk read the charges, and the judge asked how the defendant pled. If the defendant pled "guilty," sentence was immediately dispensed. If the defendant pled "not guilty," the arresting officer testified, the defendant (or his counsel, but not, Matt noted with a smile, his mother and/or father) was permitted to cross-examine the uniform, and when that was done, the judge immediately decided guilt or innocence and handed out the sentence.

Then the next case was called.

A hand tapped Matt's shoulder. He looked around and saw a middle-aged man he instantly decided was a lawyer. The lawyer was pointing to the cracked-open double doors of the courtroom. Matt saw the enormous sergeant beckoning to him.

He and Olivia made their way through the standees in the rear of the courtroom and out the door.

"You're the cop from Philadelphia?" the enormous sergeant asked in a thick southern accent.

Matt saw that he had a highly polished name badge reading "Sgt. D. Kenny" pinned to his crisply pressed shirt.

This is the guy I talked to when I called from outside Olivia's apartment.

"*Cops* from Philadelphia," Matt said. "This is Detective Lassiter, and my name is Payne. I'm a sergeant."

The sergeant stopped Matt from producing his identification with a wave of his huge hand.

"The chief says that Sergeant Paul doesn't know anything about the peeper; that court will probably last until about ten-thirty, maybe later; and that you can wait for him if you want but that he'd much rather talk to you in the morning. About eight."

"Can I ask you two questions, Sergeant?"

"You can ask."

"Is your peeper going to make bail and walk out of here tonight?"

"No."

Matt took his laptop out of his case. The enormous sergeant watched silently and without expression as Matt turned it on.

"I'd really be grateful, Sergeant, if you could tell me if this knife looks familiar to you."

Matt turned the laptop's screen so the sergeant could see it. It was one of the digital images Matt had taken from the camera the doer had left in Cheryl Williamson's apartment. It showed a visibly terrified young woman lying on a bed, tied to the headboard with plastic binders. Her breasts were exposed. Lying between them was a large knife, its tip almost touching the soft skin under her chin. There were several thumbnail-sized drops of a thick, milky white fluid on the highly polished blade.

The enormous sergeant looked at the image, then at Matt, and then back at the computer screen. Then he handed the laptop back to Matt.

"Wait," he said.

In two minutes, he was back with the chief.

Matt wordlessly raised the almost closed laptop screen and extended it to the chief.

"Where'd you get this?" the chief asked.

"Our doer forgot his camera when he left the scene," Matt said. "Possibly because by then he knew he'd killed Miss Williamson and was a little frightened."

"Sonofabitch!" the chief said, instantly adding, "Excuse me, ma'am."

Olivia made a gesture indicating she understood.

The chief, taking care that Olivia could not see the screen, returned the laptop to Matt.

"You're the sergeant who talked to me and Sergeant Kenny this morning, right?"

"Yes, sir. I'm Sergeant Payne, and this is Detective Lassiter."

"Let me tell you how it is, Sergeant. Sometime tonight, in there, a man is going to appear before the judge to have both the suspension of his DUI sentence and the suspension of the revocation of his driver's license challenged by me. I personally got him again for DUI two nights ago, and one of my not-too-smart officers let him go on his own recognizance after he'd had time to sober up. He's a lawyer, and he's got a damned good lawyer, and nothing would make either of them happier than for them to show up only to hear that I'm not there. I think they're sitting in a car someplace waiting for some other lawyer to call, telling them I've gone. You follow me?"

"Yes, sir. Another continuance. And you don't want that to happen."

"No, I don't."

"I understand, sir. I was a little concerned that your peeper would get out on bail."

"That's not going to happen, not tonight," the chief said. "Kenny, you bring these officers up to date on what happened last night. We can do that much. And later tonight, if you'd like, or in the morning—which would be better for me—we can talk about what we're going to do about this Peeping Tom Jabberwocky caught."

"Yes, sir, Chief," Sergeant Kenny said.

"And tell the people in the lockup that the only person who can let Mr. Homer C. Daniels out of his cell is me."

"Yes, sir, Chief."

Sergeant Kenny led them through a corridor, then a locked door into what was obviously the administrative department of the Daphne police department. It was a fairly large room with several rows of desks. Offices opened off it, and Matt saw signs identifying those of the chief, the deputy chief, and then—just as they reached it—one reading "Sgt. Kenny."

He waved them inside, closed the door, and gestured for them to sit down.

"Okay. I don't know how much you know—"

"Not much," Matt said.

"I don't know how many *details* you have, so if I start telling you something you already know, stop me."

"Sure."

"I don't think the chief *dislikes* Colonel Richards," Sergeant Kenny said, "but the chief doesn't know what a fine officer the colonel was when he was in Special Forces. I do."

"And does the chief know that you know—"

"I don't think that's ever come up in conversation, come to think of it."

"I understand."

"Good," Sergeant Kenny said.

He met Matt's eyes for a long minute.

"Okay. I wasn't there at the Yacht Club, but the dispatcher called me at the house and told me what had gone down. So I came here. And while they were booking him, a concerned citizen who didn't identify himself called me and said he smelled that this peeper was more than a peeper."

"Interesting."

"Well, after they booked him . . ."

"On what?"

"Peeping. It's a misdemeanor."

Matt nodded.

"Our detective sergeant and the chief interviewed him. I got to listen."

"'Your' detective sergeant?" Olivia asked.

"Yes, ma'am, we have two. A detective and a detective sergeant."

"I see."

"This was three o'clock in the morning. And this guy said he wasn't going to say anything, even give us his name, without a lawyer."

"He'd been Mirandized?"

"Sure. Well, hell, I thought that was a little strange. This wasn't even serious. Not even like DUI. This was peeping. We catch peepers every couple of weeks. The judge fines them two hundred dollars and court costs, and threatens them with having to register as a sex offender if they get caught again. I can't recall any peeper ever going to jail."

"I understand."

"Then the chief tried to identify this guy through the car, and got nowhere. That made him a little more suspicious, so he charged him with leaving the scene of an accident, which is either, depending on the circumstances, either a first-class misdemeanor—thirty days in our jail, max—or a felony.

"Anyway, they left him in a cell to think things over. I guess he did, because in the morning—just before you called—when the chief got him a lawyer, he'd changed his tune. Now he was all remorse. He was ashamed, and was going to be embarrassed when all this came out, and all he wanted to do was take his punishment."

"Had you identified him by then?"

"He gave us his name, and said he was from Las Vegas, and that he'd borrowed the car from Fats Gambino in Mobile, said he was doing business with Gambino, told us Gambino would confirm that, and practically begged us not to tell Gambino *why* he'd been arrested."

"And then you had to wait for Gambino to come to work?"

"Yeah. And while we were waiting for that, you called. And asked about the knife."

"Okay."

"Anyway, Fats confirmed what he had told us, and said he'd loaned him the car to go to Biloxi to play blackjack. And offered to go his bail."

"And?"

"We told him bail hadn't been set, that he hadn't been arraigned. And then, an hour after that, Fats called back, said he'd just got the New Orleans newspaper, the *Times-Picayune*. It had the picture of old Mr. Galloway standing over him in it. And Fats wanted to know if the guy on the ground was the one who was driving his car, and the chief said yes, it was, and Fats threw a fit. He wasn't going to make bail for a pervert, et cetera, et cetera, and asked was there any way he could get his car back without his name being connected with it. The chief told him he'd see what he could do, but couldn't make no promises."

Sergeant Kenny let this sink in for a moment, then went on.

"By this time, the chief—who's a nice man—is starting to feel sorry for this guy. And the mayor says that enough people have been laughing at Daphne and Jabberwocky, and that if he had his druthers the municipal judge would set bail high enough to hurt him when he jumped it, but not too high that he couldn't afford to make it or jump it—something on the order of a thousand dollars, maybe less—and that would be the end of it.

"The chief was willing to go along. There was your phone call, but you told the chief you were going to send a telex saying who you were, and you didn't, so he thought it was likely you were some wiseass reporter. . . ."

"I completely forgot about that," Matt said. "When I showed my lieutenant the newspaper, the next thing I knew Olivia and I were on the way to the airport. I'm sorry."

"And then you showed up here," Sergeant Kenny said. "And that changed things."

"We're really anxious to bag our doer, Sergeant," Olivia said. "Dr. P . . . the psychiatrist who did a profile said that the doer was going to be really frightened when he realized he had killed someone, and do one of two things—go underground for a long time, or keep doing this sort of thing, knowing that he could only be executed once. If this is our doer, he obviously wasn't frightened into going underground."

Sergeant Kenny considered that for a moment.

"Can I ask how you got involved in this, ma'am? Just curious."

"I was next up on the wheel at Northwest Detectives when the brother found the victim," Olivia said. "So I got involved that way."

"You know what she means, Sergeant?"

"No, but I'm guessing she was the first detective on the scene, and then you got involved because it was a homicide."

"Right."

"So why do you two think this guy is your man? Because of the knife?"

"That would be incriminating if it's the same one in the pictures we have," Olivia said. "But we have more."

"Well, let's see if it is," Kenny said. He got up, walked to a steel door, and unlocked two locks. He came out with a Jim Bowie replica knife wrapped in plastic film.

"We got the Mobile police lab to take prints off it this afternoon," he said, "they're better equipped to do that than we are. They're also having their expert see if there's a match between Mr. Daniels's prints and the ones they took off this."

He unwrapped the Jim Bowie replica as Matt opened his laptop and turned it on.

"Well, what you have here is a big knife that looks just like the big knife in the picture," Sergeant Kenny said. "I don't suppose they made more than five or ten thousand knives just like this."

"In the photo, Sergeant," Olivia said, "those . . . spots, I suppose is the word . . . on the blade are sperm. We can make a DNA comparison."

He looked at her for a long moment but said nothing.

"Was there a camera, Sergeant?" Olivia asked.

"Yes, there was. Looked like brand-new. One of those digitals."

"Our doer left a digital camera at the scene. We took those photographs from it," Matt said.

"And a mask?"

"A black ski mask."

"What we believe, and what the psychiatric profiler believes, Sergeant," Olivia said, "is that our doer has previously done what he did in this case. That is, stalk a young woman until he feels comfortable in breaking into her home. He then ties her to her bed with plastic ties . . ."

Kenny turned and went to the closet, returning with a Ziploc bag full of plastic ties.

"Like these?"

"Like those," Matt said.

". . . and when she is terrified sufficiently, and her clothing has been cut off," Olivia went on, "he humiliates her sexually and takes photographs of various stages of the assault."

"And then kills them?"

"No. We don't think so," Matt said. "We think he didn't mean to kill our victim. It just happened."

"Would you agree, Sergeant," Olivia asked, "that there is a similarity in the *modus operandi* of our doer and what this man was apparently about to do last night?"

"I think you could reasonably conclude something like that," Kenny said. "So what do we do now?"

"I don't know," Matt confessed. "I have no idea what the legal procedure is. But I know there's enough here to tell my lieutenant about it."

Sergeant Kenny pointed to the telephone on his desk. Matt started to reach for it, then stopped.

"Would it be possible for us to have a look at this man?" he asked. "I don't mean interview him. I just have a feeling I ought to have a look at him."

Olivia looked at him in surprise and disapproval.

Kenny considered Matt's request a moment, then nodded, stood up, and nodded again, this time toward the door.

"If you've got weapons," he said, as he unholstered his pistol and laid it on his desk, "it'd be better to leave them in here."

Matt and Olivia laid their pistols on his desk, which gave Matt a chance to take a closer look at Kenny's shiny revolver. It was, Matt saw, more than a little surprised, a Smith & Wesson Model 29 in .44 Magnum caliber. Identical, except for the five-inch barrel on this one, to the weapon Clint Eastwood had made famous in the movies.

Well, hell, why not? As big as Kenny is, he probably doesn't even feel the recoil.

Sergeant Payne's experience with jails was limited to those in Philadelphia, and a cell in the Spring Lake, New Jersey, jail in which, at sixteen, he and Mr. Chadwick T. Nesbitt IV, also sixteen, had been confined overnight, charged with disturbing the peace of that seashore community by taking a midnight swim in the Atlantic without bathing attire.

The Daphne jail was like none in his experience. It reminded Matt more of a hospital than a jail. It was spotless. The walls were of white tile. The bars on the six cells were white. The in-cell toilets were of stainless steel, and there was no graffiti on the walls.

The first cell was empty. Sergeant Kenny pointed to the second. It held a large, crew-cutted man wearing white coveralls on the chest of which was embroidered DAPHNE JAIL in red.

Matt stepped in front of the cell and looked in. Olivia stepped up beside him.

Homer C. Daniels, as if he was trying to be friendly, at first smiled—if a little uneasily—at the young couple standing with Sergeant Kenny looking into his cell.

Then the smile vanished.

"Who are you?" he asked, and when there no response, angrily demanded, "Sergeant, who the fuck are these people?"

"Watch your mouth, Mr. Daniels," Sergeant Kenny said. "You see the lady!"

"I'm Sergeant Payne, Mr. Daniels," Matt said. "And this is Detective Lassiter. We're from the Homicide Unit of the Philadelphia police department."

"What do you want with me?" Daniels asked.

"I'm sorry, sir. But that's about all I can say to you without your attorney being present."

He turned and walked toward the door through which he had entered the cell block. He stopped just inside, out of sight of the cell, and gestured almost frantically for Kenny to follow him, but Kenny waited until Olivia had turned away from the cell and started for the door.

They both looked at Matt in bewilderment.

Matt frantically silently mouthed something to Sergeant Kenny. He had to do it three times before Kenny understood, thought it over, shrugged, and then dutifully repeated what Matt had mouthed.

"You think that's your man, Sergeant?" he said, speaking a little more loudly than he normally did.

"No question about it," Matt boomed, confidently. "That's him. It all fits. The knife, the mask, the digital camera. Same *modus operandi*. All we'll have to do is match the DNA, and there's no challenging DNA. I'll start the extradition paperwork tonight."

Olivia shook her head in disbelief.

Matt gestured for Olivia and Kenny to go through the door. When they had, he closed it.

"Now we call the Black Buddha," he said to Olivia.

Olivia rolled her eyes.

Oh, shit! There goes my automatic mouth again.

" 'The Black Buddha' is what we call my lieutenant," Matt said, "who is an African-American gentleman slightly larger than you, Sergeant, and generally regarded as the best homicide investigator between Bangor, Maine, and Key West, Florida."

"Bigger than me?" Kenny asked.

"Bigger than you, Sergeant," Olivia said.

Kenny smiled. "How do you start the extradition paperwork?"

"I haven't a clue," Matt confessed. "I'll ask Lieutenant Washington."

"What was that business in there?" Kenny asked.

"When I saw that sonofabitch, the idea of him getting a good night's sleep, thinking he was going to bail himself out of here tomorrow, annoyed me. And then I remembered what Washington told me—"

"The Black Buddha?" Kenny interrupted.

Matt nodded.

"—about the likelihood of a suspect who has (a) time to reflect on his sins and (b) not had much sleep telling you a lot more than he would if he had had neither."

"You're not actually thinking of interviewing him?" Olivia asked.

"I'll do exactly what Washington tells me to do," Matt said.

"Hello?" a female voice said. Matt recognized it to be that of Martha Washington.

"Matt, Martha," Matt said.

"*Martha* Washington?" Sergeant Kenny asked, smiling. Matt smiled.

"He's in the shower, Matt. And you, I understand, are in the Deep South?"

"About as deep as you can get," Matt said. "Standing here with a sergeant who looks like your husband's twin brother. I really have to talk to him. When should I call back?"

"I'll just hand him the cellular," she said. "Hold on."

"I'm already annoyed with you for not having checked in earlier," Washington's voice came over the line. "And I dislike being interrupted when I am in the midst of my ablutions. That said, you may proceed."

"This is our doer, Jason."

"You will forgive me for asking, Matthew, but do you believe this because of something more than your intuition?"

"Sergeant Kenny showed me the knife he had. It's a twin of the one in the pictures. He had a digital camera—a new one—and a package of plastic ties. He was trying to pry open a window in a young woman's apartment when the Citizens' Watch guy caught him."

"Who is he?"

"His name is Homer C. Daniels. White male, six feet one inch, two hundred pounds, mid-thirties. He's a dealer in exotic cars, from Las Vegas, and he drives all over the country doing business."

"On what charges are they—presumably the Daphne police—holding him?"

"Peeping, a misdemeanor, and leaving the scene of an accident, which is a little heavier."

"Is there a chance, however slight, that he might be allowed to post bail?"

"Not tonight."

There was a thirty-second pause.

"I will be calling you back shortly, Matthew. May I presume your cell phone battery is fully charged?"

"You may so presume."

"Splendid," Washington said, and the line went dead.

Matt hung up the telephone on Sergeant Kenny's desk.

"He's going to call me back," Matt said.

"You want to wait here?"

"I think maybe I'd better."

"We keep a pot of coffee going," Sergeant Kenny said.

Matt's cellular buzzed fifteen minutes later.

"I have just spoken with Mrs. Solomon," Washington said. "Placing what I truly hope is justified confidence in your analysis of the situation, she is dispatching an assistant district attorney—probably, if she decides Peter Wohl will just have to do without his services for a day or two, Steven Cohen, Esq. As we speak, a teletype message is being prepared asking the Daphne authorities to hold Mr. Daniels. Travel arrangements similarly are under way. You will be advised of the details."

"Yes, sir," Matt said.

"I devoutly hope this is not premature: Good job, Matt!"

"Thank you, sir."

"Please share that with Detective Lassiter."

"Yes, sir."

CHAPTER 18

[ONE]

"We're going to have to check out of the hotel," Olivia said, almost as soon as they got into the Mustang. "We never should have gone in there in the first place."

"The alternative would seem to be sleeping on the beach," Matt said.

"The alternative was any of the motels we saw when we turned off the interstate into Daphne."

"Every time I stay in a motel off an interstate, I am invariably denied sleep by the sounds of unbridled passion, a crying baby, or a barking dog—often all of the above—coming from the next cubicle. What's wrong with where we are?"

"An assistant D.A. is coming tomorrow," she said. "I don't want him going back to Philadelphia and saying, 'When I got down there, Payne has got his squeeze in a plush hotel.'"

"I hadn't thought about that," Matt confessed. "And the cold fact seems to be that I do seem to have my squeeze in a plush hotel. You're right, we better get out of there before our shameful secret becomes public knowledge. But in the morning. Not tonight."

Matt looked at Olivia, expecting a smile. She was not smiling.

"Is that how you think of me, as your squeeze?"

"That was your term, Mother, not mine."

Neither said anything else for the next ten minutes, until they were off four-lane U.S. 98 and driving through Fairhope.

"Hey, look at that!" Matt said, cheerfully, pointing. "Trattoria."

"What?" she asked.

"I wouldn't be a bit surprised if that was an Italian restaurant," he said. "It doesn't sound Polish. How about it, squeeze? A little linguini, a nice bottle of red, maybe even candles romantically flickering in a bottle covered with dripping wax?"

"Don't ever call me that again," she said, coldly.

"Sorry," Matt said. "I was about to add, '*Then* we can go to the hotel and fool around.' Does that interest you at all, Detective Lassiter?"

"Just go to the hotel, please."

"You want to tell me what I've done wrong?"

"From your perspective, probably nothing."

"And from yours?"

"I've been thinking."

"About what?"

"Us."

"What about 'us'? This afternoon—Christ, from the time I first laid eyes on you—I thought 'us' was nice and dared to think the feeling was reciprocal."

"It's happening too fast," she said. "And you're dangerous."

"How the hell am I dangerous?"

"You don't think, that's your problem," she said.

"Give me a for example, Mother."

"You never should have talked to the doer without permission."

"Were you there when I said, 'I can't talk to you without your lawyer being present' or words to that effect?"

When she didn't reply, he asked,

"Anything else I've done dangerously?"

"When you chased the guy in Philadelphia, you were drunk."

"I wasn't drunk. And you will recall I caught him."

"After you fell down twice."

"I fell over a goddamn wire."

She snorted.

"And the Highway sergeant gave you mints. He saw you were drunk."

"Isn't that what they call the pot calling the kettle black?"

"At least I admit it."

"Okay. I admit it. I was drunk. Happy?"

"And we never should have gone to the hotel in the first place. You should have thought what it would mean to me if it ever got out."

"I wasn't aware that our going to a hotel—in which, by the way, we have separate rooms—was going to see you branded forever with a scarlet A on your forehead."

"It would damned sure keep me from staying in Homicide," Olivia said.

"Look, you better be prepared, Olivia—Christ, you're naive—for all sorts of clever remarks from the guys in Homicide about our 'vacation' in Alabama. Whether we move into some dump of a motel or not, there are going to be suggestions that we fooled around."

"What they're going to think, is (a) I walked into Homicide, and (b) took one look at the hotshot sergeant, who calls the first deputy commissioner 'Uncle Denny,' and (c) jumped into his bed. And you know it, and you know that'll keep me from staying in Homicide. And you don't care."

"As much as I would like it to be otherwise, I think you have absolutely no chance of staying in Homicide."

"Is that so?"

"That's so. The only reason I'm in Homicide is because Mariani had that brainstorm about giving the top-five guys on the sergeant's exam their choice of assignment."

"It had nothing to do, right, with your 'Uncle Denny' Coughlin?"

"No, goddamn it, it didn't. He tried to talk me out of it, as a matter of fact." She snorted again.

"And he was probably right. There is no one more aware of my limitations as a homicide investigator than I am."

"Amazing! That's the first modest thing I've ever heard you say."

"Oh, screw you!"

"Fat chance!"

The doorman of the Grand Hotel opened the door for Olivia.

"Olivia, would you like to have dinner with me?"

"I think I'll have a sandwich in my room. But thank you just the same."

She smiled at the doorman and walked into the hotel.

[TWO]

Matt drove back into Fairhope and had linguini with Italian sausage and a bottle of Merlot—all of a bottle of Merlot—in La Trattoria, while considering the differences of the mental processes of the opposite sexes.

And then he drove very carefully back to the Grand Hotel, asked for any messages—there were none—and then went into the hotel's Bird Cage Lounge, where he sat all by himself in an upholstered chair at a table and had the first of five drinks of Famous Grouse on the rocks. The prospect of a scotch—or even an Irish—martini did not have much appeal.

Between drinks three and four, he used the house phone on the bar to call Miss Olivia Lassiter. The hotel operator said she was sorry, but Miss Lassiter had left word that she didn't wish to take any more calls tonight.

Between drinks four and five, his cellular buzzed.

It was Detective Joe D'Amata.

"The Black Buddha said to call, Matt. Meet Delta 311 at the Mobile airport—"

"Mobile?"

"That's what he said. Mobile. Arriving at twelve-thirty-five."

"They pronounced that 'Mow-*beel*,' not 'Mow-*bile*,' by the way."

"No shit?"

"Tell him I'll be at the 'Mow-*Beel*' airport. Who's Mrs. Solomon sending down? Did she make up her mind?"

"I dunno," Joe said. "This is the doer, huh?"

"It sure looks like it, Joe."

"Good for you, Matt. Having a good time?"

"Absolutely, Joe."

"Yeah, I bet you are," D'Amata said, chuckled, and hung up.

After drink five, Matt signaled for the waitress and signed the bill.

"I've had all the fun I can stand for one night," he said to her.

He left a call for half past seven and went to bed.

He woke with a hangover and a clammy undershirt.

He wondered about that and sniffed, and when he first encountered a really foul odor, remembered he had had a nightmare.

I always smell like death warmed over when I have one. And this was one of the better ones:

A Ford van driven by Warren K. Fletcher, white male, five feet ten, thirty-one, of Germantown was backing up toward him with the obvious intention of squashing him between the van and the Porsche. First he couldn't get the .38 snub-nose out of its holster no matter how hard he tried, and then when he finally got it out he couldn't make it fire no matter how hard he pulled on the trigger, and then when he finally got it to fire, he fired five times and missed all five times. . . .

He'd seen the movie before, and when he missed with the last shot, and the van was about to squash him, he usually woke up.

But I don't remember waking up last night.

Probably the booze.

And Fletcher as the star of my nightmare? Usually it's Susan.

Is there some significance in Fletcher showing up again?

The sweat soaked T-shirt smelled so foul that he didn't want to pack it with the rest of his clothing. He took it instead into the shower with him and started to wash it.

To hell with this! I'll just buy another T-shirt!

He tossed the T-shirt into a trash can and then took a long shower, considered again the gross injustices of the world as he found it, then had an inspiration.

"Screw her!" he said aloud, and when he got out of the shower, he walked still naked and dripping to the bedside telephone and called the concierge.

The concierge said the pro shop of the Lakewood Country Club would have clubs to rent and golf shoes for sale.

"And how about a tee time? As early as possible?"

"Well, perhaps tomorrow, sir. The rain'll probably stop in time for the course to be playable tomorrow. Shall I reserve a tee time for you then?"

"I'll be gone, I'm sorry. Thank you very much."

Having the telephone in his hand reminded him of two calls he had to make, and he made them.

First he called Colonel Richards and told him he thought the peeper was the man they were looking for, and that an assistant district attorney was en route from Philadelphia. And then he called Sergeant Kenny and told him that he would be meeting whoever was coming from Philadelphia at the Mobile airport a little after noon.

"I think whoever's coming will want to see the chief right away. Is he going to be available then? As soon as I can get from the airport to the station?"

"He'll be here then, I'm sure."

"If he needs to talk to me, you've got my cellular number."

"Right," Kenny said. "Mind telling me what you'll be doing?"

Until that moment, Matt had no idea—since golf was out and it was raining—how he was going to spend the morning. But it came to him.

"I'm going to take statements from the colonel, the old guy . . ."

"Mr. Chambers Galloway," Kenny furnished. "I'll give you his number."

"And anybody else . . . maybe Fats Gambino, if I have time on the way to the airport."

Kenny chuckled, deep in his throat, reminding Matt of Jason Washington.

"That'll make Ol' Fats's day. His place is right on Airport Boulevard, a couple of miles short of the airport. You can't miss it. I wouldn't suggest you tell him you're coming."

"And anybody else you think would be a good idea."

"I'll think on it, and tell you when you come in."

"Thanks, Kenny."

"My pleasure."

Matt considered for a moment having a room-service breakfast, but decided against it, but not because of the thought he had on the way to the dining room, which was that after he ate a leisurely breakfast, he would call Detective Lassiter and suggest that if she was now awake, they had work to do. He would then meet her in the lobby, and she could have a McMuffin and canned orange juice for breakfast at the McDonald's on their way to Daphne.

She came into the dining room a minute after he took a table, even before the waiter had brought coffee.

Jesus, that's a good looking woman!

"Good morning," Matt said.

"Good morning, Sergeant," Olivia said. "May I?" she asked, indicating a chair.

"Of course."

He smiled at her. She smiled back, but her smile was a momentary curl of her lips, completely devoid of anything resembling warmth.

Okay, if that's the way you want to play it. Screw you.

Olivia sat down.

"What we're going to do this morning is take statements from Colonel Richards and Mr. Galloway," Matt said, and then, without waiting for a reply, devoted his entire attention to the breakfast menu.

[THREE]

Detective Payne had just about finished his Belgian waffles with strawberries and cream, which he had ordered to accompany his chipped beef over toast with poached eggs, and glanced to see if Detective Lassiter was finished with her whole-wheat toast, when he thought he heard his name being spoken.

He looked toward the headwaiter's table in time to see the woman behind it nod in his direction, the nod guiding a young man in a business suit toward him.

"Sergeant Payne?" the young man asked.

Matt nodded.

"My name is Roswell Bernhardt, Sergeant. I'm an attorney. Specifically, I'm Mr. Homer C. Daniels's attorney."

"I don't mean to be rude, counselor, but I don't think I should be talking to you," Matt said.

"I understand," Bernhardt said. "Certainly. But what I was hoping you could do is give me the name of someone in your district attorney's office with whom I could speak."

"I wouldn't know what name to give you, Counselor, in the D.A.'s office. Except for that of the D.A. herself. That's Mrs. Eileen McNamara Solomon."

"I understood someone's on the way here," Bernhardt said, then added. "Sergeant Kenny told me that."

If Kenny told this guy my name and where to find me, and that somebody's coming, he must like him. What the hell!

"I'm going to meet someone from the D.A.'s office at the airport, Mr. Bernhardt . . ."

"Someone with the authority to discuss a plea bargain?"

". . . at half past twelve," Matt went on. "I don't know who, or what authority he or she might have. But if you'd like, if you give me your card, I'll pass it on, and tell whoever it is you'd like to speak with him/her."

Bernhardt produced a card, gave it to Matt, thanked him profusely, and left.

"I wonder what that was all about?" Olivia asked.

"I really have no idea," Matt said. "Are you about finished with your breakfast?"

She stood up and walked away and waited by the headwaiter's table until he had settled the bill.

"If you'll give me the keys to the car, please, I'll put my luggage into it," she said.

He wordlessly handed her the keys, then went to his room, packed, and then settled the bill. He made no attempt to rush.

When he got into the Mustang, she didn't speak.

Jesus, she's good-looking.

Is she going to stay pissed all day?

For good?

That seems a distinct possibility.

Well, if that bitchy, irrational behavior last night was an indicator of the future, maybe that's not such an all-around bad thing.

"'Tis better to have loved and lost, than not to have loved at all," as they say.

You don't believe that for a minute, and you know it.

Just keep your mouth shut, and maybe she'll cool off. Or warm up.

A familiar face came through the revolving doors into the persons-meeting-passengers area, but it was not that of Steven Cohen, Esq., but rather that of Michael J. O'Hara.

"Sherlock goddamn Holmes in the flesh!" Mickey greeted them. "And the beauty with the beast!"

"I won't ask what brings you to the Redneck Riviera, Mickey," Matt began.

"What did you say? 'The Redneck Riviera'?"

Matt nodded. "That's what they call it."

"Great! I'm going to do a long piece, and that's great color."

"But frankly," Matt went on, "I was expecting Steve Cohen or somebody else from the D.A.'s office."

"They're in the cheap seats," Mickey said. "They'll be off in a minute."

He turned to Olivia.

"Stanley said to tell you he's sorry as hell about the *Ledger* and that Phil Donaldson asshole, and that he'll try to make it up."

"Stanley?"

"Stanley Coleman, aka—"

"That's very kind of Mr. Colt, but not necessary," Olivia said.

"Who's 'they,' Mick, as in 'they'll be off'?" Matt asked.

O'Hara turned and pointed.

Steven Cohen, Esq., and Lieutenant Jason Washington were about halfway down a long column of arriving economy-class passengers.

"I didn't expect the boss," Matt said.

"They don't want any mistakes made with this one. For your sake, Matty, I really hope this guy is the one you're looking for."

"He is, Mick. I'm sure. How did you find out?"

"A little Irish bird named Denny told me."

"Welcome to the Redneck Riviera, boss," Matt said. "Hello, Mr. Cohen."

"By calling me 'Mister,' Matt, are you implying I'm not welcome in the . . . what did you say—'Redneck Riviera'?" Cohen replied, putting out his hand.

"I am really delighted to see you. And yeah, that's what it's called. They've got a really spectacular seashore. Ol—Detective Lassiter and I saw it when we drove over from Pensacola."

Cohen offered his hand to Olivia.

"Matt says he's sure this is the doer," Mickey said.

"I really hope so," Cohen said.

"Well, let us go see this fellow," Washington said. "Mick has reserved a car."

"The chief of police will be available," Matt said.

"Perhaps *after* we check into the hotel," Washington said. "Mick's made reservations for us at the Marriott. Is that where you are?"

"No, sir," Matt said, looking smugly at Olivia. "We're in the Eight Dollar Motel right in Daphne. Detective Lassiter thought the Marriott was a little too rich for us."

"Actually, it's the Nine Dollar Inn, Sergeant," Detective Lassiter corrected him.

"Actually, it's the $37.50 motel, after you pay up front and they give you the AAA discount," Matt said. "But what the hell."

They collected their luggage and went to the Hertz counter, where a Lincoln Town Car awaited Mr. Michael J. O'Hara.

"I think the best way to handle this, Detective," Washington said, "would be for Sergeant Payne to drive us in Mr. O'Hara's car. En route, he can fill us in on what we should know. In the meantime, you could go to the police station, advise them of our arrival, and tell them we are anxious to speak with the chief at his earliest convenience."

"Yes, sir," Detective Lassiter said.

Matt handed her the keys to the Mustang.

"Thank you," she said with a somewhat brittle smile.

The Mustang stayed on the tail of the Lincoln all the way from the airport through Mobile, across the I-10 bridge over Mobile Bay, and into Daphne, where it turned off U.S. 98 at the Joseph Hall Criminal Justice Center.

En route, as Washington intended he should, Matt told them everything he thought they should know. He pointed out the Gambino Motor Mall, and told them he had spoken with the proprietor, and that Fats had shown him the Peterbilt truck Mr. Daniels had driven into Mobile.

"I called the chief, and he said he just got a search warrant for the truck from a judge in Mobile, but he thought he'd wait until I could go along before he had a look."

"You didn't enter the vehicle?" Washington asked.

"No."

"Good," Cohen said.

"He certainly had to fuel the truck somewhere," Washington said, thoughtfully. "If he did so in Philadelphia and used a credit card, that would establish his presence there. On his way down here, as careful as we must presume he is, he probably paid cash. But he may not have had that much cash, and he may have used a card. It's worth looking into."

"Yes, sir," Matt said.

"I've got to have a picture of that truck," Mickey said. "How do I find my way back here?"

"After we have accepted the chief's kind invitation to witness his search of the vehicle, I will arrange something with Detective Lassiter to get you back here," Washington said.

"I'd like a picture of you two searching the truck," Mickey said.

"Sergeant Payne and I have had quite enough personal publicity lately, thank you just the same, Michael."

"There is good publicity and bad publicity, Jason," Mickey said, "and you two could certainly use some of the good kind."

"If you'll pardon me, Michael, what I am trying to do is develop a variety of good reasons that will suggest to Mr. Daniels that denial of his participation is no longer one of his options."

"That may be easier than you think, Jason."

"You will remember, *Sergeant*, to address me as 'Lieutenant' when we are about our official business?"

"Yes, sir."

"Oh, beware! Beware!" Mickey said. "What we have here is the Black Buddha in a bad mood. Cheap seats a little too small for you in the beam, were they, *Lieutenant?*"

Cohen laughed.

Washington ignored the remark.

"Why will I find it less difficult to reason with Mr. Daniels vis-à-vis confessing all that you—with your vast experience in these matters—think will be the case?"

"Because he sent his lawyer to see me vis-à-vis copping a plea," Matt said.

"Try to behave, Steve. We're in the company of the only two cops in Philadelphia who say things like 'vis-à-vis' in normal conversation," O'Hara said.

"Shut up, Mick. I want to hear about this lawyer," Cohen said. "What did you say to him, Matt?"

"I told him I would give you—whoever Mrs. Solomon sent down here—his card."

"That's absolutely all?"

"That's absolutely all."

"No suggestions, anything, that I would be interested in a plea bargain?"

"Nothing. And the only reason I said I'd pass on his card was because Sergeant Kenny told him where to find me."

"And Sergeant Kenny is who?"

"Local cop. A good one. Been very helpful."

"And when and where did this conversation take place?" Cohen asked.

"At breakfast."

"If he ran Matt down at the Nine Dollar No Tell Motel," O'Hara said, "he must be really interested in copping a plea."

"Actually, it was in the Marriott. We stayed there last night."

"And got out before somebody arrived from Philadelphia who would wonder what you were doing in the Grand Hotel? And might talk?"

" 'The Grand Hotel'?" Washington asked.

"Marriott's Grand Hotel. One of the stars in the galaxy of Marriott Resorts. When I told Stanley I was coming down here, he said to stay there. He said it's great."

"I have to ask, Matthew. You haven't behaved inappropriately with Detective Lassiter down here, have you?" Washington said.

"Two rooms. She slept in her bed, I slept in mine."

That's the truth. Admittedly not all of it, but the truth.

"But you do have something going with her, right?" Mickey asked.

"Go to hell, Mick."

"Answer Mr. O'Hara's question, please," Washington said.

"I thought for a while there might be something, but if there was, there ain't no more."

"While I confess I find this discussion of Matt's sex life absolutely enthralling," Cohen said, "can we get back to this guy's lawyer? You said you've got his card, Matt?"

Matt found it and handed it to Cohen in the backseat.

"Do Philadelphia cell phones work down here?" he asked.

"Mine does," Matt said, and handed Cohen his cellular telephone.

[FOUR]

When Matt saw Sergeant Kenny standing beside a thirtyish man in a business suit in the tile-walled outer room of the Daphne police department, he was surprised to see how they resembled each other.

"I got to get a picture of that guy with you, Jason," O'Hara said.

"Sergeant Payne," Kenny said. "This gentleman would like a word with you and the other people from Philadelphia."

The man with Kenny smiled, stuck out his hand, and marched up to Matt.

"Sergeant, I'm Special Agent Bendick of the Federal Bureau," he said.

"Federal Bureau of what?" Matt's mouth, on automatic, asked innocently.

"Investigation, of course. The *FBI*."

"How can I help the FBI?" Matt asked.

"It's how the FBI can help you, Sergeant," Special Agent Bendick said. "A telephone call would have saved you a trip all the way down here. But no real harm done. We'll handle it from here."

"Jesus Christ!" Mickey O'Hara said. "You guys really have no shame at all, do you?"

"I beg your pardon?"

"You heard me, J. Edgar Junior. Anything to get the FBI favorable notice in the papers, right? You can already see the headline, right? 'FBI Apprehends Philadelphia Murderer.'"

"Who are you, sir?" Special Agent Bendick asked.

"O'Hara's my name."

"And are you some sort of law enforcement officer?"

Mickey shook his head, "no."

"I couldn't get on the cops. My parents were married," Mickey said. He took out his digital camera and aimed it at Special Agent Bendick, Sergeant Payne, and Lieutenant Washington.

"I'd rather not have my photograph taken, if you don't mind," Special Agent Bendick said, holding his hand out in a vain hope—Mickey nimbly dodged around it—of covering the lens so that a photograph would be impossible.

"Jesus, didn't they tell you about the freedom of the press at the Quantico School for Boys?" Mickey asked.

"Sir," Washington said, "if we feel that any assistance from the FBI would be useful to us in this investigation, I will seek same through the appropriate channels."

"And you are?" Special Agent Bendick demanded.

"My name is Jason Washington. I'm a lieutenant with the Homicide Unit of the Philadelphia police department."

"I'm Special Agent Bendick of the Mobile office of the FBI, Lieutenant . . ."

"So you said."

"And inasmuch as this case crosses state lines, the FBI—"

"I don't believe this case meets the necessary criteria for the unsolicited involvement of the FBI, Mr. Bendick," Steve Cohen said.

"And may I ask who you are?"

"My name is Steven Cohen. I'm an assistant district attorney in Philadelphia."

"I don't really understand your attitude," Special Agent Bendick began.

"They're understandably a little pissed, J. Edgar Junior, that you tried to steal their pinch for the glory of the FBI. Unfortunately, you picked the wrong guys," Mickey said.

He quickly snapped another photograph.

"If you will excuse us, Mr. Bendick," Washington said. "We have an appointment with the chief."

"Right this way, Lieutenant," Sergeant Kenny said, waving them toward one of the steel doors.

"Mr. O'Hara," Washington said. "This is official police business, to which, unfortunately, I cannot make you privy at this time. Perhaps you'd like to stay here and continue your conversation with Mr. Bendick?"

Sergeant Kenny waited until Cohen and Matt had gone through the steel door, then followed them through it.

Special Agent Bendick looked at the closed door, then at Mickey O'Hara, who was again raising his camera, and then, mustering what dignity he could, marched out of the building.

"I have a confession to make," Washington said. "I was not overjoyed when Commissioner Coughlin told me Mickey was coming with us. But now?"

"He was magnificent," Cohen said.

"What did Mickey call him, 'J. Edgar Jr.'?" Matt asked, laughing.

"I don't think we've heard the last of him," Cohen said.

"Fuck him," Washington said, coldly.

Matt was surprised. Washington very rarely used vulgar language.

Washington turned to Sergeant Kenny and offered his hand.

"My name is Washington, Sergeant," he said.

"How are you?" Kenny said. "Payne said you were about as big as me."

"And this is Mr. Cohen, an assistant district attorney."

They shook hands.

"Detective Lassiter was supposed to tell you we would be here as soon as we got ourselves settled. . . ."

"She's in with the chief. Come on, I'll take you in."

"Thank you."

"You got any kin down this way, Lieutenant?" Kenny asked.

"Not so far as I know, but a first glance at the genetic evidence does seem to make that a distinct possibility, doesn't it?"

[FIVE]

Mr. Walter Davis, a tall, well-built, well-dressed—in a gray pin-striped, three-piece suit—man in his middle forties, who was the special agent in charge (the "SAC") of the Philadelphia office of the Federal Bureau of Investigation, sensed his secretary's presence at his office door and raised his eyes to her from the documents on his desk.

"Yes, Helen?" he asked, a slight tone of impatience in his voice. He had asked not to be disturbed if at all possible.

"I know, I know. But it's Burton White, the SAC in Mobile. . . ."

"Put him through. Thank you, Helen."

Walter Davis had known Burton White since they had been at the FBI Academy in Quantico, Virginia, and they had crossed paths often since. They had risen through the ranks together. Not quite as high together, as Philadelphia was a more important post than Mobile.

It is always pleasant, Davis thought, as he waited for the light on his telephone to illuminate, *to touch base with a peer who has not risen quite as far as oneself.*

The light came on, and Davis grabbed the phone.

"Burton, you old sonofabitch! How are you, buddy? How's things down there in the sunny South?"

"It's raining, and this is the Heart of Dixie, Walt. It says so on our license plates."

"Well, it's good to hear your voice, buddy. What can Philadelphia do for our outpost in the Heart of Dixie?"

"I'm having a little problem with the local cops. *Your* local cops. I thought you might be able to help me—the Bureau—out on this."

"Do whatever I can, you know that. My local cops? What are they doing way down there?"

"You had a murder up there. . . ."

"We have a lot of murders up here."

"This one was of a young woman raped and murdered in her apartment. It was on the NCIC, looking for a similar *modus operandi.*"

"That one made the front pages. It seems like the cops were actually on the scene, but couldn't take the door because there was no sign of forced entry. They took a beating for a while in the press."

"Well, one of my agents heard about the case, and then there was a similar *modus operandi* in a little village across the bay from here, and he went to check it out. . . ."

"And it was the man the locals here are looking for? Good for you, Walt! A little favorable publicity never hurts the Bureau, does it? You're sure you've got the right man?"

"When he got over there, your locals were already there."

"You don't say. That's odd. I had lunch with the Commissioner—Commissioner Ralph J. Mariani—yesterday, and he didn't say anything to me."

The sonofabitch! There's no way Philadelphia cops would go all the way to Alabama without Mariani knowing all about it. And he didn't say a goddamn word!

"There were Philadelphia Homicide cops there, plus an assistant D.A."

"Well, your man took over, didn't he, Burton?"

"He ran into a stone wall, Walt. I was hoping you could speak to somebody up there."

"You didn't get any names, by chance?"

"There was a Lieutenant Washington, a Sergeant Payne, and a female detective—I don't have a name on her—an assistant D.A. named Cohen, and some wiseass of a reporter named O'Hara, who accused my agent of shamelessly trying to steal the arrest. Do you think you could say a word in the appropriate ear up there?"

Of course I could. And then Mariani would shove it down my throat. With great joy.

"No. I don't think I could, Burton."

"'No'? Just like that? 'No'?"

"Let me tell you about the locals you're dealing with, Burton," Davis said. "Starting with the sergeant. You remember a couple of months ago, when one of my people had to put down a terrorist?"

"The guy with the machine gun? A real O.K. Corral shoot-out?"

"That's the case. Well, he had with him a local cop who, it has been reliably reported to me, said, 'Some of my best friends are FBI agents, but I wouldn't want my sister to marry one.'"

"A real wiseass, eh?"

"Whose father is a senior partner in what is probably our most important law firm. That's the sergeant. The lieutenant is probably Jason Washington. Is he a great big black fellow?"

"That's the man. My agent says he's enormous."

"Who is married to a lady who moves in the same exalted arty circles as our mayor, and incidentally is the best homicide investigator I've ever known."

"I see."

"Mr. Cohen is one of our two-hundred-odd assistant district attorneys. He specializes in the prosecution of homicides. He is generally held in high esteem—on a scale ranging upward from one to two hundred, he would be mighty close to two hundred, in other words—by those who know him. Including me."

"Well, they didn't behave with anything like professional courtesy, no matter who they are. They stood right there while this belligerent reporter—"

"And that would be Mr. Michael J. O'Hara, Burton, the Pulitzer Prize–winning reporter of the *Philadelphia Bulletin*," Davis interrupted, "whom I have been assiduously attempting to cultivate since they made me the SAC here. Without conspicuous success. I can only hope your agent didn't antagonize him."

There was silence on the line for a long moment, before Davis continued.

"So, for the reasons mentioned, Burton, no, I cannot say a word in the appropriate ear here. My advice, for what it's worth, is to stay away—far away—from these people unless they ask for your assistance, in which case I suggest you be the spirit of cooperation."

[SIX]

"Chief Yancey," Jason Washington said, "I would be very grateful if there were someplace private where I could confer with Mr. Cohen and Sergeant Payne for a few minutes before we talk to Mr. Daniels."

"You're welcome to use this," the chief said.

"You are very kind, sir," Washington said, and waited for the others to leave.

"What's this, Jason?" Cohen asked the moment the door closed.

"With the caveat that what I suggest would have to have your approval—not implied approval, and certainly not grudging approval—I am going to suggest a scenario for the initial interview."

"Shoot."

"Sergeant Kenny will handcuff and shackle Mr. Daniels in his cell, and bring him . . . Here, I suppose, inasmuch as they do not have an interview room as such, would be as good a place as any, and I think the chief would make it available to us—and handcuff him to a heavy and, it is to be hoped, uncomfortable chair, if such can be located.

"Here, for ten minutes, he will wait—with Sergeant Kenny standing out of his sight behind his chair—while absolutely nothing happens. It will, I think, in his frame of mind, seem like much longer.

"It is possible that he will feel the call of nature, and I hope this indeed happens, because it will give Sergeant Kenny the opportunity to lead him—after he takes, say, five minutes getting permission to do so, while another silent officer stands behind the chair—back to his cell, and then back here, all the time in handcuffs and shackles. The ten-minute time clock will start again, if this happens, on his return here.

"I think his only experience with being either handcuffed or shackled was when he was first detained by the concerned citizens. There is a feeling of both helplessness and humiliation when one is shackled and handcuffed."

"You don't want to go too far with that, Jason," Cohen said.

"Handcuffs and shackles are a normal security precaution. Nothing will take place that could possibly be construed as a threat of physical violence.

"His attorney will next appear. Mr. Daniels will almost certainly ask him what's going on, to which Mr. Bernhardt will give the only reply he knows, that they are waiting for the police—I hope the word 'homicide' is used—and another ten minutes will pass.

"Then Sergeant Payne will enter the room and prepare to begin the first interview—"

"Sergeant Payne?" Cohen asked, incredulously, "and where am I?"

"Pray indulge me. I will be grateful for any objections or suggestions you might have, but let me finish, please, first."

"Go ahead."

"Payne will unlimber a recording device, not hurrying at all. One with two microphones would be good, and if we can find one with four, that would be even better."

"A little theater, Jason?"

Washington nodded.

"When the recording device is set up, Matt will respectfully summon you from the corridor. When you come in, Matt will say, 'Mr. Daniels, this is Mr. Cohen, an assistant district attorney for Philadelphia, who specializes in prosecution of those charged with murder.'

"And then he will turn on the tape recorder, and go through the routine there. . . . 'This interview of Mr. Homer C. Daniels, in connection with the murder of Cheryl Williamson,' et cetera. You both know the routine."

Both nodded.

"And then Matt will say, 'Mr. Daniels, I understand that you have been advised of your rights as established by the United States Supreme Court, commonly called 'the Miranda Decision,' but just to make sure that you are fully aware of your constitutional rights in this situation, I'm going to go over them again with you in the presence of your attorney.'"

"And re-Miranda-ize him?" Cohen said. He was now smiling.

Washington nodded.

"And then Matt will say something to this effect: 'Mr. Daniels, I'm Sergeant Matthew Payne, Badge Number, of the Homicide Unit of the Philadelphia—'"

"Won't he have already said that?" Cohen interrupted.

"Possibly, but redundancy is sometimes useful," Washington said, and went on: "—and what I am going to do now is tell you why we believe, beyond any reasonable doubt, that in taking the life of Miss Cheryl Williamson you are in violation of Paragraph 2502(b) of the Criminal Code of Pennsylvania; that, in other words, you are guilty of Murder of the Second Degree.'

"At this point, I really hope Mr. Daniels will think he sees a slight glimmer of hope. 'Second Degree? That can't be as bad as First. Maybe I'm not going to be executed after all.'"

"I think I see where you're going, Jason," Cohen said.

"At this point, Steve, you will disabuse him of this hope by interrupting Matt and handing Mr. Bernhardt a Xerox of page thirty-four of the Crime Codes, and saying, one lawyer to another, 'I didn't know if this was readily available to you, Counselor, you might want to look it over.' And when he has had a moment to do so, you will add, collegially, 'You'll see that the only difference between Murder of the First Degree and of the Second, is that the First is premeditated, and Second while the accused was engaged in the perpetration of a felony. A little farther down the page, you'll see that 'perpetration of a felony is defined as—'"

"'—engaging in, or being an accomplice in the commission of,'" Cohen picked up, quoting from memory, "'or an attempt to commit, or flight after committing, or attempting to commit robbery, rape, or deviate sexual intercourse, by force or threat of force, arson, burglary, or kidnapping.'"

"So by now he understands he's really in trouble," Matt said.

"Which understanding you will then buttress," Washington said, "by proceeding something like this: 'Mr. Daniels, I'm not going to be asking you, right now, many questions, because frankly I don't have to. What I'm going to do is run through what we know right now, and then give you the opportunity to confer with your attorney, and after that you and he, and Mr. Cohen, can confer, if you like.'"

"And then I go down what we do have," Matt said. "Starting with what?"

"I would suggest the camera. 'We have the camera you left at the scene, Mr. Daniels, and the images it contained. We know that you bought the camera at Times Square Photo and Electronics, on . . .' Do you have the date?"

"It's in here," Matt said, indicating his laptop.

Washington nodded.

". . . 'and we have your signature on the sales slip. Among the images in the camera are those of the knife you used, and which the police took away from you here. One of the images shows sperm on the blade of the knife. We think it's reasonable to believe it's yours, and that we can convince a judge there is sufficient cause for him to issue a search warrant, which will give us a sample of your tissue so that a DNA comparison can be made' . . ."

"I get the picture," Matt said.

"Overconfidence is dangerous, as I've tried to point out to you before," Washington said. "That is especially true of someone like you, who has an abundance of confidence in himself that is not entirely justified."

Matt looked at him but didn't say anything.

"Does this scenario have any appeal at all to you, Counselor?" Washington said.

"It might even work, Jason," Cohen said.

"I will accept that as meaning it has your full approval," Washington said, but it was more a question than a statement.

Cohen thought this over for a moment, then nodded.

"Matt, you go someplace quiet—Mickey's car, perhaps—with your laptop, and refresh your memory about the details. Your performance will be more effective if you can readily recite from memory, for example, the date he bought the camera."

"Yes, sir."

"I don't have to tell you, do I, not to have your laptop with you? I don't want it subpoenaed."

"No, sir."

"Refreshing your memory should take no more than ten minutes, and during that time, I will set the stage in here and give Sergeant Kenny an understanding of his role—and how important it is—in our theatrical production."

"Yes, sir," Matt said.

Cohen waited until he was gone and the door had closed behind him.

"Jason, you and I have marched down this path together for a long time," he said. "And you know I'll go to the wire and beyond for you. But will you tell me why you're sending Matt to do this? He's a nice kid, and I really like him, but . . ."

"Primarily, Steve, for the educational aspects of it. This is his first homicide job."

"And if he blows it?"

"I don't think he will. He's smart, he can think on his feet, et cetera."

"But if he does?"

"Then we will both—Matt and I, I mean—know he doesn't belong in Homicide, won't we?"

"Then it's sink or swim time, right?"

"I shall have to make note of that phrase," Washington said. "It is so profound."

"What about Daniels, if Matt blows it?"

"Then, psychologically guided interrogation having proven ineffective, I fear I shall be forced to revert to the rubber hose system."

Cohen chuckled.

"That's really not so funny," Washington said. "I really would like to work that walking obscenity over with a rubber hose."

CHAPTER 19

[ONE]

When Sergeant Kenny led Homer C. Daniels from what the Daphne police department called the "Detention Area" into the administrative area and toward the chief's office, Daniels was even more firmly cuffed and shackled than Jason Washington thought he would be.

The chief of police had gone into his supply room and come out with a white canvas bag labeled "Prisoner Restraint System." It held three belts made of thick saddle leather and heavy canvas, a Y-shaped chain, and some other accessories. The system looked as if it was rarely used, if it ever had been.

Washington could now see how it worked when installed. The waist belt buckled in the back. On the front, connected to it with heavy chains, were handcuffs. Daniels could move his cuffed wrists no more than a few inches. Daniels's ankles had smaller versions of the waist belt around them. A short length of chain connected the two ankle restraints together, so that he had to walk with small steps. Another chain ran up his back, split into two, then went over his shoulders and connected with the waist belt. His ability to bend was severely restricted. Washington wondered how he was going to sit down in the restraint.

When Sergeant Kenny led his shuffling prisoner through the door of the chief's office, Washington said, "Time," and punched one of the buttons on his Tag Heuer chronograph.

"I never saw anyone actually push the buttons on one of those fancy watches before," Steve Cohen said in mock wonderment.

Washington held his wrist up so that Cohen could see the dial.

"It is also extremely useful when preparing soft-boiled eggs, Steve. One needn't make wild guesses about whether three and a half minutes have passed or not."

"I'm impressed."

"And well you should be."

Three minutes and forty seconds later, Sergeant Kenny came through the door, a very large Daphne police officer went in, and then Kenny walked to his office.

"He wants to take a leak," Kenny said.

"Time," Washington said, punched several buttons on his watch, and then said, "Splendid."

Precisely five minutes later, Washington said, "Sergeant Kenny, will you please escort Mr. Daniels back to his cell, so that he may relieve the pressure on his bladder?"

"The more I think about how that guy gets his kicks, the more I'd rather have him piss his pants," Kenny said.

"That, while a very interesting thought, would almost certainly, as Mr. Cohen would quickly tell us, violate Mr. Daniels's civil rights," Washington said.

"Let him have his leak, Kenny," Cohen said.

It took seven minutes and twenty seconds for Mr. Daniels to be shuffled back and forth to his cell.

"Time," Washington called, as Daniels shuffled through the door into the chief's office.

Not quite ten minutes later, Washington said, "Matt, go tell the chief that if Mr. Bernhardt wishes to consult with his client . . ."

"Yes, sir," Matt said, and left Kenny's office.

"Jason, what does your screenplay have to say about Daniels wanting to talk privately with his lawyer?"

"I don't think he will," Washington replied. "But if he does, it can only accrue to our advantage. I don't think he's seen him since the chief got the search warrants. He would tell him that, I'm sure."

Roswell Bernhardt, Esq., came into the room. The large Daphne police officer standing outside the chief's office opened the door for him and he went inside.

"Time," Washington said, and pushed buttons on his watch.

Matt appeared a minute or so later.

"You are prepared, I presume, Sergeant Payne? You're on in eight minutes and fifteen seconds."

"Yes, sir."

Eight minutes later, Washington said, "Good luck, Matt."

Matt, carrying a tape recorder and two microphones, walked across the room, waited for the Daphne uniform to open the door, then walked into the chief's office.

And four minutes after that, came out again.

"You're on, Steve," Washington said.

"Yeah, but I'm not going to get canned if I give a lousy performance," Cohen said, and walked across the room.

Five minutes after that, Chief of Police Charles Yancey came into Sergeant Kenny's office.

"Am I going to be in the way here?"

"Of course not," Washington said. "And it gives me the opportunity to tell you again how appreciative we all are for all your assistance."

"This isn't my first murder," Yancey said. "But I've never been around a sleazeball, murdering pervert like this before. Or seen big-city cops at work."

"We work exactly the same way as you do."

"The hell you do. Kenny told me what you did—are doing. Is it going to work?"

"Sometimes it does, and sometimes it doesn't. It largely depends on the interrogator."

"And that young sergeant is that good?"

"We are about to determine that," Washington said.

"Kenny told me about the run-in you had with the FBI. Does that happen all the time?"

"I don't know about *all* the time. But it happens far too frequently, I'm afraid. They seem to be very concerned with their image."

"They always—between you and me, a couple of cops—seem to look down their noses at us."

"Odd," Washington said. "I seem to have heard that before somewhere."

Yancey smiled at him.

"You want to go get a cup of coffee while you're waiting?"

"You're very kind, but I'd rather stay here."

"Hell, I'll get it," Yancey said.

He hadn't made it out of the administrative area when the door to his office opened and Matt Payne—carrying the tape recorder and microphones—and Steve Cohen came out.

Cohen walked to Washington.

"Mr. Daniels asked to confer with counsel, privately," he said.

"How did it go, Steve?"

"Matt did a hell of a good job, and I'm not saying that for any reason but giving credit where due."

"I expected nothing less," Washington said. "What are they going to talk about, would you think?"

"Probably my refusal to offer more of a deal than life without the possibility of parole."

"You didn't tell me about that."

"You didn't ask," Cohen said. "The boss wants this guy off the streets permanently. I told her I had the feeling that there are unsolved rapes, maybe even murder-rapes, all over the country that are going to surface now that we've caught this guy."

"Detective Lassiter spent fruitless hours on the telephone . . ."

"Calling big-city departments. I don't think she would have gotten around to Daphne anytime soon."

"I grant your point."

"Well, anyway, Eileen said we couldn't count on that, and she decided we have enough to go with here with no deal except life without parole."

"Eileen's tough," Washington said, admiringly.

"Personally, I'd like to see the sonofabitch strapped to the gurney," Cohen said. "But that's emotional. The interests of the people are best served by ensuring that he's behind bars permanently, rather than taking a chance that he'll walk, or get out in ten years."

"Isaac 'Fort' Festung," Washington said. "He was sentenced to life and he's walking around France eating grapes."

"Yeah."

"Any developments there?"

"The goddamn French are still dragging their heels. I think it has more to do with giving us the finger than anything else."

"Anyone but Eileen would have probably given up," Washington said. "She's as tenacious as she is tough."

He smiled.

"What's funny?" Cohen asked.

"I just remembered 'appealing to a higher jurisdiction,'" Washington said.

Cohen laughed.

When the Hon. Eileen McNamara Solomon had been on the bench, a just-convicted felon, facing a long prison term, had jumped up from his seat in her courtroom, run to a window, crashed through it and jumped to his death in the interior courtyard of City Hall.

When asked by the press how she felt about this lamentable incident, Judge Solomon had replied, "I can only presume he was appealing to a higher jurisdiction."

Matt came into Kenny's office.

"I forgot one thing before I went in there," he said. "The minute I opened my mouth, my back teeth began to float."

Cohen laughed.

"That happens to me," he said. "Usually ten minutes into a thirty-minute concluding statement."

"Your bladder problem aside, Matthew," Washington said, "how would you assess your chat with Mr. Daniels?"

"I don't know," Matt said.

"You 'don't know'?" Washington asked, incredulously.

"I think he knows we have him," Matt said. "But what his reaction to that will be, I have no idea. He may decide to take his chances. What has he got to lose?"

Washington grunted noncommittally.

Three minutes later, Roswell Bernhardt, Esq., came out of the chief's office and said that in exchange for a written guarantee that the City of Philadelphia would not seek the death penalty, his client was prepared to make a full statement, cooperate fully with the investigation, and waive extradition.

[TWO]

At five-thirty-five, Mr. Walter Davis walked up the marble steps of the Rittenhouse Club and entered the building through its revolving door. He stopped long enough to check the Members Board, and to see that the brass nameplate reading MARIANI, R had been slid to the left, so that it was now under the IN heading.

He found Commissioner Mariani in the paneled bar with First Deputy Commissioner Coughlin, which didn't surprise him. But with them at one of the round tables was Brewster Cortland Payne II, Esq., which did.

Mariani waved Davis over. The men shook hands. Davis sat down. A waiter appeared and Davis ordered a scotch, rocks. The others held up their hands in a silent gesture meaning they didn't need another one just now, thank you.

Davis wondered how long they had been here. He sensed that the drinks on the table were not the first round.

"We're having a little celebration, Walter," Mariani said. "I'm glad you were free to join us. I didn't give you much notice."

"It's always a pleasure, you know that. What are we celebrating?"

As if I didn't know.

"Mr. Homer C. Daniels has agreed to waive extradition."

"And he is?"

As if you don't know.

"You don't know?"

"I'm not sure," Davis said.

"He's the man who tied the Williamson girl to her bed with plastic ties, committed obscenities on her body, and then killed her."

"And you've got him?"

"The Daphne, Alabama, police have him. He was apprehended by one of those civilian neighborhood watch outfits, apparently in the act of trying to break into some other young woman's apartment. He's a dealer in fancy cars, from Las Vegas."

"I wouldn't be at all surprised, Walter," Coughlin said, "if he's been doing this sort of thing all over the country."

"A civilian neighborhood watch outfit? If this wasn't so serious, that would be almost funny. You're sure he's the doer, Ralph?"

"We're sure. We sent Sergeant Payne down there to check him out. Payne said everything fit, but just to make sure, I sent Jason Washington down there, and Eileen Solomon sent Steve Cohen. Not only does everything fit, but he gave Payne a statement and, as I said, has agreed to waive extradition."

"Washington and Cohen are in Alabama?" Davis asked.

"I thought you would have heard, Ralph," Mariani said, innocently. "Washington said the FBI had been there to offer their assistance."

Davis shook his head, "no."

"But whatever assistance we can provide, Ralph," he said. "All you have to do is ask."

"Thanks, Walter," Mariani said. "We appreciate that."

He smiled at Davis and went on:

"So what *I'm* celebrating is that an hour ago Eileen Solomon called to tell me that she had just spoken with the Attorney General of Alabama, who told her—in case Daniels changes his mind about waiving extradition—that the governor of Alabama would authorize his extradition just as soon as we place the request before him. And just a few minutes ago the homicide detective . . . Joe D'Amata, I think you know him?"

"Yes, indeed."

". . . called Denny from the airport to say he and the others, including several lab people, are indeed going to be aboard the five-fifty flight to Alabama. Joe's carrying the request-for-extradition packet with him in case it's needed."

"You apparently have this pretty well sewed up," Davis said.

"It looks that way, Walter. And what Denny and Brewster are celebrating is young Payne's faultless performance—starting with his finding this fellow down there—on his first time out as a homicide supervisor."

Mr. Davis's scotch rocks was served.

He raised his glass to Brewster Cortland Payne II.

"To Sergeant Payne," he said. "And at the risk of making Denny angry, Brewster, you know how much I would like to have your son working for the Bureau. And the offer is still open."

"So is Mawson, Payne, Stockton, McAdoo and Lester's, Walter, but the police department seems to have him firmly in its clutches."

[THREE]

"Before Steve and Matt get into the wine and become incoherent," Washington said, "I think an analysis of where we are and where we have to go would be in order."

Mr. Cohen gave Lieutenant Washington the finger.

They were sitting in upholstered chairs around two tables pushed together in the Bird Cage Lounge at the Grand Hotel.

Perhaps understandably, they were the object of some curiosity on the part of other guests. There were two enormous black men who looked like brothers, one of them in police uniform. There was a second uniformed police officer, a small man. There was an attractive young woman in the otherwise all-male ensemble, but she seemed to be sitting as far away as was possible in the circumstances from the only young man in the group. And finally, there was a dignified man in a double-breasted gray suit and finely figured necktie sitting beside a man with wildly unruly red hair, who was wearing an open-collared yellow polo shirt and a yellow-and-red plaid jacket.

"Where do we stand legally, Steve?" Washington asked.

"Joe D'Amata's in the air right now," Cohen said. "He's got the warrant for Daniels's arrest and the request-for-extradition packet, in case Daniels changes his mind about waiving extradition—"

"And if he does?" Washington interrupted.

"Eileen has talked to the Alabama attorney general," Cohen replied. "He told her the governor will sign the extradition order as soon as he gets it. If we have to go that route, I'll have to go to Montgomery, which raises the question 'How do I get there'?"

"Mr. Cohen," Chief Yancey said, "if you have to go, we can get you there in probably a little less than three hours. It's a straight shot up I-65. The troopers would be happy to carry you."

"The state troopers?"

Yancey nodded. "We do it all the time. We call it a handoff. A car would pick you up here, then go as far as he usually patrols up I-65. Another trooper car would meet you there. And maybe another one before you got to Montgomery. But they'll get you there, and be happy to do it."

"Well, that would really solve that problem," Cohen said. "But let's hope it doesn't prove necessary."

"Kenny?" the chief asked.

"I'll set it up, in case we need it," Sergeant Kenny said.

"Okay, that settles that," Cohen said. "Now, where was I? Okay. With Joe on the airplane are two lab technicians, we don't know who yet, and two detectives, ditto. They're going to change planes in Atlanta, fly to Pensacola, pick up a rental car, probably two rental cars, and then drive here, to the world-famous $37.50 No-Tell Motel, where Matt and Olivia are staying."

"I had a call from Peter Wohl, Steve," Washington said. "We know who the detectives are. Mutt and Jeff."

"Really?" Matt asked. "What are they going to do when they get here? And what about Stan Colt?"

"All I know is Inspector Wohl said that's who he's sending, and what they're going to do is sit on Daniels's truck as long as it's here, and when we locate a truck, or trucks, large enough to haul Daniels's truck—with contents—back to Philadelphia, they're going to ride back with it."

"When are you going to search the truck?" Chief Yancey asked.

"Where we are legally with that, Chief," Cohen said, "is that Matt has statements from Fats Gambino and you, Fats's stating that he saw Daniels lock the truck and trailer in his locked and guarded lot, and the truck has been there, under guard, since then. Yours states that the keys in your possession believed to be those to the truck and trailer were taken from Daniels at the time of his arrest and have never left police possession since that time. Tomorrow, the lab technicians will make an examination to see if anyone has forced any locks, and be prepared to testify they saw no evidence of such. I don't know for sure, but what they will do then is probably see what prints and whatever they can get from the exterior of the truck—stuff that might get lost between here and Philadelphia—and then conduct a cursory search of the interiors of the truck and tractor. If they don't find a body—which is not entirely out of the question here—or something else spectacular, they will seal both tractor and trailer as well as they can, and supervise the loading of it onto whatever we finally get to haul it back to Philadelphia."

"That seems like a hell of a lot of work," Yancey said. "Taking everything to Philadelphia."

"It is," Cohen agreed. "My boss is concerned—and so am I—about preserving the chain of evidence. We've got three jurisdictions here. Philadelphia; Daphne—Baldwin County; and because the truck is in Mobile, Alabama—Mobile County. But I think it's under control. Legally, the search will be executed by the Mobile police, using the search warrant the Mobile County judge issued. Matt and I—and to cover all the bases, Mutt and Jeff, too—will be there. And if you can send somebody—"

"I think Sergeant Kenny and I can find time to be there," Yancey interjected.

"Then any of us, or all of us, can testify under oath that Philadelphia police and Daphne police witnessed the search—and had control of the evidence—from the time the Mobile police exercised their search warrant—and put Daniels's keys in the locks."

"Kenny and I will be there," Yancey repeated, and then asked, "How are you going to get him to Philadelphia?"

"That's yet to be determined," Washington said. "I have given Sergeant Payne a list of other people from whom he and Detective D'Amata should take statements, which should keep them gainfully occupied for the next day or two. Detective Lassiter and I have reservations for a flight leaving Mobile at one-fifteen tomorrow afternoon. That may or may not provide time for me to speak with Detective D'Amata. . . ."

"I'm going back tomorrow?" Olivia asked.

"At one-fifteen," Washington said.

She was obviously surprised at the announcement. So was Matt. But when he looked at her, there was no mistaking what the coldly furious glint in her eyes meant.

She thinks I knew all about it. Hell, she thinks I asked Washington to send her home.

"... but inasmuch as Mr. Cohen and Detective D'Amata will have three hours together in a car coming back here, I don't see that as a problem. Do you, Sergeant Payne?"

"No, sir."

"In that case, our business having been completed, you may summon a waiter and you and Steve can begin to drink yourselves into oblivion."

"If that's all, sir, may I be excused?" Olivia asked.

"Olivia, I hope you understand that was an attempt at humor. We're going to have a very few drinks, and then dinner."

"I have a headache, sir."

"I'm sorry. Is there anything I can do?"

"No, thank you. I just don't feel—"

"I understand," Washington said, as, ever the gentleman, he rose to his feet. "I'm sure you'll feel better by morning."

"Would you like me to take you to the motel, Olivia?" Matt asked.

"I'll get a cab, thank you just the same."

"I don't know if they have cabs," Matt said.

And really hope they don't.

"We have the next best thing," Chief Yancey said. "Kenny?"

Kenny spoke to the microphone pinned to his shirt.

"Barbara-Anne, send whichever car is closest to the Grand Hotel to give Detective Lassiter a ride to her motel. She'll be outside the front door."

"Thank you very much," Detective Lassiter said.

They watched her walk out of the Bird Cage Lounge.

"Didn't want to ride with you, huh?" Mickey O'Hara asked. "Is that what they call 'a lover's quarrel'?"

"Go to hell, Mickey," Matt snapped.

"What is bothering her, Matt?" Washington asked. "Something obviously is."

"I think she thinks I arranged for her to be sent back," Matt said.

"I can quickly straighten that out, if you'd like."

"She wants to stay in Homicide," Matt said. "Is there any chance she can? She's a pretty good cop."

"Your loyalty is commendable. . . ."

"Is that what it is, 'loyalty'?" Mickey said.

"Mickey," Washington said, coldly angry, "sometimes, as now, you don't know when to stop." He turned to Matt. "As for her staying in Homicide, that, I'm afraid, is self-evidently out of the question. And you should know it is."

Matt couldn't think of a reply.

"And I just thought of something else," Washington said. "When I spoke with Commissioner Coughlin, he suggested that your father might like you to call. And I had the feeling that the commissioner would not consider a call from you to be an unwelcome intrusion on his time."

"Well, I guess I'd better do that right now," Matt said. "Before I become incoherent."

He got up from the table and went through a plate-glass door to an area between the hotel building and the bay. They could see him taking out his cellular.

"I think what we have here is raging testosterone," Cohen said. "And I'm not making fun of him."

"For that reason, I was deaf to his insolence," Washington said. He looked between Chief Yancey and Sergeant Kenny.

"I think a word of explanation is in order. Sergeant Payne is carrying his father's badge. Shortly before Matt was born, his father was killed on duty, answering a silent alarm. Deputy Commissioner Coughlin was his father's best friend. He is Matt's godfather."

"Being a cop's in his blood, huh?" Sergeant Kenny said.

"Prefacing this by saying I am—perhaps too obviously—fond of our young sergeant, I sometimes wonder if he's not flying a little too high for his experience."

"He did a good job with Daniels, Jason," Steve Cohen said. "Absolutely professional."

"And now he knows it. That's my point, Steve. Our Matty is not burdened with over-modesty."

"And he's going to be money in the bank on the stand," Cohen pursued. "If we're taking a poll, I'd say Matt is a hell of a good cop."

"I associate myself with the shyster," O'Hara said. "Now, can we get something to drink, for Christ's sake?"

[FOUR]

"The Nesbitt residence," the Nesbitt butler answered the call.

"Brewster Payne, Porter. Is Mr. Nesbitt available?"

"I'm sure he will be at home for you, Mr. Payne. One moment, please."

Several moments later, Chadwick Thomas Nesbitt III, Chairman of the Executive Committee of Nesfoods International, Inc., who had been practicing with a new putter on the practice green behind the left wing of his home, came on the line.

"If you weren't my lawyer, I'd be happy to hear from you. What's the bad news you really hate to have to tell me this time? IRS, or something else?"

"Actually, Tom, this does have a certain IRS connection."

"Oh, God, now what?"

"Your assets have been seized and you may have to go to prison."

"I don't think that's funny."

"I had drinks with Denny Coughlin at the Rittenhouse just before I started home."

"Jesus, I didn't even say the appropriate things about Matty, did I? It was all over the TV. You must be proud as hell of him. Hell, we all are."

"I am. I just spoke to him. He confirmed what Denny Coughlin told me. There's no doubt this is the fellow who killed the Williamson girl."

"And now what happens to him? He pleads he had an unhappy childhood, and they award him damages?"

"I don't think that's going to happen. As a matter of fact, the only thing Denny seemed worried about is how to get him back to Philadelphia."

"He's going to fight extradition? Do we have diplomatic relations with Alabama?"

"The problem is one of transportation, Tom. Bringing him back on the airlines poses a number of problems, as you can well imagine. The press, for one. The restrictions on even policemen carrying firearms on airplanes, for another."

"Cut to the chase, Brewster. Your pal Denny Coughlin would like to use Nesfoods's Citation to bring this character back here, right? And suggested you call me?"

"No, he did not. I really don't think using your airplane has ever entered his mind."

"This is your idea?"

"Which I had moments ago, just before I called."

"After drink number what?"

"Four, possibly five."

"You're my legal counsel—counsel me. Why should I?"

"Well, for one thing, all expenses would be fully deductible."

"As you have so often pointed out to me, you have to spend money before you can claim it was spent for business purposes and is thus deductible from income. You know how much it costs to operate that airplane."

"It would have undeniable good public relations aspects, Tom."

"And your pal Denny had nothing to do with this idea of yours, right?"

"I told you he didn't, Tom," Payne said. There was a chill in his tone.

"So you did. And I'm still listening."

"My thought is that there would be benefits to both parties if you were to telephone Alvin Martin and say it has come to your attention—you may use my name, if you like—that the police are having a problem transporting this fellow back here, and that Nesfoods International, as concerned, good, corporate citizens of our fair community . . ."

"And you just happen to have the mayor's unlisted number, right?"

"No, but I have one he gave me in case I ever wanted to get in touch with him, day or night."

"Let's have it."

[FIVE]

Homer C. Daniels looked up as the door to his cell slid open. A moment later, the enormous black sergeant and the nearly-as-big white cop who followed him around appeared at the entrance, carrying the prisoner restraint system.

"You want to stand up, please?" Kenny ordered.

"Is all of this necessary?" Daniels asked. "I'm cooperating. I'm not going to try to get away."

"It's procedure," Sergeant Kenny said, gesturing with his finger for him to turn around.

If I had my way, you white trash pervert, you'd spend the rest of your life in this thing.

"If you have to go to the john, do it now," Kenny ordered. "You won't have another chance for a while."

"Where am I going?"

"You agreed to waive extradition to Philadelphia, right?"

Daniels nodded.

"That's where you're going."

Daniels relieved his bladder.

Sergeant Kenny and Officer Andrew Terry put the belts on Daniels. Then each put a hand on his arms and led him, shuffling, out of the Detention Area, down a corridor, and through another door.

They were now outside.

There was a line of police patrol cars, two with Daphne police department insignia on their doors, two with STATE TROOPER lettered largely on their trunks, and two black sedans—a Ford and a Mercury—with several antennae on their trunks and roofs but without police insignia. There were also, incongruously, both a red Ford Mustang convertible and a Lincoln Town Car in the line of cars.

A flash went off and Daniels saw that a redheaded man in a loud sports coat had taken his picture with a digital camera.

The rear door of the Daphne police department car nearest to the door was open, and Sergeant Kenny led him to it, taking care that he didn't bump his head, and then got in beside him, pulled the seat belt over Daniels's lap and then closed the door. The big white cop got behind the wheel.

When he looked out the window, Daniels saw the young homicide sergeant from Philadelphia, the homicide detective who'd shown up a couple of days before, the assistant district attorney, and four other men in civilian clothing who could have been detectives or lawyers.

As he watched, they distributed themselves among the other cars.

There was another flash, and Daniels saw that the redheaded man had taken his picture again.

Sergeant Kenny spoke to the microphone pinned to his shirt.

"We're ready here."

"Where are we going?" Daniels asked.

"You have to sign the waiver before a judge," Kenny said.

The line of cars began to move, in a sweeping circle, through the parking lot. Daniels saw that the lights on the roof of the state trooper car leading the procession were flashing red and blue, but only on that car.

They came out of the Joseph Hall Criminal Justice Center onto a four-lane highway. Two more Daphne police cars blocked traffic in both directions to permit the convoy to enter the highway.

The convoy turned left and moved at just under the speed limit out of Daphne and toward Fairhope. Several times, cars ahead of the convoy spotted the warning lights and, thinking it was a funeral procession, respectfully pulled left and slowed—or stopped—and looked in vain for the hearse and flower car.

In Fairhope, at a shopping mall, the convoy turned left off U.S. Highway 98, and then, a half-mile down a two-lane macadam road, turned left again into a complex of one-story brick buildings.

Daniels saw a sign: "Baldwin County Satellite Courthouse."

The car with Daniels in it stopped about halfway down the building. As Kenny got out of the backseat, bright lights came on, and when Daniels got out, he saw that he was being videotaped by cameras bearing the logotypes of three different television stations.

With Kenny holding one arm and a state trooper the other, Daniels shuffled into the building and was led to a small courtroom. The courtroom, to judge by the signs on the walls, was often used as the place where driver's license tests were administered.

Roswell Bernhardt, Esq., was sitting at one of two tables facing the judge's bench. He stood up, gave his hand to Daniels, and then watched as Kenny removed the Prisoner Restraint System, and then motioned for him to sit beside Bernhardt.

The Philadelphia assistant district attorney, and another man who looked like a lawyer, sat down at the other table facing the judge's bench, laid briefcases on it, and then checked their contents. The young homicide sergeant and others took seats in the first couple of rows of benches.

A large man in a two-tone brown police-type uniform—he had both a badge and a large-caliber revolver—looked into the room, pulled his head back, and then, a moment later, stepped inside.

"All rise!" he ordered.

Everybody stood up.

A pleasant-looking man wearing a judge's robe—who looked as if he was no stranger to heavily laden tables—entered the room and sat down in a high-backed leather chair.

"The circuit court of Baldwin County is now in session, the Honorable Reade W. James presiding," the man in the brown uniform intoned.

"Good morning," Judge James said. "Please be seated."

Everybody sat down.

"The court recognizes the presence of the attorney general of Alabama," Judge James said. "And why are we so honored?"

The man standing beside Steve Cohen stood up.

"Good morning, Your Honor. If it pleases the court, may I introduce Mr. Steven Cohen, who is an assistant district attorney of Philadelphia, Commonwealth of Pennsylvania?"

"Good morning, Mr. Cohen. Welcome to Alabama. You have business to bring before this court?"

"Good morning, Your Honor. May it please the court, a warrant has been issued in Philadelphia for the arrest of Mr. Homer C. Daniels alleging violation of Paragraph 2502(b) of the Criminal Code of Pennsylvania, which is Murder of the Second Degree. It is my understanding, Your Honor, that Mr. Daniels, who is present with counsel in this court, is willing to waive his rights to an extradition hearing and prepared to return to Philadelphia to answer this and other related charges."

"Which are?" Judge James asked.

"In brief, Your Honor, Murder of the Third Degree; Rape; Involuntary Deviate Sexual Intercourse; Robbery; Theft; Receiving Stolen Property; Aggravated Assault; Simple Assault; Recklessly Endangering Another Person; Burglary; Criminal Trespass; Possession of Instrument of a Crime; and Abuse of a Corpse."

"Mr. Bernhardt," Judge James said, "may the court presume that the man beside you is Mr. Homer C. Daniels, and that you are serving as his counsel?"

Bernhardt stood up.

"Yes, Your Honor."

"Mr. Daniels—" Judge James said, and interrupted himself to say, "would you please rise, sir?"

Homer C. Daniels stood up.

"Have you any problems with Mr. Bernhardt serving as your counsel?"

"No, sir."

"Are you aware of the nature and specifics of all the charges being brought against you in Pennsylvania?"

"Yes, sir."

"And has Mr. Bernhardt explained that, should you desire, you have the right in the law to ask for an extradition hearing, at which you may offer evidence as to why you should not be returned to Philadelphia to face any and all charges laid against you there?"

"Yes, sir."

"And having been made aware of your rights in the law in this matter, you wish to waive same, which means that sometime within the next ten days, your person will be turned over to appropriate Pennsylvania law enforcement officers, who will then return you to Pennsylvania, there to face whatever charges have been laid against you."

"Yes, sir."

"This court is satisfied that Mr. Daniels is aware of his rights in this matter, and is voluntarily waiving same," Judge James said, and made a gesture which Steve Cohen correctly interpreted to mean that he could now place the appropriate documents before Mr. Daniels.

He walked to Daniels's table, laid a bound legal folder before Daniels, and handed him his pen. Daniels quickly scrawled his signature on them.

"May I approach the bench, Your Honor?" Cohen asked.

Judge James waved him to the bench. Cohen handed him the legal folder. James looked at it for a moment, then signed it.

"You understand, Mr. Cohen, that the Commonwealth of Pennsylvania must take Mr. Daniels into custody within ten days?"

"Your Honor, Sergeant Matthew Payne, of the Homicide Unit of the Philadelphia police department—and other Philadelphia police officers—are present in this court, and prepared to take custody of Mr. Daniels within the time prescribed."

"Then that would seem to conclude this matter," Judge James said, and stood up.

"All rise!" the man in the two-tone brown uniform ordered.

Everyone stood up.

Judge James left the courtroom.

Sergeant Kenny began to place Daniels in the Prisoner Restraint System. When he was finished, Kenny and the state trooper led him shuffling back through the satellite courthouse and put him back in the rear seat of the Daphne police car.

Then the convoy left the satellite courthouse complex, went back to U.S. Highway 98, and turned left onto it. Three miles farther along, it turned left onto a two-lane macadam road, and half a mile down that turned into the Fairhope Municipal Airport.

There the convoy drove onto the parking tarmac and up to a Cessna Citation. There was an almost identical Citation on the ramp, and half a dozen other business aircraft.

Mickey O'Hara jumped out of the Lincoln and ran up the line of cars to be in place when Daniels was taken from the Daphne police car.

He was there in plenty of time to see the little ceremony.

The attorney general of Alabama got out of one black Mercury and walked toward the Daphne car holding Daniels. The driver and the state troopers moved quickly to stand behind him.

Steve Cohen walked up to the car. He had ridden with O'Hara in the Lincoln. Matt Payne and Joe D'Amata took up positions behind him. Chief Yancey, several of his officers, and Detectives Martinez and McFadden stood to one side.

At a nod from the man in civilian clothing, one of the state troopers opened the door of the police car and helped first Sergeant Kenny and then Mr. Daniels out.

"Mr. Daniels," the man said. "I'm Baxley Williams, Attorney General of the State of Alabama. And this is Sergeant Matthew Payne, a Philadelphia, Pennsylvania, police officer, who has a warrant for your arrest."

Daniels did not reply.

Williams turned to Matt.

"You may now take custody of the prisoner."

Matt put his hand on Daniels's arm. Sergeant Kenny took his hand off.

Cohen signaled D'Amata with a finger. D'Amata took handcuffs from his belt, went to Daniels, and put them on him.

"Sergeant Kenny, you want to help me with this?" D'Amata asked.

Kenny began to remove the Prisoner Restraint System.

When he had finished, D'Amata said, "Come with me, please," and led Daniels toward the Cessna Citation.

Matt walked quickly to the airplane, got there first, and went inside.

When Daniels came into the cabin, Matt showed him where he was to sit, the rearmost seat, usually occupied by the steward. Then he took handcuffs from his belt, added one cuff to Daniels's left wrist, and snapped the other around the aluminum pipe work of the seat.

D'Amata watched.

Steve Cohen came aboard, followed by Mickey O'Hara.

"Let's go," he said.

Matt walked forward and knocked on the cockpit door. A man in a blue shirt with first officer shoulder boards opened it.

O'Hara took his picture.

"Any time," Matt said.

The copilot walked through the cabin and operated the door-closing mechanism.

O'Hara took his picture.

Before the copilot could get back to the cockpit, there was the whine of an engine starting.

Joe D'Amata went to Homer Daniels.

Mickey O'Hara took their picture.

"The law says you cannot be restrained during takeoff, flight, or landing," D'Amata said. "The law also says I have the authority to use what force is necessary to ensure that you remain in custody. What I'm going to do now is take those cuffs off you. What you're going to do is fasten the seat belt. If you even look like you're thinking of getting out of that seat, I'm going to shoot you. Do we understand each other?"

Daniels nodded.

D'Amata took the cuffs off.

The Citation started to move.

From where he was sitting, Matt could see everybody waiting for them to take off.

He didn't think they could see him through the darkened windows of the Citation, but he waved anyway.

The Citation taxied down the runway, turned around, and immediately began the takeoff roll.

Matt could see that at least half the law enforcement officers on the tarmac were waving goodbye at them.

When he stopped looking out the window, Mickey O'Hara took his picture.

[SIX]

There weren't quite as many people, or representatives of the Fourth Estate, on hand to meet the Citation at the Northeast Philadelphia Airport as there had been when Stan Colt's Citation had arrived. But almost.

The Hon. Alvin W. Martin was there, sitting with a group of prominent officials and citizens at tables in the Flatspin Restaurant whose windows provided a view of aircraft using the main runway.

These included Police Commissioner Ralph Mariani—who was there primarily because he heard over Police Radio that the mayor was headed for the airport—and First Deputy Commissioner Dennis V. Coughlin—who was there because he wanted to be.

Sitting with them was Mr. Chadwick Thomas Nesbitt III, Chairman of the Executive Committee of Nesfoods International, who was there at the invitation of the mayor who intended to thank him publicly—that is, before the assembled TV and still cameramen—for his generous public-spirited offering of the airplane. Beside Mr. Nesbitt III was Mr. Chadwick Thomas Nesbitt IV, a vice president of Nesfoods International, who was there because he had called the Nesfoods International aviation department and asked to be informed of the arrival of the Citation.

When word was passed that the Nesfoods Citation had just requested landing and taxi instructions, Mr. Nesbitt IV was engaged in conversation with Mr. Stan Colt, the film actor, who had somehow acquired a zipper jacket with the legend PHILADELPHIA POLICE DEPARTMENT on it.

Also sitting in the VIP section of the Flatspin, so to speak, were the proprietor, Mr. Fred Hagen; Mr. Brewster Cortland Payne II, Esq., and Amelia M. Payne, M.D. The latter two had been informed of the arrival time by Commissioner Coughlin. Mr. Payne was there as a proud parent. Dr. Payne was there both because she wanted a look at an interesting example of mental disorder and also because she wanted to see her little brother's moment of triumph.

The Hon. Eileen McNamara Solomon had also found time in her busy schedule to be in the Flatspin, primarily because she wanted to have a look at Mr. Daniels, with an eye to evaluating how he might be evaluated by a jury should he change his mind—which she thought was a distinct possibility—about his confession, and claim his right to be judged by a jury of his peers.

Outside the restaurant, just inside the airport property—where a four-engine B-24 Liberator stood permanently parked as a memorial to Captain Bill Benn, USAAC, Mr. Hagen's uncle, who had gone down flying a B-24 in World War II—a small coterie of more junior white shirts and their cars was also waiting for Mr. Daniels.

Captain Henry Quaire and Lieutenant Jason Washington of Homicide stood beside Captain David Pekach of Highway Patrol and the captains commanding the Eighth Police District and Northeast Detectives between the B-24 and the tarmac in front of the Nesfoods International Aviation Department hangar where the Citation would park.

Twenty or so uniforms—and their cars—waited in front of the hangar itself.

About three quarters of them, Deputy Commissioner Coughlin thought privately, had no real business being here. All that had to be done was to get Daniels off the airplane and into a patrol car and haul him off to the detention room in the Roundhouse basement. Sending a car—or even two—to go with the car with Daniels in it—there was a slight but real possibility of a flat tire, or a vehicular accident—would seem justified, but this was more like a circus than it should be. Homer C. Daniels was not the first—by a long shot—accused murderer to require transportation.

But Coughlin knew there was nothing he could do about it, even if he had the authority to order them all to go away. He understood their curiosity, their sense of proprietorship. This was a homicide, thus Quaire and Washington. Northeast Philadelphia Airport was in the area of responsibility of both the Eighth Police District and the Northeast Detectives Division, thus the presence of both of those captains commanding. And Highway Patrol had citywide authority, which is why Dave Pekach had felt free to come and watch Homer C. Daniels be returned to Philadelphia.

Mr. Michael J. O'Hara, who had gotten out of his seat the moment the Citation's wheels had touched ground to take a final shot of Daniels in his seat— and had nearly lost his footing when it decelerated rapidly—was the first person off the plane.

He took up a position to get a shot of Daniels getting off the plane very much as Eddie, Colt's "personal photographer," had taken when Colt had landed at the Northeast Airport.

Mr. Steven Cohen got off next, followed by Detective D'Amata, then Daniels, again wearing handcuffs, and finally Sergeant Payne.

The Eighth District commander and the Highway Patrol commander walked up to the airplane and a Highway car, an Eighth District car, and then another Highway car drove up.

Detective D'Amata put Daniels in the Eighth District car, then got in beside him. The three cars then drove off, leaving Mr. Cohen, Sergeant Payne, Mr. O'Hara, and the two captains standing beside the airplane.

"They want you over there," Captain Pekach said, indicating the grouped VIPs.

Sergeant Payne looked carefully around the field. He did not see Detective Lassiter.

There had not been much for the press to record for posterity. It had taken less than a minute to get Daniels off the plane and into the Eighth District car. Having nothing else to do—something the mayor had counted on—the press turned their attention to him.

The mayor smiled first at Steven Cohen, Esq., and shook his hand, and then smiled at Sergeant Payne and shook his hand. District Attorney Solomon, also an elected official, was photographed shaking Mr. Cohen's hand.

The mayor waved Mr. Nesbitt III to his side.

"I have a brief statement to make," the mayor began. "A terrible tragedy took place in our city, and nothing can ever make that right. But I want to take this opportunity to say how proud I am not only of our police department and the office of the district attorney but of our concerned, involved citizens as well.

"As soon as it came to his attention that as the result of some really first-class investigative work by the police department, and some really first-class legal work by Mrs. Solomon and her associates, the man charged with this heinous crime was in custody in Alabama, Mr. Nesbitt, of Nesfoods International, called to offer the use of his corporate aircraft—at no cost whatever to the city—to bring the accused murderer to Philadelphia to face justice. Thank you, Mr. Nesbitt."

"It seemed the least we at Nesfoods could do, Mr. Mayor," Mr. Nesbitt said. "Nesfoods International likes to think we are responsible corporate citizens of Philadelphia."

"And I have to say this," the mayor went on, "there has been some unfortunate, and in my judgment, unfair comments in some of the press lately to the effect that certain police officers were spending too much time protecting my good friend Stan Colt from the ardor of his fans, when what they should have been doing was trying to apprehend a murderer. I think this proves beyond any doubt that our police can do both things at the same time."

Mayor Martin did not take questions. He turned and ducked quickly into his waiting limousine.

Mr. Nesbitt III shook hands with Sergeant Payne and ducked into his waiting limousine. District Attorney Solomon said, "Good work, you guys," and got into her unmarked Crown Victoria.

Commissioner Mariani shook Sergeant Payne's hand and got into his Crown Victoria.

Captain Quaire and Lieutenant Washington walked up.

"What next, boss?" Sergeant Payne asked.

"Come to work in the morning," Washington said, "after you finish your detail with Dignitary Protection. I understand Mr. Colt is leaving at eleven-fifteen tomorrow morning."

"I was supposed to leave after the last thing tonight," Stan Colt said. "But I didn't want to leave without seeing you. I want to hear everything that happened."

"There's not much to tell," Matt said.

"Bullshit. After this thing tonight, I'm throwing a little thank-you party at La Famiglia. You, Mickey, your pal Nesbitt Four, Terry, a handful of others."

"Stan, I don't know . . ."

"It's all laid on. You can't say no now. I gotta go. One more lunch—which I'm already late for—and this thing tonight, and then I'm done."

Commissioner Coughlin nodded, which Detective Payne correctly interpreted to mean was an order to him to attend Mr. Colt's little thank-you party tonight. And to tell him everything that happened.

Mr. Colt then punched Sergeant Payne in the shoulder and got in his limousine. Highway Patrol officers kicked their bikes into life and, sirens growling, led the way out of the airport.

"If my children," Brewster C. Payne said, "don't mind having lunch with a couple of old men, Denny and I are about to have ours."

"He doesn't have any choice in the matter," Dr. Payne said. "I want to hear about this guy."

"So do I," Deputy Commissioner Coughlin said. "How about right here at the Flatspin? They do a really nice Mahi-Mahi."

CHAPTER 20

[ONE]

There was a telephone in a niche in the low fieldstone wall around the patio of the Payne house in Wallingford, but when it rang, Patricia Payne really didn't want to answer it.

Feeling just a little ashamed of herself—*this has to be prurient interest*—the truth was that she was fascinated by the interrogation of her son by her husband and her daughter concerning his encounter with Homer C. Daniels.

She had known Amelia M. Payne, M.D., from before she had taken her first steps—and was in fact the only mother Amy had ever known—and she had given birth to Matt. They were her children.

And she had taken maternal pride in both. Amy was a certified genius, and while Matt wasn't as smart, he had been graduated *summa cum laude* from Pennsylvania. And she knew that her husband was a very good lawyer, and Amy a highly regarded psychiatrist, and Matt was carrying his father's sergeant's badge.

But knowing that hadn't prepared her for sitting with them and listening to them speak of this unspeakable crime, and the man who had committed it, and his motivations, and the legal aspects of the whole sordid series of events as professionals, rather than father and son and daughter.

And it wasn't just an idle conversation. They had been at it over an hour, ever since Brewster's sedate black Cadillac had unexpectedly led Amy's battered Suburban and Matt's unmarked police Ford into the drive. When he had called from the Flatspin Restaurant where they had had lunch, she had asked what the chances were of having "the children" home for supper. He had said he'd see. From his tone of voice, it had seemed unlikely.

But then they'd appeared, surprising and pleasing her. Brewster had said Matt couldn't come for supper, he had to be with Stan Colt, so they'd come now. They'd immediately gone out to the patio, arranged themselves on the comfortably upholstered lawn furniture, and started talking about Homer C. Daniels.

Without being asked, Mrs. Newman, the Payne housekeeper—a comfortable looking gray-haired woman in her fifties—had produced a pot of coffee and a tray with toasted rye bread, liverwurst, mustard, and sliced raw onions, and then taken a chair by the door. Patricia was pleased to see Mrs. Newman was as fascinated with Mr. Homer C. Daniels as she was.

And then the phone rang, and Patricia didn't want to talk to anyone, and said as much.

"Grab that, please, Elizabeth," she called. "And get rid of whoever it is. I'll call them back."

Mrs. Newman took her walk-around telephone from a pocket in her dress and spoke into it. Then she got up and walked to them.

"Mrs. Nesbitt for Mr. Payne," she said. "She won't take 'no' for an answer."

"Damn!" Brewster C. Payne, Esq., said.

"Not you," Mrs. Newman said. "*Young* Mrs. Nesbitt for *Young* Mr. Payne."

"Shit," Young Mr. Payne said.

"Matty!" his mother said.

Mrs. Newman handed him the phone.

"And how is the somewhat careless caretaker of my goddaughter?"

"God, you're such an asshole, Matt . . ." Daffy Nesbitt said.

"Thank you for sharing that with me. I'll tell Mother what you said."

". . . but despite that, I'm going to do you a favor."

"Oh, God!"

"I probably really shouldn't tell you this, but Chad said I should."

"You're in the family way again?"

"No, goddamn it!"

"Can we get to the point of this fascinating conversation, please?"

"We're having a few people in here before we make an appearance at the Four Seasons thing," Daffy said.

"What people?" Matt asked.

"Old friends of ours, of yours," Chad said.

"And I want you to show up in black tie and spare us your usual bad manners," Daffy said.

"What's in it for me?"

"Terry," Chad Nesbitt chimed in.

"She's the door prize?"

Chad laughed.

"I can't imagine why," Daffy said. "But she really likes you. She asked if you would be coming."

Now, that's interesting!

Detective Lassiter's cellular phone was reported out of service. And messages left on her answering machine and at Northwest Detectives asking that she call him had brought no response.

"Tell me more," Matt said.

"You could take Terry to the Colt dinner at the Four Seasons and then to La Famiglia."

"Whose idea is that?"

"Mine," Daffy said. "She's not throwing herself at you."

"Well, I don't know. I like it better when they throw themselves at me."

"Suit yourself, you bastard," Daffy said.

"What time is this drunken brawl of yours?"

"Five-ish," Daffy said.

"What was that all about?" Dr. Payne inquired, asking the question her mother had just, reluctantly, decided was none of her business and couldn't ask.

"Daffy wants me to go by Society Hill before the Colt dinner at the Four Seasons. They're having people in. What I think they really want is for me to entertain one and all by telling them all about Homer C. Daniels."

"That's unkind, Matt," Patricia Payne said. "They're your oldest friends."

"And they're playing cupid again," Matt said, "trying to pair me off with Terry Davis."

"So you're not going?" Amy asked.

"As Mother says, Chad and I go back a long way," Matt said, realizing as he said it that it sounded transparently lame.

[TWO]

At 11:48, when Matt Payne left La Famiglia—an upscale restaurant on South Front Street just below Market Street, overlooking the Delaware River—he was just about convinced that he was going to get lucky with Terry Davis.

Everything had gone well, from his immediately being able to put his hands on the little box with the studs for his dress shirt when he hastily changed into a dinner jacket at his apartment—that almost never happened—through the drinks at Chad and Daffy's place until now.

Terry had looked very good indeed when he went into the party, and she did in fact seem glad to see him. And he'd even gotten along with the people Chad and Daffy had in. Many of them he'd known all his life. Usually, however, when he saw them socially, they gave him the impression that he'd done something terrible that had moved him far below the salt. Like being a cop. So he didn't often see them socially. When he did, he often, in Daffy's words, showed his ass, and embarrassed everybody.

Tonight there had been none of that, with one minor exception.

"I didn't know, Payne, until I saw you on the tube, that you were a sergeant," J. Andrew Stansfield III had said, coming up to where Matt was looking out the windows onto the Delaware.

"That's right, Stansfield."

Matthew M. Payne, Chadwick Thomas Nesbitt IV, and J. Andrew Stansfield III had graduated from Episcopal Academy together. Stansfield had gone on to Princeton, then the Harvard School of Business Administration, and then found employment with Stansfield & Stansfield, Commercial Realtors.

"I'm afraid I actually don't know what that means," Stansfield said.

"It means I make four percent more than I made when I was detective," Matt said. "It comes to right over two thousand a year."

"That's all?" Stansfield said, genuinely surprised.

Then his face showed that he suspected Payne was pulling his leg.

"Well, there are certain professional privileges," Matt said.

"For example?"

"For example, when Terry and I leave here for the Four Seasons, my car is parked right outside on the cobblestones of Stockton Place," Matt said. "If you tried to park there, Stansfield, you'd be towed."

"Yes, I know," J. Andrew Stansfield had said, nodding and seeming a bit confused. Terry Davis had squeezed his arm, and when he looked at her, her eyes were smiling.

And Terry had smelled very nice indeed in his Porsche on the way to the Four Seasons, where he was able—because Sergeant Al Nevins of Dignitary Protection was there awaiting the arrival of Stan Colt and wanted to talk to him—to park very near the door.

"We're playing games later," Nevins said. "The limo will take Colt and the Bolinskis—"

"Bolinski as in 'The Bull'?" Matt interrupted.

Nevins nodded.

"—the limo will take them back to the Ritz, where they will go inside, get on the elevator, go to the basement and out into the alley, where they will get into a Suburban and go to La Famiglia."

"Clever," Matt said.

"With a little luck it will work," Nevins said.

Casimir Bolinski, L.L.D., Esq., whom Matt had never met before, turned out to be a very nice guy who would have been perfectly happy to stay in an anteroom off the dining room with Matt and Terry—whom he knew—during the banquet, had not his wife found him.

"Honey, we're going to La Famiglia after this. I don't want to eat any of that fancy French food. . . ."

"You're going to go in there and sit next to the cardinal and the monsignor, you're going to drink only water, and when they introduce you, you're going to hand him this."

She handed him an envelope containing a check.

"Jesus Christ, Antoinette! That much?"

"You graduated West Catholic," Mrs. Bolinski said. "You owe them. They tossed Mickey and Stan out. They don't. Anyway, it's deductible."

Mrs. Bolinski, looking not unlike a tugboat easing an aircraft carrier down a river, had then escorted her husband into the dining room.

Terry Davis again smelled delightfully in the Porsche on the way from the Four Seasons to La Famiglia, but there he couldn't park the Porsche in front, and instead had to take it to the adjacent parking lot.

There were red plastic cones—the kind used to mark lanes on highways—in the first half-dozen parking places by the entrance.

But Terry held his hand as they walked from where he finally found an empty slot, which he decided was more than enough compensation for the inconvenience.

At dinner, he found himself seated beside Casimir Bolinski, Esq., and across from Michael J. O'Hara, who, sensing they had an appreciative audience in Terry Davis, entertained her with stories of their time at West Catholic High School.

The cardinal had not come to La Famiglia, but Monsignor Schneider was there, sitting beside Stan Colt.

More than once, during a meal that began with an enormous antipasto and ended with spumoni onto which a shot of Amaretto had been poured, Miss Davis's knee brushed against Matt's. Often enough to allow himself to think it wasn't entirely accidental.

And there was another indication of good things to come at the first of the two goodnight and farewell sessions. The first was held inside the restaurant.

"You're just going to have to come to the coast, Matt," Stan Colt said. "You make him come, Terry."

"I will," Terry had said, and squeezed his arm again.

Matt was surprised when they actually left the restaurant that the Classic Livery body wagon with darkened windows wasn't waiting on the sidewalk for Colt and party, but then he saw Sergeant Nevins and half a dozen men he knew to be detectives discreetly lining the path to the parking lot.

When they got there, Matt saw that the body wagon, Mickey O'Hara's Buick Rendezvous, a black Oldsmobile, and three unmarked cars were in the spaces that had been blocked off by the red lane markers.

There was a second goodnight and farewell session there. Monsignor Schneider seemed reluctant to say good night, making Matt wonder how deep the cleric had gone into the wine.

But finally everybody was loaded into the vehicles, and they left. Terry took Matt's hand again and then leaned against him, suggesting an arm around her shoulders would not be unwelcome. They walked through the parking lot toward the Porsche.

The only problem now seemed where to go:

My apartment's a dump to begin with, and a mess after that quick shower and jump into the dinner jacket. And there's probably something, hair, lipstick on a towel, whatever, that'll give away that Olivia—screw her!—has been there.

Terry's staying at the Ritz-Carlton, but if we go there, she may not want them to know I went to her room, and it will be a brief kiss and I had a lovely time.

Can I suggest another hotel?

Screw it. The apartment it is.

He opened the door to the Porsche for her, then got in and started the engine. He saw that the parking slot in front of him was empty.

If there's not a concrete block in the way, I can just drive through.

There was not and he did.

He turned left—the only entrance/exit was where he came in, and he would have to drive to the end of the line, and then out that way—and flicked the headlights onto high.

"What the fuck is that?" he asked aloud, and then he accelerated rapidly and braked as quickly.

"Oh, my God!" Terry said. She had seen what he had.

There was a man propped up against the rear of one of the parked cars, his legs sprawled in front of him. A woman was kneeling beside him, wiping at his face. He was bleeding from the mouth.

Matt jumped out of the car.

"What happened?"

"What does it look like?" the woman snapped. "We were mugged."

"I gave him my wallet, why did they have to do this?" the man asked, and spit. What looked like part of a tooth came out of his mouth.

"Have you got a cell phone?" the woman demanded. "We need an ambulance."

Matt reached for his cell phone.

"My God, they're coming back!" the man said.

Matt saw where he was looking.

At the extreme end of the parking lot, there were two young men in dark clothes.

"You're sure that's them?" Matt asked.

"That's them, that's them, that's them," the woman said.

"Stop right there," Matt called, loudly. "I'm a police officer."

The two started running.

One of them had what could be a sawed-off shotgun, or a softball bat.

"Where the hell were you when we needed you?" the woman asked.

Matt ran back to the Porsche and got in. He tossed his cellular into Terry's lap.

"What the hell are you doing?" Terry asked.

He had the car moving before the door had closed.

He wound it up in first, and touched the brake only as he reached the end of the lane of cars. As he turned left, the windshield of the Porsche suddenly reflected light all over.

There was a boom.

"You cocksucker!" Matt said, slamming on the brakes.

The object in the man's hand obviously was not a softball bat.

There was another boom. Part of the windshield fell out.

Matt dove out of the car, and half rolled, half crawled, between two parked cars.

He pulled his Colt Officer's Model .45 from the small of his back and worked the action. A cartridge flew out. He'd had one in the chamber.

That leaves five.

He ran between the cars, dropped to his knees, and peered very carefully around the bumper of one.

The two were climbing the chain-link fence at the end of the parking lot.

Matt stood up, held the pistol in both hands, and called out, "That's it. Just drop to the ground."

One of them dropped to the ground and one didn't.

For a moment, Matt didn't know what to do.

Then the second one dropped to the ground, reached into his jacket, and came out with a semiautomatic pistol and started firing it wildly.

And then there was another boom, immediately followed by the sound of heavy lead shot striking metal and glass near him.

Matt fired four times, taking out the shotgunner first, and then the man with the pistol. The shotgunner went down and stayed there. The man with the pistol didn't. He began to scream in agony.

Matt took the spare clip to the .45 from where he had concealed it behind the white handkerchief in the breast pocket of the dinner jacket—ejected the empty clip from the pistol, and slipped in the spare.

Then, holding the weapon in both hands, he carefully walked up to the two men on the ground. The one with the shotgun was on his back, his head in a pool of blood. One of Matt's shots had struck him, straight on, in the right cheek.

The other one was screaming.

Matt saw the pistol—at first glance in the dark, it looked like a Browning .380—and keeping his eye on the man, bent over, carefully picked it up with two fingers on the grips, and then put it in his hip pocket.

"You got anything else?" he asked, and patted the writhing man down to make sure he didn't.

Then he went back and picked up the shotgun on the ground near the body, and turned and walked quickly toward the Porsche and the victims.

The first thing he saw was that only one headlight was working. And then he saw the pellet holes in the hood and door and windshield frame, and what was left of the windshield. Then he first smelled and then saw gasoline running from under the Porsche.

"Jesus," he said. He laid the shotgun on the roof and jerked Terry's door open.

She looked at him without comprehension.

And then he saw that her face was bleeding.

"Are you all right?"

"All right?" she parroted.

He unfastened her seat belt, reached into her lap, reclaimed his cellular, and then pulled her out of the car.

There was blood on her dress, but when he put his hand to it, she pushed him away, as if he was taking liberties with her person. He led her around the corner and sort of leaned her against a Ford van.

Then he went to the victims.

"It's over," he said. "Everything's going to be all right."

"All right? All right?" the woman snapped at him. "What the hell is the matter with you? Are you drunk, or what? Can't you hear that screaming?"

"I'm calling for assistance," Matt said. "Help will be here soon."

He punched in 911 on his cellular as he walked back to Terry.

"Police radio." Mrs. Angelina Carracelli, who had been on the job for twenty-two years, answered his call on the second ring.

"This is Sergeant Payne, 471. Shots fired. Officer needs assistance."

Mrs. Carracelli waited for the sergeant to provide greater details. When none were forthcoming, she said, "Sergeant?"

"Radio," Sergeant Payne said, a little distantly. "That's not exactly accurate. I'm doing fine. I don't need assistance. But there are people here who do."

"You said 'shots fired,' Sergeant?"

"Oh, yes. Lots of shots fired."

"What is your location, Sergeant?"

"I'm going to need two ambulances—no, three. And the fire department. There's spilled gas."

"What is your location, Sergeant?"

"I'm in the parking lot next to La Famiglia Restaurant on South Front Street."

"Are you injured?"

"No, I'm fine, thank you."

"Are you in uniform, Sergeant?"

"Oh, no, I'm not in uniform," Matt chuckled.

Mrs. Carracelli made several quick decisions. First, that the call was legitimate, not someone's idea of a joke. That there was something wrong with the sergeant. His voice was strange, and he sounded a little disoriented. He might be injured, or even wounded.

She muted the telephone line and pushed the appropriate switches.

Every police radio in Philadelphia heard three shrill beeps, and then the call:

"Assist the Officer, South Front Street, parking lot by La Famiglia Restaurant unit block South Front Street. Shots fired. Assist the Officer, parking lot by La Famiglia Restaurant unit block South Front Street. Shots fired. All officers use caution, plainclothes police on the scene."

The three shrill beeps and the call were also heard in the Buick Rendezvous, which was carrying Mr. and Mrs. Casimir Bolinski up Market Street toward the Ritz-Carlton Hotel.

"Shit," Mr. Michael J. O'Hara said, as he put the Rendezvous into a screeching U-turn. "That's where Matty is!"

As they followed the black Suburban up Market Street in their unmarked Crown Victoria, Lieutenant Gerry McGuire and Sergeant Al Nevins heard the same call.

McGuire found the microphone.

"Dan Seven-four and Dan Seven-five, stay with the assignment," he said into it, and then he tossed the microphone to Nevins as he desperately looked for a hole in the oncoming traffic on Market Street in which he could make a U-turn.

"Radio," Sergeant Nevins said to the microphone, "Dan Seven-one in on the Assist Officer on Front Street. Be advised there is probably an officer in plainclothes on the scene."

Mrs. Carracelli opened the telephone line.

"Sergeant, identify your unit and give conditions."

"My name is Payne. Homicide," Matt said. "There was an armed robbery, two black males, one pistol, one shotgun."

"Are there any injuries?" Mrs. Carracelli asked, trying to keep her voice calm.

"One of the doers looks dead; the other's alive. He'll need fire rescue. At least one of the victims is going to need an ambulance. Maybe three victims. And I'm going to need the fire department. There's gas on the ground."

"Are you injured?"

"No, I'm fine. They missed me."

"Help is on the way."

"I can hear the sirens. Tell them I'm deep inside the parking lot."

"Help is on the way," Mrs. Carracelli said, and muted the telephone line again.

Three more shrill beeps went out over Police Radio.

"All units responding to the Assist Officer on the unit block of South Front Street, be advised shots have been fired at police and there are plainclothes police officers on the scene. One is inside the parking lot. All units be advised, the unit block of South Front Street, shots have been fired at police and there are plainclothes officers on the scene. One is inside the parking lot. Suspects in the shooting are two black males. Both have been shot and are still at the location."

Matt looked down at Terry.

She looked up at him with horror in her eyes.

"Help is on the way," he said. "You can hear it. . . ."

"What about the . . . man who's screaming? Can't you do something for him?"

"I'd like to put another round in the sonofabitch, is what I'd like to do."

"My God, I can't believe you said that. You really are a cold-blooded son of a bitch, aren't you?"

Matt decided there was no point in arguing with her.

"There will be help in a minute," he said, and started walking back toward where he'd put the two men down.

Halfway there, he pulled his bow tie loose and opened his collar.

He was sweat-soaked.

He looked at the cellular and punched in an autodial number.

[THREE]

Detective Payne's call was answered by Inspector Peter F. Wohl in his residence in the 800 Block of Norwood Street in Chestnut Hill, in Northwest Philadelphia.

When Wohl's cell phone—in a charging cradle on his bedside table—chirped, he was not wearing any clothing at all, and was engaged in chasing a twenty-eight-year-old female around his bedroom with the announced intention of divesting her of her sole remaining article of clothing, black nylon underpants.

When the cell phone tinkled, Wohl said "Shit" and the young woman—having only moments before decided to let Peter work his wicked way with her—softly said, "Amen."

Amelia Alice Payne, M.D., knew Inspector Peter Wohl well enough to know that not only was he going to answer the phone, but that the odds were that it was something that would keep them from ending what had been a delightful evening in what she had thought was going to be a delightful way.

The look on Peter's face as he listened to what the caller was saying confirmed her worst fears, as did his almost conversational response to what the caller had said:

"Was it a good shooting?"

Amy had been Peter Wohl's on-and-off girlfriend, lover, and the next-thing-to-fiancée long enough to have acquired an easy familiarity with police department cant.

She knew, in other words, that "a good shooting" was one in which the police shooter was not only fully justified in having used deadly force in the execution of his duties, but in circumstances such that his justification would be obvious to those who would investigate the incident, which was officially the Internal Affairs Division of the police department and the Office of the District Attorney, and unofficially Philadelphia's newspapers, radio and television stations, and more than a dozen civil rights organizations.

"Well, you know the drill," Inspector Peter Wohl said to his caller. "They'll take you to Internal Affairs."

He clicked the cell phone off and tossed it on the bed, then raised his eyes and looked at Amy, who was still where she had been when the phone tinkled, standing on his mattress, holding on to the right upper bedpost.

"Sorry," he said.

"Fuck you, Peter!" she said, furiously.

"Maybe we can work that in a little later," Wohl said. "But right now I have to go to Internal Affairs."

"No you fucking well don't!" Amy went on. A part of her brain—the psychiatrist part—told her that she had lost her temper, which disturbed her, while another—purely feminine—part told her she had every justification in the world for being angry with the male chauvinistic sonofabitch for choosing duty over hanky-panky with her, particularly at just about the precise moment she had decided to let him catch her.

He looked at her with a smugly tolerant smile on his lips, which added fuel to her anger.

"I 'fucking' well don't?" he parroted, mockingly.

"Peter, you've got a deputy," she said, when she thought she had regained sufficient control. "Under you and your deputy, there are three captains, and probably four times that many lieutenants."

"That's true," he said.

"There is a thing known in management as delegation of authority and responsibility," Dr. Payne went on reasonably.

"I agree. I think what you're asking is why do I, as the Caesar of my little empire, have to personally rush off whenever one of my underlings has need of a friendly face and an encouraging word?"

"That's just about it, yeah," she said.

"Ordinarily, I would agree with you, having given the subject some thought after your last somewhat emotional outburst."

She felt her temper rising again, and with a great effort kept her mouth shut, as Peter found clean linen and started to put it on. Only when she was sure that she had herself under control did she go on.

"Let me guess. This is an exception to the rule, right?"

"Right."

"Fuck you, Peter. It will always be 'this is an exception to the rule.'"

"That was Matt on the phone," he said.

"Oh, God!" she said, her anger instantly replaced with an almost maternal concern. "Oh, God, not again!"

"It looks that way, I'm afraid," Wohl said.

"What happened?"

"Matt said—right after the Colt party—he was in the parking lot next to La Famiglia Restaurant?"

She nodded. She knew the restaurant well.

"And he walked up on an armed robbery. They shot at him, and he shot back, and put both of them down—one for good."

"Why the hell couldn't he have just, for once, for once, looked the other way?"

"He's a cop, honey," Wohl said.

"Is he all right?"

"He sounded all right to me."

She jumped off the bed and looked around the room.

"Where the hell is my damned bra?" she asked softly, more of herself than of him.

"It's probably in the living room," Wohl said.

She looked at him, then picked up her skirt and stepped into it.

"I gather you won't be here when I get back?" Wohl asked.

"I'm going with you," she said.

"I don't think you want to do that," he said.

"Don't think you know what I want to do, please," she said. "What it is, is that you don't want me to go with you."

"Okay," he said. "I don't. And I don't think Matt will want to see you right now, either."

She slipped her feet into her shoes, then went out of the room, returning in a moment in the act of putting her brassiere on.

She backed up to him.

"Fasten it, will you, please?"

"Funny," he said after fussing with the catch for a moment. "I didn't have this much trouble opening it."

She didn't reply until she was sure he had fastened the catch, and then she turned and faced him.

"I can't believe that you're as unaffected by this as you're trying to make out," she said. "You know what this is going to do to him."

"I'm really unhappy about it, if that's what you mean," he replied. "But no, I don't know what this is going to do to him. I hope that it was a good shooting, and I'd like to think he's already worked his way through the questions something like this brings up."

"You mean, after the first couple of *good shootings* it gets easier?" she asked, more than a little sarcastically.

He didn't reply for a moment.

"I hope, for Matt's sake, it does," he said, finally.

She looked at him for a long moment, then walked out of the room again and came back pulling a sweater over her head.

"Your call," she said. "We can take two cars, or I can go with you."

He looked at her in the mirror—he was tying his tie—but didn't say anything until he was finished.

Then he turned around and looked directly at her.

"Thank you," he said.

"What for?"

"You know what for," he said.

He took a tweed sports coat from his closet, then followed her out of the bedroom, and through the living room to the door.

His apartment had once been the servants' quarters above what had once been the stables, and then the five-car garage of the turn-of-the-century mansion now divided into "luxury apartments."

They went down the outside stairs and to his unmarked Crown Victoria. He unlocked her door for her, and she reached up and kissed him.

"Sorry to have been such a bitch," Amy said.

"Hey, I understand."

He closed the door after her and went around the front and got in the car, and drove up to the drive, past the mansion to Norwood Street, and turned right.

"No flashing blue lights and screaming siren?" Amy asked.

"We'll probably get to Internal Affairs before he does," Wohl said.

He reached under the dash and came up with a microphone.

"S-1," he said.

"Go ahead, S-1," Police Radio—this time a masculine voice—replied.

"On my way from my home to Internal Affairs," Wohl said.

"Got it."

He dropped the microphone on the seat.

"Can you get Denny Coughlin on that?" Amy asked.

He picked up the microphone.

"Radio, S-1. Have you got a location on Commissioner Coughlin?"

"S-1, he's at Methodist Hospital."

"What's going on there?"

"An officer was shot answering a robbery in progress on South Broad. And be advised, there's a new assist officer, shots fired on Front Street. Just a couple of minutes ago."

"Okay. Thank you."

He put the microphone down.

"If the root of your question was 'Does he know?', the answer is if he doesn't, he will in a matter of minutes."

"He does a much better job of telling Mother and Dad about things like this than I do."

"They're almost certainly asleep at this hour. You really want to wake them up?"

"No," she said after a moment. "But they'll be hurt and angry if someone doesn't tell them."

"You really want to wake them up?" he asked again, and went on. "All you're going to do is upset them. You—or Coughlin—can do it in the morning, when things have settled down."

"Good morning, Mom!" she said, sarcastically. "Guess what happened, again, last night?"

He chuckled.

"Was it a good shooting, Peter?" she asked, almost plaintively.

"From the way Matt talked, it was," he said. "We'll soon find out."

[FOUR]

Mickey O'Hara beat the first police unit—a marked Sixth District car—and the second—Lieutenant Gerry McGuire's unmarked Dignitary Protection Crown Victoria—to the parking lot by a good thirty seconds.

He was well into the parking lot, camera at the ready, before the uniformed officer, McGuire, and Nevins got of their cars, drew their weapons, and cautiously entered the lot.

O'Hara saw Matt Payne long before Matt Payne saw him—or, perhaps more accurately, acknowledged O'Hara's presence.

Matt was standing at the far end of the lot, pistol drawn, looking down at what after another second or two O'Hara saw was a man writhing on the ground.

"Matt! Matty! You all right?"

O'Hara decided that the crescendo of sirens was so loud Matt couldn't hear him.

But finally, just when O'Hara was close enough to be able to hear the anguished moans of the man on the ground, Matt turned and looked at him.

O'Hara instantly—and certainly not intentionally—turned from concerned friend to journalist.

Jesus, that's a good picture! A good-looking young cop in a tuxedo, tie pulled down, gun in hand, looking down at the bad guy! Justice fucking triumphant!

He put the digital camera to his eye and made the shot. And three others, to make sure he got it.

"What took you so long, Mickey?" Matt asked.

"What the hell happened, Matt?"

"These two guys . . ." He raised the pistol and indicated the second body. Then he waited patiently while Mickey took images of the dead man before going on:

"These two guys mugged a nice middle-class black couple out for dinner. The guy gave him his wallet, and one of these bastards knocked his teeth out with a gun anyway. I walked up on it, tried to grab them, and they let fly with a sawed-off shotgun and what looks like a .380 Browning—"

"Jesus, Payne," Lieutenant McGuire asked. "What went down here?"

"—and shot the shit out of my car and almost killed my girlfriend, and I put them down," Matt finished, almost conversationally.

O'Hara, Nevins, and McGuire looked at him curiously.

"Are you all right?" McGuire asked in concern.

"I'm fine. They missed," Matt replied. "The victims are over here."

Sergeant Nevins squatted beside the man on the ground, who glared hatefully at him.

"It looks like you're off the ballet team," he said. "But you'll live. Fire Rescue's on the way."

He stood up.

"They had guns?" he asked. "Where are they?"

Matt carefully took the Browning from his hip pocket and held it out. McGuire took it.

"I put the shotgun on the roof of my car," Matt said.

"Mickey, get the hell out of here!" McGuire ordered.

O'Hara ignored him.

"Around here, Matt?" he asked.

"Just around the corner," Matt said. "Two angry females. The victim's wife, who wanted to know where I was when I was needed, and my girlfriend— perhaps ex-girlfriend would be more accurate—who just described me as a cold-blooded sonofabitch for shooting these two."

"O'Hara, I told you to get the hell out of here!" McGuire shouted after him.

"I presume the firemen are on their way?" Matt said to McGuire. "In addition to the other damage, they apparently shot out a fuel line. There's gas all over the ground. Or maybe they got the tank."

McGuire approached him warily.

"Why don't you let me have your weapon, Payne?" he asked.

"Oh, yes, of course. I forgot."

He handed the Colt to McGuire butt-first as three uniforms and two men who were dressed much like those they hoped to arrest for illegal trafficking in controlled substances ran up to them, pistols in hand.

McGuire removed the clip, counted the rounds it held, then worked the action and ejected the round in the chamber.

Matt reached into the breast pocket of the dinner jacket, came out with another magazine, and handed it to McGuire.

"This is the magazine, now empty, that was in my weapon," he said. "And somewhere over there is a live round I inadvertently ejected when this started."

"The crime scene people will find it," McGuire said.

Holding Matt's pistol carefully by the checkering on the wooden grips, he started to put it in the pocket of his suit coat.

"I think you're supposed to give that back to me," Matt said.

"What?"

"Regulations state that the first supervisor to reach the scene of an incident like this is to take the weapon used from the officer who used it, remove the magazine, count the remaining rounds, take possession of that magazine, then return the weapon to the officer, who will then load a fresh magazine into his weapon and return it to his holster."

"Sergeant, this is evidence," McGuire said.

"With all respect, sir, that is not what the regulations say."

"Shut up, Sergeant," McGuire said.

"Yes, sir," Sergeant Payne said.

A Fire Rescue ambulance began backing into the parking lot.

A Sixth District lieutenant, a very large man, came running up.

"My name is McGuire," McGuire said. "Dignitary Protection Unit. I'm the first supervisor on the scene."

"I've seen you around," the Sixth District lieutenant said.

"I have relieved Sergeant Payne of his weapon, and am now going to transport him to Internal Affairs."

"You're the shooter, Sergeant?" the lieutenant asked.

"I think all the questions to him are supposed to be asked by Internal Affairs," McGuire said. "Nevins will tell you what we know. Will you come with me, please, Sergeant Payne?"

"Yes, sir."

Lieutenant McGuire put his hand on Sergeant Payne's arm and walked with him through the parking lot to where the unmarked Dignitary Protection Crown Victoria sat, its engine running and its headlights and concealed blue flashers still on.

He put Matt in the backseat but didn't close the door.

Nevins came to the car a moment later.

"You drive, Al," McGuire said. "I'll ride in the back with Payne."

They exchanged questioning glances, then shrugged, and then Nevins got behind the wheel, and McGuire got in the backseat with Matt.

CHAPTER 21

[ONE]

In Philadelphia, any discharge—even accidental—of a police officer's weapon is investigated by the Internal Affairs Unit. Even if the discharge of the police officer's weapon results in a death, Internal Affairs still retains the responsibility for, and authority to, conduct the investigation. The Homicide Division "assists."

This policy came into being when various civil rights organizations charged that police shootings—fatal and nonfatal—were being covered up when investigated by Homicide or Detective Divisions, and that only Internal Affairs, an elite unit already charged with the investigation of police malfeasance, could be trusted to investigate shootings fully and fairly.

When the first "assist officer, shots fired" call was broadcast to every police vehicle in Philadelphia, it was received in the Crown Victoria assigned to Inspector Michael Weisbach, of the Internal Affairs Division, who was at the time returning to his home from a social event at Temple Beth Emmanuel.

He did not respond to the call, primarily because he was a considerable distance from South Front Street, and realized that by the time he could get there, at least twenty, and probably more, other units would be on the scene.

But he did turn to his wife and say, "I really hope no one was hit. I'm really beat."

By the time he got to his home, however, other radio traffic had made it clear that he wasn't going to be able to go to bed anytime soon. And after he'd dropped his wife off and headed for the Internal Affairs office on Dungan Road in northeast Philadelphia, there came, several times, official confirmation.

"I-2, Radio."

"I-2, go."

"We have two suspects down, one dead, at the assist officer, shots fired, unit block South Front Street."

"Okay. I'm on my way to IAD."

. . .

Then his cellular telephone chirped the first bars of "Rule Britannia."

"Weisbach."

"Inspector, this is Captain Fein, Sixth District."

"Hello, Jake."

"Two suspects down, one dead, at the assist officer, shots fired on South Front."

"I'm on my way to IAD. Thanks for the heads up."

"Out of school, Mike, it looks righteous."

"I sure hope so. Thanks again, Jake."

He had just laid the telephone down on the seat when it played "Rule Britannia" again.

"Weisbach."

"Kimberly, boss. I just got a call from Lieutenant McGuire of Dignitary Protection. He was the first supervisor on the scene in the shots fired on South Front, and he's transporting the shooter here."

"I'm en route."

"You're not going to like this, boss. The shooter's Sergeant Matt Payne."

"Oh, hell."

"You want me to call the FOP?"

"Yes, please. And put Payne in an interview room and don't do anything else until I get there."

"Yes, sir. There's more, boss."

"Let me have it."

"Stan Colt and his entourage were there. The press has hold of it and they're all over the scene. I'm watching it on the television here in the office. They broke into the prime-time shows to cover it live. It's a real cluster fuck out there."

[TWO]

Under the contract between the City of Philadelphia and Lodge #5 of the Fraternal Order of Police, it is agreed that whenever any police officer, regardless of rank, is detained for any reason that might result in criminal prosecution, the detaining unit will, at the same time it notifies senior police officials, notify the Fraternal Order of Police.

The Fraternal Order of Police will then dispatch an attorney to ensure that the rights of the police officer being detained are not violated in any way, and to assist him in any way deemed necessary.

There are lawyers under contract to Lodge #5 to provide counsel on call. There are other lawyers in Philadelphia who provide their professional services, *pro bono publico,* to Lodge #5.

Perhaps the most distinguished of this latter group is Armando C. Giacomo, Esq., a slight, lithe, dapper Italian who once served his country as a Marine Corps fighter pilot, then came home to become either the best and most successful criminal defense attorney in Philadelphia, or the second best. The other contender for that unofficial title being Colonel J. Dunlop Mawson, Esq., of Mawson, Payne, Stockton, McAdoo & Lester.

The difference between the two was essentially in their clientele. Colonel Mawson, who often defended individuals accused of stealing, misappropriating, embezzling, taking by fraud or deception, or otherwise illegally acquiring huge sums of money—and was compensated accordingly—declined to offer his professional services to anyone with any connection, however remote, to organized crime, or the illegal trade in controlled substances.

Arguing that even the most despicable scoundrels were entitled under the United States Constitution to the best defense possible, Armando C. Giacomo defended, very often successfully, the most despicable scoundrels alleged to be connected with organized crime and/or the illegal traffic in controlled substances, and was compensated accordingly.

Mr. Giacomo's understanding with Lodge #5, Fraternal Order of Police, was that he wished to offer his services only in cases worthy of his talent. As the ordinary thug could not afford to avail himself of his services, neither should the cop charged with, say, drunken driving, or slapping the wife around, have his professional services made available to him, *pro bono publico.* He preferred to defend officers charged with violating the civil rights of citizens, and—above all—officers alleged to have illegally taken life in the execution of their official duties.

When the official of Lodge #5, Fraternal Order of Police, was informed by Captain Daniel Kimberly of Internal Affairs that a sergeant was being detained for investigation of a shooting of two suspects, one of them fatal, he immediately began searching for Mr. Giacomo's unlisted home number in his Rolodex. And he was not at all surprised, despite the hour, that Mr. Giacomo said he would go directly to IAD, and that the FOP representative should meet him there.

[THREE]

The city editor of the *Philadelphia Bulletin*, Roscoe G. Kennedy, responded to a computer message from Michael J. O'Hara—

```
Kennedy—
Hold space page one section one for three column pic, plus jump for
350–400 words, + 3, 4 more pics
Ohara
```

—in several ways, the first being annoyance. O'Hara's message was very much in the form of an order, rather than a request or suggestion.

No matter how much money and perquisites O'Hara's pal Casimir Bolinski, the football-jock-turned-sports-attorney, had beat the people upstairs out of in exchange for the services of Michael O'Hara, Roscoe G. Kennedy felt that this in no way changed the fact that Michael J. O'Hara was a staff writer, no more, and Roscoe G. Kennedy was the city editor, and thus entitled to tell the staff writer what to do, and when, not the reverse.

The second cause of annoyance was that in order to see what immortal prose Michael J. O'Hara believed was worthy of a three-column photograph on page one of section one—plus a jump with more pictures—before O'Hara saw fit in his own sweet time to send it to him, he would have to go to O'Hara's office.

This was actually a double irritant. Mr. Kennedy did not think a lowly staff writer was entitled to an expensively furnished private office—O'Hara's $2,100 exotic wood and calfskin-upholstered Charles Eames chair was more salt in the wound here—in the first place, and to get to it, he was going to have to get up from his desk and walk across the city room, which meant past a large number of other staff writers, all of whom would see that he was calling on O'Hara rather than the other way around.

The third irritant was that Roscoe G. Kennedy knew that if O'Hara thought he had something worthy of space on page one of section one, and with a large jump to be placed elsewhere, the sonofabitch probably did.

Roscoe G. Kennedy was honest enough to admit—if sometimes through clenched teeth—that Mickey O'Hara was really a hell of a good writer, and had earned his Pulitzer Prize.

So Mr. Kennedy resisted the urge to summon Mr. O'Hara to his presence to discuss his latest contribution to the *Bulletin,* and instead got up and walked across the city room and knocked politely at the door.

He saw that Mr. O'Hara had guests in his office, Casimir "The Bull" Bolinski and presumably Mrs. Bolinski, and he smiled at them.

"What have you got for me, Mickey?" Mr. Kennedy asked.

O'Hara raised one hand from the keyboard of his computer terminal, on which he was typing with great rapidity, and pointed to the screen of his personal (as opposed to the *Bulletin*'s) computer.

There was a very clear photograph of a well-known Philadelphia police officer on it, this one showing him in a dinner jacket, with a cellular phone in one hand and a .45 Colt in the other, standing just a little triumphantly over a man lying on the ground.

"There's more," O'Hara said.

The city editor looked at the other images from the parking lot, then read Mickey's story on the computer screen. He didn't speak until O'Hara had finished and pushed the Transmit key. Then he said,

"Great stuff, Mickey! Really great! The Wyatt Earp of the Main Line Does It Again."

Mickey stood up.

"What did you say?" he asked.

"For a head, how about 'Main Line Wyatt Earp 2, Bad Guys 0 in Shoot-out at the La Famiglia Corral'?"

"You sonofabitch," Mickey said. "That's a cop doing his job."

"Watch your mouth, Michael," Casimir said. "Antoinette . . ."

"A goddamn cop in a tuxedo who obviously likes to shoot people."

"You sonofabitch, you're no better than the goddamn *Ledger!*"

"Don't call me a sonofabitch, O'Hara. I won't stand for it."

"Then don't make wiseass remarks about a cop liking what he has to do to do his job, you arrogant, elitist, bleeding-heart . . ." Mickey paused, searching his memory for the most scalding insult he could think of, and then, triumphantly, concluded, ". . . Missouri School of Journalism sonofabitch!"

"Michael, I'm not going to tell you again," Casimir said.

"You can't talk to me like that, O'Hara!"

"I just did. What are you going to do about it?"

Mr. Michael J. O'Hara assumed a fighting crouch and cocked his fists.

Mr. Roscoe G. Kennedy rose to the challenge.

He threw a roundhouse right at Mr. O'Hara. Mr. O'Hara nimbly dodged the punch, feinted with his right, then punched Mr. Kennedy in the nose with his left, and then in the abdomen with his right.

Mr. Kennedy fell, doubled over, to the floor, taking with him the *Bulletin*'s computer terminal.

Casimir J. Bolinski, Esq., erupted from Mr. O'Hara's $2,100 Charles Eames chair, rushed across the office, wrapped his arms around Mr. O'Hara, and without much apparent effort carried him across the city room—past many members of the *Bulletin* staff—and into an elevator. Mrs. Bolinski followed them.

Mr. Kennedy regained his feet and sort of staggered to the door.

"You're fired, you insane shanty Irish sonofabitch! Fired!" he shouted. "When I'm through with you, you won't be able to get a job on the *National Enquirer*."

Mrs. Bolinski stuck her tongue out at Mr. Kennedy.

Ten minutes later, after an application of ice had stopped his nosebleed, Mr. Kennedy gave Mr. O'Hara's latest—and as far as he was concerned, certainly last—contribution to the *Bulletin* some serious thought.

And then he called his assistant and told him to save space on page one, section one, copy to come, for a three-column pic, plus a four-hundred-word jump inside with three or four pics.

[FOUR]

When Inspector Weisbach came into the Internal Affairs Unit Captain Daniel Kimberly was talking with Lieutenant McGuire and another man he sensed was a police officer. He didn't see Payne.

Kimberly anticipated his question.

"I put Sergeant Payne in an interview room and asked him to wait," Kimberly said. "Nothing else. And I called the FOP."

"Good," Weisbach said.

"Who called back just a moment ago to inform me that Mr. Armando C. Giacomo is en route here to represent Sergeant Payne."

"How fortunate for Sergeant Payne," Weisbach said.

"Inspector, this is Lieutenant McGuire. . . ."

"How are you, Lieutenant?"

"Good evening, sir. Or good morning, sir."

"And this is Sergeant Al Nevins, Inspector," McGuire said.

"You were the first supervisor on the scene?"

"Yes, sir."

"A uniform got there ahead of you?"

"No, sir. Mickey O'Hara got there first—by about thirty seconds. When Nevins and I got there, he had already taken Payne's picture, standing over the man Payne put down."

"I understood there were two men shot?"

"Yes, sir. One fatally. Payne blew his brains out."

"How do you *know* that, Lieutenant?"

"Well, sir, Payne told us. And we saw the body. The bullet struck right about here."

He pointed at his own face.

"Did Payne also tell you what happened?"

"He said there had been an armed robbery of a couple picking up their car in the lot; that he'd walked up on it right afterward, told the robbers to stop. They ran, he went after them. They fired at him with a shotgun and a semi-automatic pistol, and he put both of them down."

"Did they hit him?" Weisbach asked.

"No, sir," McGuire said, and hesitated.

"Go on, Lieutenant," Weisbach said.

"He was a little shaken up, sir."

"How shaken up?"

"Acted odd, you know," McGuire said.

"No, I don't know."

"Well, there was the business about his weapon," McGuire said.

"What about his weapon?"

"I took it from him, of course," McGuire said, and pointed to one of the desks in the room. There were two Ziploc bags on it. One of them held Matt's Officer's Model Colt .45 pistol, and the other a magazine.

"Of course?" Weisbach asked.

"Yes, sir, and he gave me some lip that I was supposed to give it back to him. He didn't give me any trouble, but he told me I was supposed to give it back to him after I counted the rounds left in the magazine."

"At that time, Lieutenant, did you believe that Sergeant Payne (a) posed a danger to others or himself, and/or (b) that he had committed a crime of any kind?"

"No, sir. From what I saw it was a good shooting."

"Two things, Lieutenant. There is no such thing as a good shooting. They are all lamentable. Some of them are unfortunately necessary, but there is no such thing as a 'good' shooting."

"Sir, I meant—"

"Secondly, Lieutenant, you might find it valuable to refresh your memory regarding the regulations dealing with taking a weapon from an officer in a situation like this."

"Sir?"

"The sergeant was right, Lieutenant. Absent any reason to believe that the shooting officer poses a danger to himself or others, or belief that the officer has committed a felony, the regulations state that his weapon will be returned to him by the supervisor after he counts the rounds remaining in the magazine, and takes possession of that."

"Inspector, I thought it was evidence. . . ."

"So you implied. The point here is that a clever lawyer, such as Mr. Giacomo, may make the point that your disarming of Sergeant Payne against regulations is proof of bias."

"Jesus, I didn't know."

"Obviously. Now, was there any other indication of what you considered odd behavior in Sergeant Payne?"

"He was . . . sort of out it, sir. Distant, maybe, is the word."

The telephone on one of the desks rang, and Captain Kimberly went to answer it, and the door opened and Inspector Peter Wohl and Amelia A. Payne, M.D., came into the room.

"Hello, Mike," Wohl said. He nodded at the others.

"Where is he?" Amy asked.

"Honey!" Wohl said, warningly.

"Peter, as I understand it, Sergeant Payne is no longer assigned to Special Operations," Weisbach said.

"That's right."

"That makes me ask, you'll understand, what you're doing here?"

"What we're doing here?" Amy flared. "Jesus H. Christ! I want to see my brother, is what we're doing here."

"And what Dr. Payne is doing here," Weisbach continued.

"Inspector," Captain Kimberly said. "That was Captain Hollaran on the phone. He and Commissioner Coughlin are en route here. He asked who was the supervisor. I told him you were."

Weisbach nodded his understanding.

"Unless you can tell me you have official business here, Peter," Weisbach said, "I'm afraid I'll have to ask you and the lady to leave."

"I'm not a *lady*, goddamn it, I'm a physician. And I demand to see my brother."

"Take it easy, honey," Wohl said. "Mike's just going by the book. He has to."

"Screw his book. Screw him. I demand to see my brother."

"Peter . . . ," Weisbach said.

"Inspector Weisbach, with your permission," Peter said, "I'd like to stay here with the lady until the arrival of Commissioner Coughlin."

The door opened again.

Armando C. Giacomo strode in. He was wearing a tweed jacket, gray flannel trousers, a pajama top, and bedroom slippers.

"Sorry it took me so long to get here," he said. "Hello, Mike. Amelia. Peter. What brings you two here?"

"They won't let me see my brother," Amy said. "Tell them they have to."

"Do I correctly infer that it is Sergeant Payne who was allegedly involved in this unfortunate incident?"

Weisbach nodded.

"I'm not sure if they have to give you access to your brother, Amy," Giacomo said, "but I am absolutely sure that I have the right to see the detainee, accompanied by the physician of my choice. Isn't that correct, Inspector Weisbach?"

"I think you can have a police physician, Counselor," Weisbach said. "I'll have to check about Dr. Payne."

"You're splitting hairs, Inspector. If the police department can seek, as they have on several occasions that come readily to both our minds, the consultation of Dr. Payne in the investigation of crimes, the only reason I can see why you refuse her, as my consultant in this matter, access to the detainee is that you are personally biased against my client, determined to deprive him of his full rights under the Constitution, or, perhaps . . ."

"He's in there, Counselor," Weisbach said, pointing to the closed door of the interview room.

Amy walked quickly to the door and pulled it open.

Sergeant Payne was sitting at a table.

Tears were running down his cheeks.

He smiled like a child when he saw Amy.

"I guess I did it again, huh, Amy?"

He suddenly slammed his left hand on top of his right and stared at it angrily. After a moment, he took the left hand away and looked at the right. The right hand rose, trembling, from the table. He slapped it down again.

"I have no idea what's the matter with it," he explained with a shy smile. "It just keeps doing that."

"Jesus Christ," Armando C. Giacomo said.

He turned to Inspector Weisbach, who looked almost as horrified and unhappy as he felt.

"Inspector, I believe that Dr. Payne is about to advise me that in her professional medical opinion, Sergeant Payne, having suffered understandable pain, fear, and anguish as the result of tonight's events, not only is not able to intelligently respond to any questions posed by anybody, but is in urgent need of medical attention. Would you have problems with that?"

"No, sir," Weisbach said. "I'll call an ambulance."

"No, goddamn it!" Amy called from the interview room. "He's had enough sirens and flashing lights for tonight."

The men looked away in embarrassment.

Doctor Payne was holding Sergeant Payne in her arms, stroking his head. He was sobbing uncontrollably.

After a moment, Peter Wohl entered the room.

"Take him," Amy ordered.

Very gently, Wohl pulled Matt from Amy's arms and took him into his own.

She went to Kimberly's telephone and dialed a number from memory.

"This is Dr. Payne. I will require a private room immediately, anywhere but in psychiatric. I will be there shortly with the patient."

She hung up, but stood there with her hand on the telephone in thought.

Captain Frank Hollaran and First Deputy Commissioner Coughlin walked into the room.

"Amy, honey!" he said when he saw her. "I'm not sure you should be here. . . ."

"Just shut up, Uncle Denny," she said, levelly. "Now *I'm* taking care of him."

Then she raised her voice.

"Get him on his feet, Peter. We're going to take him out of here."

In a moment, Wohl appeared in the interview room door, his arm around Matt.

Matt smiled shyly at everybody as Wohl led him across the room and out the door, but no one spoke or moved.

[FIVE]

Sergeant Matthew Payne was lying on his side in the hospital bed, his arm over his face, when the door opened.

He first looked annoyed, and then curious. His hand reached out and found the bed control. As the back of the bed rose, he rolled onto his back, then folded his arms over his chest and looked somewhat defensively at the two physicians who entered the room. One was his sister, the other a short, plump, somewhat jowly man in his fifties.

He was Aaron Stein, M.D., the Moses and Rebecca Wertheimer Professor of Psychiatry at the Medical School of the University of Pennsylvania, and a former president of the American Psychiatric Association. Dr. Stein had surprised many of his peers—and annoyed as many more—when he selected Amelia Payne, M.D., for a psychiatric residency under his mentorship. She had then just turned twenty-two years old.

She had worked under him—he always insisted on saying "with him"—ever since, and it was widely believed that Dr. Stein had been responsible for Dr. Payne's current position as the Joseph L. Otterby Professor of Psychiatry.

"I must really be off my rocker if Amy called in the heavy duty reinforcements," Matt said.

"How do you feel, Matt?" Dr. Stein asked.

"I feel as if I was drugged," Matt said. "I can't imagine why."

"All I gave you was a sleeping pill," Amy said.

"Did it say 'for elephants' on the bottle?"

Dr. Stein chuckled.

"How long have I been here?" Matt asked.

"You slept through yesterday," Amy said.

"Let me guess," Matt said. "Light began to come through the windows a couple of hours ago. This is the morning of the second day?"

"Yes, it is," Stein said, smiling.

"I normally tell time by looking at my watch," Matt said. "But that seems to be missing. And both the telephone and the TV seem not to be working."

"You needed rest, Matt," Dr. Stein said.

"Is that a polite way of telling the lunatic that he was really bouncing off the walls?"

"It's just what I said," Stein said. "You needed rest, Matt. And not only don't we heavy-duty psychiatrists use that word anymore—actually it means 'affected by the moon'—but you're not loony, bonkers, gaga, or whatever else you're thinking."

Matt had to smile. He remembered what his father said about Dr. Stein: "He looks, and acts, like a beardless Santa Claus."

"Then what is wrong with me?" he asked.

"In layman's terms," Dr. Stein said, "do you know what thoroughbred race-horses and overachiever workaholics like yourself have in common?"

"We make a lot of money for other people?" Matt asked, innocently, after a moment.

Stein laughed.

"You don't know when to stop. You don't understand that you have limits like ordinary horses and other human beings," he said.

He turned to Dr. Payne.

"He's all right," he said. "I'll talk to him now. I'll page you when we're through. And on your way out, have them send two breakfasts in here." He turned back to Matt. "I've never known you not to be hungry. What would you like? Take advantage of my presence. I get whatever I want."

"I am a little hungry," Matt said.

"Send in the ward nurse," Dr. Stein said. "She's getting a little too big for her britches, and it will do her good to take our breakfast order."

"Okay," Matt said. "Amy's gone. That was a very nice breakfast, thank you very much. And now, I hope, you're going to tell me what's wrong with me?"

"I already told you what I know is wrong with you. Do you want to hear what your sister thinks is wrong with you?"

"I'm afraid to ask."

"She's been really worried for some time about you, and she's been coming to me for some time to tell me why she's worried."

"Is that ethical?"

"Ethical, schmethical. She loves you. She's a pretty good doctor. We're friends. She came to me. It's done—she can't undo telling me. You want to hear what she thinks?"

"Okay."

"She has developed quite a theory—basically that you don't know who you really are."

"Who does she think I really am?"

"Essentially, the psychological heir of your mother."

"I don't know what she can mean by that."

"That your psychological makeup is gentle, kind, even intellectual, maybe. Anyway, the antithesis of warrior."

Matt threw his hands up to indicate he had no idea what Amy was driving at.

"She thinks you have been conditioned all your life by your role models to believe you were destined to be a warrior," Stein said.

"What role models?"

"Commissioner Coughlin for one, the cop's cop," Stein said. "But primarily, the legend of your biological father, who died heroically in the line of duty. Your uncle, the cop captain, what was his name?"

"Dutch," Matt said. "Captain Dutch Moffitt."

"Who similarly died heroically in the line of duty, right?"

"He had just finished telling some kid to put the gun down, he didn't want to have to kill him, and some goddamn junkie shot him with a .22, of all goddamn weapons."

"But heroically, right?"

"I suppose."

"And he died heroically right at the time when the Marine Corps told you, 'No, thanks, you don't measure up to our standards,' right?"

"They found something wrong with my ear," Matt said.

"All of these things combining, in the Dr. Amy Payne theory of what's wrong with Little Brother, to compel you to join the police force to prove your manhood, that you're a warrior."

"Jesus!"

"And then you met another man, who became your mentor, Inspector Peter Wohl. Another warrior role model."

"Okay."

"Now, being as intelligent as you are, you could not have been unaware, in Amy's theory, that Role Model One, Commissioner Coughlin, had arranged for a job for you that was not really police work. You weren't walking around dark streets in a uniform with a gun and a nightstick, in other words. And you subconsciously understood this to mean that Coughlin and Wohl, Role Model

Two, didn't think of you as a fellow warrior, but rather as sort of a wimp who had to be protected."

"She told you all of this?" Matt asked.

"And then you shot the Northwest serial rapist, trying to prove that you were indeed a warrior and a man."

"I wasn't trying to prove anything. I shot that sonofabitch because he was trying to run me over with a van."

"But still, even after this warrior act, neither Coughlin nor Wohl was convinced that you were a warrior. The proof of this, your subconscious believed, came on the memorable day when the real cops, the real warriors, were about to face down the bad people and they sent you a block away to safety, allegedly to protect a journalist."

"I must be crazy, I'm starting to think she may be onto something."

"I'm not finished. She's given this a lot of thought."

"Go on."

"And again you risked your life to prove you were a man, a warrior, when a bad guy appeared in the alley and you faced up to him."

"He was shooting at us! What was I supposed to do?"

"You're an intelligent young man. You should have ducked, run away. You were driven by the need to prove your masculinity."

"My God!"

"And going off at somewhat of a tangent, Dr. Payne feels that your interest in so many members of the opposite sex is really a manifestation of your need to prove your manhood, carnally. And that, of course, is another proof, she feels, that you doubt your own manhood."

"And all this time, I thought she was my friend."

"She spoke to me as one physician to another. Give her that much, Matt. This was not idle gossip."

"What else did she have to say?"

"You next began to prove your manhood by becoming a detective, and then a sergeant, in the latter case studying obsessively because it was obsessively so important to you that you do well—preferably better than anyone else—on the examination."

"Anything else?"

"You told her, I think, that you were having nightmares about what happened in Doylestown?"

"And ten seconds after I did, I realized it was a mistake."

"You ever have them about the other shootings, Matt?"

"What the hell, the cow's out of the barn. Yeah. Most of them are about Doylestown, but every once in a while I have one about the guy who tried to run me down in the van, and now I suppose I'll have them about the guy I just shot outside La Famiglia."

"You said, 'The guy in the van, the guy I just shot.' But 'Doylestown'?"

"I didn't shoot anybody in Doylestown," Matt said. "The guy we were after shot the girl who took us to him."

"That's all she was to you?"

Matt thought that over, then shrugged.

"No. I thought I was in love with her. I had to prove my manhood, I guess."

Dr. Stein grunted.

"Amy thinks that your weeping over the girl in Doylestown was the first manifestation of your impending, uncontrollable psychological problems, and she feels the nightmares tend to confirm that theory."

Matt looked at him but didn't reply.

"You then were promoted to sergeant, and given your choice of assignment, and chose homicide, primarily because homicide is considered the *ne plus ultra* of warrior assignments in the police department."

Matt shook his head.

"The warriors—Amy's term—are Highway, the Bomb Squad . . . not Homicide," he said.

Dr. Stein shrugged but did not respond directly.

"Where you were immediately plunged into things beyond your capacity to deal with," he went on, "and to which you applied all of your best efforts. That, she believes, would have, so to speak, pushed you over the edge in and of itself, but then you became involved in this last incident, two nights ago, and that finally produced the inevitable result. You experienced an emotional meltdown, so to speak."

"Well, I guess she's got my number, doesn't she?"

"She believes she has correctly assessed the situation."

"And what does my all-wise sister think I should do about it?"

"That's pretty clear to her too. She thinks you should face who you really are, and that done, take the appropriate action, which would be for you to resign from the police force, go back to law school, and assume a more suitable life for someone with your psychological makeup."

"And you agree, right?"

"I didn't say that. Are you interested in what I think?"

"Yes, of course I am."

"I don't want you quoting me to her, Matt. I'd like your word on that."

"Sure."

"Your sister is a fine psychiatrist and a fine teacher. Perhaps for that reason I was terribly disappointed in just about everything she had to say, and certainly with her theories. They weren't at all professional—although she is so good that some details were valid—but rather the near maternal musings of a loving sister. Furthermore, she should have known that, and that you should not even think about treating someone you deeply care for. It clouds the judgment. In this case, spectacularly."

"You're saying she's wrong about everything?"

"Just about everything."

"She makes a lot of sense to me," Matt said. "So what do you think is wrong with me?"

"I told you when I first came in here. You're like a thoroughbred racehorse. You think you have a bottomless pit of energy from which to draw strength, physical and emotional, and that you're unstoppable. You don't and you are."

"I've found out that I'm stoppable, Dr. Stein. Did she tell you how I came apart?"

Matt mimed the rising of his trembling hand and slapping it down.

"In detail. Including how you wept and allowed yourself to be comforted as she held you like a mother. In short, Superman, you showed typical symptoms of emotional exhaustion. The treatment is basically rest and the admonition 'Don't push yourself so hard from now on.'"

"That's all?"

"I think you ought to see Dr. Michaels a couple of times. He said he'd be happy to, and you won't be the first cop he's talked to about something like this, because you are by no means the first cop something like this has happened to."

[SIX]

"Come in, Doctor," Aaron Stein said to Amy Payne. "We have to discuss the patient in 1411, and your relationship with the patient."

"What did Keyes Michaels have to say?" Amy asked.

"Dr. Michaels and I agree the patient was suffering from understandable emotional exhaustion, from which he—being of sound mind and body, so to speak—will recover rapidly with no lasting ill effects."

"Well, I don't agree with that, Aaron."

"As his attending physician, and after consultation with Dr. Michaels, I have decided that further hospitalization is not indicated, and I have ordered his release."

"Without consulting me?"

"That brings us to that, Doctor," Stein said.

"I beg your pardon?"

"You're Matt's sister, Amy, not his physician. You seem to have forgotten that. It's unethical—not to mention stupid—for a physician to treat anyone with whom the physician has a familial or other emotional connection. It clouds the judgment. You know that. Or at least knew it. You seem to have forgotten."

"All right," she said after a moment. "I was wrong. Sorry."

"Have you ever heard the phrase 'Physician, heal thyself,' Doctor?"

"Of course I have."

"Would you be interested in my advice in how you can do that, Doctor?"

"I'd be interested to know what you think it is that needs healing, Doctor," Amy said, growing angry.

"I'll tell you what I'll do, I'll give you the formulation I would recommend, and from that, if you're half the intelligent, dedicated psychiatrist I think you are, you'll be able to deduce what I think is wrong with you."

"Please do, Doctor."

"Marry the cop, Amy. Have a baby. Have several babies."

She looked at him in genuine shock.

"You're serious, aren't you?"

He nodded.

"You're a young woman of childbearing age. Do what nature intended for you to do. Apply your very healthy, very normal maternal instincts to your own child, not your brother." He paused. "In my judgment, that would make you even a better psychiatrist than you already are."

She met his eyes but didn't reply.

"The formulation you developed for your brother applies to you. You're the overachiever workaholic, refusing to believe your well of strength can ever go dry. And the first symptom of your inevitable—unless you do something about it—emotional meltdown has been your delusionary relationship with your brother. You're not his mother, and you're not his doctor."

"Marry the cop? Have babies?"

He nodded again. After a moment, he added:

"I'd like your word, Doctor, that insofar as the patient in 1411 is concerned, you will from this moment regard yourself as his sister, not his physician."

"Jesus!"

"I will interpret that as meaning 'Of course.' Now, take your brother home, and see if you can get him to take it easy."

[SEVEN]

"You free, Denny?" Police Commissioner Ralph J. Mariani asked from First Deputy Commissioner Coughlin's door.

"Of course."

"What do you hear about Matt?"

"His sister just called. They're about to let him out of the hospital. She's going to take him out to his parents' place in Wallingford."

"That was quick, wasn't it?"

"They say he's all right—that he was emotionally exhausted, is all."

" 'They say'? His sister, you mean?"

"No. He was examined by both our psychiatrist, Dr. Michaels . . . You know him?"

"Sure. Keyes Michaels. Good man. Comes from a whole family of cops."

"And Dr. Aaron Stein, who's the head shrink at UP Medical Center."

"I'm getting the feeling, Denny, that you don't like—"

"Between us?"

Mariani nodded.

"Dr. Michaels is really proud he took his psychiatrist residency under Dr. Aaron Stein. I would be very surprised if Michaels disagreed with Stein about anything. Even if he did."

"Meaning?"

"You weren't at Internal Affairs when Matty came apart," Coughlin said. "I was. I wanted to cry. I have trouble believing he's all right so soon."

"They're psychiatrists and you're not, Denny," Mariani said.

Coughlin shrugged.

"You asked, Ralph."

"Well, it was a good shooting," Mariani asked. He laid a folder on Coughlin's desk. "That's Mike Weisbach's initial report. Payne did everything by the book. One of the victims—the wife of the guy that got pistol-whipped—even wants to apologize for what she said to him—'Where the hell were you when we needed you?'—when he walked up on it. She said she was upset, and wants to apologize. The only thing that wasn't done by the book was when the Dignitary Protection Lieutenant . . . What's his name?"

"McGuire."

". . . took Payne's weapon as evidence."

"Oh, Jesus."

"Payne's got a legitimate beef about that."

"He won't say anything," Coughlin said. "He's a good cop."

"But you're worried about him, right?"

"I'm worried about him. He needs a rest. A long one."

"That poses a problem. If Dr. Michaels has pronounced him fit for duty, that means . . ."

Coughlin nodded, and finished the sentence:

". . . he's supposed to come to work tomorrow."

"You don't know if he's got any vacation coming?"

"Something over four hundred hours. I just checked his jacket."

"See that he takes thirty days of that, Denny. Make it an order."

Coughlin nodded.

[EIGHT]

Patricia Payne held both of her son's arms and looked intently up at him.

"Are you all right, sweetheart?"

"Amy says I have to wear the straitjacket only when I leave the property," Matt said. "She has it in her truck."

"Don't be such an ass, Matt," Amy said. "You heard what Doctor Stein said."

"Which was?" Patricia Payne asked.

"That what Matt and a jackass have in common is that they don't know they have limits, and Matt reached his. All he needs is rest."

"He said 'thoroughbred racehorse,'" Matt said.

"And all he needs is rest?" Patricia Payne asked.

"That's it, Mom," Amy said. "Really."

"Can you get some time off?" Patricia Payne asked.

"I'm sure I can," Matt said.

"Well, go tell your father. He's pacing back and forth on the patio, waiting to know what's up."

Matt walked toward the patio, and Patricia Payne led her daughter into the house, where she sought—and got—confirmation that all that was wrong with her son was that he had been pushed, or had pushed himself, beyond his limits, and that all he needed was rest.

Matt had just finished telling his father this, and was about to tell him that Amy had another medical theory that he thought had a lot of merit, despite what Drs. Stein and Michaels said, when Deputy Commissioner Dennis V. Coughlin, trailed by Captain Frank Hollaran, came onto the patio.

Coughlin was carrying in his hand what looked like a briefcase but was the size of a woman's purse. Matt wondered what it was.

"I just had a talk with Dr. Keyes Michaels, the department psychiatrist, Brewster," Coughlin said. "Good man. Comes from a family of cops. Knows cops. Says the only thing wrong with Matty is exhaustion, and all he needs is some rest."

He turned to Matt.

"By order of the commissioner, you are now on vacation. Thirty days."

"Great," Matt said.

Coughlin handed him the purse-size leather briefcase.

"This is yours," he said.

"What is it?"

"Your pistol. You forgot it at IAD."

"Oh, yeah," Matt said. "Thank you."

He laid the purselike thing on the fieldstone wall of the patio.

"Matt," Brewster Payne said, "why don't you go inside and get us something to drink?"

As soon as Matt was out of earshot, Brewster C. Payne sought—and got—confirmation from Dennis V. Coughlin that all that was wrong was that Matt was emotionally and physically exhausted, and all that he needed was rest.

As Matt rolled the bar cart across the fieldstones of the patio, Armando C. Giacomo, Esq., arrived.

He was now his normal, sartorially elegant self.

"Brewster, I realize I'm barging in—"

"Nonsense, Manny, you don't need an invitation here."

"Actually, I came to see my client," Giacomo said. "How are you doing, Matt?"

"I'm fine."

"I have been informed, unofficially, of course, but reliably, by both the cops and the D.A.'s office that nothing you did in the La Famiglia parking lot in any way violated any law of the Commonwealth of Pennsylvania. In legal terminology, it was a righteous shooting, Matt, and you're off the hook."

"Manny, we appreciate how quickly—" Brewster C. Payne began.

Giacomo waved his hand to signal thanks were unnecessary.

"But you will have a taste, Manny, right?"

"I thought you would never ask."

Next to arrive were Lieutenant Jason Washington and Detective Joe D'Amata. As Matt was pouring their drinks, the telephone in the niche in the fieldstone wall rang and Brewster C. Payne answered it.

It was Mr. Stan Colt, calling from the Coast. The monsignor had called him, Mr. Colt said, and said he'd heard that Matt was a little under the weather, and "could I talk to him, if he's up to it?"

Sergeant Payne assured Mr. Colt that he was fine, that he had just been a little exhausted, and that he would make a real effort to go out to the Coast, and soon.

Inspector Peter Wohl appeared next. He was intercepted by Mrs. Patricia Payne and Dr. Amelia Payne as he walked up the now car-clogged drive toward the house.

"Amy told me what you did for Matt the night . . . it happened," Patricia Payne said, "and I just wanted to say, 'Thank you.' "

"Absolutely unnecessary," Wohl replied. "I was just glad I was there. I think of Matt—I think of all of you—as family."

"And we do, too, Peter," Patricia Payne said, emotionally. "Don't we, Amy?"

"Yeah," Amy said, looking intently at him. "I guess we all really do."

Her tone was strange, and Peter looked at her with a raised eyebrow, and as if he was about to say something. But then he saw something else, and smiled instead.

"Look who's here," he said. "Mutt and Jeff."

Detectives Charles McFadden and Jesus Martinez got out of their unmarked Special Operations Crown Victoria and started up the drive.

They stopped, and looked uncomfortable when they saw Wohl.

"Sir," McFadden said, biting the bullet, "Captain Sabara said it would be all right if we took the rest of the day off—we just took the truck to the impound lot—and came out here and saw how Sergeant Payne was doing."

Wohl nodded.

"How's he doing?" McFadden asked.

"He was exhausted, really exhausted," Amy said. "But he's fine, and he'll be glad to see you."

Detective Martinez unrolled the newspaper he had in his hand and extended it to Dr. Payne.

"My mother saved this for me—Charley and me was driving up from Alabama when this happened," he said. "I didn't know if Pa . . . Sergeant Payne had seen them or not."

It was the *Philadelphia Bulletin,* with a three-column picture of Sergeant Matthew M. Payne in a dinner jacket, standing, pistol in hand, over a man on the ground.

With an effort, Mrs. Payne smiled and said,

"No, I don't think he has. It was very kind of you, Detective, to think of bringing this."

An hour—and several bottles of spirits—later, everybody had gone, and Matt and Brewster Payne found themselves again alone on the patio.

"Well, I don't know if that was the rest Aaron Stein prescribed for you, but I don't see how it could have been avoided, and in the long run, I think it was good for you," Brewster C. Payne said.

"I'm all right, Dad."

"What are you going to do for thirty days? Given it any thought?"

"Aside from getting the Porsche fixed . . . It's in the impound lot, Peter told me—"

"You're going to have it repaired?"

"I don't know. There was a lot of damage."

"You have time to decide."

"I may get another car, something less ostentatious, suitable for a starving law student."

Brewster Payne looked at him for a long moment without saying anything.

"When did you decide that?" he asked finally.

"In the hospital," Matt said.

"May I comment?"

"I sort of expected 'Finally, thank God, he's come to his senses!'"

Brewster C. Payne chuckled, then said, "I would be delighted if that's what you finally decide to do, Matt, but I suggest to you that that's a very important decision to make, and important decisions should not be made impulsively."

"Okay."

"Why don't you go to the Cape May house and take *Final Tort* out of sight of shore and watch the waves go up and down for a couple of days? That always helps me to think when I really need to."

Matt thought that over for a moment, then nodded.

"You're probably right. You usually are. But I really think my days as the Wyatt Earp of the Main Line are over."

CHAPTER 22

[ONE]

The theory that using *Final Tort V,* the Payne fifty-eight-foot Hatteras, as a platform from which, as he watched the waves go up and down, Matt could do some really serious thinking—and, his father hoped, incidentally get some rest—would be an excellent idea did not work out well in practice, largely because of her captain.

Her captain, retired Coast Guard chief petty officer Al Bowman, who had been with the Paynes since Matt was ten, when the family boat was *Final Tort II,* a much smaller Hatteras, was on vacation.

Matt had learned small-boat handling from Chief Bowman, and took not a little pride in knowing he had met Chief Bowman's criteria in that area. Usually, when they went out on *Final Tort V* together, the chief would come to the bridge only to hand Matt another beer.

Standing in for him in his absence was another, much younger retired Coast Guard chief petty officer, who was visibly nervous when Matt went to the control console, fired up the engines, and asked him to let loose the lines, with the obvious intent of taking the vessel to sea with himself at the helm.

Even when Matt managed to get the *Final Tort V* away from the wharf and into the wide Atlantic without running her aground, the stand-in captain never got far from Matt or the controls.

What was worse, however, was that the replacement captain had seen in the *Bulletin* both the photograph of Matt getting off the Citation with Homer C. Daniels and the photograph of Matt, pistol in hand, in the parking lot near La Famiglia, and naturally presumed Matt would be delighted to tell him all about the murdering rapist, exchanging gunfire with a couple of armed robbers, and what it was really like to be a real-life Stan Colt. And incidentally, what's Stan Colt really like?

Compounding the problem was that the replacement captain was a really nice guy, the sort of man to whom one could not say, "I wish you'd shut the fuck up!" although that thought did run more than once through Matt's mind.

And finally, if there were fish in the Atlantic, none of them showed any interest whatever in the bait supposed to tempt them to any of the four lines Matt put in the water.

At 2 P.M., Matt said, "I think we'd might as well call it a day. You want to take her in?"

The replacement captain had been obviously pleased with the request for his professional services.

Matt, sitting in a fishing chair with his feet on the stern rail, watching the churning water, had time for two beers and some private thoughts before he saw that they were nearly at the dock and he would have to go forward and handle the lines.

He had reached no profound conclusions, except that he didn't want to do this again tomorrow.

When he went forward, he saw a familiar vehicle, a Buick Rendezvous with an antennae farm on its roof, sitting beside the house.

Michael J. O'Hara himself was sprawled in a lawn chaise on the wharf, drinking from the neck of a beer bottle. The chair was from the deck of the house. There was a portable cooler beside Mickey that he'd obviously brought with him.

He waved, but rose from the chair only when Matt called, "Hey, Mickey, want to grab the line?"

On the third try, he managed to do so, whereupon he inquired, "What am I supposed to do with it?"

Matt resisted the temptation to tell him the first thing that came to his mind, and instead said, "Wrap it, twice, around that pole, and then hang on to it."

When he saw that Mickey had done so, he went aft to handle the stern lines.

I wonder what he's doing here. Who cares? I really am glad to see him.

"You didn't answer your phone," Mickey said, by way of greeting. "I was about to call the cops."

"On the water, you call the Coast Guard, not the cops," Matt said. "Write that down."

"So why didn't you answer the phone?"

"I didn't have it turned on, for one thing," Matt said, helping himself to a beer from the cooler, "and for another, I was probably out of range."

"You're not supposed to be," O'Hara said.

"Well, sorry. My profound apologies."

"I meant of this," Mickey said, and patted his shirt pocket, which held what looked to Matt like a bulky cellular telephone. "They advertise world-wide service. They use satellites."

"Then I guess I didn't have my phone turned on."

"I guess not," Mickey said.

It occurred to Matt that unless they got off the wharf before the reserve captain got off *Final Tort V,* he would probably be joining them for whatever happened next, which included a couple of beers, for sure, and then probably dinner.

Worse, that he would probably recognize Mickey's name, and start asking questions about what it was like being a famous journalist, and even worse than that, Mickey would delight in telling him.

"All I had for lunch was a ham and cheese sandwich," Matt said. "Let's go get something to eat."

"Steamed clams," Mickey announced. "I didn't have any lunch at all, and steamed clams seems like a splendid idea."

He picked up the portable cooler and started down the wharf.

"Are we going out tomorrow?" the reserve captain called down from the *Final Tort V.*

"I'll call you," Matt said.

In the Rendezvous, Mickey asked,

"You okay, Matty?"

"I'm fine."

"I heard you came apart for a while."

"I came apart for a while, but I'm fine now."

Mickey handed him his cellular telephone.

"Call Denny Coughlin and tell him. He's worried about you."

"He sent you down here to keep me company?"

"He told me how to get here," O'Hara said. "You have to dial Zero Zero One first."

"Zero Zero One first?"

"That's the United States," O'Hara explained.

"I thought that's where we were."

"That's a worldwide telephone. You have to dial the country code first. Call Denny, for Christ's sake."

Matt punched in the numbers, including the Zero Zero One country code, then the Philadelphia area code, and then Commissioner Coughlin's number, and was finally connected with him.

He told him that he was fine, thank you; that Mickey had found him; that they were in his car en route to get some steamed clams; and that he felt fine, thank you, nothing has changed in the thirty seconds since you asked me that the first time.

"Is Mickey going to be in the way, Matty? He really wanted to see you. I thought maybe you'd like some company, so I told him where to find you."

"I'm glad you did. Thank you."

"Well, have a couple of beers, but get some rest. And give me a call every once in a while, okay?"

"I'll do it," Matt said, and pushed the Off button.

They sat at the bar of the Ocean Vue Bar & Grill and viewed the ocean while eating two dozen steamers and drinking two Heinekens each. Aside from "Hand me the Tabasco, please," there was not much conversation.

Matt pushed the second tin tray of empty mollusk shells away from him, finished his beer, signaled for another round, and then asked,

"Can I ask you a personal question, Mick?"

"Shoot."

"Have you ever been out of the country?"

"No. Why should I have been?"

"Then what's with the worldwide dial Zero Zero One as the country code telephone all about?"

"I'm thinking of going to Europe," Mickey said.

"Really? What for?"

"Actually, Matty, that's one of the reasons I came all the way over here. The other was to apologize for not coming to see you after Doc Michaels told me that he let you out of the loony bin. I was busy."

"You have been discussing my mental condition with Dr. Michaels, I gather?"

"He said medical ethics prohibited his discussing your case with me, but apropos of nothing whatever, there was nothing wrong with you that a little rest wouldn't fix. He's a good guy."

"And he suggested you come to see me?"

"No," Mickey said, his tone suggesting that even the question surprised him. "What happened was after I heard that you'd been in and out of the loony bin, I called your mother, and she gave me the runaround about where you were, so I called your father, ditto, and I began to have visions of you in a rubber room somewhere, so I went and saw Doc Michaels, and he told me . . . what I told you he told me . . . so I called Denny and asked him where you were, and he told me. So I came."

"Tell me about Europe."

"I told you I was busy. What it was was that I was involved in a contractual dispute with my employers."

"About what?"

"I knocked my city editor on his ass," Mickey said. "With a bloody nose."

"Why?"

"It was a matter of journalistic principle," Mickey said. "The lawyers for the *Bulletin* said it was justification for my termination, unless I apologized to the sonofabitch, which I will do the morning after the Pope gives birth to triplets."

"So where does the matter stand now?" Matt said, smiling.

"Casimir responded that in this era of political correctness, it is not professionally acceptable behavior for a supervisor, before a room full of his fellow employees, to call an underling 'you insane Shanty Irish sonofabitch' . . ."

"He actually called you that?" Matt asked, on the edge of laughter.

Mickey nodded, smiling, and went on, obviously quoting Bolinski verbatim,

". . . 'and to threaten a distinguished Pulitzer Prize–winning journalist such as Mr. O'Hara, before the same gathering of his peers, with using his influence to ensure that Mr. O'Hara would never find employment again, even with the *National Enquirer,* a periodical generally held in contempt by responsible journalists.'"

"He did that?"

"As blood dripped down his chin from his bloody nose onto his shirt," Mickey said.

"What set you two off?" Matt asked.

"That's not important. The sonofabitch has never liked me, and vice versa. It just happened."

"So what's going to happen?"

"We have entered a thirty-day cooling-off period, during which they hope that I will change my mind about apologizing—they know I won't—and the

Bull hopes Kennedy will make a full and public apology for his reprehensible remarks and behavior to me—which he just might. During this period, I have withdrawn my professional services from the *Bulletin*. I still get paid, of course."

"So what can we two rejects of society as we know it do for the next thirty days?" Matt asked.

"That's what I came to talk to you about," Mickey said.

"Whiskey and wild, wild women? You want to go to Atlantic City? What about Vegas?"

"Casimir has this nutty idea—has had it for years—that I should write a book."

"You told me about that, Mick. And I told you it doesn't sound nutty to me at all."

"The original idea was a collection of stuff that I've done, Matt, and I even started putting stuff together for that."

"I know."

"But what Casimir did now was call some publisher and tell him that what they really needed was a book about Fort Festung, and I was just the guy to write it."

"Why him?"

"Casimir said the Frogs can't stall much longer—he looked into it, I suppose—and they're going to extradite the slimy sonofabitch."

"I agree with the Bull," Matt said. "If they send Festung back, it'd be national news. That'd sell a lot of books. And you are just the guy to write it."

"Yeah, well, anyway, they threw a lot of money at me—which I don't have to give back, by the way, even if I don't write the book, or they don't like it—and I'm going to France to have a look at him."

"Hence the worldwide telephone?"

"Yeah. My mother goes bananas in the nursing home unless I call her once a day. I think it's nine dollars a minute or something when you use it, but what the hell."

"The more I think about this, it's a great idea," Matt said.

"Come with me," O'Hara said.

"What?"

"Come with me. What else have you got to do?"

"Wow!" Matt said. "That came out of left field."

"You've been there, right? You even speak a little Frog?"

"Very little," Matt said. "*Ouvrez la porte de mon oncle.* That means 'open the door of my uncle,' if you're taking notes."

"That's more than I speak. Come on, Matt. Everything on me, of course."

Matt didn't reply.

"I already know all I have to know about the sonofabitch, so all I have to do is take a quick look at this farmhouse, maybe get a couple of pictures of it, him and his wife, then we can go to Paris, or wherever, drink a lot of wine, and *cherchez la femme.*"

"Mick, if I didn't think this was be nice to poor, loony Matt time, I actually think I'd go with you."

"I want you to go because I don't want to go by myself, okay?" O'Hara said.

Jesus, he means that. Mr. Front Page himself, the battling brawler of the city room, is afraid to leave Philadelphia by himself.

What the hell, why not? What else have I got to do?

"What the hell, Mick, why not?" Matt said.

Mickey took out the cellular, pushed one button, and then put the instrument to his ear.

"What happened to the Zero Zero One routine?" Matt asked.

"The Bull's got one of these, too. They store a hundred numbers of other people with one of them," Mickey explained, then held up his hand to cut Matt off.

"Antoinette, this is Michael. Would it be possible for me to speak with Casimir, please?"

It took several minutes for Mr. Bolinski to get on the line. He explained he was floating around the pool.

"Matt says he'll go, Casimir," O'Hara said. "Set it up."

Bolinski said something Matt couldn't hear.

"You got a passport? Is tomorrow night too soon for you?" Mickey asked.

"Yes and no," Matt said.

"That's fine with Matt, Casimir. Set it up."

Bolinski said something else Matt couldn't hear.

"He's fine. He was exhausted, is all."

Mickey broke the connection after Bolinski said something else.

"The Bull says he's glad to hear you're okay."

"That's nice of him."

Mickey pushed another button on his worldwide telephone and put it to his ear.

"Hi, Mom!" he began. "How you doing?"

He spoke with his mother for five minutes, then handed the cellular to Matt.

"You want to call your mom?"

"Not particularly."

"She's your mother, for Christ's sake. Call her."

Matt called his mother and told her that he was fine, thank you, and that he was going to Paris tomorrow night with Mickey O'Hara.

[TWO]

When Air France Flight 2110 deposited them at Charles de Gaulle International Airport in Paris the second morning later, French customs showed great interest in Mr. O'Hara's brand-new luggage—a last-minute purchase after Matt suggested that if they were going to be gone a couple of weeks Mickey would need more space than his zipper bag with the Philadelphia 76ers logotype would provide—and went through it suspiciously before gesturing they could pass.

Outside Customs, a man in a chauffeur's cap was waiting for them, holding a sign lettered "M. O'Hara."

He drove them, in a new Mercedes, to the George V Hotel, where they were installed in a two-bedroom, two-bath, sitting room suite on a corner of the building. From two windows in the sitting room, if they looked carefully, they could see the Champs Elysées, a block away.

They unpacked their luggage and then walked over to the Champs Elysées, took a quick look at the Arc de Triomphe at the other end, and went in search of breakfast.

Then they went to the U.S. Embassy at the foot of the hill, where—after Mickey threatened him with calling Pennsylvania's junior senator right then and on his worldwide telephone—the press officer somewhat reluctantly promised to be prepared to give him the latest developments vis-à-vis the extradition of Isaac Festung once a day when Mickey called.

As they left the embassy, Matt said they were within walking distance of two famous Paris landmarks, the Louvre Museum and Harry's New York Bar.

"Let's take a quick look at the museum," Mickey said. "Just so we can say we saw it. And then we'll go to the bar and hoist a few."

They went into the museum a few minutes before eleven and left a few minutes more than eight hours later, when at closing time three museum guards—immune to Mickey's argument that he was the press, for Christ's sake, and entitled to a little consideration—escorted them out.

He immediately announced to Matt that they were going to have to come back tomorrow.

"I could spend all goddamn day in there just looking at Venus de Milo," Mickey said.

They called their respective maternal parents while sitting at the bar in Harry's. When Matt told his mother they had spent most of the day in the Louvre, and had only minutes before arrived at Harry's Bar, she chuckled knowingly.

"Have a good time, sweetheart," she said. "But get some rest."

When they left Harry's four beers and an hour later, and were walking toward the Opera, where Matt remembered a restaurant his father particularly liked, Mickey offered a philosophical/historical/literary observation:

"Did you know that's the joint where Hemingway used to hang out?" he asked.

"I heard."

"Did you know that before he became a writer, he was a newspaperman?"

"I heard that too."

"I don't mean some schmuck on a small-town rag, he worked for the *Herald-Tribune,* here, " Mickey said. "He gave a speech one time where he said he thought working on a newspaper was the best training he ever had to become a writer."

"I didn't know that, but I'm sure he was right," Matt said.

"Yeah," Mickey said, thoughtfully. "He probably was."

Am I in the company of the next Tom Clancy? The next Whatshisname, the guy who made millions writing about dinosaurs?

"When do you want to go to Cognac-Boeuf, Mick?"

"What's that?"

"That's where Festung is."

"Soon, but not right away. I told you, I want to go back to the Louvre. You can't see half what they have in that place in one day, for Christ's sake."

Over the next five days, they developed a routine. On waking, while Matt ordered their room-service breakfast, and while waiting for it to be delivered, Mickey first got on the phone to the embassy's press officer, then would get on the Internet with Matt's laptop, go to the *Bulletin*'s Web site, and catch up on what was happening in Philadelphia.

After breakfast, they took a cab to the Louvre. Matt thus got to see more of the museum than he'd seen in his previous—more than a dozen—visits to the City of Lights. Once they went out of the museum to lunch, but that took too much time for Mickey, so the other days they had eaten lunch standing up at a museum concession.

He did manage to get Mickey briefly to the top of the Eiffel Tower—to which Mickey's reaction was "What's the big deal?" and "Are you sure it's safe? It's rusty all over"—and to Napoleon's Tomb, but that was about all.

They called their respective maternal parents daily, usually from Harry's New York Bar after the Louvre closed. And then they went to dinner, and after that, twice, to jazz places on the East Bank.

Matt realized that he was having a good time, largely because Mickey was what his father described as "a good traveling companion."

On the morning of the sixth day, Mickey called, "Hey, you better take a look at this!"

Matt, munching a croissant, walked to where Mickey was at his laptop. The screen showed the front page of the *Bulletin,* and for a moment Matt didn't understand what he was being shown. And then, in the "Inside Today's Bulletin" box, he saw: "Police Arrest Two in Fast-Food Restaurant Murder. Page 3, Section 2."

There wasn't much of a story there, even though it had a double byline on it.

TWO ARRESTED IN FAST-FOOD DOUBLE MURDER

BY RICHARD HIGBEE AND BETTY-JO WOLFF
BULLETIN STAFF WRITERS

Philadelphia—Police Commissioner Ralph J. Mariani announced the arrest early this morning "without incident" of Lawrence John Porter, 20, and Ralph David Williams, 19, at their homes in the Paschall Homes Project. The two, who are cousins, have been charged with the double murder of Ms. Maria M. Fernandez and Police Officer Kenneth J. Charlton during a robbery of the Roy Rogers restaurant at South Broad and Snyder Streets earlier this month.

"We've had the two under round-the-clock surveillance for some time," Commissioner Mariani said, "but delayed arresting them while assembling irrefutable evidence against them."

Mariani said that evidence included the murder weapon, a .38-caliber handgun, which police divers, assisted by the Philadelphia Treasure Hunters Club, recovered later yesterday from the silt banks of the Schuylkill River, where it had been thrown.

Mariani cited the involvement of the Treasure Hunters, who joined the police in searching the murky waters of the Schuylkill, as another example "for which I am grateful and proud" of civilian cooperation with the police.

Philadelphia mayor Alvin W. Martin, in a separate statement, said that all Philadelphians "can and should take pride in the professionalism and dedication of the officers of the Special Operations Division Task Force, which I ordered formed, in apprehending these individuals under extremely difficult circumstances."

"Jesus, what a shitty story," O'Hara said. "And it took two of them to write it."

"There's not much, is there?" Matt said. "For all the effort that went into that job."

"On the other hand," O'Hara said, more charitably, "it might have been my pal Kennedy's editing. I know the broad. She's got talent."

O'Hara looked thoughtful for a minute, and judging by the look on his face, Matt was not very surprised at what came next.

"Matty, unless you really want to go back to the Louvre . . . You've been there before a lot, right?"

"Yeah, I have."

"How would you feel about making arrangements to getting us to where . . . I forget where you said . . ."

"Cognac-Boeuf," Matt furnished.

"Right. Where this sleazeball Fort Festung is."

"Sure, Mick. Good idea. We better rent a car. I don't know if we can find one to rent down there."

"See if you can get us a Lincoln, or a Cadillac. These Frog cars look tiny to me. What I'd really like to have is my Rendezvous."

[THREE]

The concierge in the lobby of the George V said it would be impossible to provide either a Cadillac or a Lincoln—much less a Porsche or a Buick Rendezvous—and he would therefore recommend a Mercedes.

"Unless M'sieu would like a Jaguar?"

"Tell me about a Jaguar," Matt said.

He put the Jaguar rental on his American Express card, because every time he'd tried to pick up a bill, O'Hara had been adamant that the whole trip was on him. "Put your goddamn money away," he'd say.

Signing the receipt triggered the memory of what Detective Olivia Lassiter had said to him in Alabama about his not even looking at the bill there before he signed it, and his first reaction was, *"Screw her!"*

But she stayed in his mind all day, and about six-thirty, as he sat in the hotel bar in the vain hope that Mickey would leave the Louvre before they threw him out, he remembered that Mickey had left his worldwide telephone in the suite. And after one more drink, he went to the suite, dialed Zero Zero One, and after some difficulty was connected with the Northwest Detectives Division of the Philadelphia police department.

"Detective Lassiter, please."

"Who's calling?"

"Sergeant Payne."

"Hello, Matt. How are you?"

"I'm fine."

"I heard—"

"I'm fine, Olivia. Thank you for asking. I was about to send you one of those 'having lovely time in Gay Paree wish you were here' postcards, but I figured what the hell, I'd call you."

"Matt, I'm working."

"Can I call you later?"

"I don't think that would be a very good idea," Olivia said. And hung up.

The next morning at ten, Matthew M. Payne and Michael J. O'Hara, both more than a little hungover, watched their luggage being loaded into a powder blue Jaguar XK8 Cabriolet. Then they got in and, with Matt at the wheel, drove across Avenue George V onto Rue Pierre Charron, then turned right onto the Champs Elysées and headed for French National Highway A20.

They stopped for lunch in Orléans, then drove on, this time with Mickey at the wheel. At seven-thirty, by which time it was already too dark to take pictures, they pulled into the cobblestoned forecourt of Le Relais in the village of Cognac-Boeuf.

"It looks," Matt said, "as if it's been here for centuries."

"It looks like a dump," Mickey said. "Is this the best we can do?"

"This is it, unless you want to go back to Bordeaux."

Mickey wordlessly turned the engine off and got out of the car.

The only accommodation available was one room. It had two single beds and a washbasin. The bath and water closet were in separate rooms down a narrow corridor.

"And I'll bet you snore, too, don't you?" Mr. O'Hara inquired.

Their dinner—roast lamb—was very good, and so was the wine. At nine o'clock, they retired to their room.

"I want to get up early, find their house, and take a couple of shots," Mickey announced, "then hang around for a while to see if I can get a couple of shots of Festung, and then get the hell out of here."

They called their respective maternal parents, turned off the worldwide telephone because the battery was running low, and then got into bed.

"You know what else—besides forgetting to charge the phone in the car— you made me do when you decided to drink everything in Paris last night?" Mr. O'Hara inquired across the dark room.

"I can hardly wait to hear."

"I didn't call that jackass in the embassy."

"You can call the jackass in the embassy in the morning," Matt said.

They were both asleep by half past nine.

[FOUR]

When it is half past nine in Cognac-Boeuf, France, it is half past three in Philadelphia, Pennsylvania.

At 3:33 P.M., Dianna Kerr-Gally, Executive Assistant to the Hon. Alvin W. Martin, stepped to the mayor's door and coughed.

"What's up?" he inquired.

"I've got Eileen Solomon on the line," Dianna said.

"Put her through," he said.

"She wants to know if there is any reason you can't see her right now."

"See me? As opposed to talk to me?"

Dianna nodded.

"Did she say what she wants?"

Dianna shook her head, "no."

He shrugged.

"You think I should talk to her?"

"I think you should tell me if there's some reason you can't see her right now."

"Tell our distinguished district attorney that my door is always open to her," the mayor ordered. "And stall whatever's on the schedule until she shows up."

The Hon. Eileen McNamara Solomon, trailed by Detective Al Unger, appeared ten minutes later in the mayor's outer office, and was immediately shown into the inner office by Dianna Kerr-Gally, who stood just inside the door.

"This is between the mayor and me," Eileen Solomon said. "Do you mind?"

Mrs. Kerr-Gally smiled somewhat thinly and left the office.

Our D.A. is really pissed off about something. I wonder what? And what does it have to do with me?

"You seem a little upset, Eileen," the mayor said.

"'Little' is an understatement, and 'upset' a euphemism," she said.

"Well, let's see what we can do to make things right," the mayor said. "What's happened?"

"I had a call just now from Walter Davis," Eileen began. "He told me he was really delighted to be able to tell me that Isaac Festung would soon be returned to Philadelphia."

"Well, that's certainly good news after all this time."

"Specifically, that he was reliably informed by the legal attaché of our embassy in Paris . . . You do know, don't you, Alvin, that for reasons I never really understood, they call FBI agents assigned to embassies 'legal attachés'?"

"No, I can't say that I did," Martin confessed.

"Rephrasing, *the FBI agent* at our embassy has told Davis that the French court is about to extradite Isaac Festung."

"And for some reason I don't understand, you're annoyed about that?"

460 · W. E. B. GRIFFIN

"Davis said that as soon as the French court orders his extradition, the legal attaché—read FBI agents—there will take custody of his person, and then they and U.S. marshals will escort him home."

"You're going to have to explain to me, I'm afraid, what's wrong with that."

"When I was on the bench, Alvin, after Festung jumped bail, I spent a lot of effort—and a lot of taxpayers' money—trying to find him. After he was convicted in *my* court of murder in the second, and—surprising me not at all—the FBI had not been able to find him, much less bring him back here and lock him up, I spent even more effort and taxpayer money trying to find him and bring him back here."

"And the FBI was not very useful in this, I gather?"

"What they did, Alvin, was notify Interpol. 'Hey, fellas, the local cops here are looking for this guy. If you stumble over him, give us a call, huh?'"

Mayor Martin was tempted to smile, but wise enough to know that this was not the time to do so.

"And since I became D.A.," the D.A. went on, "my people—my fugitive guy and others—have spent a fortune running this sonofabitch down all over Europe. *We* found out from the French cops that he was—wherever the hell he is, in some village in the South of France—and when Interpol and the FBI did nothing to get him back, I sent two assistant D.A.s over there—at the taxpayers' expense—to light a fire under them."

"I see," Alvin W. Martin said, although he really didn't.

The only thing he knew for sure was that he had never seen the Hon. Eileen McNamara Solomon so angry before, and from which he drew the conclusion that one could anger Mrs. Solomon only at great peril.

"I have no intention of standing there, smiling in gratitude, when the FBI or the marshals take him off the plane," Eileen McNamara Solomon declared.

"I understand how you feel, Eileen," he said.

"I want a Philadelphia cop's handcuffs on him," she said. "I want a Philadelphia cop to bring him back."

"I can understand that," the mayor said.

"Those bastards try this sort of thing all the time. They even showed up in Alabama, trying to steal Jason Washington's pinch of Homer C. Daniels."

"I didn't know that," the mayor said, truthfully. "Is that what it's called, 'stealing a pinch'? That sounds like something that would happen at a high school junior prom."

It was evident on District Attorney Solomon's face that she did not share Mayor Martin's sense of humor.

"Well, what can we do about this, you and I, Eileen, to make things right?"

"What you can do, Alvin, is call Ralph Mariani and tell him to get a cop—preferably one from Homicide—over to France before the FBI gets away with this."

"Is there going to be time to do that?"

"There will have to be," Eileen McNamara Solomon declared.

[FIVE]

"Homicide, Lieutenant Washington."

"Mariani, Washington. Is Quaire there?"

"No, sir. He is not."

"Come up here, please, Jason. Right now."

After he had explained the situation to Lieutenant Washington, Commissioner Mariani was surprised, and a little annoyed, at the amused look on Washington's face.

"This is not funny, Lieutenant. We better be able to do something, and do it right now."

"As it happens, Commissioner, there does happen to be a man from Homicide in France right now."

"How did that happen?"

"Sergeant Payne—two days ago, anyway—was in Paris, sir."

"I ordered him to take thirty days' vacation time!"

"Yes, sir. That's what he's doing. He and Mr. O'Hara. Sergeant Payne told his mother, and she told me, that Mr. O'Hara is quite taken with the artistic treasures of the Louvre."

The commissioner waited for him to go on.

"There is a rumor circulating, sir, that Mr. O'Hara and Mr. Kennedy, the city editor of the *Bulletin*—"

"I know who he is," Mariani interjected impatiently.

"—exchanged blows in the city room of the newspaper . . ."

"No kidding?"

". . . and that Mr. O'Hara is on a thirty-day sabbatical from his duties. According to my information—again via Sergeant Payne's mother—Mr. O'Hara is thinking of writing a book about Festung. Anyway, sir, the two of them are in France."

"How do we get in touch with them?"

"They are—or were—in the George the Fifth Hotel in Paris, sir," Washington said. "And Mr. O'Hara, I understand, has one of the new worldwide satellite telephones. It shouldn't be any problem."

Commissioner Mariani picked up his telephone.

"Put in a person-to-person call to either Sergeant Matthew Payne or Mr. Michael O'Hara in the George the Fifth Hotel in Paris, France," he ordered.

Ten minutes later, Commissioner Mariani was informed that both Mr. O'Hara and Mr. Payne had checked out of the hotel that morning and left no forwarding address.

"I knew that was too good to be true," Mariani said. "What about this around-the-world telephone of O'Hara's? Can you get the number?"

"I'm sure that won't be a problem, sir."

"Well, get it. Get them on it. Tell them to call me."

"Yes, sir."

"And you better see who else has a passport. . . . Do you?"

"It's being renewed, sir."

"Get somebody else started, in case we can't get through to Payne. Hell, they may be on their way home."

A half hour later, Lieutenant Washington telephoned Commissioner Mariani to report that he was having trouble getting O'Hara's number but he was working on it, and hoped to have it shortly.

He also reported that they had made reservations for someone to fly to Paris. It had yet to be determined who would go, but there would be plenty of time to make the decision. The next available seat to Paris was on a flight leaving New York tomorrow afternoon. When he added that only first-class seats were available, he anticipated the commissioner's next question:

"It would appear we're in the tourist season, sir," Washington concluded.

"In that case, I would suggest that you make every effort to get O'Hara's phone number," Commissioner Mariani said. "Keep me advised, Lieutenant. I'm about to tell the mayor we are making every effort to comply with his wishes."

"Yes, sir."

Two hours after that, Lieutenant Washington called the commissioner again.

"Sir, I have the number. I had to get it from Mr. Casimir Bolinski. But when I call it, the recording says that it's been turned off. Probably overnight, sir. I'll try again in the morning."

"No," Commissioner Mariani said, "you, or some one you delegate, will try that number every thirty minutes until someone answers."

"Yes, sir."

[SIX]

Mr. Michael J. O'Hara rose at first light and, without disturbing Sergeant Payne, went down the narrow corridor to the communal bath, took one look at it, and decided he would just have to remain unwashed until they found a decent hotel.

Then—with less trouble than he expected to have—he got directions in the form of a hand-drawn map to the Piaf Mill, and got in the Jaguar and drove there.

He had a little trouble getting the shots he wanted. There were half a dozen French gendarmes guarding the place, and when they spotted him, they tried to run him off. But he finally got what he wanted, and even a shot of Isaac "Fort" Festung, standing in the doorway of the ancient mill house.

Then he drove back to Le Relais with a sense of mission accomplished. He had all he needed. He'd wake Matty up, they'd get some breakfast, and then "Sayonara, Cognac-Boeuf! Or whatever the hell this place is called."

He had already stopped the Jaguar when he remembered he had forgotten to take the telephone with him. He had planned to see how much of a charge it would take plugged into the Jaguar's cigarette lighter hole.

He went to their room, turned the light on, woke Matty and told him to get his ass out of bed, as soon as they had breakfast they were out of here, and took the telephone down—the battery of which was now really dead, he having apparently failed to turn it off correctly the night before—to the Jaguar.

The clever Englishmen had designed the interior to frustrate him. It took him almost five minutes to find the cigarette lighter hole. It was in the ashtray, mounted in such a position that it couldn't be seen by the driver unless he bent nearly flat and looked around the gearshift lever.

Matt was just coming into the combined bar and dining room of Le Relais when Mickey finally went in.

Mickey explained that he had had difficulty finding the cigarette lighter holder, but that he had finally succeeded, and the phone was now being charged.

"Maybe not, Mick," Matt said. "Sometimes the lighter hole is hot only when the ignition is on."

"Shit!"

Mickey went back out to the Jaguar and immediately discovered that Matt had been in error. The cigarette lighter hole was hot, even with the ignition off. The proof was that the once dead-as-a-doornail device was chirping.

Mickey wondered what the hell Casimir—the only person who had the number—wanted this time of night. It was eight-fifteen here, which meant that it was 2:15 A.M. in the States.

"What's up, Casimir?"

"That you, Mickey?"

"Yeah. Who's this?"

"Jason Washington."

"What the hell do you want?"

"Is Matt somewhere around? And how is he?"

"He's fine. We're about to have breakfast. Can I give him a message?"

"Can't you just give him the phone, Mick?"

"I don't think the battery will last that long," Mick said. "This is important? Nothing wrong with anybody?"

"It's important, Mick. Nothing's wrong with anyone."

"Hang on, I'll get him."

"This afternoon, huh?" Mickey asked after Matt returned from the Jaguar and reported the gist of his conversations with Lieutenant Washington and a somewhat sleepy-sounding Commissioner Ralph J. Mariani. "It's a sure thing?"

"So says Mariani. He says Eileen Solomon told him she talked to the embassy."

"That bastard in the embassy never said a goddamn word to me."

"Possibly because you forgot to call him."

"Screw you, Matty. Did they say where?"

"The Palais de Justice in Bordeaux."

"Well, we better drive over there after we finish breakfast," O'Hara said.

"Actually," Matt said, thoughtfully. "It makes a pretty good last act. The fat lady sings. The last act of the Wyatt Earp of the Main Line. I'm quitting the job, Mickey."

"You're not going to bring that crap up again, are you?"

"Again?"

"You had a couple of drinks—eight or ten—too many the other night, pal, after you had your little chat with the lady detective."

"And I told you?"

"You were . . . somewhat loquacious . . . Matty. You would never love again, and you were quitting the job. *Ad infinitum.*"

"I don't remember that."

"And thus you don't remember what I told you?"

"No."

"I said you were probably lucky Detective Whatsername dumped you—I never liked her; she's one of those dames who's never satisfied—and as full of shit as a Christmas turkey about quitting the job. You could no more do anything else than I could become a ballet dancer. You're a cop, Matty. A good one. It's in your blood."

The conversation was interrupted by the entrance into the combined bar and dining room of Le Relais of Mr. Isaac Festung.

He was accompanied by two gendarmes.

He was wearing what looked like a dirty white poncho and baggy blue cotton trousers, and was barefoot in leather sandals.

He looked around the room and spotted Mickey.

He walked to the table.

"You were at my home this morning," he challenged. "Taking pictures."

"Yes, I was."

"Morbid interest? Or journalistic? Or is there a difference?"

"I'm a reporter, if that's what you mean," O'Hara said.

"Well, I'm sorry to tell you that I'm not granting any interviews right now."

"That's good, because I'm not asking for one."

"Then what are you doing here?"

"I just rode down here with him," O'Hara said, nodding at Matt.

Festung turned his attention to Matt.

"You're a reporter?"

"No, I'm not, Mr. Festung," Matt said. "I'm a police officer. I'm here to take you into custody when the court of appeals denies your appeal."

"Well, then, I'm afraid you've wasted your time, too, my young friend. That's not going to happen."

"We'll know for sure about that this afternoon in Bordeaux, won't we? And I'm not your young friend, Mr. Festung. I'm Sergeant Matthew Payne, Badge 471, Homicide Unit, Philadelphia police department."

Festung met Matt's eyes for a long moment, and when Matt didn't blink, apparently lost his appetite for breakfast, for he suddenly spun around on his heels and stalked out of Le Relais, with the two gendarmes on his heels.

"That felt good, admit it," Mickey said.

"I don't know about 'good,' Mick, but it felt right."

"Let's get the hell out of here," Mickey said.

And they left.